BRONCO

NOLA REBELS MC NEW ORLEANS

BOOK 12

MACKENZY FOX

Copyright © 2025 Mackenzy Fox

All rights reserved. No part of this publication may be reproduced, distributed, or transmitted in any form or by any means, including photocopying, recording, or other electronic or mechanical methods, without the prior written permission of the publisher.

Please purchase only authorized electronic editions and do not participate in, or encourage, the electronic piracy of copyrighted materials. Your support of the author's rights is appreciated.

This book is a work of fiction. Names, characters, places, brands, and incidents are the products of the author's imagination or used fictitiously. Any resemblance to actual events, locales, or persons, living or dead, is entirely coincidental.

Cover by: @mosadesigns
Exclusive photo: Eric Battershell Photography
Model: Alex Perez
Formatting by: Kiki Edits
Editing: Daisie GCD Editing
Proofreading by: Kiki Edits

Alpha reader: Michelle A (The Outgoing Bookworm)
Beta Readers: Dakotah F, Kylie T, Tara B, Anshul S

*Please note. This book is written by me (Mackenzy Fox) I do not use AI to write my books or in any book content, nor do I use AI for book covers. Any book you pick up that is copyrighted by me - is written by me - and always will be 😊

ISBN: 978-1-923015-59-3

DEDICATION

He might be her best friend, but let me tell you, this man is not to be messed with when it comes to keeping her safe... that is all.

AUTHOR'S NOTE

CONTENT WARNING: Bronco is a steamy romance for readers 18+. It contains mature themes that may make some readers uncomfortable.

It includes: cult themes and religious sects, domestic violence (not on page) mentions of miscarriage, mentions of female infertility, abusive ex, child trauma, mentions of child abuse (not on page) torture scene of enemy (on page) gun violence, knife violence, consensual graphic sex scenes.

All of my books are heavily focused around the love story first, and the MC second.

My bikers are all possessive with their own quirks. Bronco is Amber's best friend, but he is also fiercely protective, and if you touch her, you will die. Amber is tough, but also vulnerable. She's been through a lot. I also love it when she makes the first move, and that kiss-cam moment... swoon.

I absolutely love writing 'friends to lovers'; suffice to say that in love with the two of them. Oh, and Bronco has a cool rescue dog called Titan who is just so sweet (yes, he's protective too!)

If you loved my best-selling Bracken Ridge Rebels MC series, you're sure to love this new spin-off too.

You also don't have to have read Bracken Ridge to enjoy this new series as it is written to be read stand-alone.

SYNOPSIS

Bronco: NOLA REBELS MC – (New Orleans Series Book 12)

Bronco is a gritty, motorcycle romance with friends to lovers, fake dating, kiss-cam moment, protective hero and a sassy heroine who's escaping a dark past.

The men of the NOLA Rebels MC will do anything for their club. They're a brotherhood, a club who stands mighty, and above all else, they take care of business, New Orleans style. The bikers may rule this city, but the women of the club have their hearts, and the men will do anything to protect what's theirs.

It is part of a series but can be read stand-alone with a HEA. This book is recommended for mature readers 18+

BLURB

Bronco

It's the kiss that did it
Falling for her wasn't my fault
I mean, she's my best friend
And I didn't plan on falling in love with her
But that's exactly what happened
She's always been in my life
But never like this
The more I get to know her
The more the secrets unfold
The past is never in the past
Not when the most precious person in the world
Could be the one to get hurt
And that would be my final undoing
The pact we made?
It's about to be tested
And I'm ready to fight

Amber

I'm to blame for the kiss-cam moment
I kissed him, after all, not the other way around
I shouldn't have
But we crossed a line
It was supposed to be one night
We made a pact that went something like this:
No feelings
No commitment
Definitely no heartstrings
He's my best friend
The man who's always kept me safe
He'd die for me
But I've found something to live for
And he was right under my nose all along
Then a dark shadow suddenly casts over us
One we can't escape from
And I'm left wondering if I didn't drag him into this
Only to lose him before our love story even began

NOLA MC COMMITTEE MEMBERS:

NOLA MC Committee members:
Cash – Founder & President
Ryder – Vice President
Harlem – Enforcer
Tag – Sergeant at Arms
Jett – Treasurer
Hawk – Road Captain
Riot – Secretary
Nevada – Tail Gunner
Bronco – Tail Gunner

Priest – Club Chaplain

Other regular club members:
Manny (Club chef)
J.J.
Bullet
Rock
Chains
Haze
Brew
Bandit
Pipes
Hustler

Current prospects:
Giggs
Rodeo

Ol' ladies of the club (so far) and their bikers:
Deanna (Cash)
Summer (Jett)
Jas (Hawk)
Indigo (Harlem)
Luna (Tag)
Aspyn (Rock)
Crystal (Ryder)
Bella (Priest)
Star (Nevada)
Halo (Riot)
Lace (Manny & Bandit)
Audrina (Hustler)

1

BRONCO

If you'd told me I'd end up with a giant, black Cane Corso — the last dog to be adopted at the New Orleans Faux Paws Rescue adoption event — I'd have told you that you're nuts. I wasn't looking, but I felt sorry for the dude. He played on my heart strings the second I saw him.

Okay, I admit he does look a little scary, but with a name like 'Diablo' how can one blame him? It's a terrible name because even though he looks like he might be a guard dog for the devil himself, he's surprisingly soft and playful and completely docile. He prefers to sleep for twenty-plus hours a day on a huge pillow the size of a Buick rather than be a working dog.... Albeit, he doesn't seem to mind other dogs, but he's a little hesitant with humans. The breed is known for their loyalty, temperament and their ability to protect; yeah, you could say I've done my research.

He's only three, and was surrendered because his owners didn't have the time to train him properly. They're a strong breed, but he's smart, and he loves his walks. For the last six months, I've been taking him to obedience training and we've learned a lot about each other. I also changed his name to

Titan. Suggesting he's anything like the devil is just an insult, and I hate how dogs are misunderstood just because their owners are complete fuckwits.

Titan would likely lick you to death before he ever charged at you; once he got to know you, that is. Then again, Nevada, my MC club brother, keeps telling me we need to train him as a proper guard dog and not mollify him so much, but I kinda like it. It's nice having company at night; he lies in the doorway of my bedroom taking up all the room until he deems it safe enough to leave his post and jump onto the bed.

"You know, you spend more time gazin' at that dog than you do tryin' to score pussy these days," Ryder, the VP and one of my best friends, laughs. He plonks down on the chair next to me at the bar. The clubhouse is quiet at this time of the afternoon because most of the members are out at their day jobs.

Titan doesn't even look up. He's used to most of the guys around here, it's only new people he's not sure of. He lets out a huge sigh as he falls back asleep, his legs in the air as he rolls onto his back.

"That's not entirely true," Amber says, from around the corner. Amber is one of my best friends and the only girl I really talk to about deep and meaningful shit. She's restocking the bar for the weekend and I had no clue she'd appear right then. "I think that new girl, Cupcake, right? Pretty sure she has a crush." She wiggles her eyebrows and I groan.

"She does not," I say, hoping this news isn't true. I really don't need any woman drama right now, and since I've worked my way through most of the sweet butts over the last few years — the women who hang around the club for booze, grub and sex — I don't need another clinger. *Cupcake?* What kind of name is that? "At least, I hope not."

Ryder rolls his eyes. "The fact you'd rather hang around your damn dog is telling enough for all of us." He slaps me on the back. "You savin' yourself for marriage? I can highly recommend it."

Well, he would know. He's been married to Crystal for years and his dick hasn't fallen off. They've got a kid together, Ade; a cute, lovable little terror.

Amber snorts and I give her the evil eye. I don't like talking about other women around her, not that we're a thing or are ever gonna be a thing, but we're friends. I don't know how it happened, but it did. She's a cool chick. I also almost tattooed her ass one drunken night a few months ago, and ever since I caught sight of one of her bare ass cheeks, I haven't been in my right mind. *Thank you, tequila shots...*

But me and Amber? That ain't ever gonna work. She's so far out of my league, I'm not ever gonna reach the summit. Plus, *we're friends.* I've never been friends with a woman before. I didn't think it was remotely possible, but she's not naggy or annoying like most of the women around the club or in my life. She actually listens without judgment or ridicule. We can hang out and there's no pressure or expectation.

"I've just been busy," I lie.

"Riiiiight." Amber laughs as I throw my hands in the air.

"Seriously? You're gonna dump on me, too?"

She shrugs. "Someone's gotta keep you honest."

Ryder chuckles. Clearly he thinks he's won. "The woman talks sense."

"No, she doesn't. She's cute so she gets away with sayin' whatever flies out of her mouth." I gesture toward Amber and she pokes her tongue out.

"You're just being nice because I know all your secrets."

Ryder shoves me in the shoulder. "What about bro-code?"

Amber laughs out loud. "Oh my God, you did not just say that."

"Bro-code is not sayin' *bro-code* out loud, asshat." I shake my head. "And anyway, she's not talkin' about club business, right *AJ?*" I've always called her that because her full name is Amber-Jane. Nobody else calls her AJ and strangely, I like that idea.

"Ooh, the dreaded *club business.*" She waves her hands at us and we both can't help but laugh. "Heaven forbid."

Club business is exactly that; stuff the club discusses in the meeting room that's between the members. Usually, it involves what shit and mayhem is going on at any given time, and while we're not a 1% club, we do have our fair share of ups and downs.

Ryder points at her. "You know you said a mouthful there, sister?"

She rolls her eyes. "Puh-lease, do you know how much swearing, groveling, punch ups, brawls, drunken rants, broody behavior, stalking tendencies, bullet wounds — not to mention tears — from *bad ass* bikers I've seen over the last year?" She snorts. "Trust me, I know *all* of your secrets, that's the perk of being the bartender who listens. Kind of a rite of passage when you think about it."

God, she's fantastic.

Ryder stands, holding up his hands in surrender. "Can't argue with that. Gotta run and collect Ade from preschool." He gives us a two-finger salute and takes off.

After he leaves, I turn to look back at Amber. She has her long, chestnut hair tied up in a ponytail, thick curls falling back. Her tan skin and big, hazel eyes are pretty without even trying. Maybe I am a misogynist and I like her because she hasn't slept around the clubhouse; that idea evokes a small heart tremor in my chest which is news to me. I'd also be lying if I said I wasn't protective of her, but I am over all the girls. It's how my mama raised me.

She's average height at around five-six, with limbs that appear longer than they are because she's slender, but has these hips and breasts that go for fucking days...

She snaps her fingers. "Ogle much?"

I lift my eyes. "Sorry, you wore a white tank with a black bra. I am a man, after all."

She leans on the bench, ignoring me. "I have a date tonight actually."

"Oh?" This is news. "Who with?" We've often shared our haphazard dating life over the last couple of years, but lately Amber hasn't exactly had much time to hang out with her niece showing up unexpectedly. She's cagey about it, and doesn't want anyone to know because her sister-in-law, Erica, could be in trouble. I've been sworn to secrecy, and I'd never say anything to anyone, but I feel like I should do more and help her out. But how?

She gives me a look. "It's a blind date."

The fact she's not offering any more than that is telling. "Did you meet him on Tinder?"

"Nope, I deleted that app. If I just wanted wild sex I'd take JJ or Bullet home, or both of them." She shrugs.

I frown. "Two guys at once? You been talkin' to Lace?"

Lace, my club brother Riot's sister, is in a poly relationship with Manny, the club chef, and another club brother, Bandit. They're happy and I'm stoked to see Manny, who's been at the club a long time, thriving in a relationship where he's appreciated. He's a good guy and everyone loves him.

She snorts. "Yeah, on second thought, I think one guy at once is enough."

"Clearly you haven't seen my dick." I lean back in the chair and she gives me a withering look.

"Let me guess, it's nine inches and goes all night?" Yup, she's heard my usual spiel one too many times.

"A physical inspection could be on the cards." I waggle my eyebrows. "You know, just so you have something to compare to."

"Hey, I have sex."

"Uh, huh, when? And don't include dildos or vibrators."

She does that cute thing where she bites her lip and looks up to the left, thinking about her answer. "Okay, maybe I haven't in a while, but I could if I wanted to."

I laugh. "Oh, I'm fully aware of that, sweetheart. Trust me. You're hot, but guys only want one thing, no matter how nice they seem."

She wiggles her butt. "This?"

"Uh, huh. And you're a good girl. Gotta stay away from those pretty boys, they're the worst."

She laughs. "Are you gonna come save me again?"

"You know I got arrested for you."

"You never let me forget it."

I rest my chin on my hand, not ready for this conversation to end just yet. "So tell me about your date. What's he like?"

She shrugs. "It's a blind date, I have no clue. But apparently we have a lot in common, according to my best friend, Abigail. He's also best friends with her brother."

"So he could be a complete psycho for all you know?"

"Abi wouldn't set me up with a psycho." She rolls her eyes. "But it's better than a bar. If you have a first date with a guy in a bar, he's expecting sex."

I like that she doesn't have sex on the brain for a first date. I don't like that she has a date at all, but at least it'll be inside a crowded place... I'm guessing. It's what they could get up to afterwards that makes me wanna follow her to make sure she's safe. The streets aren't safe for a woman these days. She's got Olive to think of now until her mom comes back for her.

That gets me thinking. "So when can I meet Olive? I could get tickets to the Pelicans this weekend, they're playin' at home."

She blinks and her demeanor changes; her eyes drop and her smile vanishes. "I think for now it's best that she settles in.

She just started a new school and I'm kinda struggling with what to tell her about her mom and when she's coming back."

"Babe, don't look so glum. I'm just sayin' I'm here, and if you wanna go to a game, with or without me, the offer is there."

She swallows hard. "I'll actually be going to that game already." She cringes, then adds, "I scored a couple of tickets and invited him."

I cross my arms over your chest. "Wow. You don't even invite your best friend to a Pelicans game? Don't tell me the seats are ringside?" I'm not a huge sports nut like Amber, but I don't mind going to a game every now and again.

"They're not ringside," she huffs. "And I would've invited you, but when I told Abi about the tickets, she suggested we have our date there."

"All men expect sex no matter where you meet," I tell her. "Don't be fooled into thinkin' otherwise."

She raises her eyebrows. "Oh, really? So when you just invited me to the Pelicans game, is that what you were expecting?"

Of course she's smarter than me, that's a given. But unlike this freak she's meeting up with, I'm not expecting shit. Men are men, no matter what she says. *Best friend's brother?* What a fuckin' cliche.

"Very funny. That's what you get for tryin' to be a nice guy. I was just tryin' to do somethin' to take your mind off all of this."

She sobers for a second. "I know, Bronc, that's why I love you."

I snort. "Right. That's why you stuck up for me back there with my VP?" I thumb behind me toward the clubhouse doors.

"Aww, poor baby!"

"There you go again. So what else do we know about this dude aside from he could potentially be a serial killer."

"You watch too many late night shows," she sighs. "And for the record, it feels kinda weird leaving Olive for the first time. Audrina and West offered to babysit, as well as Harlem and Indi because she's made friends with Cami and they want to do a sleepover..."

Audrina is West's ol' lady, and Nevada's mom. Harlem is the club's Enforcer; his ol' lady Indigo runs NOLA Sweet Treats Bakery.

"So? Nothin' wrong with havin' a night out, it might be good for you. Long as he's a gentleman."

"I'm not looking for a hook-up," she says matter-of-factly. "Though if I was, I wouldn't tell you about it." She throws a dish rag at me. I'm fast, catching it before it hits my face.

"Why not? We tell each other everything."

"Because you'll only rub it in my face when he doesn't call."

"Like I say, he'll only not call after the deed if he's after a booty call, babe." I point at her. "And you're better than that."

This time she lobs a coaster at me, narrowly missing my head. "Very funny, you're practically a club whore so you have no room to speak."

"*Was,*" I state matter-of-factly. I place a hand over my heart. "Past tense. I'm a changed man."

"Aww, does having women running around doing your laundry get old? Poor baby." She flicks her bottom lip with her finger... *How have I just noticed her mouth?*

I tear my gaze away from dangerous territory and screw my face up. "They don't do my laundry." Then under my breath I add, "*Anymore.*"

She sighs. "You're hopeless, Bronco. I think that's why you're single."

"You think?"

"Uh, huh. I knew you were a momma's boy when I first met you."

I grin. "Is it that obvious?" I can't deny it. Whenever my mom is in town, she spoils me rotten because I'm her baby. It hasn't helped me a lot in the real world, but it's still nice that she fusses.

"I have a sixth sense."

"Fuck I hope not, otherwise you'll know I was checkin' out your rack just before."

She wiggles her breasts at me. "Read 'em and weep."

My eyes drop and my dick stirs at the same time. I almost glance down at my wood and say, 'Bad boy!' But I refrain. *I can't be having thoughts about Amber. She's the only friend I have that isn't a big dumb ass.*

Titan glances up, realizes I'm not talking about him, and flops back down again, heaving another sigh like he's hard done by.

"So much for a guard dog," Amber laughs. "I think he's missing the killer instinct."

I laugh, too. "You should see him around kids, though. He's like their own personal protector."

I smile when I think about the day Ella; Hawk and Jas's kid, Lexi; Hawk's niece, and Kai; Harlem's boy, were all over for a playdate and Titan sat outside watching them play basketball, not letting anyone get on the court who didn't belong there. It leads me even further to believe my dog is just misunderstood.

"Oh, I can imagine."

"So what's his name?"

"My date?" She starts to unbox the drinks.

"Who else?"

Her eyes flick to mine. "Ben."

"Ben?"

"Yes, that's his name."

"Benjamin?" I draw out the syllables like I'm five years old.

"Yep."

"He sounds like a weirdo who wears corduroy, has a five dollar haircut and lives in his mom's basement because he's addicted to online gaming, or porn."

"You got all *that* from Ben?"

"Just make sure you take that pepper spray I got you."

"You know, you're worse than my grandpa," she says, indulging me with another roll of her eyes. "He used to guard us with a shotgun when we were little."_

"I'll wear that badge with honor then." I give her a lopsided smile. "And if your date sucks ass and you want an excuse to leave, I'll call half an hour into the game and pretend that I'm one of your girlfriends whose boyfriend just left them or somethin'. I'll be a hysterical mess and need you immediately."

She laughs out loud. "You'd really do that for me?"

"Of course I would, dummy."

"Huh, well, in that case, I'm gonna think about hooking you up with one of my friends," she says.

My eyes widen in surprise. "Oh, yeah?" I don't know why that doesn't feel as good as it should. All of Amber's friends are pretty and smart like her. Any guy would be happy to get a potential date with one of them. But for some reason, all I can focus on is this fucking Ben dude and what he's all about. Does he even have a job? I just don't have a good feeling about this.

"You don't have to sound so enthusiastic," she mocks. "Or are you really taking a break from the ladies like you keep professing?"

I can't lie to her, and I won't, but I run the risk of sounding like a complete loser in the process by being totally honest, so I use work as an excuse. "I've been so busy at the shop ever since we opened, I'm workin' twelve to fourteen hour days, seven days a week. Last thing I've got time for is a date." I bang my knuckles down on the bar. "But I'd make an exception if it's that Katie chick."

I know full well Katie is dating some hot-shot lawyer and I'd never stand a chance, but it'll throw her off the scent of the real reason why I'm not wanting to spread my wings and fly from our little nest. The real reason being I don't want hook ups anymore. They're old and boring and have been for a while. And if I'm honest, even if things aren't romantic with me and Amber, I still like having her all to myself. Ben can go fuck himself, but one thing he won't be doing is fucking her. Not if I can help it.

"She has a boyfriend."

I rub the scruff on my chin. "She does, huh? That's too bad."

She narrows her pretty eyes. "You know Katie's not single. Are you trying to dodge my matchmaking skills on purpose? I have nice friends and I'll have you know I have a hundred percent success rate."

I scoff. "Right. I'll believe that when I see it. If you're so good at match-makin', then why haven't you found your own Prince Charming?"

She starts putting the bottles into the cooler, her back to me. "Well, maybe I just have to kiss a lot of frogs before I find my happily ever after."

Something in her words sounds sad; like she truly believes it and it isn't just a joke anymore.

"Let's make a deal," I say, leaning over the bar toward her. "If your date doesn't work out, and all of your friends are too prim and proper—"

"Hey! They're not prim and proper!"

"—then I think I should stand in and be your date, you know, like a worst-case scenario."

She stops what she's doing and turns. "Bronco, get outta here."

"What? I'm serious. It's like those pacts you make when you're twelve with your best friend and one of you is moving away. If we're not married by the time we're forty, we'll meet again and get hitched because we're the only single people left," I laugh. "Not that I'm suggestin' we get hitched."

"You know you're only making me more determined to make Ben and me work, right?"

I fucking hope not. I grit my teeth and smile. "I still think he sounds like he's a history teacher."

"So he'll be smart."

"Smart enough to stay out of your panties, if he knows what's good for him."

She puts her hands on her hips. "Thanks for the pep talk, *babe.*"

I wink. "Anytime. My door is always open."

She shakes her head. "We don't have a pact."

"Oh yes we do. You might not agree with it, but I'd be bettin' you'd have more fun on a date with me than *Benjamin.*"

"You really do keep me amused," she jokes. "I don't know what I'd do without you."

I really fucking hope to keep it that way.

2

AMBER

Four months ago
The rescue

I CHECK THE TIME ON MY WATCH. *GODDAMN IT.* THE guy I was supposed to meet is late and this isn't exactly the kind of bar where you're going to potentially meet the love of your life. I could be wrong, but Skinny Dick's Saloon isn't ringing my bells.

This is exactly what you get when you don't plan ahead. I need to stay off dating apps, and I have successfully for a while now, but I got curious. I haven't had a date in a long time and frankly, I'm in the mood. I just didn't plan on having to wade through a bar with women barely dressed, handing out drinks on silver trays to creepy looking men who make the biker bars I'm used to look like Disneyland. I cringe. I don't know what the hell possessed me to not look this place up before I accepted a drink invitation, but this is not looking good.

I need to get the fuck out of here because I'll probably catch hepatitis just from drinking out of a glass.

I glance around, unable to see my way through the crowd

gathering, the loud music practically rattling my bones. *This is why you should stay home, it's safer that way.*

Stupid me for thinking that this could be a good idea. In a city like New Orleans with over 350,000 people, you'd think I'd be able to have one decent date. Over the years I've been single, it's only gotten worse. Coming out of a bad relationship three years ago, I swore I'd never get into anything heavy again. Heavy, to me, is scary. It makes me want to run, and running is something I told myself I'd stop doing once I left the compound.

My husband wasn't a good man, and it didn't take long to realize that once he had me in his sights, I was destined to be doomed. My family wasn't overly religious until my older brother, Steven, became my guardian after Mom died, and then our dad split. Dad was a drunk, as well as a good-for-nothing. After our family dynamic changed, Steven became involved with a church and as I was only fourteen at the time, I had no choice but to go with him. At twenty-two, he was an adult and like I say, he was now my legal guardian. I was already mourning the loss of my mom, and dealing with our dad leaving, too. I trusted Steven, and to be fair, I really don't think he knew what he was getting himself into until it was too late.

I steel myself. Now isn't the time to think about any of *that*. It's in the past. I've moved on.

It's been three years and I deserve a night out. I'm clearly just not looking in all the right places. Being new in town, I'm not familiar with any of the bars or clubs or wherever it is you go to meet people these days. I make my way through the crowd when I feel a hand at my elbow.

"Hello, beautiful."

I turn as a big guy with tattoos on his hands puts them on me and I try to wriggle away.

"Not looking," I state, shoving his hands off my hips.

"Really?"

"Really."

"C'mon, baby, don't be a spoil sport."

I've half a mind to knee him in the crown jewels, but I refrain. *For the moment.*

"I'm here with someone," I lie.

"I've been watching you." He tries to grope me again and I shove his chest when he reaches for me. I don't miss the distinct smell of stale beer permeating from him. *Jesus, get the fuck out of here. It ain't worth this shit.*

"Keep watching, bozo," I holler, dodging around a couple dancing so I can get the hell outta dodge.

The hustle and bustle of bodies makes it almost impossible to make it to the front door, but I finally do and take a breath when I make it outside and slump against the wall.

"This is so fucked," I say to myself. And the dick didn't even show up, or if he did, he took one look at me and left. We both said what we'd be wearing, and it isn't hard to miss a red dress like the one I'm wearing. I realize now that I'm a tad overdressed.

I'm honestly starting to question why I put myself through this. I thought a nice quiet drink at a bar would be just the ticket, but I'm too dumb to do research beforehand and got distracted by his pretty face. It's probably not even his face. It's probably AI because now I'm thinking about it, he was a little too perfect.

I sigh, pushing off the wall, turning just as the doors open and loud music spills out. My heart rate accelerates when I see the guy who groped me, and another man by his side. They're both looking around, but their eyes stop when they spot me. I start to walk quickly up the street, hoping to blend into the crowd but the meat head has his eyes on me and gives me a chin lift. I hurry my pace, leaving them behind, but as I glance back once more, to my horror they're coming my way. *Shit! Shit, shit, shit.*

Okay, now is not the time to panic. Now is the time to stay in a nice, well-lit area and not go off down any dark alleyways.

My phone buzzes in my hand and I glance at it quickly.

BRONCO

Hey, pretty girl. How did the date go?

It's my buddy from the motorcycle club where I've been bartending a few nights a week at the clubhouse. I've come and gone a few times, taking other jobs in between, but the MC has always been good to me. Crazily enough, they've been the most respectful out of all the people I've worked for over the years. It's good money, and the bikers aren't all that bad. Okay, a few of them have tried hitting on me, but that's to be expected. There are women everywhere at that club, but I can't honestly complain and say they're shitty to work for because they're really good.

I turn again. The guys are gaining on me and the big beefy one who touched me looks like he's on a mission. His jaw set, his face tense; I'm guessing he didn't like my rejection. I turn back just in time to not hit somebody on the sidewalk.

I hit the phone icon and call Bronco.

"Goin' that good, huh?" He snickers.

"Bronco, I think I'm in trouble."

"What? *Fuck.* Where are you?"

I glance around. "I... I don't know, I was supposed to meet a guy at this joint..."

I can hear him shuffling around, voices in the background, then it's quiet. I'm figuring he's at the clubhouse and he just stepped outside. "Which bar?"

"Uh." I rack my brain to think of the stupid name again. "Skinny Dick's."

"For fuck's sake, Amber!" he cusses. "Please tell me you're jokin'?"

"These guys." I turn again, my mouth dry as they continue their pursuit. "They followed me out, and now I'm running up the street away from them."

"Fuck. Okay, this is what you're gonna do. If you see a cop on the street, you go tell him what's goin' on, got me?"

I glance around. "I don't see any."

"This is fuckin' New Orleans, where are the fuckin' police when you need them?"

"They're gaining on me, Bronc. The larger of the two tried to grope me inside."

"Go into the nearest cafe or restaurant and stay there, pick a crowded one, but not a bar."

"Okay—"

"A bar is too easy for one of them to snag you."

"Shit, Bronc!"

"Tell me the name of the street you're on."

I glance up. "I don't— I don't know... the same one Skinny Dick's is on."

"I'll be there in five minutes."

"Okay, there's a fancy restaurant, Clarice's, I'm going in there..." I step inside and shut the door behind me. A few of the tables close by turn to look at me, but at least I'm dressed for the occasion.

"Okay, tell me if they come in." I hear the distinct sound of straight pipes in the background as he fires up his Harley Davidson.

The maitre de at the front glances up at me and smiles. "Good evening, miss. Table for—" She glances down at my attire.

"One." I hold up a finger.

"Please, right this way."

"She's taking me to a table," I whisper behind her into the phone.

I take a peek toward the door and sure enough, my assailants are looking through the window.

"Did they come in?" he barks over the noise of his engine.

"No— They... they're outside..."

"Good. I'll be there soon. Do not move from that spot and if they come inside, you call the police."

"Okay."

He hangs up and I smile sweetly at the server as she takes me to a table, thankfully, in the middle of the restaurant, surrounded by other diners. This is good; it's well lit and it's doubtful they're going to come in here and cause a scene.

I've never been so frightened in my entire life. I'm sure they're not following me to ask if I'd like to have a drink with them while chasing me up the street.

I chew on my thumb as I fake-peruse the menu, knowing I'm not ordering anything, and also hoping Bronco will get here before I have to start making excuses.

This could only fucking happen to you. Trouble follows you wherever you go.

Ain't that the truth. I've been around long enough to know that I do possess a certain bad juju where men are concerned, and it was only a stroke of luck that I happened to see Bronco's text when I did. I'm not good in times of pressure. Don't get me wrong, I escaped a cult so I know how to run and hide, but this is a little too close for comfort.

It feels like forever, and I've already told the server I need some more time, when my eyes dart to the door and I see Bronco's larger than life body in the doorway, his gaze scanning the restaurant for me as I stand. I've never been so relieved to see anyone in my life.

I practically leap into his arms when he reaches me. "Oh, thank God," I sigh.

"You okay?" He checks me over; the frown between his eyes deepening.

"Just rattled," I admit. "Maybe I'm being paranoid, I don't know."

"You're not bein' paranoid. There are too many creeps in this fuckin' shit hole." He glances around as some of the patrons stare at him.

I can't help but smile. Bronco is dressed in his motorcycle jacket; his dirty patch on the top left corner reads 'Tail Gunner,' with his name underneath it. I never knew what a Tail Gunner was until I started working at the clubhouse. Apparently, this club needs two motorcycles to ride at the back to ensure the safety of the riders when they're out on their club runs. I think it's kinda hot. He also sports a fitted long sleeved, black Henley and a dark pair of jeans with a lot of wear and tear, and his black boots finish everything off. Then there's the hair; his pride and joy. It's short at the sides but longer on top, neatly disheveled and his goatee closely trimmed. The man is a sight for sore eyes, not that I've not noticed before; I've got perfect vision.

Bronco and I kinda just clicked right away. He was probably one of the few who didn't hit on me, and also didn't stare at my tits while I talked. Don't get me wrong, not all the bikers are like that; a lot of them are in relationships or married, but the single guys in the club can be a little loose.

"I feel silly calling you to rescue me."

He frowns. "We're friends, *AJ,* of course I'm gonna come to your rescue. This city is wild. What did the guys look like?"

I shake my head. "The bigger one was beefy with tattoos on his hands, short, almost shaved, hair. As for his counterpart, I didn't get a good look at him but he was a bit of a mini-me of his friend, shorter with tattoos."

He quirks a brow. "Mini-me?"

"Let's just go before the server comes back." Just as I say it, the server arrives at the table, her eyes growing wide when she takes in Bronco and his grasp around me.

He leans over and drops a ten-dollar bill on the table, giving the surprised looking girl a wink. All I had was a free glass of water. "Plans have changed," he tells her. "Gotta get my girl home."

My girl?

I know he's just playing a part so as not to upset the other patrons, but he's raised enough eyebrows in here to make sure we're definitely being watched and talked about in quiet whispers. Leaving no time to ponder that, he takes my hand. "Stay with me, I'm parked across the street."

Where does he think I'm gonna go? Though, I think he's just trying to reassure me.

I don't argue with his words. Bronco is safe, and all my embarrassment over calling him dissipates when we step outside and I can fully appreciate how warm his hand is in mine.

It's like home, although it shouldn't really feel like home. I don't know what fucking home is. I've been carving out this new life for myself for so long, you'd think I'd have a handle on it by now. Clearly, I've been living in delulu land because this is the first time anyone has made me feel safe.

"You good?" His gaze finds mine after he glances up and down the street. We're still under the small entryway of the restaurant.

I glance around too, finally meeting his gaze. "I don't see them."

"Okay, let's go." He squeezes my hand as we step out onto the street and make a dash across the road toward his motorcycle.

It's then I stop in my tracks mid-way across the road.

"Amber?" he barks. "You're on the fuckin' street!"

"I see them!"

"Where?" He looks around, but it doesn't take long. He spots them because they're right there, staring at us.

Dragging me off the street, he positions me beside his motorcycle and says, "Don't move."

"Bronco, don't!"

He charges toward them and before I know what's even happening, he's tackling the bigger dude like he's a quarterback and the big man goes stumbling backward, surprise taking him off guard. I shriek, my hands over my mouth as Bronco starts pounding his face with punches. The smaller guy is behind, yanking Bronco off his not-so-tough friend who's unconscious on the ground, then he turns and takes one swing and the guy doubles over, crying out like a mama's boy when Bronco strikes.

"You think it's fuckin' funny to stalk women down the street?" He kicks him in the ribs as I stare, horrified.

"Bronco!" I yell as two policemen rush toward him.

He turns, cussing as he reaches into his back pocket and tosses me his keys. "Gonna need these."

I stare at him. "I can't drive your Harley!"

"Not you! Call one of the girls, get a prospect down here to drive it, babe."

Oh.

I gape at him as he drops down on his knees, folding his arms behind his head before the cops even reach him. "Are you actually insane?" I scream, moving toward him.

He grins. "Not like they're gonna try that again anytime soon, right?"

I've never had a man defend my honor before, it's a new experience. Even if he did go a little postal on their asses, being chased by two drunk men isn't exactly cool behavior.

"You're getting arrested for me?" I cry, my voice an octave too high. Panic runs through me as I try not to hyperventilate.

I've never seen anything like that, and if I wasn't so shocked, I might be a little impressed.

He doesn't even have a mark on him, though his knuckles look red and a little swollen. He grins at me, his face showing absolutely no remorse. "Not just for you, for women everywhere."

I think I just died a little bit right there on the pavement. I watch in horror as the cops tug his arms behind him and slap cuffs on his wrists. He doesn't protest or say anything, but the two sprawled out men by their feet are indication enough of what he did.

"He didn't do anything!" I tell the police. "These guys were following me all the way up the street and making me feel uncomfortable. I had to make a run for it."

"Ma'am, you can make a statement downtown," one of the cops says, then barks something into his receiver as I glance at Bronco. He's not giving them a lick of trouble, but once they see his MC patch they call for backup. Typical.

"Call one of the girls," he repeats. "Can't leave my sled here all night."

"Got it, Bronc." I pull my phone out and with shaky fingers I call Luna, who's Tag's — the club's Sergeant at Arm's — ol' lady.

I think I've had just about all the dating that I can stand.

Bronco rubs his wrists as we walk out of the station. Of course the club has a lawyer, Payden, who's friends with Luna and helps the MC out from time to time. I used to think the two of them had something going on, but then Payden got a boyfriend, putting that rumor to bed.

He whistles a tune like nothing has happened. Like he

wasn't just in jail for beating up two people, and essentially defending me.

"That was intense," I say, feeling guilty that he'll have a criminal record if the charges go ahead. I explained to the cops what was going on, and once the two miscreants are treated at the hospital, they'll be able to make a statement, too. I won't hold my breath that anything will happen to them. The police don't usually do anything until it's too late.

"It wasn't nearly as intense as it could've been." He smiles when he sees his beloved motorcycle parked out front. "Which motherfucker drove my sled?"

"Pipes was the only one free," I say, even though he's not technically a prospect anymore, he's the most trustworthy out of the members who don't sit around the committee table.

"Not pissed about that."

"He said as much."

He glances down at my dress. "You gonna get on my sled in that?"

I glance down at myself. "I didn't think I'd be hopping on the back of your motorcycle tonight, did I?"

The cops let me ride with them to the station but now I need to get home.

"Clearly." He rubs his chin. "You look pretty in red, it suits you."

I balk. "Uh, thanks?"

"Why do you say it like it's a question?"

"Um, probably because you've never said anything like that to me before."

He shrugs. "Doesn't mean I haven't thought it."

"I guess not." I shift awkwardly.

"So, you gonna hitch that skirt up, or want me to do the honors?" He smirks.

I slap his arm. "How long have you been waiting to ask me that?"

I like the sound of his laughter, his eyes creasing at the corners as he waves his palms at me. "Fine. You do it yourself, but don't blame me when that pretty skirt gets ripped. Skintight and motorcycles don't exactly mix well."

I huff as he swings one leg over the body of his bike and then pulls a bandana up around his neck, covering his chin. Okay, that's hot. I've seen him wearing it higher over his mouth when he rides, but up close and personal... okay, that shouldn't be doing things to me.

This is my fucking friend. I refuse to be attracted to him because he's the only male I truly trust. I don't want to jeopardize a friendship by sleeping with him and ruining what we have; which is what will inadvertently happen if we let it.

"You gonna get on or just gape at me all night?"

Just to prove he's wrong and I'm right, I start to shimmy my skirt up my legs and his eyes dip. He scratches his chin, then palms the back of his neck as the material slowly rises.

"See?" I do a twirl and he laughs.

"Put this on." He hands me a helmet and I frown.

"C'mere." I move toward him and he pulls the helmet down slowly, fixing the strap so it's tight and won't go anywhere.

"You really are some kind of saint," I sigh.

He smirks. "Nah, I'm pretty sure they kicked me outta heaven for misbehavin'."

"Of that I have no doubt." Moving behind him, I swing my leg over, and at the same time my dress gives way and the ripping sound rings in the air.

His shoulders shake. "Told ya."

I whack him on the shoulder. "You were just dying to be right for once, weren't you?"

"Come on, I'm gonna take you to get a burger, then you're gonna burn that dress and never wear it again."

My heart hitches in my chest as I settle in behind him, my

coochie practically on display because my dress is now rucked up around my hips. "Hey, this is my go-to dress which cost a lot of money, and I can still fix it. "

He turns to the side, patting me on the thigh. "That's not what I meant."

"Oh?"

His voice is husky when he says, "If this dress doesn't exist, it'll be better for everyone concerned." With that, he starts the engine as it roars to life, deafening any reply I have on my tongue as I wrap my arms around his waist.

This man really will be the death of me in more ways than one.

3

BRONCO

Present day

"So, you think you can cover it?" the pretty girl named Cara asks as I try not to crack a smile.

I'm a professional, but having a Butthead tattooed on your body without Beavis is a crime in itself. I'm kinda known as the cover up guy in the ink slinging world. Truth be told, I didn't plan on being the cover up guy, it just sorta worked out that way.

"You like the design, right?" I check, just to be sure. I know she's nervous and she has good reason to be after her last tattoo disaster, but I'm not some amateur.

She bites on her lip. "I love it, I just don't want it messed up again."

I sigh inwardly. I get it. Cara's been duped before. Then again, she did admit that she got drunk in Vegas and went to a cheap tattoo shop; the end result was the shittiest tattoo I've probably ever seen. Covering it up will be a challenge, but I'm always up for something that will push my limits.

She chose a red rose design with intertwining stems,

intricate detailing and a golden dragon raging through the center. Apparently, there's a fantasy book out that has taken the world by storm and this chick wants to commemorate it on her skin. I've no idea what the fuck *Fourth Wing* is, but she's the client, not me, and if that's what she wants, I'm going to give it to her.

"I promise I'm not gonna mess it up. You've seen my work and the reviews on my website," I reassure her. "But you can think about it if you need a little more time. I want you to feel one hundred percent sure before you do anything, okay?"

She shakes her head. "I'm ready. I just want this gone." Her plea has me feeling sympathy for her.

I mean, this ain't pretty. "Just promise me you won't go gettin' anymore late night, drunken tatts anywhere, got me?"

She nods solemnly, tears in her eyes.

"Say it." I hold my pinkie toward her; at least that renders a smile.

"I promise." She links her pinkie with mine and I think I've helped lighten the mood as she settles back onto the chair. The stencil is ready, and I place it on her shoulder blade, over the existing monumental mess she's currently sporting. Cara takes deep breaths as if she's about to give birth.

My shop is fucking epic. It's been a long time coming, but Iron & Ink has been a long dream of mine. Thanks to the club's help, I was able to secure a great location downtown and finally start working for myself. I still help around at the clubhouse, but doing what I wanna do has been a life changing event.

I really hope she's not a crier, but as I start the needle, she tenses and I may have to go and get Josie, one of my artists, to come and hold her hand. Why she didn't bring a gaggle of friends, I'll never know. Usually, that's what girls her age do.

"I can stop at any time," I tell her. "Just let me know, okay? It's gonna feel a lot different than when you were drunk." I've used numbing cream, and I think she may have had a shot of liquid courage before she got here, but if this chick wants a normal life — or to wear a strapless sundress again — she needs this covering.

She nods. "Okay, thanks Bronco, you've been really sweet."

I get this a lot, but I've always been a good listener. It's the one thing my mama taught me in life, especially when it comes to women, and it's served me well. I want her to feel good about herself, and that's why I'm here. To help people.

"Sweet's my middle name," I joke. "Just relax, and when you need a break, you just let me know."

"It's gonna hurt, right?"

God, how passed out was she that night? "Uh, yep, it'll sting a little."

The appointment runs overtime because I have to keep stopping and starting so many times. She's a trooper though, and we get the session finished; something I wasn't sure I could do in one sitting. It looks fucking epic. The red of the roses drips, while the golden dragon roars through the middle, bright bursts of yellow and orange in his wake. It's a work of art. Sometimes I really don't give myself enough credit for what I do. To think she had fucking Butthead tattooed there hours ago.

I help her up once I'm done cleaning her skin, then pass her a handheld mirror as I guide her to the huge hanging mirror across the room. "What do you think?"

She gasps, tears falling down her cheeks. "Oh, my God!" She jumps up and down, and I'm still unsure if she's happy or madder than before, but then she reaches for me and starts hugging the crap out of me as I laugh. For a little thing, she sure has a mean grip.

"Okay, you like it? Phew." I swipe my forehead with the back of my hand. "For a second there I got a little worried."

"This is fucking amazing!" She bounces up and down on her toes, releasing me as she has another look. "I love it!"

I laugh. "Fantastic. I'll give you some care instructions—"

She palms the side of my face. "I can give you some instructions with what I'd like to do with that big dick energy of yours."

Big dick energy? Am I really giving off BDE?

I open my mouth and close it again. I want to peel her hands off me, but she hasn't paid me in full yet, and I don't wanna piss her off. But I'm not sleeping with her. For one, she's a client, she's also not my type, and she's far too young.

"Honey, I don't mix business with pleasure, but you are really sweet. I'm glad you like it." I try my softest voice that usually works on most of the women in my life.

As if I didn't get the memo, she blurts, "*Like* it? I love it! I could suck your dick for how fucking epic this looks!" She's back to checking herself out again in the mirror. Her smile is a mile wide.

I chuckle. "Let me get those after-care instructions as I need to go over them, okay? It's really important."

She's nodding again, taking in every word as I guide her back to the chair so I can wrap the tattoo properly and let the healing begin. I know she's a bit of an airhead, so I make sure that I tell her she needs to take off the saran wrap after 24 hours.

"So you're gonna take this off tomorrow and wash it with soapy water, we don't want any bacteria or an infection settin' in," I tell her. "The swelling and tenderness will go down in a week or so, and healing is between two and four weeks. You need to keep it clean, dry and I don't recommend re-wrapping it. If you want it re-wrapped over the next day or so, then come back into the shop anytime and we'll do it for you. The skin will need to breathe, regenerate and heal itself."

"Okay, I mean, I can show it off to my friends, though, right?"

I smile. "Of course, just don't take this off until tomorrow night, and don't leave it on any longer."

"Got it."

I hand her the booklet with the care instructions and her little takeaway bag with some of our merch and social media paraphernalia; courtesy of Jett's ol' lady, Summer, who helped me get it all together. Jett is Club's Treasurer, and Deanna, our club Prez's ol' lady, is an interior designer who did an awesome job of making the shop look like a high-end tattoo parlor.

We went with a deep burgundy on the walls with gold and black accents; a chandelier hangs in the main foyer with dark, original floorboards that we had sanded back and refinished. There's motorcycle memorabilia all around the shop and a vintage Harley in the window; my own little tribute to the club that has become my family.

I love my mom, and with my dad not in the picture growing up, I didn't have a lot of male influence. My dad's family was a nightmare, so we moved away. I have one brother, Ansel, who lives in Mississippi near my mom. I often get shit over my real name, Torin, but I'm named after a bull, which is also my star sign, Taurus. Mom is a hippie from way back, but I don't hold that against her. She raised us with all the love and affection she possibly could, and it wasn't easy with two boys only a year apart. Ansel is the older one; he and I couldn't be more like chalk and cheese if we tried. He works for an insurance company and has settled down with a wife and a new baby. I don't get to see them as much as I'd like, but we're on good terms. My mom, however? She's always popping by unannounced to check up on me and bring me food. That would be cool if the food she made was edible. Since going vegan a few years ago and experimenting with things like mung beans and lentils, I've gotta suck it up and eat what she makes so I don't upset her. I just make sure I get my protein in after she's left the state.

When I finally manage to get Cara out of the shop, after slipping me her number even though it's already on her file, I sigh with relief. I'm glad she's happy and it makes me feel good knowing there's one less horrible tattoo in the world. There'll always be cover ups until the day is long, that's the unfortunate thing in this business, but there's no way you can't feel good about what she just walked out with and I take pride in that.

My phone buzzes in my pocket and I smile when I see Amber's name pop up.

AJ
How's it hanging?

ME
9 inches last time I checked

AJ
😁 9 inches?

ME
You asked

AJ
Stupid me

ME
What's up?

AJ
My date has the flu

I rub my chin. *Good.* I haven't heard better news all day because her going out on a date with her best friend's fucking brother's best friend, just spells a happily ever after. Not that I don't want that for her, I do, but I don't trust dudes. Especially ones named Ben. It's too squeaky clean, and when something sounds too good to be true, it usually is. I know what dudes are like and Amber is the kind of girl who lands herself into trouble before she can even blink.

ME

What a shame

AJ

I can just hear the sarcasm in that text

ME

Would I do such a thing?

AJ

Yes, you would. Before I cancel the babysitting, I wondered if you'd like to go to the game with me?

Remembering the pact I suggested, not that she agreed to it, I smile. Sitting back in the chair behind the desk, I rub my chin. Hanging out with Amber this weekend sounds great. I'm not gonna pass that opportunity up.

ME

I like how I'm your second choice

AJ

Haha, are you coming or not? Otherwise, I'm gonna have to sell the tickets. Olive hates sports so she won't come with me

ME

Is this the part where I keep you hanging?

AJ

No, this is the part where you decide if you're not gonna be a complete dick

ME

Not the first time I've been called that today, though my client did offer to service me bc I made her so happy

AJ

OMG, what???????

ME

Happens all the time

AJ

Uh, huh, Mr. Bighead. I might have to cancel if your head isn't gonna fit through the door, there's clearly no point in being seen in public with you

ME

Apparently I'm also sweet

AJ

You know how to schmooze, that's not the same thing

ME

Schmooze? Them's some big words. I promise, I'll deflate my head just for you

I wait for her reply and I realize that whenever me and Amber text or call one another, I'm smiling. Not just smiling. Grinning like a fucking Cheshire cat. What the fuck is up with that?

AJ

So that's a yes?

ME

To me schmoozing you, or the date?

AJ

It's not a date, and yes, the game, you asshat

I chuckle. Amber always gives it to me straight; it's one of the things I dig about her. I also want to drag this out a little and make her sweat.

ME

Why isn't it a date? Am I not good enough boyfriend material?

AJ

Of course you are, but with my baggage at the moment, there's no way I'd put that on you. Plus, I've seen you around the club…

Again, she startles me with the truth. As if her, or Olive, could ever be that. *Baggage?* Right now, they are a package deal, I get that, but I hardly see it as baggage.

I dance over the snide club comment because lord knows I've been no angel. I just wish she'd tell me what the fuck is really going on and why there's all this mystery around this little girl being dumped in her care without prior warning.

ME

Don't see any baggage. Ben is a dumb fuck if you ask me, but maybe it's fate lending a helpin' hand and stepping in before it's too late

Yeah, some of my mom's woo-woo shit rubbed off onto

me. I know more about crystals and essential oils than any man should know, courtesy of Mama dearest.

> **AJ**
> Or he really did catch the flu

> **ME**
> It's fate

> **AJ**
> You and your hocus pocus

> **ME**
> You read your star signs every day, who's the weird one now?

Amber is a Virgo, and often displays attributes associated with the sign; she's always cleaning, she's never late, and will go out of her way to make others feel appreciated. Perfectionism is her middle name, her only downfall is her tendency to worry. She does that a lot. Amber's a giver.

> **AJ**
> You, weirdo. You're the one who wears crystals on their body

I glance down. The shungite at my wrist is made up of pure carbon and assists with keeping bad elements away, according to my mom, and electro-magnetic field energy from computers and the outside world. The black obsidian is in a small pouch that tucks under my shirt. It's made from volcanic glass and lava. It's said to cleanse dark energy, has grounding properties and helps relieve stress. I was a skeptic until I tried it out for myself.

> **ME**
>
> Walkin' on sunshine over here, Little Lady. My mom knows when I haven't been wearing them and she'll only send me more

I can just picture Amber laughing her ass off at me, but that's how we are. We tell each other every little detail, and basically leave nothing out. Except for the darkness I know Amber carries with her. I know she had an awful ex, and her childhood was shitty, but aside from that she keeps quiet about her past. And Olive. I want to help. If her sister-in-law is in trouble, I'm here to assist in any way. I'm also not a mind reader and it's frustrating the ever-living shit out of me.

> **AJ**
>
> Your mom does sound adorable

> **ME**
>
> Wait until you meet her for real

The last few times she's been in town, Amber has been busy at work, or out of town. Since I talk about her all the time, Mom is convinced she's my secret girlfriend. She doesn't understand that men and women can be friends without anything happening.

> **AJ**
>
> Can't wait. So, are you keeping me hanging?

> **ME**
>
> Fine. You twisted my arm. But I'm only doing this bc you'll now have to measure up every date you have after this one to see if it compares

> **AJ**
>
> It's not a date!

> **ME**
> Yeah, you keep telling yourself that

> **AJ**
> Just keep the cheering down to a dull roar, I've got sensitive ears

I chuckle again.

> **ME**
> Yes, ma'am

I shove my phone in my back pocket to go tidy in the back to get everything ready for the next client. Aside from me, I have five other ink slingers working around the clock. We're open until late every night, and close on Sundays. It's taken time to get the right crew together, but we got there in the end. Now I have a full staff and the shop is always busy.

As I clean my work area, I can't help but feel a little smug that I'm the one that gets to go out with Amber to the game. It's not like we haven't spent a lot of time together over the last few years, but now she's talking about seriously dating someone, I feel even more protective than I ever have.

Amber has come a long way from when she first turned up at the clubhouse looking for a job. She's no longer a shadow of her former self. While she's never gone into the details of her abusive ex, I know that living with him was no picnic and she fled to get away. It hurts her to talk about it so I don't pry, but a part of me wonders. I mean, if I knew where he was I could fuck him up. It might not fix things, but it'd make me feel better, and quite possibly her, though Amber doesn't have a mean bone in her body. She's perfect just as she is.

I spend the rest of the day working until dark, then take my sorry and sore ass home. Titan, who sleeps the whole day in my office, sits next to me in the truck on the days I bring him to work. He usually whimpers when I leave him behind, but sometimes he's mad at me for no apparent reason and ignores me, preferring to have some 'me' time every now and again. He hates me being gone for long periods, but it's just one of the things I love about him.

I slide into bed late, turning the TV off in my room. It's been playing merely for background noise, but I prefer quiet when I'm sleeping. Titan jumps on the end of the bed. While I've tried to make him comfortable on his own bed right below me, he's not having any of it, preferring to lie half on top of me while he snores loud enough to wake the dead. He also barks at the slightest little noise, whether it be a potential burglar or a leaf blowing outside, we'll never know the difference.

I sleep naked, preferring to be comfortable in my slumber. I live alone so it's not like I've got the chance of offending anyone.

My hand slides to my dick, and though I'm exhausted, I should rub one out. I'll feel better and I'll inevitably fall asleep quicker.

I lean over, reaching for the baby oil in the top drawer, along with the tissue box close by.

Okay, maybe I did get a little cheeky, but I'd be close to it. It isn't like I've ever measured before, but chicks always tell me I'm fucking massive. I grip my dick, sliding my hand up and down my cock as it grows harder. Sometimes I'll watch porn to get off, sometimes I'll check out the Victoria Secret website. But tonight, I don't have the energy as I grow hard in my hand, grunting as I rock my hips, hoping to get this over and done with fast.

It'd be easier to open my phone and look at the hot chicks file I have; tits being my thing. My mind wanders to Amber in her tight tank top the other day and my dick pulses. *What the fuck?* I've never pictured her while getting off. Not that she isn't fucking beautiful, I just want to be able to look her in the eye the next time I see her. But as I remember her jiggling those generous tits in my direction when she was teasing me, my mind wanders to what they'd look like naked and if she'd enjoy me sucking her nipples while underneath me. Before I know it, I'm spilling cum all over myself before I can even blink. *Holy shit.* I'm breathing hard, my chest rising and falling rapidly as I reach for the tissues.

No.

That can't happen. Not with Amber. She's my touchstone. A delicate rose that I can't toy with. I made that promise to myself when we first started getting friendly. No fucking friends. It'll only end in disaster, and I'll do well to remember that.

4

AMBER

The Past - Three years ago

"You can't be serious?" Erica stares at me, her voice low. "If they find out what you're doing, they'll hang us both."

I rip up the sleeve of my dress, exposing my bruised skin. "Do you think I want to live like this for the rest of my life?" I stammer. "Being afraid of the husband I was forced to marry? And what about you? Steven is completely insane!"

"I don't know, Amber. This is extreme."

I huff. "You're just saying that because the time has come to make our escape and now you're getting cold feet."

"I swear to you, I'm not. But this? This is nuts!"

"It's our only shot."

"In a delivery van?" I can hear the incredulousness in her tone. "You've lost your ever-loving mind!"

"Can you think of anything better?" I challenge. "We both need to get out of here. Do you want what happened to us to happen to Olive?"

Erica shifts her gaze. Long in thought, she eventually

meets my eyes again. "I don't want to get caught and be punished. If we do, they'll take Olive away."

"They're too in love with their own egos to think we'll ever stray. Besides, I've been acting like a good little wife now for ages."

Erica regards me with suspicion. "You have?"

I huff slightly. "I love how you always think the worst of me."

"I don't think the worst of you, but Vince is fully aware of your schemes, as are the rest of the village."

"Do you honestly like being a prisoner here?" I whisper. "Erica, you can't tell me this is how you thought life would be. We can both admit that my brother and Vince went too far in this thing, now they think they're some kind of Messiahs to the masses."

"Shh!" She looks around the empty garden as if someone could stumble upon us. All the men are at work or at the ministry.

"Nobody can hear us!"

"You don't know that," she mouths.

I can't say I blame Erica for being paranoid. After twelve years of living in the compound, shit kinda gets to you. When my brother became a minister in the church, the power went to his head. He's always been controlling and has looked upon me with disdain. I truly think that he brought me here after our dad left to dump me so I'd become someone else's problem. Then he got friendly with Vince and the rest is history.

I also know she's talking about Sara and Jude; Steven's other two wives. Yes, the men in our village can take as many wives as they like, and we're supposed to put up with them putting their hands on us whenever they feel like it. Steven has never beaten Erica to within an inch of her life like Vince has done to me, but he has slapped her around. He thinks because he hits her with an open hand it's not abuse. I fucking hate him, but I hate Vince more.

I hold Erica's shoulders. "Listen to me. Things are only going to get worse. I was promised to Vince at fifteen! I was a fucking child, and we know full well what happens to girls in this fucking place. Olive is ten now," I say. "It won't be long before she'll be sacrificed to some old geriatric and forced to marry just like we were. There are more women than men in this shit hole for a reason."

She stares at me, her face draining as she takes in my words. Surely, she's thought about this before? It isn't like she's incapable of doing the math.

When Vince took me and Steven in, I thought he was a good guy. He always had a kind hand and words to match, complimenting me and making sure I never went without. He's fifteen years older than me, an old man in my eyes, but especially when I was fourteen years old at the time we joined. I was forced to marry him at sixteen. *Sixteen!* I suppose I should've been grateful that I wasn't any younger. Of course, it was what the Good Lord wanted from us. The fact I couldn't fall pregnant, however, that was a huge problem and still is. I'm all but shunned and Vince has done everything, including beating the living shit out of me, trying to get me to produce an heir. I've always been his favorite wife; my sister wives Becky, Anne and Linda all have children. I guess the Lord just isn't ready to bless our marriage. The more the years rolled on, the more I realized exactly how lucky I was to not fall pregnant. I've had two miscarriages, and they were no picnic, but the more I've thought about it, the more I realize that it isn't meant to be. If I do ever have a child, it won't be with him. He makes my skin crawl.

Erica chews on her bottom lip. "I don't want that for my daughter." Her face grows redder as she speaks, her anger bubbling. "She's a child, just like you were."

"It doesn't matter about that." I brush it off. If I think about the injustices that were done to me over the time I've been here, I'd never leave my own house. Somewhere deep inside, I know there's a better life out there for me. "He will get what's coming to him, they all will. This isn't God's plan: it's *their* plan."

She nods. "I'm sorry. I didn't mean to imply that you couldn't get us out of this, but I'll admit that I'm afraid."

I clutch her hands. "Now's our chance. We can't let this slip away."

The delivery van comes into the village once a month, along with other delivery trucks for bigger items like hay for the animals and feed. Vince and Steven organize all the supplies with several of the other ministers. We have no shops and no contact with the outside world. Nobody has a phone or any technology. It's like the Mormons and the Amish gave birth to a baby and that's where we find ourselves. We're literal prisoners.

We're the outcasts because we both have spirit. That's another thing the hierarchy doesn't like about women; opinions don't matter. You're here to cook, clean and reproduce. We're not even allowed books unless they're approved by the church.

I screw my eyes shut, my anger just as robust as Erica's. We both want to leave so badly.

"There you are!" We both jump as we hear Sara call over the wall.

What the heck is she doing here?

"Sara." I fold my arms over my chest. I don't mind Sara, but loathe Jude. If she was the one to catch us out here, innocently watering the garden, she'd be running off to our husbands to make up lies about us. "To what do I owe the pleasure?" It is my home, after all. My sister wives are out assisting some of the other women with the weekend festivities over Easter. It keeps them out of my hair for a bit while I pretend to be helping out at home getting the baked goods ready.

"I was just trying to find Erica." She smiles a little tightly, she's afraid of me and for good reason. I fight back, and she of all people knows that I'll smack her in the face if she ever touches me or says a bad word in front of my face.

"What for?" Erica puts her hands on her hips. "I'm foraging with my sister for the decorating table. I said I'd be back after lunchtime."

"Steven needs you."

Erica is very good at hiding the panic from her face. "Whatever for?"

Sara shrugs. "I don't know, he didn't say. I would assume it's about the weekend and where he wants all of us."

I try not to let the panic show in me, too, but I'm a little easier to read.

"Is that all?" I huff. "We're busy, I'm sure this can wait."

"Can I help?" She looks over at our empty baskets, a small frown on her face.

"No," I say at the same time Erica says, "Of course."

Sara looks between us both. It's no secret that Erica and I are close, and I don't like sharing my time with her with anyone else. She's the only one in this godforsaken place that's worth talking to, the fact that she hasn't ratted me out when I first came to her to tell her my plans, just goes to show you what kind of person she is. We've both been brainwashed, but somehow we can see the wood through the trees. I've known for a long time she isn't happy, and she's been worried about the implications for Olive.

I give Erica a sharp look. "I'm sure Sara can run along and let my brother know you're with me. It'll put his mind at ease while we fill our baskets."

We both know Sara came to spy. I guess we should be grateful it's not Jude. She'd be all over us like a rash.

"That's probably best." Erica smiles and Sara smiles back. My eyes almost roll into the back of my head at how superficial this all is. How all of us walk on eggshells around one another, afraid to speak freely. But that's how it is around here. Trust nobody, only each other.

I shoo her with my hand. "Bye now, thanks for stopping by."

She frowns slightly, then waves and takes off. I look over the wall to make sure she's really gone.

Erica turns to me. "Did you have to do that?"

"What?" I act as if I've no clue what she's talking about.

"Giving her pause to cause a fuss will only arouse suspicion."

"Suspicion for what, exactly?" I scoff. "They don't know what we're up to. Nobody does."

"You know how Steven is. If he gets wind of any of this..."

"I think all of this devious behavior is making you more paranoid than normal," I tell her. "It'll be fine."

"So we just hitch a ride with the delivery guy? I don't think you've thought this through."

"He won't know. We'll climb in the back, and if you have any other suggestions, other than scaling the wall, let me know."

"Oh, my heavens, please do not tell me that's your next plan?"

"What?" I shrug. "Have you got a better one? The gatekeepers won't be concerned with him, they don't even check his truck anymore. Plus, everyone will be so busy with the festival that they won't notice a thing. Trust me."

The gatekeepers are just that; two men that sit at the gates situated at the entrance to the village. Their only job is to oversee who comes and goes, maintain order and make sure nobody escapes. They don't put any of that in the welcome booklet, though.

The men can come and go as they please, of course. Women, however? We can only leave if in the company of our husbands. I've only been outside these gates twice in ten years and that was with Vince by my side when we had to go to the doctors to get tests. That was when we learned I'm basically infertile.

"I just... I know you're right. I'm just afraid."

I cup her cheeks, forcing her to look at me. "Erica, we have to do this. You know my brother won't give Olive an exception and she'll be married off young, too. They're both talking about taking on more wives, expanding the compound. Since I can't give Vince an heir, he wants to take another wife."

"What?" she whisper-shouts. "A fifth wife?"

"He's demented," I say. "The pigs in the mud are of higher status than he is."

"But how will we survive out there? What will we do for money?"

We've already discussed this, but I know she needs reminding from time to time. "I have a little saved from what I've managed to stash away when Vince is drunk," I say. "It'll be enough to buy a bus ticket to somewhere. *Anywhere*. We'll get help, they have refuges and things. I just know we will be okay. We have to have faith. Anything is better than this. Don't back out on me now, we need to stick together."

"I'm not," she whispers. "But you have to promise me, if anything happens and we get split up—"

"We won't."

"You get Olive out," she finishes. "All that matters is she is safe and away from here."

I nod. "You know I'll guard her with my life."

She stares at me, her golden eyes sad as we make our preparations to get the fuck out of here. "Okay. I'm in."

"For real?"

"Yes! For real."

I pull her into a hug, barely able to contain my excitement. It's a crazy plan, but I've talked to Carlo, the driver, a few times. He delivers the flour, eggs and milk when we run out of our own supplies; usually Christmas and Easter. Making our getaway has never looked so promising and I'm kicking myself that I haven't thought of it before. If he catches us? I don't know… I haven't thought that far ahead.

I take a breath. *It's going to be okay. We're going to survive this.* I don't really know if that's true, but I have to stay strong for Erica. She's with me but I feel as if this kind of convincing could only mean she's not certain. Heck, I'm not certain of anything, just that we have to try.

"Tell me you mean that," I stammer, my eyes glazing over. I've dreamed of this day for so long.

"I mean it! I swear, I mean it. I just don't have the… I don't know… killer instinct like you do. I would never attempt this by myself."

I want to laugh in her face. I don't have a killer instinct; all of it is bravado. A mask that I've perfected over the years to protect myself. I've become so used to this lie that I truly believe we will be okay. We have to be because I can't live for one more second like this. I can't. I won't. I'd rather die than be Vince's sex slave who can't keep her mouth shut.

One day I'd love to come back with a baseball bat and hit him with it until he's suffered like all his wives have. I may not like my sister wives, but I don't hate them enough that I think it's right what he does to all of us. Ruling with an iron fist is the way of the church. They don't want the women getting too ahead of themselves, heaven forbid if they had a mind of their own. All this is, I've come to realize, is a ploy to lure people in and suck them dry. They take all the money, control everything and we have to just sit by and take whatever they dish out. It isn't fair. I was a child. I didn't sign up for this, but my own brother sold me like a slave on the black market.

"I will get us out of this," I promise. Those are some big words, but Erica needs to hear that right now, and I can give it to her. "I'll get us away from here and we can start living how we want, you just have to trust me."

She nods. "I trust you." The look in her eyes; deep devotion and respect, makes my heart lurch. She's my best friend and the sister I should've had. Betraying her husband, *my brother,* isn't anything I've taken lightly. It's a big fucking deal.

I pull her into another hug. "Whatever happens," I whisper, "we stick together. We have to stick together."

"And if we get caugh—"

"No, don't think like that. We won't get caught. The men will think we're enjoying the festivities, the women won't care what we're doing because they'll be too wrapped up in the celebrations."

I know she's nervous, but if we don't leave now, we may never escape this place. "I'm in."

I smile. "We ride at dawn."

Well, dawn takes a little longer than expected, and I'm growing more nervous on the coming Friday when the delivery truck arrives early. *Shit!* I can't pack a bag because someone will want to know where I'm going, and if I dump it and someone finds it, we're doomed. I literally have to leave with the clothes on my back and the money I stole tucked into my underwear.

I feel like I should take a weapon for when we get out, just in case, but I have nowhere to hide it.

I sprint across the village, all under the guise of prepping for the main event. We're baking fresh bread ready for tonight's supper, and I thought we had a few more hours up our sleeves.

I make it to Erica's and to my dismay, I run into Jude. "What on earth?" She gives me a once over, disapproval written all over her face.

"I'm running late," I say, panting from my sprint.

"I can see that, but it's not very lady-like to be running around out of breath. Shouldn't you be helping your sister wives?"

I want to punch this woman in the face. It's literally killed me this past month to be super nice to everyone and extra cooperative. I owe her nothing but because she's Steven's first wife, she thinks she has some hierarchy over the rest of us. "I've been helping them all week. Sara, Erica and I have always worked together over Easter, it's a tradition."

She scowls at me and it takes all my might not to reach over and scratch her eyeballs out. Like I need her permission to do jack shit. "I disagree, traditions should stay within your own home."

"Let's keep in with the Easter tradition of giving," I sing-song, pushing past her to go find Erica. I'll do and say anything to get away from the witch and I'm losing precious time.

"You won't find Erica here!" she hollers after me.

I stop in my tracks. "Where is she?"

"She went into the village." Why she looks so smug I'll never know.

"Fine. I'll go look for her there." It kills me, but in the sweetest tone I can muster I add, "Do you need anything brought back?" *Like a hole in the head?*

Even Jude can't rebuke my generosity; it isn't the Christian way. "Uh, no, th— thank you, I have all I need." Then, because she's a sour-faced bitch who can't help herself, she adds, "It's not like you to be so thoughtful."

"Oh, I'm full of surprises!" I yell, taking off down the laneway toward the village. I need to find Erica and fast. We don't have much time.

As I'm running by the tables being set up outside the church, I have to think fast. Of course Jude wouldn't have told me where Erica was even if she did know, so I have to put my thinking cap on. She knows today is the day, but she won't be at the meeting point for two more hours, and by then, the van will have been and gone. With all the activity going on today, we won't get another opportunity like this until next year. If I have to live another night here, I'll scale that wall myself and suffer the consequences, I don't even care anymore.

Erica wouldn't be visiting friends, not today. She also wouldn't let Olive out of her sight either, so they're definitely not at the school, which is out for the holiday break anyway.

Suddenly, I know where she'll be... My lungs burning and my legs killing me, I finally find the two of them, paint brushes in hand, putting the finishing touches on the table decorations at the shed where we store the outside tables and chairs.

"Erica!" I'm barely able to get the words out.

She turns and when she sees me, she pales. "Amber, are you okay?"

I double over, trying to catch my breath. There's nobody else in the barn, only Olive who gives me a wave. She doesn't know anything about what's going on because we couldn't run the risk of her accidentally telling anyone. Kids can be too honest, and the last thing we need is all of our prepping blowing up in our faces.

"The van," I wheeze. "It's here."

Her eyes grow wide. "Already?"

I nod.

She places a hand over her mouth, unable to talk.

"We have to move, we've got maybe forty-five minutes."

"To get through the entire village?"

"Yes, if we leave now, we'll make it to Mcgregor's farm."

"No, we won't." Panic starts to rise in her. "It's too far!"

"Mama?" Olive says, looking up from her painting. "What's wrong?"

Erica wipes a tear. "Nothing, sweetie, nothing at all. I'm just having a talk with Amber." She grabs my elbow and leads me away. "Go play with Anna." Anna is her ragdoll she won't go anywhere without.

"It's too soon. They'll see us!" she spits.

"No, they won't, nobody will be there. The Mcgregors aren't even at their place. Carlo will drop the bags off in the barn and that'll be his last stop. It's perfect."

"You're crazy," she hisses. "I should never have agreed to this!"

I pull the collar of my dress to one side, showing her the fresh marks Vince left on my skin. "Do you think I agreed to *this?*"

Her scrutiny falls upon my skin and I see the sorrow there in her face. I know this is all she knows, but we've both lived in the outside world, we know that there's more than this. Now is the time to truly believe that anything is possible.

She wipes her tears and puts on a brave face. "No, you didn't, and neither did I."

I take her hands. "We need to run for our lives."

5

BRONCO

Present day

Cupcake crawls across my lap as I wait for my turn at the pool table. I really wanted to avoid female drama tonight. I've had a long fucking day and I don't need to deal with her petty shit.

"What are you doin'?" I'm tempted to yank her off, but it's not like she's done anything wrong... technically. I'm just a sour bastard. We've never fucked, and as she's new at the club, she wouldn't know anything about my vow; keeping away from sweet butt pussy. It's not that I don't like sex — hell, I fucking love it. But if I'm being honest, the club chicks just aren't doing it for me anymore. They haven't for ages and I can't pinpoint how or when it happened. It's like my libido just died overnight and hasn't regained momentum.

Cupcake is gorgeous. She has a mixture of pink and blonde hair, a pretty face with pouty lips — that are one hundred percent silicone — lashes, nails, the works. She also has a pair of ten-thousand-dollar titties that are half hanging out the scrap of material she's calling a top.

All in all, she would've been my type six months ago. Hell, I probably would've fucked her right here on the couch while waiting for my turn at the pool table. But that was the old me.

"Aww, poor baby looks a little tense," she purrs against my neck. "Would you like me to suck that big dick of yours to relieve some of the tension?"

I glance down at her as she grinds against me, her tiny skirt rising farther. "How do you know it's big?"

She giggles. "I've heard the rumors." She sits up, swinging her arms around my neck. "I'll make it good for you."

"I need to take my shot." I gesture behind her.

"Your shot can wait." Not an inch of her face moves and I always think it's sad that a girl as young as her, not a day older than twenty-two, has so much botox in her face that she's expressionless. It's not like she'd have a damn wrinkle on her pretty face anyway. "I've been dying for this dick."

"Then you're gonna be sorely disappointed," I grunt, trying to untangle her arms.

"Ooh, someone's a little feisty tonight," she sing-songs, my brush-off doing absolutely nothing to make her grip any less tight. "I like a little fire in the bedroom."

I snort. "Get off me, Cupcake. I'm serious."

She sighs, then before I know what's happening, she's flipping up her top; her giant titties bouncing right in front of my face. I mean, they're nice tits, I'm not gonna deny it, but like everything about her; it's all plastic. I'm a natural man myself, and I love big tits. Even though I've seen a lot of breasts over the years, you can't beat a natural rack. They just feel better. Look better... Who the fuck cares? Cupcake ain't gonna give me any attention once I flip her off. My mind suddenly flicks to Amber shaking her rack at me behind the bar the other day in jest. My dick twitches and I hope that Cupcake can't feel that because it ain't for her. I didn't realize it was for fucking Amber either until this very moment.

"Don't be so mean." She cups her tits as I put my hands on her hips to steer her backward.

"Fuck, man, nice rack!" Bullet hollers as I turn and see him, JJ, Pipes and Giggs, one of the prospects, hooting and gawking. "Throw some of that my way!"

They all laugh as I steel my jaw. I don't know why, but I look over toward the bar, knowing Amber is on shift tonight. I don't see her, but I also don't want her seeing Cupcake on my lap like this. I know our date isn't a real date, but I don't want her to think I gave in to temptation. She needs me right now, and that's what I'm trying to focus on. Being a better man. This sudden awakening all happened the night I beat the living shit out of those two assholes bothering Amber in the street. The charges against me were dropped and deemed self-defense, even though I didn't have a scratch on me. Security footage showed exactly what happened when the two jerks chased her up the street and waited for her to leave the restaurant. The thought sickens me that something more sinister could've happened. One of the guys, the bigger dude who fell like a sack of shit when I hit him, has already been inside for sexual assault. Seems he didn't learn his lesson and he's back in the slammer because he was on parole.

"I'm not bein' mean."

She's still cupping her ginormous tits. "Don't you like these?"

My dick is still hard, but not from her tits. That one flash back of Amber shaking hers, plus that time she dropped her pants and I saw her butt cheek, is all it took to get me rock hard. I don't like it. I don't like having these thoughts about her because I'm never gonna act on them. You can't fuck and be friends.

"Sure, they're great, I'm just... I'm... seeing someone." The words blurt out before I can stop myself.

She frowns. "You are? Who?"

I wave a hand. "Just someone."

Her frown turns into a grin. "Would I like her?"

I growl. "No, you wouldn't, so go flash your titties over at Bullet, I'm sure he'd love to take you for a ride."

She huffs. "Sure you're not gay?"

"If I was, I wouldn't be ashamed of it," I counter. "Also, have a little self-respect. Pullin' your tits out like that when there are ol' ladies present isn't gonna win you any favors."

Her nose wrinkles. "You sound like a bitter old man." She tucks her tits back into her top angrily. "I bet you can't even fuck if you wanted to."

"Oh, he can," Amber says, leaning over to pass me another drink. "And I would know."

I stare at her open-mouthed as Cupcake gapes.

"You?" she stammers, one hand placed on her hip. "Are you fucking him?"

We're not, obviously, but I'm glad Amber jumped in to save my reputation. Sometimes I'm known to stick up for the ladies a little too much. I mean, we've all been sucked off and even fucked on this very couch with people around, but those days are very much behind me. The club is more PG now we're all getting older and settling down. We still like to party, but I still think the likes of Cupcake and the other girls who wanna act this way should show a little restraint. That's what the rooms upstairs were made for. Fuck away in private.

"What if I am?" Amber fires back, narrowing her eyes.

Cupcake, like a lot of the sweet butts here, are a little intimidated by Amber. She's a tough chick and I dig that she can stick up for herself. She backs up just a fraction and I smile to myself.

"Nothing, I mean... I didn't know." Cupcake bites on her lip. "Sorry, Amber."

Amber rolls her eyes. "Just don't let it happen again."

"I won't."

"Good."

Cupcake trots away in her sky-high heels over into the waiting arms of Bullet. He owes me one, but I'm glad she's gone. I let out a sigh of relief.

I pique an eyebrow. "So not all heroes wear capes?"

Her lips tip up in a smile she's trying to fight, collecting the empty glasses around the table. "Apparently not."

"Thanks. So now you're my fake girlfriend?"

"It looked like you needed an out."

"I did, she's a clinger," I say, which makes it sound like I know. I didn't mean it to sound like that, but Amber doesn't look like she really cares.

She gives me a withering look. "I didn't just do that for you. I did it for the rest of the women who are getting pretty sick and tired of chicks like her flashing their boobs anytime of the day and night without giving a shit about the rest of us."

The pounding in my chest increases. *What is going on?*

"I think you'll find I practically told her the same thing. You may have missed that part."

"I'm curious." She taps her chin as I try to keep my focus on her face, and not on her body. She's wearing a cut-off t-shirt so I can see her belly button, along with tight, black patent leather pants and boots. Her hair is tied back into a thick ponytail, but some curls have escaped. As usual, her face is pretty and her skin flawless. The way her eyes narrow when she's either mad at me or asking a serious question, like the one in progress, makes me smile every single time. "Do you think she's throwing herself at you because she can't have you?"

"Reverse psychology?" I cup my dick and thrust into my hand. "Everyone wants this dick, babe, haven't you heard?"

"Oh, God, I am never sticking up for you ever again."

I laugh. "I think you kinda enjoyed that as much as I did."

"Listen to you with a big ego. I told you, there won't be a next time if your head doesn't fit through the door."

I laugh. "I'm not playin' hard to get. I don't want her."

She pats my arm and I realize my hard-on has got worse. *No, fuckface. This is Amber and we don't get hard over her. She's our friend...* The fact I'm talking in third person to my dick is actually insane. "I know, you're saving yourself for marriage."

She rolls her lips, collecting more glasses from around the pool table as I watch her go. I've never really noticed until recently how well her ass fits into the tight pants she wears. It's a fucking tribute to the nation. *Focus!*

I stand, ready to take my shot as Nevada misses. Damn asshat is practically a pool shark, which is why I've been waiting so long to take my shot. I see in my periphery Cupcake and Bullet taking off upstairs and my shoulders sag in relief. I'm all about the vibe in things, and I can't feel something just because someone wants me to. Maybe that's why my club brothers keep saying I'm going soft. Fuck them.

I block Amber's retreat, taking my shot as she's caged in between me and Nevada who's leaning back against his stool, watching me closely because he thinks I cheat.

"Question is, why do you care what Cupcake does?" I say, lining up my shot as I sink the ball into the side pocket. I turn my head as she watches me, that look of defiance on her face.

"I don't, but like I said, I don't wanna see her big, fake tits bouncing around when I'm trying to work."

"Most of the guys around here won't wanna hear you sayin' that."

"You think I give a shit?" she sasses. "We both know I can't get fired. Cash loves me and I'm the only reliable staff member here who doesn't ball every guy in the place and work for blow jobs."

"What the fuck?" Nevada laughs.

We ignore him and I don't miss the grin forming on her lips as I smirk. "I guess you've got me there, no competin' with that."

"Plus, she's annoying," Amber goes on.

"Right again."

She sighs. "So if that's all, can I go now?"

I move, standing taller but resting my hand on the table so she still can't go anywhere. "Nope."

"Take your shot, asswipe!" Nevada calls, throwing a couple of Cheetos at me.

"Fuck off!" I yell over Amber's head.

"That's right, you're talking to your *fake* girlfriend now, use your manners," Amber says sarcastically.

"You know what I do to chicks who talk back?" I grin.

"Do I really want to hear this?"

"It's not what you think, by the way."

"Uh, huh, most guys talk about Fifty Shades, but they just can't seem to pull it off."

"I'm more of a vanilla man myself with a little dark chocolate on top." I waggle my eyebrows. "Does that shock you?"

She leans in. "I'm not sure telling a girl you're *vanilla* is the right way to lure them into your bed."

"What about when I deny them an orgasm because of their lip?"

Her own lips part as she dips her eyes down to my crotch, then back up again. "You are so full of shit."

I laugh. "What? Is that too boring for you? Trust me, ain't no lurin' here, babe. Women come willingly."

She waves her hands at me. "It's not me who wants it. This is hypothetical."

"Enlighten me." I lean down, taking another shot. I miss this time, not that I mind because it gives me more time to give her shit. My gaze back on her, I move away from the table, but don't let her pass me.

"Vanilla *is* considered boring. In the romance books I read, they like wild, dirty sex... No hero ever said he'd give them good old plain, boring vanilla." A smile tugs at her lips and I palm the back of my head, considering her words.

"I bet I can prove you wrong about that. I'm sure there are plenty of vanilla romance books out there ready to shock your pretty little mind into submission."

"Right, like you would know." She's really on a roll. "Oh, and porn doesn't count as reading, Bronc."

"I read."

"What, *Playboy*?" She thinks she's so funny.

"I'll have you know there's a lot about me that would surprise you if you dug deep enough. It isn't about how many times I can make a woman come. It's about the connection."

She blinks at me for a fleeting moment, then we're back to sarcasm. "What's your record, *hot shot?*"

I lean closer. "If you must know, it's fifteen."

She bursts out laughing. "Fifteen?"

Clearly, she's never had a decent lover before. "Yup. The first three weren't even using my hands."

She swallows hard and I'd like to think she's thinking about my ability when I realize this innuendo is hitting differently. We've always bantered and given each other shit about lovers and sex and shitty experiences, but now I want to know how good or bad her lovers have been in the past. I realize I know nothing about that part of her life. Not even her ex.

"Are you sure you're not lying to try and get your balls back after Cupcake's little display?"

I cup my dick in front of her for the second time tonight. "Nope, balls are still safely hangin'."

"Glad to hear it."

If I'd have known our innuendo would make me stiffer than ever, I wouldn't have engaged in it in the first place. I blame her, and I tell her as such. "This is all your fault, by the way."

"How do you figure that?"

I lean closer to her ear. "That time you wanted me to tattoo your ass."

She laughs, but it comes out more like a snort and she slaps her hand on my chest. "You just can't let go of that, can you?"

"More like you should be thankin' me that I didn't take you up on that idea. Do you know how many cover ups I do? Please tell me you'll never get drunk and get tattooed."

"If I do, it'll only be with you." She pats my cheek and slips under my arm with her tray of empty glasses.

Nevada stands next to me. "You tappin' that?"

"No," I grunt, watching after her.

"But you want to, can see that look in your eyes, brother. Can't hide it from me."

"We're friends," I say, turning back to him. "This is what we do. We banter."

He snorts. "Come to think of it, I haven't ever seen her here with a dude, like ever. Have you?"

"What's your point?"

"Point is, maybe she's battin' for the other team?"

I shake my head. "She isn't."

"So why haven't you fucked her yet?"

"*Because,* asshole!" I slap him upside the head. "She's not like that and once we fuck, it'll ruin the friendship."

"Not if you fuck without feelings."

I frown, taking in his words. It's not often that Nevada

says anything prolific. Heck, until he met his ol' lady Star, he fucked anything that moved. Then he fell in love and now has twins; a boy and girl who're only a few months old. He's content now, happy and settled, which just goes to prove my point after all; that monogamy is not a dirty word.

"Fuck buddies?"

"Yeah." He slaps me on the back. "You'd make a cute couple."

Nevada knows how I feel about this whole situation, and even though he gives me shit about it, we're best friends. He knows the heart of me. I tattooed his fucking dick for Christ's sake, and that took a lot of bribing.

"Yeah, but she's too pure. Look at her, she's a goddamn dream."

"So? Ask her out, no good can come of procrastinatin' over it."

"Words of wisdom?" I mock. "Comin' from you, that's rich."

"Hey, just because I no longer play the field doesn't mean that I can't see what's right in front of me. When you know, you know, and it'll happen for you, too."

"Not with Amber," I maintain.

"Fine. She's eventually gonna find someone else." He says it like I don't know. Like I haven't considered it before. Oh, I'm well aware, and while I don't like the idea, it's because I don't want to see her get hurt. Or so I thought.

"Don't I know it."

"You've got nothin' to lose. Hell, you just rejected Cupcake's titties in your face in front of the entire club," he laughs. "Not like you could sink much lower than that."

I punch him on the arm as he laughs harder. "I love how you act like you weren't Bullet not too long ago."

He shrugs. "Like I said, shit gets old. When you find a woman who knocks you off your feet, you'll know it, and when that happens." He makes a hand gesture toward his head, impersonating an explosion. "It's magic time."

I know he's right, not that I'd tell him that. I'm well aware of brothers getting snagged by their ol' ladies but I never thought I wanted that until recently. My emotions are everywhere right now. I'm literally a lost fucking puppy with no place to land.

"We've got a date this weekend," I say.

"There ya go." He nods approvingly.

"But it's not a real date, she just had an extra ticket to the Pelicans game when her date bailed out at the last minute."

"So it's the perfect opportunity to test the waters. If you do the fuck buddy thing, I'd make it a stipulation that you're exclusive, just so she doesn't get any funny ideas."

"She doesn't sleep around." The entire club knows that, but I don't like the insinuation.

"But if she's dating other people, that means she could be gettin' friendly with another dude on the side while she's gettin' it from you." He holds up his hands because he knows it's a touchy subject where she's concerned. He knows what I did to those two assholes in the street and I'd do it again, ten times over. "I just don't want it to be your bleedin' heart smashed up and hurt when she ends it because some other guy had the nerve to give her what she wants."

I let his words hang between us. I never thought I'd admit this, but maybe Nevada is right?

I clear my throat, trying to lighten the mood. "Okay, hey, Amber. I think we should fuck with no strings attached and no feelings or expectations, but I'd also like to be exclusive and no, you can't see other people or ride any other dick but mine. We're exclusive but not together, you got me?" I roll my eyes. "That's the most pathetic thing I've ever heard. Plus, can I just say it one more time? I don't like her like that." The lies I tell are starting to make my inner being frown at me in disgust. But Nevada sees right through it.

"You're a pathetic excuse for a brother," he sighs. "With all that woo woo shit you spout about, I thought you'd see the connection a mile away. I guess I was wrong."

I glare at him in disbelief as he saunters off to take his shot, leaving me staring after him, questioning everything I thought I knew.

6
AMBER

The Past - Three years ago

I'VE NEVER HURRIED SO FAST WITHOUT RUNNING IN my life. I've also never carried an armful of fake props while I fled the place I despise the most and managed to maintain balance and poise. Luckily, I've had a lot of practice. The air feels thick today. It's a typical cold April morning, and though the sun is trying to break out, the clouds above threaten rain. It can rain all it wants once we're free of this Hell hole, but it'll only slow us down if the heavens decide to open now.

Like clockwork, it's as though every single person in the village notices us and wants to stop and chat. I've already craned my neck to check where the delivery van is. Usually he starts at the church, makes his way to the school, stops by two of the farms at the far end of our compound, and then lastly the Mcgregor's to dump the flour and whatever else can't fit in the extra storage at church.

Just breathe and you'll get through this.

I feign hardship as I carry the basket of fruit toward the village square where all the tables are being set up. The basket isn't exactly light, but then if I exaggerate too much, someone will want to help me carry it.

Olive skips along happily, unaware of the turn that her life is about to take. I can't control the adrenaline coursing through my veins, and I want to run as fast as I can, but I already did that once and now I've found Erica, I can't do it again.

Escaping in broad daylight is a bold move, but now it makes much more sense than trying to scale that wall by night. I'd plunge to my death before I made it down the other side.

All of my hopes are dashed when I see Vince at the long table, directing Becky and Anne with his orders. *Please let me go unnoticed... Please let me go unnoticed... Please let me...*

Our eyes meet and my heart falters. I've got two options here: make a run for it knowing I won't make it but I'll have the memory of dying while I tried, or appease him and make an excuse to leave. I choose the latter because time is ticking and the quicker I make an appearance, the quicker I can be gone. I can't see Steven anywhere, but he won't be far away. He never is.

"There you are!" Vince calls, his face contorted with anger. "I sent Linda out to look for you."

Why the heck can't he let me be for five minutes?

"I was just helping Olive and Erica," I tell him, keeping my voice calm and pleasant. I gesture to the fruit. "The ladies needed this for the table and now I have to get to work on the bread. You did put me in charge, after all." Vince knows the one thing I do right is baking, even he can't deny that.

He peers over my shoulder at Erica and Olive who have stopped to place their painted buntings around the tables. The best fucking guise ever. I want to smile to myself, but we're so far from the finish line, I feel if I even breathe the wrong way he'll know what we're up to.

If any of us put one foot wrong, this will all go up in smoke.

"I put you in charge and yet you're floundering around out here when you should be at home."

Yes! At home. That's where I need to be.

"I'm sorry." I hang my head. "I just wanted to help everyone."

"That's exactly what you do all the time," he sounds aggravated. "Help everyone except your own family."

I don't meet his gaze. He'd never strike me in front of people, but he would take me by the elbow and lead me to the nearest barn where he could get his belt out and punish me for not being a good wife. It's nothing I'm not used to, but the sting still does exactly that. The more I stand up to him, the worse he gets, and today isn't the day to prove myself. Today is the day I get to escape and never have to listen to him again or suffer at his hands.

To hurry things along, I add, "Let me go grab the flour from the McGregor's and I'll start on the dough."

He grunts. "The dough should've been prepared hours ago."

I don't remind him that the flour hasn't even been delivered yet, that would be enough to set him off. For once, I keep my smart mouth shut because I have everything to live for now and so much to lose.

"I'm sorry, Vincent. I'll make it up to you."

He gives me a bored look and dismisses me. My stomach drops as I see the van approaching from the far side of the road. *Crap!*

I move toward the road, smiling as I leave. Trying to remain calm has never felt so hard before, but somehow I manage it. I make my way toward home, which will have me diverting once I'm out of sight from the others, but still, I know I can do this.

Erica and Olive follow me a few minutes later as they hold hands. Olive swinging her ragdoll in one hand as I wait for them behind the bushes.

"That was close," I whisper when they approach.

"We have to hurry." Erica looks behind her at the crowd behind us. "If he comes to check and you're not there..."

"He won't," I maintain. "He's too busy playing Pied Piper to care if I'm home or not."

"I hope you're right."

We hurry along the embankment and make it to the barn before the van approaches. I hadn't thought this through, but if he doesn't stop here with the drop off, it means tackling him to the ground while we steal his van and force the guards to let us out. None of which I can see happening.

"Mom? I'm tired," Olive whines.

"Just a little farther, honey," Erica assures her. "Be a good girl now."

Olive really is a little trooper in all of this. I just hope she doesn't start yelling and screaming when we get her into the van. She's a Mama's girl through and through, so I don't see that happening, but I'm prepared for anything at this point.

We sneak through the open gate and I feel my body relax when there's nobody in the barn. The door is wide open because the delivery guy will need access, and for the first time I start to breathe like I'm not starved of oxygen.

"Okay, we need to regroup," I say, pacing. "He's going to be here any minute, so we need to hide around the side making sure we don't get seen from the road."

"This plan is nuts," Erica says. "I can't believe I let you talk me into this! All it's going to take is—"

"What are you doing in here?" Jude's voice rings out through the small space and I close my eyes for a fraction of a second. Oh, no. My back to her, I give Erica a stern look that says, 'let me do the talking,' and I turn to face her.

"We're waiting for the flour delivery," I say. "I'm baking today."

She's a suspicious little bitch by nature, but somehow I get the feeling she's been watching us for a while. "You said you were looking for Erica."

"Yep, and I found her, the mystery is solved." *Go the fuck away!* She's going to spoil everything. I won't let that happen. I've suffered at Vince's hands too much, and Erica has had similar treatment from my brother. It ends today.

"You were running through the village in a panic, now you're just here waiting for flour." Her upturned nose is aggravating, and not for the first time in my life, I want to rearrange her face.

"I didn't want to miss the delivery, we all know how Vince can get." Wrong thing to say because Jude doesn't like anyone talking badly about our husbands. Not that I care what she thinks. I'm stumbling for my words now because I'm sure I can hear the van approaching.

"Olive?" Jude ignores me and addresses the little girl. "What's going on here?"

My eyes widen as I turn my back on Jude to face Olive. Erica, still holding her hand, pats her head. "She just told you," Erica replies sternly. "The question is, why are you here?"

"Because I don't trust either one of you," she gripes.

"Don't worry, I'm not going to poison you," I laugh. "You've eaten my food before and never had a problem, and Olive here wanted to help, right kiddo?"

Jude focuses back on Olive and folds her arms over her chest and says, "Well? Speak child!"

"We're baking bread," Olive says with a defiant tone. I'd like to think she gets that from me, being her aunt and all, because she sure as shit doesn't get it from Erica. "I'm going to help roll the dough, Aunty Amber says I'm good at it."

"Yes you are," I coo, hoping her admission will make Jude fuck the hell off. "So, thanks for your concern and all but—"

"Why does she have that?" Jude points toward Olive; the little rucksack that Erica packed with some warm clothes, water and snacks is beside their feet where Erica dropped it.

"She's having a sleepover tonight, if Vince allows it," I lie. "Are there any more questions, Jude? This is starting to feel like an interrogation."

"Like I said, I don't trust you," she says. "I think you two are up to something, you're always whispering in corners to each other, scheming something."

"That's because we like each other," Erica finally speaks. "I've known her all her life, I'll protect her like she's my own blood. I'm sorry you don't have that kind of relationship with any of your sisters."

"What are you protecting her from exactly?" Jude demands. "We're your family, not her!"

An engine. I hear it...

"Well, we'd love to stay and chat, but—"

"I think I'll go find Steven and see if he approved this sleepover," she sniffs. "It sounds like another excuse for the two of you to keep Olive away from the family." She's blocking our exit, and we can't have that.

"Really?" I say, my hands balling into fists. "Did you come up with that all by yourself?"

"Always the smart mouth. Haven't you learned to keep that big mouth of yours shut? Maybe if you did, you could've given your husband the child he's always wanted instead of being a vile, barren, pathetic excuse for a wife. Not to mention a horrible little piece of work who can't even cook—"

My arm swings before she finishes the sentence, connecting with her face. I don't even think, I just launch into attack mode, socking her again straight in the middle of her nose as she yelps and falls backwards.

Erica shrieks, as does Olive. My sister-in-law covers Olive's eyes as I make sure Jude lands safely, and is still breathing. I turn back to them. "Give me something to gag her with and tie her to the machinery."

Erica is staring at me in shock as Olive hides in her momma's chest. I didn't want her to witness that, but I had no choice. Plus, I've had a decade of her insults and one can only take so much.

"Erica!"

"Okay!" They fetch some rope and I drag Jude unceremoniously over to the tractor tire, securing the rope around it tightly. I take my cap off and stuff it in her mouth, securing that with a smaller length of rope in case she wakes up and alerts the entire village to what we've done.

"Oh, my God!" Erica is shaking, comforting Olive as they stare at Jude behind the tractor.

"I'm sorry!" I spit, feeling far from it. "But she was going to tell Steven and we'd be burned at the stake if she'd gotten away. I can hear the van... let's move."

Eventually someone will come looking, and my makeshift ties won't hold her forever.

"You're out of your mind," Erica chastises me. "And just how did you learn to swing like that?"

"I'm my father's daughter," I tell her cryptically.

We sneak out of the barn around to the side, out of sight just as the van comes into view. With horror, I realize it's not Carlo who parks for a moment. *Great, could anything else go wrong?*

The older man opens the back of the van and pulls out a sack of flour, heaving it over his shoulder as he moves toward the barn. I did a pretty good job of making sure Jude couldn't be seen from the doorway, but if she's woken by now, she could stir enough noise to gain his attention.

"Let's go!" I whisper as we run across the grass toward the

vehicle. I look inside, realizing there's two more bags of flour. "Hide around the side until he's done."

I yank on Erica's hand as we do just that, crouching down on the other side as low as possible. We're in full view of anyone else from the road, but nobody really comes up here. Nobody except Jude, the nosy bitch. That might teach her a lesson to stay out of other people's business. Then again, she's been a thorn in both of our sides since we arrived here, so I don't expect her to change. My knuckles sting like a bitch but she had it coming. The amount of times I've held my tongue while she's berated me in front of people; I've lost count. The man whistles a tune as he yanks the next bag out and my heart thunders in my chest that he's going to see us. The minutes feel like hours as he returns for the last time, slamming the door shut as he takes the last bag out. I tug on both Erica and Olive's hands as I peek around the van; he's nowhere to be seen so I open it quietly and lift Olive up first.

"My doll!" she cries. In all the kerfuffle, she's left her favorite toy behind but we can't go back now.

"Shh!" Erica says, placing a hand over her mouth. "Mommy will get you another one."

Tears prick her eyes and I feel bad, she was really attached to that ugly thing. "I'll get you ten dolls better than her," I say, climbing in as I shut the door behind me. There's barely enough room, but we make it work. "We need to be quiet until we're out of here, okay?"

Olive cries quietly and I'm glad there's a partition between us and the driver's seat or we'd have some explaining to do.

The man comes back and the driver's door opens, his weight jostling the vehicle as he climbs inside. He's singing a tune to himself and I'm relieved when he pulls out and drives forward. The guard is about fifty meters away around the corner. If whoever is on the gate wants to check the van, we're screwed. I just pray we have enough time before anyone discovers Jude unconscious in the corner, tied to a tire. If I wasn't so shit scared, I'd laugh my ass off about the look on her face when I struck her. Trust me, I put all of my frustrations over the last decade into those few swings, and she bore the brunt of it. The torment and ridicule she's put both of us through, and looking down her nose at my niece. Well, her penance has been served.

Erica has her eyes closed, Olive's face pressed against her chest as they huddle together.

"Not long now," I tell them. "We're almost there."

The van stops and I know without looking that we're at the gate. *We're almost home, free.*

I hear voices, and it sounds like Ronnie, Mrs. McGregor's son. Of course the gate wouldn't be heavily manned today because it's all hands on deck. And the driver has no reason to come back here since he's done his last delivery... then I hear the driver's door open and close and we wait with bated breath as he says something else. Ronnie laughs and then to my horror he's right there; his shadow looming through the tinted window. The back door opens.

My heart in my chest, I stare right at the man who isn't Carlo, but another guy with the name tag, 'Charlie' on his shirt, under that it says; *Speedy Couriers 24/7*

He balks in surprise, then opens his mouth to say something as tears begin to fall down my face before he can speak.

"Please," I whisper, making prayer hands. "For the life of this child, please don't. Please, I'm begging you. Don't give us away. We just need a lift to town." I bow my head, resting our fate in his hands. He's an older man, maybe sixty or more, his face is lined from all weathers and his eyes are crystal blue. He has a kind face, and that's all I can hang onto. Our life hangs in the balance and no words are even exchanged.

He stares at me, his face softens when his eyes fall on Olive. Swallowing hard, he turns at the voice behind him.

"Everything okay?" I hear Ronnie ask. "Did you find them?"

The delivery guy reaches next to me, rummaging around in a large box. He pulls out a bag of skittles, takes one long look at us, then shuts the door behind him. I realize Charlie must've promised Ronnie something from the outside, because that's what all the gatekeepers ask for whenever a delivery is made, and it might just be the very thing to save us. They laugh about something and I don't hear what Charlie says. After a long pause, my ears straining to hear them... my heart pounding so hard in my chest it may burst.

Erica squeezes my hand like there's no tomorrow and Olive is sitting wide-eyed staring at us in total shock.

"Daddy hurt my mama," Olive whispers.

I swallow hard. "Yes, he did, that's why we're leaving with this nice man." My voice cracks and I realize the months of buildup have finally erupted. I'm no longer the girl I once was, and I haven't been for a while now.

"She knows Daddy is unwell. Don't you, honey?" Erica tries her best to downplay the situation, but it's no use. Olive's tears fall all by themselves as she clings to her mom.

Erica can't speak anymore, she just nods as fear and trepidation flood her face and her eyes glaze over.

We're either saved or we're fucked, I don't know which yet.

I see my life flashing before my very eyes and I don't want to be a sitting duck. If he gives us away, we're doomed and I will mount this wall, taking Olive and Erica with me if it's the last thing I do. In fact, if Ronnie is distracted, it could be the perfect time to move. Or I could be completely crazy. I start to shift but Erica grabs my sleeve. "What are you doing?"

"I'm looking for another way out!" I whisper-shout,

wiping my tears. A newfound sense of peace washes over me when I realize how close we are. "There's only Ronnie at the gate. We could overpower him."

"And the delivery guy?" she whisper-shouts back. "All he has to do is call for help. We're stowaways in his van!"

"I don't have all the answers right now!" I slingback. "But I have to do something!"

I halt my escape toward the back of the van when the door opens again and the delivery guy appears, looking right at me again. He tosses Olive's ragdoll at me and nods once. I catch it in my hand as I sink to my knees and he slams the door closed again. I hear him say something to Ronnie and he laughs. Olive hugs her doll to her chest as her face lights up.

A few moments later, our reluctant rescuer climbs in and the gate opens. I watch in stunned silence as we slowly move forward; Charlie whistling as he says his goodbyes to Ronnie out the window.

All I can hear is Erica and Olive saying the Lord's prayer as we make our way to freedom.

7

BRONCO

Present day

WTF GROUP CHAT:

> ME
> Why did I just walk into a clubhouse full of balloons?

> HARLEM
> Deanna is having a birthday party for Caprice, along with a baby shower for Audrina and a combined twins plus new baby party for Halo and Star

Okay, glad I asked...

Halo is Riot's ol' lady, she also works for Star in her P.I. office downtown.

> TAG
> Can't keep up with all the fuckin' babies around here

MANNY

Someone's a grumpy pumpy

TAG

Who let you in the group chat?

MANNY

Last time I checked, y'all patched me in, remember?

TAG

You have a private chat with the women, don't need you in this one as well

MANNY

I'm special so I get to be in both chats 😛

BANDIT

That's my boy

I roll my lips. At least that explains the balloons. Tag's always on form, night and day.

RYDER

Why are you at the clubhouse so fuckin' early?

ME

I'm an early riser

NEVADA

Since when? We all know ain't no snatch that got you up early

Trust Nevada to act like a clown and spout whatever comes into his pea-sized brain.

HARLEM

You goin' soft on us, brother?

NEVADA

He's got a thing for Amber but won't admit it

ME

Thanks a lot, asshole… and I don't have a thing

NEVADA

Right, you're 'friends' 😂😂😂😂😂

ME

Fuckface

HARLEM

Amber's a cool chick. You two doin' it on the sly?

ME

Nope. Not doin' shit. She's just a friend. Some immature idiots in this chat can't grasp the concept of that. Men and women can be friends

TAG

Fuck that. And stop blowin' up my phone

HARLEM

Men and women can be friends without fuckin'?

ME

Yeah. Tried and tested

NEVADA

Except this time you want to fuck her, and she's not reciprocating

ME

@Nevada That's a big word, did your mommy help you with that?

NEVADA

Don't try and shift the subject, your balls gotta be blue by now

MANNY

@Tag when are you having kids?

I'm glad for the subject change, which is typical Manny.

TAG

When hell freezes over

HARLEM

@Tag Come on bud, you're good with kids, they love you

RYDER

What planet are we all living on? Tag good with kids???

HARLEM

He held Caprice as a baby, and Ade, and they turned out okay

RYDER

Great, so you've probably dropped my son on his head and not said anything

TAG

Fuck off

HARLEM

He's just mad bc kids love him and he's a grump who won't admit he secretly likes the attention

TAG

Kids are annoying little germ breeders who spit, cry and smell weird. Also Ade poked me in the eye once and almost blinded me

MANNY

Aww poor baby

CASH

Every balloon is counted for, @Tag…

TAG

@Cash You think I'd pop kid's balloons for the fun of it?

MANNY

I wouldn't put it past you, you are a bit of a beast

RYDER

A monster

HARLEM

A giant

MANNY

Okay, a soft, lovable, giant beast who swears a lot and never smiles, but they still love you bc deep down they know you have a heart under all that muscle

TAG

This chat is annoying

HARLEM

Are we invited to the party?

ME

It's a baby shower combined birthday/new baby party. You wanna sit around with the women while they share birthing stories and swap gifts?

MANNY

🙇 I do, better than hanging out with the likes of you guys. No offense, but the girls have a way better time

RYDER

Hey, what did I do?

MANNY

Nothing @Ryder and Ade is adorable

RYDER

Just like his dad

BANDIT

I'm also happy to help out, what's on the menu?

MANNY

It's so cute; we have little tiny sandwiches for the older kids, muffins, pastries, I have a recipe for bolognese that Ade can't get enough of and I'm making Caprice a princess birthday cake… it's gonna be epic

CASH

Fantastic, we can expect the sugar rush to hit about what time? We can make sure we're outta there before it happens

I chuckle to myself. Sounds about right.

MANNY

I only use toxic free, natural coloring and limit the sugar intake

HARLEM

Samples are gonna be in order

TAG

Yeah, where the fuck are the samples?

MANNY

Nope, no samples if you're not planning on attending, rules from the boss' ol' lady

CASH

My baby givin' out her orders again?

TAG

@Cash When isn't she?

CASH

@Tag good point

TAG

What about cake for poker night?

MANNY

@Tag are you really going to steal cake from little kids now, too?

TAG

Who's talkin' about stealing? It's not their cake if it's in test mode

MANNY

So I'll make you a princess cake for poker night? Anything you'd like on top? Barbies, My Little Pony, Care Bears? Extra sprinkles?

TAG

Wise ass. We never get cake. @Cash, why do we never get cake?

BANDIT

@Tag I would be nice to Manny if I were you or you're never gonna get anything ever again

HAWK

I'm with Tag, we should have cake, extra sprinkles

MANNY

@Hawk nice of you to join us, Tag's requested a princess cake for his poker night so I'm kinda all caked out for a little while… he eats a lot

HAWK

He can share

TAG

Ain't no sharin' here, get your own order in fucker, spent enough time on this fuckin' chat already

BANDIT

Again, I'd be nice to the resident chef if you wanna try and pull this off

CASH

Will you all shut the fuck up about cake, what's more imporant is the ol' ladies are happy. You know how they get over the kids havin' a good time and shit, we don't need any hiccups or anyone bein' upset that some kid didn't get what they liked, then there's allergies to think of…

MANNY

Got it covered, boss. This ain't my first rodeo 😉

HARLEM

Which is why I've organized face painting, a scavenger hunt, pass the parcel, rides and a talking SpongeBob, fairies and what's that princess's name who all the kids love?

BANDIT

Elsa

HAWK

Elsa

MANNY

Elsa

RYDER

Elsa

HARLEM

Okay, got it guys 🙂

Trust Harlem, the resident Daddy who has grown up kids, and can't stop telling everyone how much he wants to knock up Indigo; much to his older kids' complete disgust. I think Stella would be okay with it. She's almost twenty now, and as much a part of this club as anyone. Kai? Not so much. He's sixteen and kinda likes doing his own thing. But Daddy Harlem, yeah, I can see that in his future.

TAG

In my day we had the egg n spoon race and musical fuckin' chairs

HAWK

And pass the parcel

RYDER

@Tag In your day they didn't have electricity

HARLEM

TAG

Very funny, fuckwit

MANNY

Well done @Harlem, I'm glad someone around here is taking it seriously

The party is on Friday night, the night before my non-date with Amber, so I should probably stop by to see if the girls need any help setting up. Usually the guys get all the tables arranged in Cash and Deanna's rose garden and they have the party at the house adjacent. Some parents still take issue with having a kid's celebration in an MC clubhouse, but there's more room here, so it makes sense to me to have it here.

HARLEM

Always happy to help

ME

I can lend a few hours tomorrow, @Manny if you need a hand bringing the food out or whatever

MANNY

Appreciate it @Bronco - may need a hand guarding the cake table

TAG

There better be cake for us

BANDIT
What are you gonna do, gatecrash?

TAG
If I have to

MANNY
I'll set Luna onto you @Tag and nobody wants that on their hands

TAG
Not scared of my ol' lady

RYDER

MANNY

HARLEM
Yeah, right

ROCK
What did I miss?

MANNY
@Rock scroll back, there's a lot to unpack

I click out, chuckling to myself as Crystal walks in the door. She's carrying a shitload of boxes, so much so, she can't see over the top. I jog over to relieve her of some of the load.

"Thanks, Bronc, I was trying to not make a second trip."

"No problem. Where do you want 'em?" I fall in step beside her and she dumps her load on the pool table.

"These are the rest of the decorations, and the tables and chairs are coming later this afternoon."

"Goin' all out, kids won't know what hit 'em. We were all

just in the group chat. Harlem gave us the rundown on the activities," I chuckle.

She smiles. Crystal is a cool chick, and she's always running around doing something. Even now Ade has started pre-school, she's here, there and everywhere, and shows no signs of slowing down.

"Oh, Daddy Harlem is a crowd favorite. He even offered to dress up as one of the kids' favorite characters when they weren't available. I swear that man is worth his weight in gold," she muses.

"Daddy Harlem." I shake my head. "He's never gonna live that down."

"Tell me about it." She gives me a look. "Speaking of which, a birdie told me you have a hot date Saturday night?"

I sigh. "Good news travels fast."

"It does."

"It's also not a date."

"Huh?"

"Amber's real date got the flu." I try not to choke the words down. "So she had a spare ticket to the game."

Her eyes are still on me, prompting me to say, "What?"

"Uh, okaaaay."

I frown. "Okaaaay? Means what, exactly?"

"Nothing."

"Crystal," I warn. "I've known you since we were in diapers, I can tickle the information out of you if I have to."

"You know that would be so creepy if you weren't like a brother to me."

"Creepy? Why does your mind always go to the gutter?"

"It doesn't! I said like a brother!"

"Which is even creepier when you think about it," I laugh.

She swats me with her hand. "I shouldn't be even saying this," her voice lowers. "But..."

I put my hands on my hips impatiently. "Spit it out, woman! Growin' old here."

"Well, Amber was asking what she should wear to the game."

I stare at her. *She was?*

"I mean, it's a basketball game. How hard is it?"

She slaps me upside the head. "Focus, Bronc!"

"Hey, what was that for?" I rub the back of my head. She manages to always get me in the right spot, just like my mama.

"Bein' a saggy scrote, that's what."

I balk. "You did not just say that."

"I did and I'll say it again if I have to. If she's asking about outfits, I'm thinking she may be a little more into this than you think."

"Okay, so what does that mean? She's into me?"

"Are you into her?" The corner of her mouth lifts.

I shift in my stance, my hands shoved into my jeans. "I like her a lot, yeah."

I swear, Crystal gives the death-stare like no other. "Do you hear what I'm saying?"

"I mean, most people just wear casual shit."

"She *wants* to know *what* to wear to your *non-date*."

I grasp the words. "She's into me, *maybe?*"

"If she didn't care, she wouldn't ask you what she should wear." The unsaid *duh* hangs in the air.

A vision of her wearing lacy underwear, her legs spread across the bar as I take in her sexy little body springs to mind, and I've gotta stop thinking about her like this. I don't know why the fuck this is happening now after years of us being friends. I didn't want this. I *don't* fucking want this. But clearly, some unspoken part of my subconscious seems to want it.

"Are you tryin' to get my hopes up?"

"Aha!" she exclaims, clicking her fingers together. "So you

do like her more than a friend?" I don't know why she has to sound so triumphant.

"I've thought about it," I say honestly. "But I'll tell you what I told my asshat friend, Nevada: I don't wanna ruin the friendship. What we have is special."

A look crosses her face; it kinda resembles when I held little Caprice for the first time and all the girls pawed over how cute it was. She squeezes my arm. "I have no idea why you're so freaking sweet and still single."

"Uh, because I wanted to be single." *Until recently.*

Of course, Crystal picks up on the one word I didn't omit out of that sentence. "*Wanted?* As in past tense."

I look around in case anybody has come in behind us, not wanting the entire world to hear what I'm about to say. "I've been having some... uh, well, *feelings*, recently, but I'm figurin' that's because it's been a while since I've fooled around."

"And why is that the cutest thing ever?"

"It's not cute."

"Yes, it is. Subconsciously you're saving yourself for Amber," she sings in a dramatic voice.

I rub my chin, thinking about her words. "I don't think I'm doing that."

She lowers her voice. "Really? Then let's examine the evidence: how long has it been?"

I blink like a deer caught in headlights. "Since I had sex?"

She nods like I'm a five-year-old.

I think back, using my fingers to count on.

"Oh, for heaven's sake! Approximately," she sighs. "I haven't got all day. I've got a kid's party to set up."

"Gimme a second, jeez, woman! This shit is heavy." I come up with the exact month. "Six months!" I declare with a grin, then it fades as fast as it appears. *Why the fuck am I bragging about that?*

"Six months!" She balks, a hand over her mouth. "Oh, wow, you have it bad."

"I don't have it bad!" I sound whiny even to myself. "I just wanna really consider the ramifications of us gettin' together and it not workin' out."

"I guess you'll never know if you don't try."

I blow out a breath. It's annoying that Crystal has gotten to the crux of it pretty quickly. I only hope she doesn't go blabbing in the group chat. I know what these women, and Manny, are like. "That's what Nevada said, only slightly less eloquent."

"Don't take advice from Nevada, it's pure luck that he scored a woman like Star, which does make me realize that miracles can happen." She smiles softly. "You can find your happily ever after if you really want it."

I don't know why I'm such a sentimental fuckface at the moment. Is it possible for men to be hormonal? Maybe there's something in the water at the moment?

Still, it's best to blow it off. I don't want to be the laughing stock of the Queens of the MC chat; not that I think Crystal is mean spirited or would do anything malicious, but the girls love to spread gossip among themselves and I'd be the subject of intense scrutiny and I don't want to put Amber through that.

"Who says I want it?"

She gives me a pointed look. "You haven't had sex in six months, and you're a good looking guy, Bronc. You want it."

Annoying little mind reader. "Fine, you wanna know what it really is with us?"

"I'm all ears." She smiles sweetly, leaning back against the pool table.

"Don't laugh at me."

Her face drops. "I wouldn't do that. It's not often a man

bears his soul. I might be a kickass in most things, but not this."

I give her a soft smile, trying not to show my vulnerability. "I don't feel good enough."

She stares at me for a few seconds. "Really?"

There's surprise in her tone. "Yeah, is that so hard to believe?"

"A little. I mean, you seem so confident in all you do."

My eyebrows rise higher. "I do?"

"Yeah?" She shrugs. "I've always thought you took life by the horns, ya know? So to say I'm surprised you don't think you're good enough for her is an understatement."

"That makes it sound like you think I'm full of myself."

"That's not what I meant." She takes a breath. "You're a good guy, you care about everyone. I've known that for a long time. Okay, maybe some of your past discretions leave a lot to be desired, but six months, Bronc? That means something."

I palm the back of my head. "Yeah it means somethin', but what?"

"I guess that's what you've gotta figure out. If she feels the same way you do, or if she doesn't, then you've got a problem on your hands."

"Which is why I maintain it's best to ignore what I'm feelin', which, by the way, has only been a recent phenomenon."

"Probably because she's started dating again for real, maybe deep down you don't want her to find Mr. Right unless it's you."

I frown. "That can't be true."

"Have you talked to her about being more?"

"It'll backfire. I don't know anyone who has a friend with benefits situation where it actually works."

"Who's talking about friends with benefits?"

"Nevada," I sigh. "He said we could be fuck buddies

basically, and then feelings wouldn't come into play, so it'd be fine."

She pinches the bridge of her nose. "Please tell me you're not going to take his advice."

"If I was, this would be just about gettin' pussy, and it isn't."

"Are you sure?" She narrows her eyes. "I mean, there is temptation there, and getting what you can't have. Some guys find that kinda thing alluring, like, the chase, ya know?"

I place my hands on my hips. "We're not in high school, and I don't chase, that shit is dumb."

"It's dumber to sit around pining for a woman you're best friends with than to admit the truth and take a shot, that doesn't add up in my mind." *God, she's so accurately annoying.* "And I think the reason you haven't tried isn't because you don't think you're good enough; it's because you're chicken shit that she could be the one. She could rock your world and your world right now is just fine, right? No commitment. No putting yourself out there. Nothing's gonna change if you don't make a move, trust me on that."

I bite on my lip, knowing she's right, but not wanting to hear the truth. "I don't know if I want to make a move." I'm being completely raw now; we're past the point of trying to hide how I feel. Crystal knows a lot when it comes to reading people and emotions, she gets it.

"Because you're afraid of getting hurt?"

I didn't know this about myself until now... *and why the fuck is there a lump in my throat?*

"I have unresolved issues with abandonment, but that's my dad, not my mom. I have a very strong love for women because of my mom and how amazing she was raising me and my brother by herself after my dad left. But I saw what that did to her. She was so completely devastated." I look down at my boots, remembering the day that he left. It took us all by surprise. We ended up moving because his family were too involved in what they thought my mom should do, even labelling her an unfit mother. It was that day, when I was seven years old, that I grew up in a lot of ways. I saw how cruel people can be, even those in your own family. Blood? It means nothing. Actions speak louder than words.

"I'm sorry, that must've been really hard," Crystal says, her eyes brimming with tears. "I know how great your mom is, she's one heck of a woman, and I'm sure she'd love to see you settle down."

"Thanks." I clear my throat. "That's enough of the heavy, we've got a party to plan."

She opens her mouth to say something else but closes it again. I'm not a guy who wears his heart on his sleeve for anyone, but talking it out feels good. "You're a good guy, Bronco," she says, eventually.

I grin. "Even with saggy scrotes?"

She snorts. "I was on a roll, and when I get on my high horse, you never know what's gonna fly out of my mouth."

I sling one arm around her shoulder for a hug. "As long as you don't ask me to blow up goddamn balloons, I'm yours for the afternoon."

"Good, you can start with helping me get the chairs off the truck when they get here."

"Spoken like a true queen of the MC, speakin' of which..."

"I won't say anything," she cuts in. "Girl scouts honor."

I glance down at her. "Ryder is one lucky man, you know that?"

She beams up at me. "I tell him every chance I get."

8
AMBER

The past
Illinois - Three days later

"We did it," I say, sagging back against the seat on our next bus. "They'll never find us now."

We've been on three buses so far, and have a little left for food but not much.

"Will it always be like this?" Erica whispers, her gaze not meeting mine. Poor Olive is asleep next to her, and I'm sitting on the opposite side of the aisle. "Looking over our shoulders?"

I shake my head. "No, it won't, I promise. It seems hard now because we have to start again, but we can do that."

I'm ashamed to admit that we raided the charity bin outside one of the shops after dark so we could dump our current clothes. I was too scared they'd see how we were dressed and march us back to the compound. I'm as full of paranoia as Erica is, I just seem to be hiding it better, which is weird; it's usually the other way around.

Erica smiles to herself, a small giggle on her lips.

"What's so funny?"

She waves a hand, then all of sudden, she's in a fit of giggles. "I'm remembering how you knocked Jude out."

I laugh, too. "Oh, that felt pretty amazing after all the shit she's pulled over the years."

"You were fearless. I've never seen anything like it."

"I didn't want the opportunity to slip away." I shudder when I think about what we almost lost. I don't like violence, but honestly? Jude had it coming. She was a few moments away from running to get help, the nosy little bitch. If our chance at freedom was jeopardized, I don't know what we would've done. I couldn't go on for another second in that place.

"She almost ruined all of it." My voice is small, it almost cracks on the last word. I glance at my sister-in-law, really taking her in. She looks tired and pale.

Her eyes meet mine. "But she didn't, and now we're here."

"Because we stuck together."

"Exactly." Erica turns to look out of the window. She looks sad in the reflection, her face falling. We've both suffered so much trauma, and we're running for our lives. Even though we're technically free, it feels like we're going to get pulled over at any second and get arrested, or worse, sent back. Then I remind myself that nobody knows us. We're not doing anything wrong.

"No matter what." I reach across the aisle as she turns, her hand gripping mine. "We're gonna get through this. We've come this far."

I know she's uncertain about the future, I am too, but we have to take each day as it comes. Nothing could be worse than the situation we've both been in for the majority of our lives. I'd rather die than go back there, and I've got so much to live for. We all do.

She nods, tears pricking her vision. "Thank you, Amber, for everything."

I smile softly. "Thank you for believing we could do it."

"What will become of us?" she asks softly.

I squeeze her hand. "I don't know, but we have to believe it's better than all of this."

She closes her eyes and for the first time in a long time, I feel safe. Ironic, really.

On a bus to who-knows-where with no money and no place to land, and it already feels like the weight has been lifted. Charlie drove us to the bus station and wished us well. He was our savior. He even pitched in money for the bus tickets because we wouldn't have enough to buy food. I know we'll get through whatever hurdles come our way because nothing, *nothing,* could ever be as bad as what we've been through.

Present day

I stare at the Amazon package, confused with what I don't remember ordering. I've drunkenly bought stuff before in the past and forgot about it until said mysterious items showed up a few days later, but as I unearth the stack of books, I frown. They're romance books; the only kind I read, but I don't have a wish list or anything... then I see the note.

So, you said that vanilla is considered boring in your smutty little books. I hope this proves you wrong... On the other hand, I could be offending a whole legion of smutty book nerds... I guess you'll let me know if my theory is correct. B x

I start laughing as I sit on the floor and take out the stack of beautiful books — each a unique mix of covers from bare-chested men on the front, couples embracing, cartoon couples and floral arrangements. I shake my head in disbelief.

"You ass," I mutter. Pulling out my cell, I text Bronco.

ME
> I know what you're doing with the vanilla thing, and I'd like to point out that you brought it up

A few moments later, I receive Bronco's reply.

BRONCO
> I know I did, and you said it was boring

ME
> I said no hero has ever said he's gonna give the heroine good old plain, boring vanilla

BRONCO
> Didn't I say vanilla with dark chocolate on top? Some men don't need theatrics, that was my point

ME
> Thank you for the books

BRONCO
> I'll have you know I spent a lot of time researching heroes with a conscience

ME
> I've never heard of such a thing

BRONCO

That's because you read Haunting Adeline for kicks

ME

Hey! How do you know what Haunting Adeline is?

BRONCO

I could tell you some things

ME

I'm getting worried about how you spend your down time if you know about that book

BRONCO

Tell me which one you're gonna read first

I look down at the stack of twelve books and shake my head. This man is excessive, I swear.

ME

I haven't decided yet, I've just opened the box

BRONCO

We could buddy read, if you want

ME

You'd do that? 😊

BRONCO

🐎What are friends for?

I don't know what to say, this man surprises me at every turn. I know he's not into reading romance books, but he just offered to do exactly that.

> **ME**
> That means you'll need a second set

Unless he plans to read over my shoulder, which I doubt, I kinda like the idea of our own little book club. Even if realistically, this will be like torture for him.

> **BRONCO**
> I'm more of an eBook kinda guy

The fact he knows I prefer paperbacks is a testament that he knows me and what I like, and despite what he says, I don't only enjoy dark romance. I like any kind, as long as it has a happy ever after.

> **ME**
> You know, if you keep being this sweet you'll get a reputation for being a nice guy

> **BRONCO**
> I'll take my chances

I close my phone and a little squeal erupts as I check out the books all over again. I love pretty things. Ever since I left the compound, I've tried to make it a thing that I spoil myself with the things I love the most, but couldn't have when I lived at the church: books. One can never have too many books. I collect half of the stash in my arms, transporting them to my bedroom. Since Olive moved in, I've had to relocate my spicy book collection.

I line them up to the far right of the shelf where the other 'to be read' treasures sit happily waiting their turn. I pick one out, running my fingertips over the raised lettering. The man even got me a couple of foiled copies with sprayed edges. It would've cost a fortune. I shouldn't be surprised, Bronco is a good guy through and through, and as much as we joke around, I do have a soft spot for him. I battle again with my feelings. I could easily go there. I could easily fall for him. Bronco is easy on the eyes, as well as smart, cute and funny; the whole package. He also has a body made for sin, and I've seen his pecs on more than one occasion. My cheeks burn a little when I think about that whole nine inches comment... he can't be *that* big. Is it even possible? Okay, I know it's possible because I've googled it, but it's not commonplace. Then again, what would I know? I've had one disaster after another, and sex with Vince wasn't exactly the kind you read about in romance books. I shudder at the idea of him ever touching my skin. I'll never let that happen again. Hell would freeze over. I've only got a few hours before we have to get ready to go to the clubhouse for the party, and I've got a spring in my step. Knowing I have a new book to come home to and read after being out makes me giddy; I am a nerd at heart, and I don't deny it. Being out is overrated, but I still have to make an appearance with Olive and I agreed with Bronco the other day that it's time they met, along with my girlfriends at the clubhouse.

The MC is a big part of my life, and I'm not ashamed of it. I just wanted to protect Olive; that's all I've ever wanted.

I've been contemplating whether it was truly a good idea bringing Olive to the party, but since Cami and Ella will be there, it seems mean to not let her come. I guess I'm just being selfish because I don't know how she'll respond to questions about where her mom is. I don't want the MC involved, though I have thought about talking to Star. She's a PI and I'm sure it's worth trying to locate Erica. If she is in trouble and I sit here and do nothing, what does that make me? Still, we have to live our lives. I can't go on shielding all of this from Olive forever, she's not dumb, but today she gets to be a kid and have fun with her friends.

That's the least I can give her in all this mess.

I crouch down, Olive holding the bag of gifts we picked out and me balancing the Tupperware of treats we made this morning on my knee. It's the first time in weeks she's been excited about something, other than hanging out with Cami. If I can give her that, and it takes her mind off things, then it's a job well done in my book. I love my niece, but I've no clue what to do with a child. I keep texting Erica's number, knowing the messages don't go anywhere, but the idea that she could get them makes me feel better. I worry about her day and night.

She'd never leave her kid, *never*. And Olive knows nothing more than I know; her mom had to go away for a little while, but she'd be back soon. The hand-written note Olive handed me said as much, but left no clues to where she was actually going. Now I have to lie to my niece and tell her that her mom had some business to take care of, and she'll be back for her soon, not knowing if that was actually true. I'm mad at her, truth be told. More than mad. Livid.

I know with a hundred percent certainty that she would never go back to the compound. It's the last thing she'd ever do.

Erica knows she can talk to me. I'm the one person she can lean on; a sister. I've always got her back, and she has mine. So why this secrecy? I'm hurt by her actions.

I squash my feelings down, knowing I've got to put up a happy front for my niece and not ruin the party by crying.

"Feeling okay, honey?" I ask as Olive looks down at me. Her pretty pale blue dress matches the color of her eyes. "You're a little quiet."

"I hope they like their presents," she admits, chewing on her lip. It's a habit she gets from me, funnily enough. "I mean, the babies won't know, obviously, but the older kids might not like them."

I cup one side of her cheek. "They're gonna love them, do you know why?"

She shakes her head, trepidation written all over her face with a frown and her eyes glazing over making her look sad. I don't want her to cry. It's a party, I'd love for her to enjoy the moment and just be a kid again instead of worrying all the time.

"Because you picked them out."

Her face softens and she envelopes me with a hug. "Thanks, Aunty A. I really needed to hear that."

I smile to myself. She's very properly spoken, which comes with years of living in an environment like we did where no-one speaks out of turn. I think when she gets a bit older, I'll help her out with some cussing. Lord knows it's helped me in the past.

"Atta girl. You're gonna be fine, plus you already know Ella and Cami, and they can't wait to see you."

She perks up at the sound of her friend's names. "Okay!"

I stand, tucking the Tupperware under my arm. "Ready?"

"Yep!"

This kid. She's been through so much in her short little life, and I hate that she has no answers. The more I think about Erica and her note, I want to scream with rage.

Dear Amber,

You know I wouldn't do this if there was any other way. Please understand how much I love you and my daughter, and to abandon her like this, although temporarily, kills me.

I don't have a choice. I wish I did, but things in my life are more complicated than you can imagine.

Know that I'm okay and I'll be back. I get you'll be mad at me for trying to fix this myself, but I have to. This is one mess I need to sort out on my own. I've told Olive I have to go away for a few weeks for work, and that we'll be moving to New Orleans permanently, so she won't be any the wiser. She'll be okay if she's with you.
Please try not to be mad at me.
I love you. I'll be back soon.
Don't look for me, I beg you, it'll only make things worse.
Your sister, Erica

I try not to get mad when I think about that letter. Heaven knows I've read it over and over so many times, the paper is wearing thin.

How could she do this to me? To Olive? To herself?

We tell each other everything, and now she does this vanishing act that, quite frankly, is scaring the shit out of me. The more I think about it, the more I need to talk to Star. It's been more than a few weeks, and every night I'm awake trying to think of something, *anything,* to calm this situation and make sense of it. That's a little hard when I've nothing to go on. Olive arrived with two suitcases of her stuff and some cash. I'm a little insulted that Erica would give me money; as if I wouldn't look after my own niece, but that's just how she is. So, yeah, I'm fucking mad at her, and I have every right to be.

I glance up as we head through the side gate at the back of the clubhouse. The garden that leads to Cash and Deanna's house is nothing short of magical. I helped Crystal, Deanna,

BRONCO

Jas and the other women set up the fairy lights, as well as the tables and chairs. It really does look like something out of a story book.

I'm not surprised when the first person I see is Crystal, running around after Ade who has swiped two cupcakes off the nearby table and is running away laughing. He's a handful, and I can't help but giggle a little. Olive does too, turning to look at me when I see Bronco heading out with two large platters of sandwiches covered with saran wrap. He falters when he spots me, his eyes shifting to Olive as he grins. He places the trays down in the center of the outdoor tables before heading toward us.

"You remember the friend I told you about?" I start, hoping Olive remembers. "My friend, who's a boy?"

"Yep, Bronco, right?" She's a smart kid and always listens.

"Right, well, he's headed this way."

He's larger than life, his hair slicked back a little off his face and he's trimmed his beard. Man oh man, I should not be noticing that, or the way his eyes light up at the very sight of us. My throat thickens; I don't know what all that's about, but I try to keep myself calm.

And there he is, standing in front of us. I don't know what I expected from their first meeting, but Bronco's grinning his head off. He's also wearing an Elsa apron that someone, probably Ade, tied over his head. It sits snug against his body and is far too small for him, but he wears it with pride.

"Hello, Amber." As he smiles, the skin around his eyes crinkles, and in this light I notice the darkening ochre of his orbs and wonder if a biker should be this pretty. Handsome doesn't even cut it. His eyes dip to Olive. "And you must be Olive? I'm Bronco."

My niece, ever the perfect child, holds out her little hand to shake his. "Pleased to meet you," she says as I roll my lips.

Bronco's eyebrows raise in surprise. "Great to meet you

also. Your aunt has told me so much about you," he says, which is true, but I've still left out a lot.

Olive casts her gaze to me for a fraction of a second, then says, "She talks a lot about you, too."

Bronco's eyebrows nearly shoot off the top of his head as he smirks. "Really? What did she say?"

I give him warning eyes, but he chooses to ignore it.

Olive shrugs. "You ride a loud motorcycle and you have a big dog called Titan."

He grins even wider. "I do. Sadly my dog chose to stay home and sleep off the donuts I fed him for breakfast instead of coming to party with us. He's also a little nuts around people he doesn't know."

Olive giggles. "You can't feed a dog donuts!"

"Did I say donuts? What I meant to say was; *dog food*, my bad."

She giggles again. "Aunty Amber says you're kind," she blurts out of nowhere. "And she wasn't sure which outfit to wear to the game tomorr—"

I put my hand over her mouth jestingly. "I think that's enough story time," I tell her pointedly.

"Oh, no, I think we should let Olive keep talking, I like story time."

I shoot him another death glare and he laughs harder. "I think we should go find your friends," I offer instead.

"What did she pick out to wear?" Bronco asks, and I want to die right there on the spot. Now he thinks this is a date, and it most definitely isn't one.

Of course, my niece answers dutifully since she was in charge of assessing the options. "Jeans, a Pelicans t-shirt, hoodie and her chucks," Olive says proudly. I mean, it's game night. What am I supposed to wear?

Bronco gives me a smile that tells me he's enjoying this a little too much. "I'm wearing something similar myself."

Olive laughs again before something distracts her gaze. "Ooh, I see Ella!" she says, excitedly.

Bronco sweeps an arm out, moving so we can pass. "Well, have fun, Olive. Great meetin' you."

She gives him a wave and tugs my hand as I begin to move.

He's grinning because he thinks he has the upper hand now.

"Don't be so smug," I mutter.

"Kind, huh? I bet that's not all you said."

"I guess we'll never know, will we, *Elsa?*"

"Hey, it's for the kids!" he yells after me. I have to admit, he does look pretty fetching in that apron.

"Sure, you keep telling yourself that!"

For the first time in a long time, the butterflies spin in my stomach.

This is *Bronco*, I remind my internal chatter. He's not someone I can crush over. Things are good right now, and I for one don't want that to change.

Still, the man bought me so-called spicy vanilla books. The spicy scene I read from the first book I started certainly *isn't* any kind of vanilla I'm aware of. Not if I ever want to eat a cucumber ever again that is. Then again, I'm sure he didn't read through the entire collection when he was selecting them off Amazon.

This is just like him, and that's why he's so very, very dangerous.

9

BRONCO

I'D NEVER SEEN AMBER IN A DRESS SINCE THE NIGHT she hopped on my motorcycle and the material ripped. She'd be pretty in a paper bag, there's no denying that, but my little bad ass looks like she just stepped out of a movie set for *Anne of Green Gables*. Okay, that's probably a little dramatic, but the pastel green floral number that clings to her body and brings out the hazel in her eyes is making me see stars. Beautiful doesn't even begin to cut it. She has her hair out in long waves; I'm used to seeing her with a long ponytail most of the time, so this is something new. Then there's Olive. She's a cute kid with manners; not something you see very often these days. She also looks like Amber with the same colored hair and eyes, and a timid smile.

Before I approached, I couldn't help but notice the slight bit of panic I saw in Amber's face as she whispered something to Olive.

Why would she be afraid of me meeting her niece? Or is it being here with lots of other people?

I like kids. Well, most of them. I try my best to make them feel at ease, and I hope I did that with Olive because I know how hard it is when you move as a kid, and have to fit in all over again somewhere else. Been there, done that. Still, there's something about them that doesn't sit right with me. Call it gut instinct, I'm not sure, but Amber hasn't told me the whole truth about her family or even her ex. She keeps that part of her life close to her chest. I never want to pry, believing that she will tell me something in her own time if she wants to, but this may be the one exception where I have to prod a little.

The party goes off without a hitch, and all the kids are running around while the moms with the babies sit in the shade, drinking iced tea and unwrapping presents. I'm not purposely spying on them, but all the guys bailed and Manny needed help with the food. Someone also had to make sure nothing ran out. I was the only man left standing, aside from Harlem who's in charge of the entertainment, but I really didn't mind. Anything to make sure that a good time is had by all.

I smell Amber's floral perfume before I see her. I'm sitting on the edge of the garden, nursing a cold beer until Manny calls me for his next errand. I can count on one hand the times I've sat in such a peaceful setting with all the roses surrounding us. Even the kids chasing each other around screaming with water guns doesn't annoy me.

"You're still here?" Amber pokes me in the arm.

I turn to look at her as she sits down next to me. "You say that like it's a bad thing."

"No. I just meant, poor you. I heard Manny roped you in because all the guys bailed once Caprice's cake was served and the games started, aside from Harlem, he's lurking around here somewhere."

I thumb behind me. "He's makin' sure all the entertainers are who they say they are. There has to be one responsible male here, after all."

She nudges me with her shoulder. "There is Manny, too."

"Very funny."

"I got a little reading time in before I came here," she says, making me grin.

"Uh huh, and did I do a good job?"

"Yes, so far so good. The current book I'm reading by Helena Hunting is fantastic. How did you know I like hockey romance?"

I give her a withering look. "Please." I tap the tips of my ears with my pointer fingers. "These aren't painted on. I pay attention."

She giggles. "It's just, men don't usually listen."

"I was brought up with a strong working mom, remember? The one thing she taught my brother and me was respect, and that listening is an art form."

"I think I like your mom a whole lot."

"She's a fiery little thing. We have Greek heritage and she blames that for her temper. My mom came here when she was about Olive's age as an immigrant, then she met my dad pretty young."

"Wow, have you ever been to Greece?"

"Nope, but someday I'd like to, it looks pretty cool."

"I haven't traveled much, either," she sighs. "Someday."

"Where would you like to go?" I prompt. "If you could pick anywhere? And don't say fuckin' Delaware or some shit. I mean, like if you had one wish and all of that."

"Paris," she says without hesitation. "It's always been a dream of mine to see the Eiffel Tower and live like a Parisian for a week or two."

"That would be pretty amazin'." I imagine what it would be like. Cobblestone streets. Local markets. French people wearing berets. Okay, they probably don't even wear those, but it would be an amazing destination, there's no denying it.

"It isn't just the food and the wine, it's the culture. The French seem to enjoy every single morsel of their lives. I watched this show where this couple moved from England and renovated a French castle..."

I turn to look down at her. "Don't tell me."

"Dick and Angel," we say together.

I put a hand over my mouth. "Okay, I'm a little embarrassed to admit that I really like that show," I lower my voice. "Just don't tell anyone I said that."

She's laughing uncontrollably. "It's a little absurd how much we have in common when you think about it."

"I know, right? Renovatin' shows. Dark chocolate. Smutty books..."

"You do not read smutty books!" she whisper-shouts.

"I do so." I put a hand over my heart. "I'm shocked, by the way, at the amount of sex in some of those books, especially the cartoon couple ones. Romance authors are hardcore."

"Ha! And you said vanilla guys are the best kind."

"You didn't text me the name of the book you're currently reading so we could buddy read," I remind her.

"Bronc, you don't have to do that."

"I want to. I mean, only if you want me to? I don't want it to be weird. Maybe one of the girls would be a better fit?"

She lays a hand on my arm and gives it a squeeze. "I know you're just being nice because you think I have no friends."

I frown. "You do have friends, but I know book nerds can be a little... uh, private about what they like to read."

"Now I'm a book nerd?"

"I've seen your collection, it's big. I also know what you girls are reading behind those pretty covers." I wink.

She flushes a little on the pretty covers comment. "And yet you sent me more books."

I hold up a finger. "I was proving a point."

"You're actually right," she sighs. "Tristan, the guy in the current book I'm reading, doesn't use cheap theatrics."

"Told ya."

"He uses a cucumber."

I almost choke on my mouthful of beer and manage to spit some out; it dribbles down my chin and I sputter. "Jesus, AJ!" I wipe my mouth with the back of my hand, then lower my voice. "A cucumber?"

She nods, biting her lip, her eyes dancing with amusement. "So I get your point. You don't have to be chained to a bed, pinned to a St. Andrews Cross, or bent over a sex chaise to get your thrills."

My heart rate kicks up a notch. *What in the ever-living fuck?* "Okay, now I'm really gonna dive deep into that bookshelf of yours. A sex chaise?"

"It's a thing."

"I'll google it later. Now, back to the cucumber. Does he really fuck her with it?"

She laughs. "Well, you'll have to read it for yourself, won't you?"

"So, you want me to buddy read?"

"Well, it's kinda cute that you offered, but I'm totally gonna let you off the hook if you want an out. I'm pretty sure Luna and Jas have both read *Fifty Shades* and other romance books similar to that, so we could maybe…" She trails off when I pout. "What?"

"I wanted to be your reading buddy." I try not to burst out laughing because frankly, I don't really wanna read about hockey players called Tristan, or cucumbers being used as sex toys for that matter. But if it takes her mind off things and causes her less anxiety, then I will. That's why I'm here and will always be here for her.

She rubs my back soothingly. "Aww. I'm sorry, you still can be. But we have to give our book club a name, those are the rules."

"Your rules?"

"Exactly."

I grin, happy again. "Bossy. Okay, how about Sex Books R Us?"

She pinches the bridge of her nose. "Romance books, *Bronc,* not sex books."

"Ah." I hold up a finger. "My bad. Just to clarify, all the books have to have a happily ever after, right? Or they're not romance books."

"Someone has been doing their homework," she teases.

I groan, remembering how I know that. "You click on one fuckin' author or reader account on TikTok, and all of a sudden you're gettin' romance book shit thrown in your face and all over your feed."

"That's BookTok," she announces. "Wow, you really have crossed over to the dark side, haven't you?"

"Unwillingly, but strangely, I'm okay with it."

"Can we think of another name, please?"

"I'm sure you've got some bright ideas?" I prod. "You know I'm only gonna come up with somethin' else dirty like Smutty Readers Unite."

"Please tell me you have a better name than that."

"How about Kiss And Tell, Swooners After Dark or R-Rated Readers—"

She whacks my arm. "Will you stop it?"

I chuckle. "Boink My Hole, Bang My Buick, Ass Tales?"

"Oh, my God, you're insufferable," she groans.

I clear my throat. "Okay, I'll be serious, but you need to pick the name."

"How about The Happy Hangout?"

I rub my chin. "You're so vanilla, *Princess.*"

"Well, it's unsuspecting, and PG when Olive is around."

"Fine." I clap my hands together. "So now we have a book club. What's the name of the book we're reading?"

She reels it off, then offers to find it on the kindle app on my phone, giving her pause to check out some of the books I have on there. They're all sci fi or murder mysteries, of course. Typical guy books.

When she finds the book in question with the cartoon cover, I narrow my eyes. "Oh, it's a series? I didn't realize."

"Yes, and you got me books one and two, well played there."

"I aim to please." I grin. I like that we have this new thing together. Sure, it'll be tough explaining it to the guys, but they can mind their own fuckin' business. Just to see her face light up when she's talking about her books is enough for me.

"There, it's on your kindle, so you've no excuses now."

"I'll text you updates," I laugh.

She laughs, too. "Can't wait. I better get back and check on Olive and the kids."

"By all means," I say. "I'll just be here reading my smutty ass book."

She laughs when I wiggle my eyebrows, and now I'm more than a little intrigued by this whole cucumber thing. Here I was thinking I'd picked smutty books without too much dark shit in there, and here she is telling me about sex chairs and fuckin' crosses. I don't want to think about Amber pinned to any kind of cross, but if she were, it'd be one of my choosing.

If she didn't want me in her book club, she'd say, right? Truth is, I want to hear about what she thinks of the books she reads. It makes her happy, and I can appreciate that. I love reading, too — maybe not smutty romance books with werewolf shifters, dragon riders or hockey gods who know how to use their tongue better than their hockey sticks, but reading has always been an escape. I like being able to shut off when I go to bed and just relax. Not even the television does that for me. It's special, and I want to share that with my best friend. *Because that's all you are, asshole.* Yes, I need to keep reminding myself of that fact. *Just friends.* Friends with their own book club...

BRONCO

I help Manny and Harlem clean up, sending Amber away to have fun with the girls. It's just like her to go into work mode, but I for one know she never has any fun. She should enjoy herself, she deserves it. The women have all worked hard at setting up, so helping them pack down is the least we can do. Even Tag, Hawk, Cash, Hustler and Riot come and help later.

The kids all had a great time, and that's what counts. I saw Olive and the others playing together, and I smiled to myself knowing it would make Amber happy to see her niece having a little fun herself.

I still don't really know what the full deal is, but I'm gonna make it my mission to find out. One day her niece just shows up and Erica is nowhere to be seen since. As Amber's best friend and new reading buddy, it's my duty to make sure she's safe, and that extends to Olive, too.

When I get home, Titan is hungry, nudging me with his head like I don't know what fuckin' time it is. "I know, bud," I sigh. Aside from a couple of leftover sandwiches the kids didn't eat, I haven't had a bite for hours. I'll get something out of the freezer and shove it in the microwave. I'm resourceful like that. I stroke his head, bending down to kiss him because that's what we do. Okay, he can be on guard dog mode when he wants to be, but when it's just us, I'm softer with him. His natural instincts kick in whenever he hears noises outside, and his bark alone would be enough to ward off any impending intruder, but he loves his cuddles. "Daddy left you alone a little too long. Maybe we should get you a girlfriend?"

He grunts as I reach up to the shelf to pour him a load of dry food into his bowl. This dog can eat — well, that's an understatement. He's a big boy, and he needs a lot of nourishment to keep him energized. I jog with him every morning, both working off our late night binges, and tonight is no exception as I pull out a frozen pizza and turn on the oven.

I'm tired, but I still have to eat and take a shower. When I decide on the latter first, I turn on the TV in my bedroom for Titan; it's the first place he'll crash when he finishes eating.

I strip as I walk toward the shower. Turning on the water, I step inside, grateful for the hot steam around me as the water pounds my sore muscles. I invested in a decent shower. Ever since my old football days, I've had back and shoulder injuries that creep up and haunt me every now and again. My body likes to remind me of the toll the game took on it. Usually when I overdo it at the gym or lift something too heavy.

I wash my hair, lathering my body with soap as I rinse, thinking about how today went. My mind flicks to Amber in her pretty green dress. There was nothing revealing about it, not like the dress she had on the night I brought her home. I hope she fuckin' burned it like I asked. This one, however, was different. Sweet. The material hugged her body, and the slight curve to her hips and plumpness to her rack was hot. *No. You've started a book club, fucker! You don't get to think like that.*

Still, my hand reaches to my dick and I purposefully do not think about her. There are plenty of women I can jerk off to. I said to myself — the last time I tamed the wild beast thinking about Amber — it was a one off, and I don't want to be weird with it. I'm not into her like that.

Or maybe I *wasn't* until recently. Still, this is just a dry spell. That's all it is. Amber's the closest woman to me in my life right now, and she's cute, sweet and sexy. It's my aching dick that's the problem. I've gone without sex for so long, the lines are getting blurred. I need to get laid, that's what it is. But every time I think about doing that very thing, I make some excuse for why I shouldn't. Not that I *can't*, but *shouldn't*.

I'm not holding out for Amber, I swear to God that's not it. I've had other women since we became friends, we've joked about shitty dates and one-night hook ups that weren't so hot, and back then, I *could* joke around with her. Now if she started telling me about a hook-up, or a date, I'd probably implode. *Why is that?* Should I explore it, or just ignore it?

As I contemplate, my dick grows harder in my palm and I brace my other hand against the shower screen. Hand jobs just aren't gonna cut it for much longer, but it's gonna have to do for a little while yet. I need to get this over with so I can go and catch up on the book Amber probably has her head buried in right this very minute. When I think about where I'd like my head buried... I jerk in my hand. *Fuuuuck.* I'm an embarrassment to myself. Instead of doing what all other normal people my age are doing — which is likely drinking, or partying, or getting heavy with a chick — I want to get this jerk-off-shower-session over with fast so I can go and read a romance book? *What the actual fuck is wrong with me?*

Maybe this is what being pussy whipped feels like. Maybe Tag was right? *Wait.* I'm gonna take that back because nobody in their right minds would say Tag was right about anything.

I need to grow some balls and stop this weak shit... but every time I think about doing that very thing, my conscience gets the better of me. Somewhere deep down inside, I know Amber needs me. She needs a friend. She's going through something she can't talk about, or *won't* talk about, and I need to be here for her when she is ready to talk about it.

Once again, I find myself imagining it's Amber in here with me. Her hands on me, caressing my body, my face. Our lips brushing, our bodies pressed together as I whisper all the dirty shit I want to do to her. It is a fantasy, after all. I grip my cock, my breathing ragged as I jerk myself to orgasm in record time. Seriously, under sixty seconds.

I'm fucked.

That's all I know.

There isn't any other excuse for me. I'm buying her books. Taking her out tomorrow night. Clapping secretly because this Ben fuckface has the flu, and now she won't get to see him. I'm a selfish bastard, that's what it is. I can't have her, so nobody else can? What are we, in grade school? I'm not proud of myself, but as I wash myself and my sins clean under the water, I can't regret any of my decisions. I just have to find a way to get through this.

Not hanging out with her isn't an option. I've vowed to keep her safe ever since that night when those two goons stalked and terrified the life out of her. She was so scared, and I never want to see that look on my best friend's face ever again.

The boys can shut the fuck up; they're all wrong. Especially Nevada suggesting we could be fuck buddies. Keeping my hands to myself has been second nature these past few years, and I'm not about to lose her because I can't control my dick now.

Not gonna happen.

I'll prove it, if it's the last thing I do.

10

AMBER

BEN
> Maybe we can reschedule? I feel really bad about tonight

ME
> It's okay, just work on getting better. Rest. Chicken soup. That kinda thing

BEN
> I'll text you when I'm feeling better, we can make another time and place

I STARE AT HIS TEXT, UNSURE WHAT TO SAY. I've seen photos of Ben from his sister, and he's cute and normal looking, but I don't know why I'm not as excited as I thought I'd be with the idea of rescheduling our date. I mean, I haven't even given the guy a chance.

ME
> Okay

BEN
> Do you mean that?

I take a breath. Maybe I'm just feeling off? I don't know what it is. Maybe I just repel men. The last time I tried a blind date, that didn't go down so well either.

ME
Of course

BEN
Okay 😊 enjoy the weekend

ME
You too

He probably won't be enjoying it if he's laid up in bed sick. I also don't have the heart to tell him I'm still using the tickets and taking Bronco. There's no point wasting good tickets to the Pelicans. I love watching them live.

When I drop Olive off at Indigo and Harlem's, they all jump up and down when Indi says she's going to take them over to her bakery; NOLA Sweet Treats, so they can pick some cakes out for the sleepover. I'm glad Olive has found her new friends because it's making the transition here, without her mom, a little easier.

Audrina is also there, heavily pregnant, and I give her a big hug. "How long do you have now?" I ask as she strokes her belly.

"Anytime now," she says. "Another week, two at the most."

"You must be so excited." I try not to think back to my previous two miscarriages, and the shame that went with it from Vince and my sister wives. Not bringing a child into the world, under those circumstances, is a blessing.

"I'm just ready to meet her," she says, smiling wistfully. "Though this pregnancy has been a breeze compared to the last time. Asher gave me hell. That was almost thirty years ago, so I could be a little rusty on the details."

Asher is Nevada's real name, but Audrina refuses to use biker names, preferring to call Hustler by his real name: West.

I laugh. "We're talking about Nevada," I remind her. "So, there's every possible chance you have it correct."

"Oh, he wouldn't keep still. He couldn't wait to come out into the world."

"How is he feeling about having a little sister with such a big age gap?"

Audrina smiles. "He's used to the idea now. Especially since having twins."

"I think that's so adorable." I can be happy for other people that are having kids, that's the thing. I've never felt a maternal instinct to have my own, and I don't think that will change anytime soon even if I could have kids. I feel content being Aunty A.

"They're so stinkin' cute!"

"I think they had a pretty good chance with the family gene pool."

We embrace again before I head off to get ready for tonight. Okay, it's not a date night, I get it. But since Olive ratted me out anyway, there's no need to keep denying that I still want to look cute. There's nothing wrong with that. Plus, usually at the live games there's tons of hot guys there. Two birds, one stone, or something like that.

I have a long soak in the tub; something else I don't really have time for, and I read some of my book while I soak. Like clockwork, texts start buzzing through my phone. After the third one in a row. I pick it up, smiling to myself when I see who it is.

BRONCO

Enemies to lovers. It's a thing

BRONCO

I don't get why they don't just bang

BRONCO

Okay, they did bang

BRONCO

They're banging a lot

BRONCO

I'm never eating a cucumber again

I laugh out loud, putting my book aside as I text back.

ME

Oh, you can't handle a little 'vanilla'? Poor baby

BRONCO

If this is vanilla, I'm fucked

ME

I did try to warn you there were vegetables involved

BRONCO

Now I know what y'all are reading, frankly, I'm shocked

ME

You are not. You just wish you could be more creative with salad

BRONCO

Careful, I'm still reeling from the St. Andrews Cross and sex chaise comment

BRONCO

ME
Don't tell me you didn't know what those things were?

BRONCO
I do now

BRONCO
What r u doin'?

ME
Soaking

BRONCO
In the tub?

ME
No in the non-existent pool outside. Yes, the tub!

BRONCO
You're naked and reading smutty books in the tub?

ME
I am usually naked in the tub, yes

BRONCO
I mean, anyone would think you had a hot date tonight and you're preparing for it

ME
I'm preparing for that hot dog you're gonna buy me at half time

BRONCO

> **ME**
>
> Fine, I'm having two just for that 😄

> **BRONCO**
>
> You can have as many hotdogs as you want, Princess, just never ask me to cut up cucumber ever again

> **ME**
>
> I'll be sure not to do that. Now go away, I'm trying to relax

A few minutes pass by...

> **BRONCO**
>
> What chapter are you up to?

> **ME**
>
> Chapter 15

> **BRONCO**
>
> Shit you read fast, maybe we should get into audio books?

I laugh out loud.

> **ME**
>
> You didn't just say that

> **BRONCO**
>
> Why not?

> **ME**
>
> You wanna hear some hot guy's sexy voice in your ears?

> **BRONCO**
>
> Won't there be a chick's sexy voice, too?

BRONCO

ME

True, it's worth the trade-off

BRONCO

I think I could be a voice narrator

ME

BRONCO

Thanks for the vote of confidence

ME

I'd love to hear you say the word cock out loud, that would be priceless

BRONCO

You think I can't be dirty, but you're sadly mistaken

ME

Taking tips from the book boyfriends? You could learn a lot

BRONCO

Why do you think I'm a member of the Happy Hangout

ME

Touché

I set the phone aside, chuckling to myself at his ridiculousness. A voice narrator? Then again, there aren't enough hot male voice actors if you ask me. Bronco may have a point. His voice is deep and manly. I just don't know if he's fully grasped what's really involved with reading some of those scenes aloud. *Audio books?* I seriously can't take this man anywhere.

I'm a Pelicans girl through and through; wearing my t-shirt and matching hoodie with my favorite jeans. I'm not dressing up for game night; this shit is important and I need to be comfortable. I pull on my comfiest sneakers and put on a little makeup, nothing too dramatic.

I was going to meet my original date at the venue, but Bronco, being the gentleman that he is, insisted on picking me up on his motorcycle. I can't say I mind. I love riding, and I don't get to do it as much as I'd like. This is also not something that usually happens to any of the women of the MC unless you're an ol' lady. It sends a message, which is why I've rarely rode with Bronco in the years I've known him. Him rescuing me that time doesn't count. This however, it feels like a real date.

When he knocks on my door at six-thirty, I ignore the butterflies in my stomach. *This is Bronco, asshat!* I've been out with him so many times I've lost count, so why does tonight feel different? Maybe because he's been showing interest in a lot more than my books lately, or am I just imagining it?

I open it and my eyes almost bug out of my head when I see Bronco in a matching sweater, and a cap, with jeans and sneakers on. I've barely seen Bronco in anything except his MC cut in all the time I've known him, plus countless Henley's and t-shirts, but never in anything so casual... and he smells like a fucking dream. The scent of pine, burnt whiskey and some kind of cedar permeate my senses and I wonder why I've never noticed it before. In fact, why haven't I noticed a lot of things about Bronco before? His face is visually perfect; the dark brow that frames those pretty amber, sometimes green eyes that seem to change color depending on his mood. He has high cheekbones, and a lovely olive complexion I'd kill for. His jaw is set, the grin on his face making him look less intense than hit six-five stature, massive shoulders that are wider than a Buick, and biceps that defy the laws of gravity.

"Hey, pretty lady." He tips his hat and it makes me laugh.

"Hello yourself." I motion to his sweater. "Nice."

"I thought since this wasn't a date, we could embarrass ourselves and look like we're twinning."

I snort, letting him inside. "I've just gotta grab my bag, come in."

My apartment is small, but it's cozy and safe. I've worked hard to be able to afford a nice place with security. That's been high on my agenda ever since I ran away from my old life.

It may have taken me years to be able to sleep properly at night, but now I have no problem at all unless I'm stressed about something. Like Erica. The need to get it off my chest almost burns a hole in place of where my heart should be. I didn't get a chance to speak to Star, but I'm going to call her first thing Monday. Hopefully we can get the ball rolling and find out where she is.

"I got you something," he says, following me up the small hallway toward the kitchen.

"You didn't have to do that, Bronc. You've bought me enough."

"Well, we can't be twinsies if you don't look the part." He pulls out another cap from the plastic bag under his arm.

I grin. "I don't know if this spells out we love the Pelicans?"

He chuckles. "You don't have to wear it if it'll ruin your hair."

I washed and dried my hair, but tied it up in a ponytail; my usual modus operandi. "It's perfect, thanks." I slide it on my head, hooking my ponytail through the back and adjust it to fit properly.

"Looks good on you."

"Most hats do. I have a gift for it, except for Kapps with a K," I blurt. *Where the Hell did that come from?*

"Kapps?" He laughs. "Like the Amish?"

I open my mouth then close it again, the blood draining from my face. Okay, I wasn't Amish, or anything close to it, but that came out of nowhere. "Uh, never mind."

"Were you in a religious cult I'm not aware of?" He leans one hand on the counter, a smirk on his face that he has no idea wrecks me to the very core.

The color drains fully now, and I stand there in complete shock until he says, "Amber?"

"It's, uh, no—" I also can't lie to him. I turn my back on him to go fetch my bag from the other room. "I'll be right back." Thankfully, he doesn't follow me, but he does hover.

I panic, my hand at my throat as I feel tears well in my eyes, my heart racing. I know it was a joke, one that I started, but I just wasn't thinking. I haven't talked to anyone about any of this, aside from Audrina, and even she doesn't know the half of it. It's a part of my life that is in the past now, and that's where it's going to stay, but it still rocks me like a grenade when I think about my time in that church.

I try not to have a panic attack. After fussing around in my room with my bag and its contents, I grab everything and head back to face the music. Bronco is exactly where I left him in the kitchen. I don't meet his gaze, but I know his face is etched with concern because he isn't moving.

"Amber, did I say somethin' to upset you?"

"No, I shouldn't have brought up the Kapp with a K thing."

"Look at me, please."

I do as he says, my gaze darting to his. To see his concern for me written in those gorgeous eyes, it constricts my heart. "I'm fine."

"Is this to do with your past? The one you never talk about."

"I have talked about it."

"Yeah, that your ex was a dick, but not much else. I get that you probably don't wanna ever speak his name again, but you know you can tell me anythin'. If I've upset you, I want to know."

I swallow hard. "You're right, I don't like talking about it, but you hit the nail on the head, okay? I was in a religious cult, and my ex was a complete nut job, is that enough for you?" I'm being rude, I *know* I'm being rude, but the words fly out before I can stop them.

"I'm sorry, I had no idea." His words are sincere.

I drop my head. "It's my fault for not thinking—"

"You never have to think before you speak around me, ever." He tilts my chin up so I'm looking at him again. "You also don't have to talk about anythin' you don't feel comfortable with, which I'm guessin' you don't since this is the first I'm hearing about it."

"I don't like bringing up that part of my life," I whisper. "It makes me sad, then I get to thinking about what happened all over again, and I never, ever want to go back there, even in my mind."

He nods. "I'm sorry—"

"You've nothing to be sorry about." A fucking traitorous tear slides down my cheek and I'm mortified.

Bronco catches it with his thumb. "Do you need me to deal with him?" His voice is low and serious.

I shake my head. "No. He doesn't live here, or anywhere close to here. Please, let's leave it alone. Can we go now?"

He stares at me for another moment, the mood has plummeted from fun and giddy to whatever this is; glum and sad. "We can go, if you still want to?"

"Of course I want to. I just..." I blow out the air in my

cheeks. "I brought something up, and now I've made you feel bad about it."

He pulls the front of my cap down, tucking the loose strands behind my ears. "I feel bad if I upset you, that's all. It wasn't my intention."

"There you go again, taking all the blame." My face softens. He truly is the sweetest creature I've ever met. "Let's just rewind. Can we go back to the part where you put the *basketball* cap on my head and said we were twinsies?"

I see his throat bob, and now I feel guilty that he's thinking about it. I hope he doesn't ask me about it again. That isn't Bronco's style, but I know it's not something you hear every day.

"You look pretty," he tells me. "Too pretty to be seen with the likes of me."

"Now you're just being kind."

"Nope." It's then I realize his hands are still cupping my face. "I mean every word. In fact, I'm happy to be your chaperone on any future dates."

Future dates?

"Yeah," I joke. "Just what I need; you in the middle when the dude is trying to hold my hand."

"Hey, someone's gotta make sure he's on his best behavior." He finally moves his hands away as if he's just realized, too.

"I'm sure nobody will make any moves when they find out you're my best friend."

"Woah, I've been upgraded from *friend* to *best friend*." He high-fives me, and I laugh. "Though I do recall Olive sayin' you talk about me all the time."

I sigh. "I wondered when you were going to bring that up."

He smirks, his eyes still a little wary, but he's trying to lighten the mood. I really want to go to the game, forget about adult shit and cults for a while and just have some fun.

He shrugs. "Kids don't lie, and I've got some questions about other vegetables on the ride over to the arena."

I laugh out loud. "The Happy Hangout is not in session when we're at the game."

He pouts. "I'm really gettin' into it. Trix has some sass, she reminds me of you."

I laugh again. "She does?"

"Uh huh, giving the main dude a hard time because she can, that and he is bein' a dick the majority of the time because he secretly likes her but won't man up."

"Oh, he mans up," I snicker.

"Yeah, thanks for that. Not only do men have to compete with vibrating toys that have thirty fuckin' speeds, and suction roses that aren't from the garden variety like I once thought, but now we have to be inferior of vegetables, too?"

I slap him on the chest lightly. "Stop it!"

"What? It's true. A man's penis is like the least appealing thing on the menu these days."

He's ridiculous, but he still makes me laugh. "That isn't true." I pat him on the chest. "Don't worry, your manhood is still safe with me."

Our eyes lock and something passes between us. I step back, removing my hands from him, clearing my throat.

"You ready, *Princess?*" He speaks before I get the chance.

"I'm ready to eat my bodyweight in hotdogs and scream for Alvarado to beat his best score or rebound record."

"Not gonna happen."

"Ye of little faith." He lets me walk ahead of him as I grab my door key and shove it into my bag. I lock the house behind us, send a quick text to Indi to check on Olive, and then Bronco is shoving a helmet on my head, fastening it before he hops on first.

I don't know how I feel.

A little numb. A little nervous. After my admission, I'm realizing that I have deep shame when it comes to my past, and maybe that will always be a part of me. I thought I'd buried it, but clearly I still have some work to do.

My gut clenches remembering his face when he thought he'd made me sad. *Why does he have to be so freaking perfect?* I know he'd lay his life on the line for me, and has done before, for so little in return. If he's not into me like a potential girlfriend, then what is his endgame? Does he have one? I know deep down in my heart that Bronco doesn't have a mean bone in his body where I'm concerned, or the ones he cares about. But I've seen him in action. I saw what he did to those two goons who stalked me, and I never want him finding out about Vince. Not that I think he'd travel to Illinois, but I wouldn't put it past him.

That's what it is. The past. It has nothing to do with where I'm at right now.

I slap a smile on my face as I press my body against his, enjoying his warmth as I wrap my arms around his waist. It shouldn't feel so comfortable. It shouldn't feel like my safe space because I don't want to put that on him, but I ignore my feelings and tell myself it's okay.

It's okay to feel good, and it's okay to enjoy the company of a man who doesn't expect anything in return. We joke around about sex toys and penises, but I know that's just our sense of humor. Bronco would never force me to do anything I didn't want to. The question is, do I want to? And if so, what do I do about it next?

11

BRONCO

Tonight already has me reeling and we've only just taken our seats.

I knew Amber had a rough past, but a religious cult? Is she for fuckin' real? My blood boils just from the way she reacted to my comment that this part of her past hurt her. I saw the fear in her eyes, the flash of cruelty she remembered suffering at the hands of her ex. I admit, I don't know much about him, but I do know that he's a dead man if he put his hands on her... Who am I kidding? Of course he did. She hasn't told me in so many words, but I've gotten the gist of it from tidbits she's told me over the years. I just don't know why she didn't tell me sooner about the cult.

Still, as I rest the tray of food on my knees, I'm trying to see past the anger I'm really feeling in order to have a good time. I lied to her. I put on a front so she wouldn't get even more upset, but I'm raging deep inside. I want her to bring it up again so I can find out more. So I can locate this asshole and wipe him off the face of the earth. I'll do it, she knows I will, which is why she brushed over his whereabouts. What are best friends for if not to stalk your ex-boyfriends and give them an ending they deserve? My temper is nuclear when it comes to women being treated like shit. I've got my mom to thank for that because she instilled in me and my brother that it is not okay to treat women like trash. It is also not okay to put your hands on a woman in anger. Period. I'm murderous when I think about someone hurting her, or that she could've possibly lived in fear from this asshole.

I'm thrown. This is the secret part of her life where the walls are still so high, there ain't no way anyone's getting over the moat or anywhere close, and that part makes me sad. I've always been the life of the party, the idiot who says the wrong thing, but a smile always ensues. The deep, dark part of me knows what I'm capable of when it comes to protecting the people I care about; I will not hold back.

"Oh, my God!" Amber groans as I look sideways, knocking me out of my reverie. She's stuffing a very large hot dog into her mouth, and I can't help but chuckle.

"You know, I can always order out if you want hotdogs anytime. When was the last time you indulged?"

She shakes her head, chewing until she swallows the huge mouthful. "I don't eat this stuff usually, and it's not the same unless you're at a game, ya know?"

I wave the huge popcorn bucket at her. I've also got two hotdogs, and a side of fries, plus our Giant sodas which are stationed at my feet. "Duly noted," I say, stuffing a handful of delicious popcorn into my mouth. "The Nuggets aren't gonna know what hit them."

"Especially when it's our home turf."

"It's been ages since I've been to a live game."

She glances at me. "We've got Ben to thank for it."

I try not to stiffen at the sound of his name. "Not a good sign that he's still sick. You don't want a dude with a weak immune system."

"Is that right?"

"Don't tell me you're gonna give this douchebag another shot once he's over his fake flu?"

She balks, the hotdog halfway to her mouth. "He isn't faking it. Katie said he'd been really sick, and why wouldn't I give him another shot? He seems like a good guy."

Uh, because I don't like the idea? And the other day when you came and saved me from Cupcake, I really liked it...

"I'm just sayin', you're better off holdin' out for someone who isn't such a flake."

"By the way, you still owe me one."

I glance at her sideways. "What for?"

"Cupcake."

I roll my eyes. "Are you still milkin' that?"

"Thanks to me, everyone thinks we're dating. The girls blew the chat up this morning. I had to let them down gently."

"We should fake date," I mutter. "It'll keep all the creeps away."

She whacks me in the arm. "I'll be single forever if I bring you along to all my dates."

"Maybe that's a wise idea, then I can check out this Ben character and give you my unsolicited opinion of him. I'm pretty good with vibes." I try not to grit my teeth when I say it.

"I'm a big girl, Bronc, I think I've got this." She continues to eat while I think about her thinking about Ben. I wonder if she really wanted him to be here tonight instead of me. Is she disappointed? Which is a given because she seems pretty hell-bent on setting up another date with him.

"Still, you gotta ask yourself why the universe is keepin' him at arm's length," I go on. "If it's not workin' out easily, then that could be a sign to stay away."

She sighs. "If I listened to you, I'd be a freaking nun for the rest of my life."

If it means not going on dates with other guys, then maybe that's not a bad idea?

"That's takin' it a bit far. I know what guys are like, how they think."

"Uh, huh, and how is that exactly?"

I give her a pointed look. "You know what I mean."

She stares right back at me. "I'm pretty dumb, you might have to spell it out for me."

"They think through their dicks."

"And chicks can't think through their anatomy as well?"

I frown. I hadn't considered it before. "I guess they can…"

"So, in your argument, only guys are horny, and all they want is to get a chick into bed?"

"That's pretty accurate for most single guys, and if you think some Prince Charming is out there, pretendin' to be somethin' else, then I'm sorry to burst the bubble, he isn't. Or at least he could be, but he definitely has sex on the brain ninety percent of the time."

She's still staring at me when she says, "But you're not like that."

My eyes slide to hers. "How do you know? Maybe I am."

"You have sex on your brain ninety percent of the time?" Her words go straight to my dick.

"Didn't say that, but men are men."

She giggles. My eyes grow wide. "I guess you have a point." She waves a hand.

I tilt my head to the side. "Glad I amuse you. What's so funny?"

"Bronc, you haven't had sex with a girl, in like, how long?"

Now I regret being so honest.

I told Crystal how long; six months to be precise, but that doesn't mean I want to broadcast it or that I want Amber knowing how pathetic I am.

I tap her cute button nose. "A gentleman never tells."

She laughs even harder. "You know what just struck me?" I wait in anticipation for what she's about to say next, but it kinda shocks me all the same. "You are kinda perfect."

My frown turns into a lazy smile. "I've thought this for some time myself."

"Oh, my God! Stop it, I'm gonna pee my pants!"

"You said it. Let's examine the evidence, or would you like to do the honors yourself?"

"I'd love to." She starts counting on her fingers. "You have a good job, and you're a committee member of the MC. Your mom's amazing. You can cook, sort of. You love the Pelicans. You're kinda good looking, but a little scary if you're not smiling. Your hair is naturally thick and lustrous. Your eyes are insanely pretty. You have your own house, car, sled, and — as far as I can tell — no crazy exes lurking around the corner. How am I doing so far?"

You're kinda good looking? My eyes are insanely pretty? Why is it like she's talking directly to my cock?

"You're observant," I joke. "But you forgot about my six pack, my record as an all-star quarterback, and my huge cock." The words are out, and I mean them in gest, but her eyes still widen.

She leans in closer, so we're whispering. "So, is it true?"

I lean in too, lowering my voice. "Is what true?"

"You said nine inches."

I sit back in my chair, spreading my legs a little wider. "I've not had any complaints."

"That isn't answering the question. I just know guys love to brag about their dick sizes, and usually it's to overcompensate because they're small."

"Trust me, I'm not."

Without hesitation she says, "That's almost twenty-three centimeters."

I shoot her a look. "You measured?"

She shrugs. "I may have."

"The question is, why are you so interested in my dick size when you've got Ben's half-mast-probably-can't-even-get-it-up noodle to look forward to." I smirk at my own joke.

She narrows her eyes, but I can tell she's trying not to laugh. "How long have you been waiting to use that line?"

"Since I found out you were goin' on a date with him."

"I don't know why this date bothers you so much," she goes on. "And don't say it's because of all your woo-woo crap."

"Hey, it's not crap. My premonitions are usually pretty accurate."

"Name one time they've been accurate," she challenges.

"I joked one day and said Star looked big enough to be carryin' twins." Okay, probably not a good thing to say to a pregnant woman, and it earned me a slap upside the head, but was I wrong?

"That is pretty freaky."

"I can also predict storms; such as the one comin' this year. We're gonna get snow, just for the record."

She balks. "Has it ever snowed in New Orleans before?"

"Two-thousand and nine was the last time. I'm a bit of a weather buff. I also predicted Tom Brady's retirement last year, who would win the NFL before the season started, and I told Cash I had a hunch about who had kidnapped Audrina, and that turned out to be true."

She stares at me. "So, you're really psychic?"

I shrug. "I don't think it's that, I think I just get a feeling about things."

"So, I shouldn't go out with Ben?"

"No."

She nods. "I won't then."

Why does my heart stutter when I hear her say the words? She's actually going to listen to me?

"I just don't like him." *Especially if I imagine his hands on you, not to mention anything else.*

"Thanks for the tip." She turns to watch as the game begins.

That's it? Thanks for the tip? I thought she'd be mad, tell me I can't tell her what to do, and who the hell do I think I am? But she says none of that. It also doesn't help matters when she brought up the nine inches thing. Has she been thinking about it? Clearly she has if she's measured. I don't wanna brag, but I would be lying if I said I'm overcompensating, or whatever it was she said.

As the first quarter unfolds, I find out that Amber is quite the cheerleader; voicing her opinion out loud, shouting out to the refs and encouraging her favorite players. She's awesome. I've never seen her like this; carefree and at ease in her surroundings. I like that she's comfortable with me, and that she chose me to spend tonight with.

At half time, I get us more drinks and food. For a slight little thing, she can certainly put some grub away. She has another hotdog, and I grab some candy and a couple of large foam fingers because I'm really just a big kid at heart. Amber's delighted when I come back and present her with one of the large hands; she laughs and takes it off me, super pumped for the next half.

She checks in with Indi on how Olive's going, relaxing when Indi texts back. I dig how cool she's being about this whole thing with Erica and Olive, and now it's clear that maybe they have something to do with this cult thing, too. *Is that the reason Erica left Olive in her care?*

If so, why hasn't Amber said anything? If Erica is in some kind of trouble, then she needs to enlist the help of the MC, or at the very worst, call the cops. Maybe she really believes Erica is coming back, but it seems sketchy.

"I can't watch anymore!" Amber cries out when her

favorite player misses a three-point shot. The scores are close, and it's gonna suck if the Nuggets win at a home game.

"Tell me about it. I'm having an anxiety attack over here," I murmur.

All of a sudden, people around us start turning our way to look at us, and I'm about to ask the dude in front what his problem is until I look up onto the big screen.

Oh, fuck no.

The kiss-cam is pointed at us. Right at the same moment, Amber realizes too and puts her head in her hands, her cheeks coloring bright red. I can't let the moment go, since it's gonna be on TV and all. I lean toward her and prod my cheek with one finger. If we try to avoid it, the crowd will only go nuts, and then the cam will only persist even more, or worse, come back later for another shot. She leans my way and presses her delicate lips to my cheek.

The crowd boos, making me chuckle with laughter as I thumb her way and mouth 'we're just friends' but before I know what's even happening, Amber grabs my face and then her lips are pressing against mine. She's fucking kissing me.

My heart skips a beat, my palms instantly sweat, and I can't feel my toes because my body is numb. Her lips are soft, sweet like honey, and breathtaking. Her mouth parts a little and it's then that I reciprocate, kissing her back as the crowd goes nuts all around us. The jolt of electricity is like nothing I've ever felt before; every part of my body is tingling, my blood feels like it's on fire in my veins. She's still cupping my face when she pulls back and smiles at me, albeit a little sheepishly.

"Sorry, I didn't want to disappoint the crowd," she gushes.

I blink. "That's the reason you kissed me?"

"Haven't you secretly had a fantasy about a kiss-cam moment? Like in the movies, though usually it's a stranger..."

"Let's not talk about kissin' strangers." The cam has

moved on, but my heart feels like it's taken up residence in my throat... and my dick. I can't adjust myself because that would be totally obvious, and I don't want Amber thinking I'm weird, even if she did just plant one on me without warning. "And don't apologize."

"I should've asked first," she says sincerely.

My hand finds the back of her neck and she turns to face me, her face still red from embarrassment. "You never have to ask to put your mouth on me, got it?"

"But we're—"

I press my forehead with hers. "Don't say it. Just for a second, let me pretend."

She doesn't pull away. Her skin is warm as she rests a hand on my thigh to steady herself. It's still too close; my dick is straining against my zipper, begging to be let out. Not for the first time, I imagine her mouth on my cock and how sweet that would feel. To see her bobbing her pretty little head up and down on me while I come in her mouth makes me close my eyes for a brief moment. *Asswipe. You're in public at a game!* I really need to save those fantasies for the shower, because then at least I can do something about it.

Maybe I'm having a delayed reaction, because... *did Amber just fucking kiss me?*

The way her soft touch had me jolting out of my seat, my cock swelling in an instant as her floral scent seemed to float around me, toying with me, making me insane.

I just kissed my best friend... and I liked it.

She pulls back. "What did you put in that root beer?"

I try to feign nonchalance, but I fail miserably. "Can't even blame the lack of alcohol, you did that all on your own."

"Your beard is surprisingly soft."

I almost spill into my underwear at her words. I open my mouth, then close it again.

"I thought it'd be scratchy," she goes on. "But you have really soft skin."

I'm like a fucking goldfish, opening and closing my mouth. *Man. The. Fuck. Up!*

I clear my throat. "You have soft lips."

"Thanks." She bites her lip, which does nothing but exacerbate my wood, and then she looks away. A few seconds later, she brings her Giant soda to her mouth and takes a huge sip. I'm a little dry myself, but I can't move in my seat. I'm too pent up. I knew kissing her would be epic, but I never truly thought it'd happen. I only dreamed it could, and she made the first move.

"Did you want anything else to eat?" I garble when I can't think of anything else to say. Neither of us are very interested in what's still happening on the court below anymore.

"I'm fine, I ate my body weight in hotdogs," she says.

I grin into my hand as I rub my face, trying to make sense of what the fuck just happened and why my ears are still ringing.

She can't just go around kissing me and then acting like it's all okay. That's some fucked up shit right there. *Is she feeling anything like what I'm feeling?*

I didn't come here tonight expecting to make out with her, and I know it was because of the peer-pressure the kiss-cam can bring, but still. I didn't force her to kiss me.

"How are the vibes?" she whispers. I side-eye her. Seeing my confusion, she adds, "Between us, do you think?"

I still don't have a grip on my emotions right now, and I'm spinning out of control. "Are you asking if I enjoyed it?"

"Did you?"

I lift the popcorn bucket off my lap and her eyes dip into my lap at my huge bulge. "What do you think?"

"Holy—"

I smirk. "Kissing is intimate, Amber, not gonna lie. It gets me goin'."

Her eyes widen slightly and I love the idea that I still have the ability to shock her. "What else gets you going?"

You.

"In bed?"

"Yes."

"Why do you wanna know?" I cock a brow. "Gonna do somethin' about what you've started?"

Her breathing, I notice, has quickened. My eyes dip for a second to her chest as it rises and falls faster than before. "I didn't start it."

I cock a brow. "Really? I seem to recall you just manhandling me like I'm some piece of meat."

"You just said you enjoyed it."

"I did, it just caught me by surprise."

"Well, I figured if Cupcake is watching, we should keep up the facade."

"We should fake date for real?"

"Why not? It'll keep the has-beens away from you," she laughs.

"Why do you care?" I pop the question, desperate to know the answer. I lean closer to her ear. "Wanna know somethin'?"

She nods, bringing that goddamn straw to her lips that I want to replace with my tongue. "I'm all ears."

"Nevada said somethin' crazy."

She laughs. "And that's groundbreaking?"

I swallow hard. "We had it out; he thinks men and women can fuck and still be friends."

Her chest hitches at the use of my words. "What do you think?"

"Were you talking about me?" she breathes.

"He was. I didn't indulge in it, other than to remind him we have a special friendship and I don't wanna ruin that."

Her pretty eyes meet mine. "But we'd be so good together."

My heart races, beating so hard it could burst out of my chest at any given moment. She has no idea the power of her words. "But sex ruins friendships, it complicates things, right?" *Please say no. Please fucking say no.*

"I don't know," she says quietly. "I've never had a 'fuck buddy' before."

I shake my head. "It wouldn't be that."

A small smile crosses her lips. It could just be me, but they seem swollen from that one illicit kiss. *Does she want more? Or am I imagining it?*

"Why? Am I too good for it?" Her tone is amused, but there is no amusement in my tone.

"Yes," I say simply. "You are. It's no secret I have you on a pedestal."

She looks away, then everyone is jumping out of their seats as the game ends and the final score sees the Pelicans winning by three points. We missed it, but I'm not sorry.

If I can hold one memory from tonight, it's not gonna be that fucking score board. It'll be the way Amber's kiss made me reevaluate everything that I hold dear. How's that for fucking vanilla?

12

AMBER

Heat.

Scorching heat.

That's what I feel running through my body. I haven't felt that way for... well, I've never felt that way. The shock and immobility I felt surrendering to the moment like that? It was like an epiphany.

I've never taken charge in my life; I never make the first move. It wasn't planned, more like a spur of the moment thing. I intended for the kiss to be a quick peck; mainly to keep the crowd happy, and so the kiss-cam would move on. But then things took a drastic turn.

The scene was set: Bronco looking and smelling like a dream, our mouths colliding in a kiss so sweet and sincere, I felt it all the way down to my toes. There was no tongue, but there didn't need to be; his soft lips were enough. And that scruff? Oh, boy, did I imagine his mouth somewhere else, not that I would even know what that's like because no guy has ever gone down on me. I've only read about it in romance books. That, along with using my imagination, has had to suffice for the last few years. The kiss wasn't longer than a few seconds, but it left me hungry and desperate for more. I wanted Bronco's rough hands on me. *All over me.*

When he said that whole thing about sex complicating things, I know he's right. But a spark lit inside me at the idea of us sharing a bed. I imagine what sex with him would be like, and I've no doubt he'd be good at it. Him and all of his nine inches. That surely has to be him just bragging, either that or he truly is gifted.

We leave the arena and take a detour because part of the main highway is closed off due to an accident.

Wrapping my arms around him doesn't help, in fact, it only makes my libido that much worse, and with the rumbling of the straight pipes underneath me? *Kill me now!* This is gonna be torture.

I try not to take in his big, strong body, and the subtle scent of his faded cologne; it's not like I could forget that woodsy aroma; I think it'll be ingrained into my brain for the rest of time.

When he kissed me back… goddamn, that was magic. My heart rate quickened like I couldn't breathe. With my eyes squeezed shut, I let my hair down and enjoyed every single second of Bronco's sexy mouth. It took me places I thought had been long abandoned. I've kissed other guys, albeit not many because the emotional scars from Vince mean that I can't form any kind of lasting relationship, nor would I probably want to. But with Bronco? He's safe. He's like home. That's what it is. I feel safe in his arms; I know he won't let me down, or expect anything, or hurt me. He lets me be myself.

I contemplate all these crazy thoughts as we speed through the city and back to my apartment. When Bronco pulls up outside my building, he doesn't kill the engine. A flood of disappointment runs through me that he doesn't want to stay, or even talk about it, or the kiss.

Maybe it's just me. He's kissed way more people than I

have. What if I'm just not that good at it? Then again, he did show me his giant wood... My skin prickles at the very idea and I groan out loud, biting on my lip, needing to squeeze my legs together, but I can't. Instead, I unfasten my helmet, anything to spend another minute with him.

"It's late, I should get goin'," he says as I climb off.

"Bronco, I think we need to talk about the kiss," I say bravely.

He piques an eyebrow. "Here I was thinkin' I was the only over-thinker around here."

I note the challenge in his tone and smile. "If you wanted to come in, that would be okay."

He scratches his chin, his bandana pulled down to his neck. He looks good enough to eat, seriously. But I fear I sound needy, and I hate myself for it.

"I probably should take off. I've gotta take the long route home with the highway backed up."

"You could stay here," I blurt. Oh, God, I didn't even mean it like *that,* but now I sound desperate! "I meant, on the couch, if you want?" It isn't like he hasn't slept on my couch before. Usually it's when he's a little drunk, and doesn't want to drive. Still, we hadn't just kissed when that happened, and all the feelings I'm now having weren't swirling around in my head like a runaway freight train.

"I don't wanna impose."

I roll my eyes. "So now you're a big shot because I kissed you?"

Relief engulfs me when he kills the engine. "My head is pretty big; I just hope everyone at the clubhouse saw it on TV."

"You mean Cupcake? I think Cherry was also checking you out not so long ago."

"I don't care about them." His words are soft as I swallow hard and hand him back the helmet.

Don't come up. Don't come up. But it's too late, I already asked him, and by the way he's now swinging his leg over the motorcycle, it didn't take too much convincing.

"I just don't want things to be weird."

"Zero weirdness," he says, taking the foam fingers I wanted to bring home off me, brushing a lock of my hair off my shoulder. His fingers still. *"Ah, shit."*

I chuckle. "So I think we failed our fake date, don't you?"

His eyes meet mine. "I think we could do better at fakin' it, but you puttin' your mouth on me wasn't part of the plan."

"Come inside, I can make us hot chocolate."

"You know how to seduce me," he laughs, swiping one hand through his hair as I feel his other hand on the small of my back, escorting me off the sidewalk.

Awkward silence ensues as we walk toward my building, and I let us in. Of course, the apartment is quiet; just as I left it. I switch on the main light as we head through to the kitchen. I place the foam fingers down on the bench and discard my bag as Bronco follows silently behind me.

"Cat got your tongue?" I can't hide my smirk. I wickedly like the idea that he's become a little unglued since I planted one on him. I wonder if he's feeling the same thing as me, but won't admit it.

"I didn't wanna make you feel uncomfortable tellin' you what Nevada said," he says out of nowhere, surprising me.

My back to him, grabbing the milk out of the fridge, I take a breath. "I mean, he's got it all wrong. I agree with you; sex complicates things, and let's face it, has anyone you know successfully been fuck buddies and made it work without someone getting hurt in the process?"

He shakes his head. "No such thing."

"So leaving it alone is probably the right thing to do." *Uh, what?* My libido is not a happy camper right now, but I feel like he wants to be let off the hook. For the first time since I've known him, Bronco looks uncomfortable.

"Exactly." The words are like poison because I don't believe a word of it.

I shouldn't have kissed him! Then I'd be none the wiser to how freaking amazing his mouth feels. Imagining his hands on me? That is pure torture.

Shit, shit, shit! When did I begin crushing big time on my best friend?

Then again, he did bring up the whole fuck buddy subject, not that I like that term, but I guess it describes the situation perfectly. Not that I'll ever get to find out.

"One person may feel something the other one doesn't, then things get weird," he says, the final nail in the coffin. Meaning, *me?*

He stares at me as I avoid his gaze, busying myself at the coffee machine as I froth the milk. Thank God I have this as a distraction, otherwise, I may very well just will the ground to swallow me whole. I try not to notice every single inch of him, but that's a little hard. He's so fucking sexy standing there in his sweats, his cap back on, and he has this kinda lost puppy look about him. It's making my insides turn to jelly.

"And you're totally right. When feelings come into play, things can get weird," I prattle on. *You also don't want to be the one being rejected.* "We'd get deeper into it, and one of us would probably want out, or we'd meet someone else and then complicate things even more. One-night hook ups rarely work, not if you're friends."

"Sounds like you've put some thought into it."

"Well, like you said before, how many couples remain friends after they've had sex? Not many, I'll bet."

He doesn't say anything, but he's also not smiling like his usual self. He's just watching me carefully. I didn't know kissing him would throw us this off course.

Eventually he speaks. "You're right on all counts, which rests my case, and the whole reason why I told Nevada the exact same thing."

"Or." I swallow hard. I just can't seem to shut the hell up. Without thinking, I power on. "We could just do it and have no feelings, no emotions, just enjoy the sex."

It's a bold statement, one I'm not sure that I mean in its entirety.

Even though he hasn't moved a muscle, I know something between us has changed. He just won't admit it.

"No feelings or emotions?"

I know it sounds cold, but it's pretty much a regurgitation of what he already said, and a part of me needs to know if he's just wanting a way out. Maybe the kiss threw him off? If that's the case, then it's pretty pathetic. I'm a big girl, I can take the truth.

"Yeah, I mean, we care about each other, but it's not like I'm asking you to marry me in the morning." Oh, no. I'm babbling. I sound like a desperate, pathetic, horny chick who is too scared to ask her best friend to bone her. And maybe I am. I don't want things to change between us, but I feel the desire deep within me to know what it would be like to be in his arms for one night. "It'd be one night, theoretically."

"Just sex?" He takes a seat at the counter.

"Yep." I pop the 'p', getting a little annoyed, truth be told. Okay, I get the idea he wants no strings attached, but I thought he'd have a few more words.

"Huh."

Embarrassment floods through me. "Clearly by the look on your face, and your body language, I've just poured cold water on the fire." I'm assuming there was fire, but maybe I imagined that, too?

"It's not that—"

"Then what is it?" I continue to make the hot chocolates,

the humiliation point is fast approaching. *I've made the wrong decision. I'm such an idiot for propositioning him like that.*

"It's like you said; it could ruin what we have." His voice is low, defeated, and that just highlights how dumb this entire thing was to begin with.

"Okay, I get it, you don't want to. It's fine, Bronc."

His eyes darken somehow when I slide his drink over to him. I stand still in my tracks, trying to gauge where this is going. "It isn't that I don't want to." *Wow. Just wow.*

"But you're a man," I finish for him. "Apparently the only one who doesn't think with his dick, because that's how all other men think, right?"

"So, you want me to think with my dick, *Princess?* Is that it? Cause I can do that without even blinkin'."

"That's not what I meant, and here we are fighting about it already. Case in point."

I don't know what's going on, or why he's looking at me like that, but I choose to remove myself from any more humiliation tonight.

"We're not fightin'. We're discussin'."

I take a slow inhale of breath. "I'm tired, it's late." I'm far from tired, but I can't stand here in front of him looking this desperate. Screw me for being honest. I guess he's proved my point with 100% accuracy: men and women can't be friends and be intimate.

I walk down the hall to the laundry cupboard and pull out a blanket and a spare pillow, and he just watches me the entire time. I've never known Bronco to be this quiet, and I'm not sure I like it. "I'll see you in the morning." My words almost shatter on the last word, but I somehow manage to keep it together.

"Amber—"

"Thank you, I had a great time tonight." I don't wait for

him to say anything more. Instead, I take off with my hot chocolate to hide in my bedroom until the end of time.

"Wait—"

"Tomorrow," I say without turning back. "We can talk about it tomorrow."

Did we just have our first real fight?

It's late and I can't sleep. Usually, I'd put myself to sleep with my vibrator, but that isn't an option with Bronco in the house... or is it? I'm aching; my heart rate hasn't calmed down since the kiss, then me wrapping my arms around him as we rode back to my apartment on his sled. I heard him walking around the living room, and I almost thought he was going to leave, but he didn't. He's out there on the couch, and I'm in here telling myself what a loser I am. How did I get the signals so wrong?

I listen closely, but I don't hear any sound. In any case, he's not right next to my bedroom, and it's my house. If I want to get off in my own bed, then I will. I'm not gonna be loud or anything, and my bullet will literally take a few minutes... then I can sleep.

I fumble around in the dark, my hand reaching into the side table until I find the small but powerful bullet. I press the top button and it springs to life silently.

I press the flat, round edge to my clit and work in circles, careful to not move too much in case the bed creaks... and nothing happens. I keep going, trying to focus, but my mind keeps wandering. Another minute goes by, and while it feels great, I can't get over the edge as much as I try. I persist, closing my eyes, letting the bullet work its magic... except it doesn't. It's not working.

I sigh out loud, huffing as I switch the thing off, my clit pulsing and my pussy slick as I lay an arm over my eyes. *This fucking sucks.*

I flip the covers off to go use the bathroom and grab some water. This is insanity! Now my vibrator won't work because my mind is playing tricks on me?

I also hate the idea that we went to bed on a sour note. I felt as if I were putting myself out there, and he just sat there like a goldfish; mouth gaping, eyes wide. I didn't realize that kissing me would leave such a bad taste in his mouth. Rejected and humiliated, I creep out of my room to the shared bathroom. Checking the coast is clear, I tiptoe across the hallway, pee, and wash my hands. I take a few calming breaths, annoyed, frustrated, and clammy from the heat surging through me. Stepping out, I shriek when I run into a brick wall in the hallway; Bronco yelping just as much as I do. I place my hand on my heart, step back and try to calm myself.

"Bronc! You scared the shit out of me!"

"You scared the shit out of me!" he fires back. Even in the dark, I can see his chest rising and falling rapidly — and my eyes stay on his chest. *Holy fuck balls.* Okay, I've seen him without a shirt plenty of times, but as my gaze lowers, I've never seen him in just his underwear.

There's a considerable bulge at the front of his white boxer briefs, and my eyes snap back up quickly.

"I was trying to find the toilet," he says, waving a hand. "My phone is lost down the back of the couch, and I didn't want to turn a light on to disturb you."

"That's big of you!" I fold my arms across my chest, adding dramatically, "Well, it's all yours."

I go to stomp off, but his hand finds my elbow and he pulls me back. "Don't go to bed mad," he says.

"Well, you were being a jerk."

"I didn't mean to. I just got to thinkin' about what you

said—" He runs one hand through his hair, and I cannot keep my eyes in my head. His body is so damn fine, rippling muscles and that deep V at the hem of his briefs with a dark smattering of hair.... *Focus! You're mad at him.*

"Hard to have a conversation when you keep lookin' at my dick."

I narrow my eyes. "You should be so lucky! As if I'd even be interested in—" I'm cut off with his next move; walking me backward until my back hits the wall and he's caging me in. Then he dips his head and his mouth is on mine. A small squeak leaves my throat as I give into his kiss. *Holy shit...* He feels so good, smells so good. It's maddening. I reach up, stroking my hands up his arms, feeling his muscles as he groans low and huskily.

"I thought you weren't affected by me," I pant when I pull away.

"You're mistaken if that's what you really think." His low rumble sends shivers all the way down my spine, and right between my legs.

"So why didn't you say something earlier? You left me hanging."

"I was tryin' to hold back, to not ruin things between us. I care about you, and if we go there, things will inevitably change forever."

"Did you want the kiss?" I can barely get the words out. "Or did I fuck up?"

He braces one palm against the wall next to my head. "You've no idea how much I wanted it."

I don't care what he says, I don't want him to stop. "So prove it."

He cups one side of my face. "You've got a mouth on you."

"Don't I know it."

His mouth crashes to mine once more and this time, the

moan sounds feral. His mouth is perfect; soft, sweet and sexy, all rolled into one. His tongue finds mine and I feel it deep in my core. My nipples pebble and he lowers one hand from my face to cup my breast.

My breath hitches as he sucks in air. "You feel so perfect, *Princess.*"

I squeeze his biceps, unable to keep my hands off him. "So do you."

"Whatever happens, we're always gonna be best friends, you have to promise." He stares at me, and even in the dull light, I see the earnest way his eyes twinkle.

"I promise," I whisper. "Always. It's just sex."

He crashes his mouth hungrily, pushing his body flush against mine, and that's when I feel the steel rod pressing into my stomach. *So, he really does have a nine inch cock.*

"These tiny little sleep shorts," he says in between kisses. "And this tiny little tank top? If you're tryin' to give me a fuckin' heart attack, you're goin' the right way about it."

We're all hands as he lifts me, and I wrap my legs around his waist, his cock digging into me as I clutch onto him for dear life. "Yes, Bronco," I cry when he kisses my neck roughly. "Right there."

He's heading for my bedroom, and when he bounces me on the bed, I know there's no going back now. I want this. I want this more than anything.

He stares at me from his standing point, and I sit up, pressing my hands into the mattress. "Come here," I coax. "I want you, Bronco. I want all of you."

He presses one knee to the bed, and it dips as his eyes find mine. I know that after tonight, we will be irrevocably changed forever, and I'm okay with that.

Right now, I just want to feel his body wrapped around mine. I just want to be enveloped in his warmth, his safety, his love. Even if it's on a friendship level. Isn't that better than with some guy I don't really care about?

"Remember what I said about vanilla?" he whispers. His voice is so low and sexy, I can't even form words. I just nod. "I lied."

He crawls over the top of me, and my breathing is so ragged, I can barely contain it.

I'm about to have sex with my best friend. This is a big deal.

Don't overthink it. Enjoy it. Enjoy him.

His mouth finds mine, and it drowns out any doubt I ever had about fucking my best friend.

13

BRONCO

My cock presses against the thin scrap of material posing as sleep shorts, and I've no idea how I'm gonna control this, because what I want to do is take my time. I want to devour this woman like she's my last meal; use my mouth for her pleasure, giving her what she needs. She deserves that much.

I kiss her neck, my hands finding her breasts as I knead them, enjoying the weight of them as she wriggles underneath me, then yanks her tank top over her head. I lean up onto one hand and stare down at her bare breasts. *Holy fuck.*

"Perfect," I mutter. Like I expected anything else. I rub my thumbs over her nipples as she groans. I lower my head to suck one into my mouth and her nails dig into my back. It sends a surge of heat straight to my straining cock. Could this woman get any more gorgeous?

I suck her nipple hard, laving it with my tongue as I pluck the other with my fingers. She tries to rock against me, and I know she's gonna go off like a firecracker, but then something digs into my knee and I groan. Digging around, I hold up the tiny bullet shaped object and frown.

"What the fuck is this?"

"Oh God!" she pants, attempting to swipe it out of my hands. "It's uh, it's nothing..."

I'm too fast, holding it in my palm as I realize what it is. "Did you just use this on yourself?"

I shift my eyes to hers. God, she looks so perfect sprawled out underneath me; her dark hair cascading on the comforter like some kind of angel. Her chest heaving as she closes her eyes, shaking her head.

"Liar."

"Okay, fine!" she gripes. "I tried to use it, and usually it works like a charm, but not tonight."

I grin. "Your little companion didn't work because you need the real thing." I press a kiss to her pulse on her neck and she wraps her arms around me. "Or how about I use it on you?"

"No, Bronc!"

"Why not?"

"Uh, because."

"I wanna see what you do to yourself."

"Well I want your dick inside me, and you're wasting time talking."

I laugh. "You think this is gonna be a quick bang?"

"Isn't it?"

I shake my head. "I've got you in bed all night, and I'm not gonna be wastin' it."

I reach down and cup her between her legs. "But first we need these little shorts off."

I peel them off her body, delighted when I see she has no underwear on. She tries to close her legs, but I push them open. "Let me see," I whisper.

She covers her eyes as I take in her beautiful body, my dick encouraging me onward, but I need to do this right. I swipe my fingers through her wet heat, shocked at how slippery she is. "Oh, yes," she groans.

"I bet if I flicked that little clit, you'd come in two seconds," I whisper.

"I need to come," she agrees.

"I haven't teased you nearly enough yet."

"No teasing."

I grunt a laugh, snaking my way down her body between the apex of her thighs. "Tell me to stop if you don't like anything."

"Wait, what are you— Oh!"

I lick through her wet center and she bucks off the bed. "Wait, Bronc!"

I left my head from between her legs. "You okay?"

"I've never— Uh, some warning, please."

"I'm gonna eat you out," I tell her. "I'm gonna make you scream as I fuck you with my tongue and this little bullet until you're beggin' to ride my cock. Is that enough warnin' for you?" Then I frown. "You never— what?"

"Nothing."

I give her a pointed look but it's wasted because her eyes are closed. "Eyes on me," I command.

They snap open, and her gaze finds mine. "This is embarrassing."

"The longer you take, the longer your orgasm waits."

She takes a long breath. "Nobody's ever gone down on me."

Huh? "Why not?"

"My husband didn't believe in any of that. It was missionary or nothing, and it wasn't pleasant or enjoyable for me. Since him, there's only been one mistake and it was ages ago. It was quick and just... well, let's just say it wasn't great."

If I needed any reminder that she needed me to go slow,

then that was it. "They're both fuckin' idiots," I say. "Real men eat pussy."

I spread her pussy lips with one hand and lick right through her wet center again. "You feel that?"

Her hands reach into my hair. "Oh. My. God."

"My tongue's gonna make this little pussy purr, *Princess*, because that's what real men do."

I circle her clit with my tongue and her fingernails dig into my scalp. I fucking love it. I bury my face, letting her ride this one out before I fuck her with my fingers. It's all about working my girl up to my cock, because she's gonna need some warming up.

I feel her pulse as I hold her hips down, her legs trying to close on my head, but my tongue works overtime, lapping over and over until she's screaming as she comes, my name on her lips as she falls apart.

"Gonna slide my fingers inside you, okay?" I grunt.

"Yes."

I slide one finger in her wet hole. In and out, in and out, then replace it with two. "Fuck, you're so wet."

I nibble her lips, enjoying the sounds she makes as I struggle keeping my dick from having his own party just by the friction against her thigh. I want in so bad.

I reach for the little bullet, finding the button with ease as I turn it on. "Usually, I let my dick do all the talkin'," I murmur. "But I wanna see what you do, so show me."

"No, Bronc!"

"Show me," I persist. "Please."

I pass it to her as she holds it in her hand, then she presses it to her clit. I keep my fingers inside her, pumping in and out slowly as I watch. "Ohhhh." She's breathy and I love it.

"Better than my tongue?" I muse, pressing kisses to her thigh.

"No, definitely not, ohhhh!" She comes quicker this time,

rocking her hips as I curve my fingers deep inside her, stroking her G-spot. "Bronco!"

I grin when she screams my name. Orgasm number two.

She pulls the vibrator away, and I turn it off and toss it to the side. Her pussy is pulsing as I revel in her aftershocks.

"I want to see your dick," she breathes."

"Spicy little thing, aren't you?" I tease. Rising to my knees, I help her sit up. She's breathless, panting like she just ran a marathon, and though I haven't fucked her yet, her hair is a tangled mess.

She pulls me in close and we kiss. This time, we're all tongues. I don't know how long we fuck each other's mouths, but my dick is so hard with need, it's about to burst. I move her hand and place it on my throbbing cock. "Take it out."

She slides her hand down my length through my underwear and I hiss. Then she breaches the elastic, her hand reaching inside as I watch. She grips me and I groan, my eyes rolling into the back of my head. Amber fondles me inside my undies, and I'm a fucking lost cause. I want to fuck her so bad. I want to shove my big dick inside her and keep her moaning my name all night long. *Patience.* I tell myself. Her experiences before me sucked, and this isn't about me anymore. It's about Amber and how good I can make her feel.

I play with her tits as she continues to stroke me, half my dick poking out the top of my undies, but it isn't enough. "All the way out," I bark.

She tugs my boxers, and I help her by shifting so I can slip them off my hips and down past my knees. My dick jerks out. All fucking nine inches of him.

"Oh, holy mother of God!" Her eyes are glued to my crotch and I smile. It's not the first time I've heard that.

"You can take it."

"I— Jesus, Bronc. No wonder your milkshake brings all the girls to the yard."

I laugh out loud, then hiss when she grips me harder. Her face determined as she stares at it, she sheaths me with that hot little hand and I feel my balls tighten. I'm on my knees, and she's still sitting, playing with me as I buck my hips. "Fuck, yeah, squeeze it, baby, that's it."

"It's so big," she marvels. "So fat."

"Hey, he'll get a complex if you call him fat."

She laughs. "I want to taste you, too."

All my Christmases just came at once and I don't waste any time rolling onto my back, bringing her with me. She straddles me, freeing me of my undies, her hand still wrapped around my base. "Ever done this before?" I grunt.

"Once."

I lift a brow in surprise at her admission. "Did you like it?"

She shakes her head.

"Why not?" I frown.

"It wasn't a nice dick like this one." She shifts her head and swipes that hot little tongue over my slit and I buck off the bed.

"Holy shit."

She does it again, her other hand gripping my balls as I close my eyes. *Do not come in her mouth. Do not come in her mouth.* My eyes spring open when I feel her lips wrap around my head. The groan that goes with it makes me pant like a man possessed. She bobs her head, taking more of me into her pretty little mouth, and it's just the right pressure. She feels fucking amazing.

"I wish we could 69 right now." I grapple for breath as she licks her way up my dick. "But if we do that, I'll come in two seconds."

"Fuck, Bronco, this dick is so sweet." She caresses it lovingly. Her tongue working its way up the other side, her other hand still massaging my balls.

I'm so pent up. I'm so ready to explode. "Need a condom," I pant. "Need to be inside you."

"I want that."

Realizing my wallet is out in the living room, I'm gonna have to go get it. "You got any here?"

She shakes her head, unable to tear her mouth off my dick. I sit up, spreading my legs as I watch her take me in and out of her mouth. "That feels so good, baby." I pinch her chin, making her look up at me. "Glad you got no rubbers here."

"Why?"

"Because you're not gonna be needin' them when you've got me."

Now that I'm in her bed, there ain't no other man coming around here, fuck no. This may be tricky considering we're just a one-night thing, but after tonight, we're both gonna want more of the same. The friends with benefits can work, we're already doing it. Even as I think about it, I don't really believe it. Amber is much more to me than just a friend.

She lets go, her tongue swiping the sticky precum at my tip and I pull her up into my lap. We kiss again, and I can taste myself on her tongue. "Would it shock you if I told you I want to come all over that pretty mouth?"

"You're such a dirty boy."

"Told you, vanilla was just a cover up."

My hands find her hips and she rubs her pretty pussy against my dick. "I'm on birth control, and I can't even get pregnant," she says out of nowhere. "When's the last time you were tested?"

"I always wore a condom." I grip her hips, moving her pussy up and down my cock without penetrating. "But I can go get one, it's no iss—"

Her mouth is on mine, her tongue warm and hot as we hold one another. This feels right, so very right. "Inside me, now."

"Fuck, babe, you're gonna take me raw?"

"Has anyone told you that you talk too much?"

I laugh, then she squeals as I roll her onto her back. "Next time, feel free to shut me up any way you please." I line my cock up, hardly able to believe she's letting me without a wrap, and I slowly work the tip in. "Relax."

Her hands roam my body, feeling every inch of me, and I wonder how I've gone this long without her touch. She's very slick, but from what I've gathered, she hasn't had sex in a long time, and the guy was useless. I want the memory of us together to be special. I slide in a little more, her breathing becoming more and more ragged as she whispers, "You're not going to break me, Bronc. I promise."

"Let's just ease into it," I murmur. "Otherwise you're gonna be sore tomorrow."

She raises her eyebrows. "Someone's optimistic."

I slide in again, this time halfway, and as Amber cries out, I still my hips, staying inside her. "Is that okay?"

"It's perfect."

"You're so tight," I mutter. "This pussy is squeezin' the goddamn life out of me."

"More, Bronc. Give me more."

I pull out and rock my hips forward again, stretching her with each and every movement. I don't want to thrust in all the way, but when her hands clutch my ass cheeks, encouraging me on every sway of my hips, I do just that. A guttural sound leaves her throat when I'm seated deep inside. I still, looking down at her.

"So full," she whispers. "Oh, God, you're so big."

"But this pussy was made to take me. See how well we fit?"

"Mmm."

I pull out, sliding back in again slowly. I rock my hips back and forth, my hands balled up into the sheets. I won't last this first time, but we've got all night. Now I'm in her bed, I plan on keeping her awake until the sun comes up. We find a rhythm and I smirk when I see the silent scream on Amber's face as I stretch her tight little pussy, edging her toward orgasm number three.

"Let me hear you," I groan. "Let me hear how good I make you feel."

She squeezes my ass cheeks as I spear my hips faster, her knees falling open as I feel my balls tighten. Then I'm spilling inside her as she calls my name over and over until I'm stilling, emptying every single drop with a growl. I collapse on top of her and she squeals.

Rolling off onto my back, I press a palm to my chest. My heart is beating so hard, I can't catch my breath.

"Holy shit," she stammers.

"Yeah."

"This is a bitch."

I laugh. "Why do you say that?"

"Because of course you're perfect at sex, as well as everything else."

"That's not a bad thing." I roll onto my side, resting my head in my hand.

"How do you figure? This was a one-night deal."

I shrug. "I mean, you can have my cock whenever you want it, babe."

She groans. "Fuck buddies?"

"You can't expect me to stay away from what we just did, unless... am I no good?"

She balks. "You're fucking amazing. That thing you did with your tongue?" She makes a guttural groaning sound. "I didn't know sex could be like that..."

"Like what, *Princess?*"

"Calm," she whispers. "Without violence or being hurt."

My blood cools. "I'll kill anyone who hurts you."

"That's what I'm afraid of."

I cup one side of her face as she turns to face me. "Is this why you didn't say anything sooner?"

She shrugs. "What use would it bring?"

"It would be a lot of use if he wasn't breathin' anymore, then he couldn't hurt anyone else."

"That's true, but then you'd be in jail."

I snicker. "You clearly don't know me as well as you think."

"I don't want to cause any trouble, and my past is in the past."

"But what about Erica and Olive?"

"You're right. I'm worried about Erica. I'm going to go and talk to Star on Monday. I need to find her."

"That's a great idea," I say. "They were living in Missouri, right?"

"Yes, Erica got a job as a teacher's aid, and I wanted to travel a little. I did that for about a year, and fell in love with New Orleans. The vibrancy of the city, the freedom I felt; I've never felt that anywhere else."

I love her passion for this city, it makes me want to hear more about her hopes and dreams.

"Tell me about the cult you were talking about earlier. What's the name of it?"

"No, Bronc, it's not important. I don't need you to rush in and play hero. It's done. I left, and I never want to see him, or anyone else from that place, ever again."

I'm making her upset, but her closing off about this won't change how I feel about it. I want him to suffer. I want everyone to suffer for hurting her.

I kiss her on the forehead. "I'm here if you need me. I'll always be here."

"I just want to forget it happened."

"And what about Erica? What if she's gone back there?"

"No, she'd never do that. She'd never leave Olive."

"You're certain?"

"Yes. She must be in some kind of trouble, though. This is out of character for her, and to just leave like that? She left me a note for pity's sake!" She takes a long breath. "We're like sisters, we tell each other everything. At first, I thought she just had to settle something by herself, and I gave her good grace to do it, but now I'm getting scared. Her phone is cut off, her emails don't go through…"

I brush the hair back off her face. "We'll find her."

"I hope so. I don't know how long I can keep this charade up with Olive. She's not dumb."

"I know, she'll work out something's up eventually. Just gotta talk to Star, then go from there. I can go with you if you'd like."

"Thanks, I appreciate it, but you don't have to take time off work just for me. I can handle it."

She has no idea the lengths I'd go for her. All she has to do is ask. "Whatever you want, but if she is in some kind of trouble, are you ready for that?"

She lets out a breath. "I honestly don't know. Erica is my best friend, I can't imagine what I'd do without her. I just want her back, safe, with me and Olive."

My gut clenches. I've got some contacts of my own, so I'll do some digging behind the scenes. Linc, who works closely with Rock and Jett sometimes, will be able to find stuff out without alerting the club. Not that I want to keep things from them, but everyone's so busy right now. Linc is an option if it comes to that.

"It's gonna be okay."

"Promise?"

"Promise."

Her eyes shine as I yawn. "Why on earth are you yawning?" She screws her face up in disgust. "You think I'm done with you already?"

I laugh as she climbs on top of me. I grip her by the hips as she presses her hot, warm body against mine. "What if *I'm* not done with *you*?"

"I said it first." She pokes her tongue.

I buck her with my hips. "We've got all night, and I'm not nearly finished with that smart mouth and tight little pussy."

"Good, then stop talking and let's get busy."

14

AMBER

I NEVER KNEW IT COULD BE LIKE THIS, AND IT ISN'T just the sex – which is completely incredible — but the way Bronco takes charge without being demanding or overbearing, it's like something out of one of my romance books. Things like this don't happen to people in real life. Okay, he fucked me into next week, but he wasn't rough, and he kept asking me how I was feeling, and if I was okay. Guys don't do that — not that I've been with that many — but I've had enough experience to know that it isn't the case. It's like Bronco takes this job as seriously as he does all the other important things in his life.

Now, as I ride him — my hands splayed out on his chest as he holds my hips — rocking me back and forth on his huge dick, I feel completely in control. I feel... *powerful*. That's how he makes me feel. Plus, I never knew this man was such a dirty talker in the bedroom. It's so sexy. If this is his idea of vanilla, I'll take it.

"Fuck, baby," he groans. Even this, me moving slowly on top of him, isn't rushed or frantic; it's controlled and delicious. He's hitting me so deep inside, I'm seeing stars. I had no clue that dicks could really be that big and be enjoyable, but he did make sure I was fully warmed up beforehand. Something I'm now appreciating.

"So good," I agree. "So fucking good."

He sits up, bringing our bodies closer. Closing his lips around my puckered, needy nipple, he groans when he suckles. The rhythm is perfect; a slow, rolling of the hips and a thrust at the end. He has me right on the edge, and I can't get enough. My clit brushes against his pubic bone over and over, and it's keeping me right there. I know when I orgasm again, it's going to be mind blowing.

"Ride me." He licks my nipple like the dirty man he is, then moves his attention to the other side. "Ride this big cock, *AJ*. Your pretty pussy ain't ever gonna go back now."

"Back to what?" I breathe. "Having sex with my bullet?"

He kisses his way over the tops of my breasts, then my neck, then covers my jaw in kisses as I bounce like fucking him is the only thing that matters in the world. And right now, it is. Right now, I'm his queen, and it feels so fucking perfect.

"You've missed dick, haven't you?"

"I've missed this dick, clearly," I pant. "It's nothing like the other—"

He holds a finger up to my mouth. "Let's not talk about fuckin' other men while I'm doin' you."

"I just meant, this is rocking my world."

He grins against my skin, pressing a kiss to my lips. "It's rockin' mine too, *bestie.*"

"This is so bad," I groan.

"Bad?"

"Us!"

"Doesn't feel that way to me. It feels very right."

"I know." I run my hands over his pecs, loving how he feels

beneath my fingertips. "It does, and I've got to look at you in daylight and pretend like none of this happened."

"But we're fake datin'," he reminds me. "So we could keep it up."

"Keep up fake datin'? Or keep up... *this?*"

"You think you can give this up?" He balks. "I'll be honest, baby, I can't."

My world rocks all over again. "Friends with benefits?"

"Better. Best friends with benefits."

"Right there," I groan as he plucks my nipples with his fingers, cupping them and squeezing them together. I start to come undone.

"Ride it, baby. Show me how much this pussy loves my cock."

Oh, my.

"Bronco!" I yell, tipping my head back as my orgasm explodes. "Yes, yes, *yes!*"

He watches me fall apart, a smirk on his face that will stay embedded into my brain for the rest of time. Oh, he's quite pleased with himself, and so he should be. I've lost count now how many times he's made me come. We had a ten minute breather, then our hands wandered, and here we are.

"You look so fuckin' sexy when you lose control," he breathes against my skin. "You make me crazy."

"You're an expert at getting me worked up," I say, my breathing ragged.

"I like to think I'm talented."

"More than talented."

"Why, thank you."

He doesn't let up. Instead, he moves his hands down to my waist and our mouths find each other. We're all tongues. It's so illicit, so bad ass, and the wild abandon side of my nature is digging it. More than he could ever know. "And anyway," he goes on. "If we say we're datin', even though we're not, it'll keep everyone off our backs."

I immediately jump on the defensive in my mind: does he not want people to know? Is he ashamed of me? Am I good enough? But I squash all those thoughts down. Bronco isn't like that, and he's right in a way; the women of the club are nosy. They'll want to know all the details, and once they know, they'll switch their attention to something else. Maybe this friends with benefits thing could really work out? Especially if I get sex like this on the regular. *Regular?* I want to facepalm myself. He's still inside me, and I'm already overthinking this entire situationship, which is what this is in a nutshell.

"You may have a point." I gasp when he lays down, tilts my hips, and rocks up into me.

I don't just see stars this time; I *am* the damn stars. He fills me to the hilt, then lifts me off. There's more pressure than before, and then he moves faster. It's so good, every single fire is alight inside me as we fuck. *Up, down. Up, down.* His hand grips my ass, the other one still resting on my hip as I go into sensory overload. And it is so fucking good.

"AJ!" he cries. "Better come because I'm barely holdin' on."

His words are my undoing as I tumble again, loudly. Gripping his shoulders, I pound down on him, rocking my hips into his as we moan and groan our way through another orgasm.

He stills, and I can feel the spurts of his cum shooting inside me as I slow my hips. I collapse against his chest, panting like I just ran a marathon. "Holy shit, we're gonna fuck each other to death."

He grins against my cheek. "Not a bad way to go."

I wrap around his body, snuggling into his neck as I breathe him in. He still has the same sexy pine scent with a hint of musk, but now it's mingled with sex. I swear, if I could bottle it, I'd be a millionaire. He's the epitome of sex on a stick.

"I know I'm gonna be paying for that tomorrow," I groan.

He kisses the top of my head. "Because my big dick broke you?"

"I haven't had sex in a long time, two years—" It was a one-night thing and I didn't enjoy it.

"I'll take that as a compliment."

"You should, because I know enough to realize that you're a stud between the sheets."

He chuckles beneath me. "Are you just buttering me up so we can go another round?"

"Another?" I gasp. "Really?"

"Don't sound so shocked. I can go all night. Just need a little minute to recover, then I'm good to go again."

"You're insane," I tell him. "I'm going to need recovery time."

"That tight pussy loves it." *Oh, his dirty words.* "You know it, and I know it."

"Shut up, *fake boyfriend*, or I won't cook you breakfast in the morning."

He traces circles on my back. "I don't expect you to cook for me."

"I want to, it's the least I could do."

"Like a down payment?"

I laugh. "Something like that. I know my vibrator can't work like that mouth can."

"You liked that, huh?"

"Mmhmm, I think we both know I more than liked it, Bronc."

"So I could be your cabana boy after all." He smirks.

I know he doesn't want a girlfriend, he's said as much over the years. Even if he has hinted at the idea of settling down, I don't know if he's truly ready for that. He's never had a real relationship before, not a serious one, so how could he know it's what he wants? And with my past forever haunting me, I'm not sure it's what I want. How would I know when all I've known since I was sixteen is violence. I've never known what love is, not truly, or if it even exists. Even when around the MC... I see and feel all of the love the men have for their women, and vice-versa. It's evidence that love is very much alive and well. Still, I can't shake how I feel.

I try not to think about that now. I don't want to ruin the happy moment I'm having being in my best friend's arms, trying not to overthink every damn thing about him that I've overlooked all this time.

Not only is he the sweetest man on the planet, as well as kind and thoughtful, he's got a body made for riding.

"Or you could tell me why a guy like you has been single for so long?" He mentioned he hadn't had sex in six months, which is quite a long time when I've seen him in action over the years. I have to admit, Bronco is one of the nicest guys in the MC. He's never treated a woman badly, none of the guys have, but he's always been upfront about it, and the girls knew what to expect. It's why sweet butts hang around, after all. I've never heard any of them say anything bad about him.

"I just haven't met the right woman."

"So, that's the reason?" I laugh. "Who knew?"

He bumps me with his hips. "Smart ass. I could ask the same thing about you, but now I know a little more about your past, I can see why."

Tears spring to my eyes. I've talked about this with Audrina briefly in a moment of panic, but not to him. Now we're this close, I want to tell him everything.

The good. The bad. The ugly.

"I'm sure you can understand why. Living in a religious cult isn't exactly screaming a happy, perfect life."

"How did you get into it in the first place?"

I sigh. "My brother. After our mom died, he was my sole guardian when dad took off. He'd always been fascinated with shit like that, and when he met Vince at a church meet, he got the idea to join Vince's little posse." I shudder at the memory. "And it was fine for a while, good, even. They had houses, a village, their own produce; a little like the Amish, but with electricity."

"How old were you when you were married?"

I hold my breath. "I—"

"You can tell me. None of this is your fault. You said you were fourteen when you moved?"

He has a good memory. I wonder what he'll think of the next words out of my mouth.

"I was sixteen."

"What the fuck?" He shifts, looking up at me as I try to bury further into his neck. "Amber?"

"I thought Vince was so charming," I whisper. "And he was good to me at first. Funny. Handsome. He always had a big, warm smile, and he treated me like a princess. But after we 'married', things slowly changed, especially when..."

His hands still on my back. "Especially when, what?"

I swallow hard. "After I had two miscarriages and couldn't get pregnant again. In their church, that's considered the work of the devil. He'd accuse me of cheating on him, he was crazy, paranoid, often leaving me for days at a time to indulge in the other women in the sect, drinking all night, coming home with a different woman...."

"Did he ever hit you?"

I've hidden enough from him, and I won't lie anymore. "Yes."

His sharp intake of breath has me wanting to retreat, but I need to do this. He needs to know some of what happened, then maybe he'll see why I am the way I am. Why I'll never get married again, have a family, or probably settle down. I never want to be controlled ever again.

"I'm sorry, baby. I'm sorry he did that to you."

"My brother didn't care," I whisper. "We'd never really gotten along, but I thought he'd stick up for me, tell Vince to lay off me, but he didn't. They both have multiple wives, and Erica was scared for Olive. Hell, I was scared; it's the main reason we decided to leave Illinois."

"This is insane, AJ. No wonder you ran for your life."

"Yeah."

"What's the name of the religious group?"

I shake my head. "No, I'm not telling you that."

He lifts my chin. "Because you know I'll kill him, and your brother."

"Yes, that's exactly the reason. Like I said before, I don't want you going to jail. It's not worth it."

"But what about all the other girls he could prey on?"

My eyes blur with tears when I think about that. "I know, trust me, that's the part that haunts me, and the women who are being used and manipulated who don't see it. One of my brother's wives tried to stop us the day we ran away." I tell him briefly what happened and his arms tighten around me.

"Even back then, you were a tough little cookie. I'm glad you knocked that bitch out."

"I wanted to do more," I admit. "I was so angry. She almost blew everything. I'd worked so hard to line this up, stash money away so we could get a bus to anywhere, and it was almost all for nothing."

"But you made it out," he reminds me. "You survived."

"Since then, Erica has always been talking about trying to bring them down. She can't let it go. It's got me worried that she may have started something."

"We need to talk to Star ASAP. Give me the name of the cult, I'll find a way—"

"No, Bronco. I know what you'll do, and I don't want that on my conscience."

"Why not? He doesn't seem to have one, or your brother."

I know his words are true, but I still couldn't stomach being the instigator of someone's death knowingly. I'm just not made that way. I know Bronco thinks I'm some kind of badass, but that isn't 100% true. I have doubt, worry, and fear all the fucking time.

"I know, but I want to handle this myself. I promise if I need your help, or if Star can't get any trace of Erica, then I'll tell you, but you have to promise me you won't do anything."

"Not gonna promise that," he says. "I'll fuckin' cut his throat in front of his entire family if we ever come face to face."

And that's exactly what I was worried about. I know he would. Bronco isn't just the big, oafy nice guy with a heart of gold. He loves hard, and if you hurt someone he cares about, you will suffer horribly. It's how he's made. I'm no stranger to what goes on in the MC, and while the club is legit and everyone works in their businesses, I'm also fully aware the club has done illegal things in the past. People have disappeared. Mafia and rival MC club wars have broken out. So-called drug fueled shootings on the news have been unsolved, or blamed on gangs, but I know the MC was involved. I've often reasoned with myself; if they only kill the bad guys, is that really considered a sin? I'm not deeply religious these days, but I still believe there is something higher than all of us. I also believe that bad people should be taken from the earth, unable to breathe the same air as us, or hurt anyone else. I do believe in vigilante justice to a degree, but Bronco is too close to this. The fear of him getting caught and locked away is too much for my heart to bear.

"Please don't say that," I chide. "It makes me nervous. I'm

sure he'll get what's coming to him. In fact, I believe it strongly."

"So he has no way of knowing where you are, right? You haven't contacted your brother or anyone else?"

I shake my head. "No. I never had a phone, so he could never contact me. I even changed my legal name."

"Were you always Amber?"

"Yes, just my last name."

He starts to stroke my shoulder again. "I hate that you suffered."

"It made me stronger."

"Even so. That shit ain't right. The fact that you escaped means they held you captive?"

I sigh. "Not in so many words. We were free to go around the village, but it was blocked off with a huge gate and fences to keep us in, and others out."

"Sounds like a prison," he huffs.

"It was in a lot of ways. Though, you have to understand, most of the people there want to be there. They have no reason to leave because it's what they want, or think it's what they want."

"How could anyone want that?"

"I was a child, I had no choice in the matter," I say. "And by the time I was old enough to know any better, I was brainwashed. That's what they do."

"It's sick."

"Yes, it is, but here we are."

He's silent for a while, then, "I'm a little mad you didn't tell me this sooner."

I laugh without humor. "You think I want to relive it? To have you do your own private investigation just to seek revenge?"

"No, but it's me." He really sounds hurt. "We've known

each other for ages, and this is the first time you've ever mentioned a cult."

"A part of me still lives in fear of him, and my brother. I was convinced they'd seek retribution for what we did. But as the years passed, I realized that finding us would be like finding a needle in a haystack," I say. "They also wouldn't leave home for long periods of time, so in a way, I knew we'd be safe if we could get out of Illinois."

His voice sounds hoarse when he speaks next. "I hate that you had to run in fear of your life, constantly lookin' over your shoulder."

I lift up and stroke one side of his face. "That's over now. They can't hurt me, I promise."

He doesn't look convinced, but he takes my head in both his hands. "I won't let them."

I know he means it. I don't need any reminders of what he's capable of when it comes to violence, but when it's toward people who commit crimes, I've no issue with it in the slightest.

It's then I realize he's still inside me. We've been lying here talking about my past, and this hulk of a man is still buried deep.

As if just realizing it himself, he smirks. "You like havin' me between those pretty thighs, don't you, babe?"

I roll my eyes. "You're not bad."

His eyebrows raise. "Not bad?" He rolls me over and I squeal, laughing as he pulls all the way out. "Ever fucked in the shower?"

"I can't say I have."

"Want to?"

"You really are insatiable." It's not a question. He's a freaking stallion.

He grins. "How is your fake, vanilla boyfriend doin' so far?"

I swing my arms around his neck. "He's the best I've ever been with."

He kisses me slowly. "Glad to hear it." He lifts himself up, offering me his hand. "Let's see how many positions we can do in one night."

I laugh. "You'll be the death of my vagina, you know that, right?"

My eyes dip to his ass as he turns. "There are worse ways to go, *Princess.*"

15

BRONCO

So I always thought I liked showering alone. I can't say I've ever showered with any of the women I've ever been with, but this is spectacular. Smelling her vanilla body wash sends me over the edge. I watch her hand roam her body, and my cock stiffens. It's not like I can keep it down when she's around. It's as if I have no control over it.

I smile to myself as she hums, completely at ease with being naked with me in her tiny shower. It's definitely not made for two, but that's where theatrics come in.

I don't like all the shit she just told me. In fact, I'm enraged. I want to cut this man, and her fucking brother, and bury them out in the bayou. Goddamn assholes. No matter what she says, I'll get to the bottom of it. What if these bastards are still doing this shit? She was married at sixteen? That's not even legal. Then when I think of Olive and her future in that damn nut camp, I really see red. Children are innocent, they deserve better than that.

I'm also still upset that she never told me. I don't want to ruin the mood, so I keep my annoyance on the down low, but I'm glad she's finally fessed up. Even if it is years after the fact.

The whole idea she held all of that from me... I really don't know what to think.

Still, she's happy tonight. I don't want to ruin the mood. I like playful Amber.

"You tryin' to tease me on purpose?" I muse, leaning back against the shower wall. We were both hot and sticky from our fuck sessions, and while I'm more than fine with her lying in my arms with my cum leaking out of her, I know she'll feel better after a shower. Not that we're gonna make it out of here without round three.

"Nope." She massages her tits, her teeth biting down on her lip as she gazes up at me.

I reach out, but she smacks my hand away. "Show me what you do."

I cock my head. "With what?"

A little smile creeps across her face. "With that big monster between your legs."

I glance down, my cock thick and heavy between my legs, and I grin. "He's a friendly monster."

"He's still big."

I run a hand down my chest and abs teasingly as her eyes follow, then I grip my dick with one palm and work it up and down my length. "Like this."

She watches me, still playing with herself as my eyes dip to her tits. "He's ready to play again."

"Oh, he's always ready to play around you." I smile. I almost tell her how hard I've been for her for a while now, but that'll give my secret away, so I hold my tongue on too much of the truth. "Ever since that kiss, my dick's been hot for you."

"Jesus, I love that dirty mouth."

"Touch your pussy."

She does as I ask, leaning back against the glass, facing me, her legs spread. She rubs her clit, keeping one hand plucking at her nipples, and I'm heady with need. Her eyes are still trained on my hand and I pick up the pace, tugging my balls with the other hand.

"You're too sexy for words," she breathes.

I laugh. "I am not."

"Like you don't know it."

"Put your fingers inside, that's it..." My strokes become faster and I grip my cock harder as I watch her. She fucks her pussy with one finger, then two, moaning softly as I take her in. I need to touch her, but I want to see if she'll touch me first.

"Bronco," she whispers. "I'm close."

"Suck my dick while you finger yourself," I growl.

Her eyes spring open, and she licks her lips. In two seconds, she's kneeling on the tiles, my cock in her hand. Spreading her legs, she continues to touch herself as she takes me into her mouth and sucks me deep. I brace a hand on the glass where she was just leaning. "Fuuuuuck."

She uses that hot tongue to tease me, lave me, nibble at my tip and I'm ready to come down her throat. I move my hips, hitting the back of her throat as she gags. I pull out.

"You okay?"

"Mmm, yes." She takes me again, sucking the tip like a lollipop. "Fuck my mouth, Bronc."

I piston my hips, moving in and out as she takes all of me. Her mouth perfect, her eyes wide, she stares up at me and it takes all my might not to spill into the back of her throat. But I need her pussy again.

"Come for me," I demand. "*Please.*"

My words are her undoing as she moves her hips, one hand between her legs, the other one squeezing my dick. Then she comes loudly, and I'm jealous of her hand working between her legs. I want to give her that. She groans, my cock locked between her lips, and I stop my ministrations the second she's done. I pull her up to standing and my lips find hers.

"Too fuckin' pretty with my dick in your mouth."

"It shut me up for a few minutes, didn't it?"

I laugh against her lips as I spin her around. She braces against the glass with her hands and I line up behind her. I slide my dick in all the way and she cries out in a long moan.

"Too big for you?" I taunt.

"Oh, you fill me so good." Her panting breath has me gripping her hips as I pull out, then push back in again.

"Wanna be fucked, *AJ?*"

"Yes, oh, God, yes!"

I can't keep it slow this time, I'm too pent up, but I also can't remember the last time I fucked three times in one night. No way. Even the overachiever that I am couldn't have predicted this.

"How does it feel? Your best friend bangin' this sweet pussy."

"About as good as having your cock in my mouth."

"Fuck." I love it when she talks dirty back. "Gonna be quick this time, you touchin' what's mine got me worked up."

"Yours?" she pants.

"Yep."

"You're confident."

"Always am." I move my hands to her tits, cupping them greedily, my thumbs pressing against her hard peaks. "Best fuckin' tits I've ever seen."

"Oh god, I'm coming, Bronc..." She does just that, her head flopping back as I hammer it home. She squeezes my cock as she comes hard.

I can't hold on. Stilling, I shoot my load thick and fast, my orgasm making me dizzy as she drains my balls, and I make noises I've never made before because this woman makes me feral.

We're panting, and when I pull out, I see my cum dripping down her thighs. I really love how that looks. I hold her wrist with one hand, then move my other hand between her legs.

"Never gonna unsee this," I mumble into her neck.

"You're a very bad man."

"Who knows how to fine tune your body."

"Touche."

I kiss the top of her shoulder. Glancing up, I frown. There's a mark on her wrist... as I lean in closer, I realize it's the arm that Amber always wears a thick cuff on. It's not a mark, it's a tattoo. "What is that?" I brush my thumb over it and she gasps.

Her reaction catches me off guard. I let go of her and she covers the tattoo with her other hand. "It's— it's nothing."

"Doesn't look like nothin'. Why have I never seen this before?"

She pushes off the glass, opening the shower door to leave.

"Amber?"

"Just drop it, Bronc, okay?"

I frown. What in the actual fuck? I run a hand through my hair, watching her wrap a towel around her. She starts to walk out, but then stops. I don't know what the fuck just happened, but it's like she'd seen a ghost.

I turn the shower taps off, and follow behind her, grabbing a towel off the rail and drying off quickly.

She moves silently, sitting on the side of the bath. "It's a tattoo," she says, her voice so faint I can barely hear her.

"I gathered that. Why the reaction?"

She looks down at it, rubbing it with her thumb. I don't know whether to move closer or back off, but she looks so hopeless.

I bend down, crouching in front of her. "You don't ever have to hide things from me, ever."

She nods. "I usually have it covered with heavy makeup, or my cuff. When I got in the shower... I wasn't thinking."

I let her talk, not wanting to fill the silence with words when it's clear she has things to say.

I do not, however, expect the next words out of her mouth.

"It's a brand." She drops her head. "Whatever you want to call it."

I frown. "A brand?"

"Yes. Vince, he—"

"He branded you with a tattoo?"

"Yes, it's the church's logo. It bound me to him, to the church."

What in the actual fuck?

I swallow hard. "Why didn't you have it removed?"

"I wanted to," she starts. "Then I got scared it would fuck up and look weird."

"But you know I tattoo people for a livin'."

"I do. I didn't want to burden you with it." It almost sounds like a protest. "And in any case, I was embarrassed."

"You're never a burden." Man, this pains me to say. "So you've been coverin' this up for years?"

She shrugs. "I always planned on getting around to it, but to be honest..." She takes a noticeable intake of breath, which in turn has my blood boiling at the jerk who did this. "I really hate needles."

I don't understand, until this moment, the power that this asshole really had over her. He fuckin' branded her with his own tattoo? I try to keep my cool, but it's hard for me. The temper boiling inside of me feels nuclear.

"I wish you told me? You can opt for laser removal if you don't want a cover up."

She shrugs, her eyes daze off into the distance looking lost for a moment. "I honestly don't know. Maybe a part of me was holding onto that old life, ya know? Even though it was toxic, and the worst time in my life, maybe I couldn't really let go because the pain reminds me how far I've come."

"How can you look at that and not see him?" I don't want to sound like an ass, but I need to know.

"I've been covering it for years, but that's no excuse. I guess I figured one day I'd pluck up the courage to ask you."

I pique an eyebrow. "You'd let me?" It brings up that whole ass tattoo thing, and here I was thinking that was cute. Now I know she'd never have done it sober because she hates needles.

"I would." She swallows hard. "I'm sorry, I'm failing miserably at being a best friend."

"You're not," I say, though the secrets hit hard. "But you're keepin' shit from me that you don't need to. I can lessen the burden if you'd just let me. If you want it removed, I'll give you the money so you don't ever have to see it again."

Her eyes fill with tears and then a sob escapes her. I feel it right down to my toes as her shoulders shake. She garbles something, but I don't understand the words.

Instead, I pull her into my arms and hug her tight. "Nobody is ever gonna hurt you again," I assure her. "I promise. Whatever you wanna do with the tattoo is fine. You don't have to do anythin', but I think it would be less of a reminder if we covered it up. Do you trust me?"

She bobs her head, her arms around my neck. "Of course I trust you, Bronc, you're amazing. I think deep down I'm always second guessing myself in case I make someone mad. It's like a subconscious thing. It didn't take much to set Vince off—"

"But I'm not him, and you'd never make me mad. You only make me worry when you don't tell me shit, and then hide tattoos for years when you should have been healin'." I feel my throat thickening. How much has this precious angel suffered?

What kind of asshole brands a woman with a fuckin' cult tattoo? I swear to fuckin' God if we cross paths, he's not only a dead man, but I'll resuscitate him only to kill him all over again until I'm satisfied he's really learned his fuckin' lesson. Then the alligators can finish off his pathetic excuse for a body.

"I have healed," she protests. "Being with the MC, they've welcomed me with open arms. And I have you and Lace, Audrina, all the girls. I've never had a family like that before. I know I've not done everything right, and I feel like I've kept things from you, but where I come from, we don't just blurt out our feelings willy-nilly. We were taught to keep those things inside."

"It's not willy-nilly." I pull back and wipe away her tears. "It's me. I'm your best friend, and I'll always be here no matter what, even if it's just to listen. There's nothin' you can say that will make me think any less of you, or what you've been through. None of this is your fault. You were a child. You trusted your brother and he let you down."

She nods, her eyes red and puffy. I can't deal with it, but I know I have to. I have to be her rock because she's got no other male figures in her life to take on this role, and I'll do it gladly. "I know, trust me, it's taken years of therapy to realize that, and I still have trust issues."

I stroke her cheeks with my thumbs. "And you can cry all you want, whenever you want. Sometimes I do that, too—"

"You do not!"

"Hell yeah, I do. Usually it's a TV commercial, especially if it has a puppy or a kitten in it, a sappy book, even a birthday card—"

She whacks me on the arm playfully. "Stop it!"

I'm trying to make her laugh; I hate seeing her like this. "What? It's true. You know I was a mess when I saw that movie about the dog who reincarnates."

"Everyone cries over dog movies, that doesn't count."

"I think I should tuck you back into bed." A tug of fear hits me in the guts that she'll regret what we did tonight. That she won't see me in the same light, and she'll push me away. She never lets too many people close. It's a habit of hers and now I know why. The same way she hasn't ever committed to anyone else. Sure, she's had dates, but I think she went on those out of obligation to the girls who set them up, or just out of curiosity.

"I think that's a great idea."

I take care in drying her off, helping her back to the bedroom as she sits on the bed and I pull on her pajamas. There's nothing sexual about any of it, but it feels intimate.

When we're settled back under the comforter, she lays in my arms. "You need anythin'?" I ask.

"No, Bronc, everything's perfect. Thank you."

She lies back, her eyes closing as silence falls between us. It only takes a few minutes, and the lull of her soft breathing tells me she's asleep.

I lay for a while, staring at the ceiling, wondering how the fuck we came to this. Not *us,* but this whole situation as well as the fucking tattoo she's been hiding. I didn't want to upset her, but I'm hurt she didn't tell me. Hell, she knows all of my secrets, and yet tonight I've only just found out two of hers. Pretty major ones. What other things is she hiding? Why did she not feel comfortable enough to share them with me?

I get that she doesn't have to tell me everything, but this is pretty big. Fucking major, when you think about it. Still, she's suffered enough trauma reliving it for one night, and after all the sex we've had, she's exhausted. I close my eyes, willing sleep to come so I don't have to keep picturing all the ways I'm going to hunt down this Vince guy and kill him for touching the woman who has sealed a special place in my heart from the moment I met her.

I don't know how I thought this was a good idea; friends with benefits? What in the actual fuck was I thinking? Clearly, I wasn't thinking through the right head. Just the head between my legs. The sex tonight was phenomenal, I'm not gonna deny it, but it's more than that.

It's the way Amber tugs at my heart, searing her way into the one place I always keep guarded. I like her more than a friend, but I know how she feels about relationships. And after what she told me tonight, she'll probably run a mile.

I start to worry I was too rough with her. I'd never hurt her intentionally, but I couldn't help myself. She's so damn beautiful, consuming her moans and groans could be my new favorite pastime.

Then I remember the other parts. The evidence that her past isn't out of her system.

I hated seeing her like that; so upset and vulnerable. Having to relive the ordeal, and having that fucking reminder on her skin every single day. I'm starting to think I'm not a very good friend, but this isn't about me. I get why she kept things to herself; I understand she's traumatized, but I thought we had trust between us. I thought she told me everything. Heck, I haven't held back.

She didn't trust me enough to tell me any of this shit, only the parts that she thought wouldn't make me mad. Why is that? Why would she care if I hunted this fucker down and cut his nuts off? It's what he deserved.

Still, as I glance at her sleeping, she looks so peaceful. I hope I put her mind at ease a little. The simple fact is, I want to tattoo her. Ever since she dropped her pants that time at my shop, I haven't been able to stop thinking about it. Even with liquid courage, she was never going to let me do it. But this time it's different.

The need in me to cover that thing up and make it the most beautiful thing she's ever seen, runs deep. Then she won't have to cover up anymore. She won't ever have to see it and be reminded of that place, or what he did. If she really wants laser, I'll organize it. I just want her to be happy.

Amber stirs, and when I glance down, she snuggles farther into my shoulder. This is how I want her; wrapped up beside me where I know she's safe. Where the demons can't find her.

I made a vow a long time ago, back when my dead-beat dad left, and I'm making that same promise to Amber that I did to my mom: I will serve and protect. She deserves a man who can give her everything she wants selflessly, and the more I think about it, the more uneasy I become. I want it to be me, and all of this is only just hitting me now.

I know I'm out of her league. I know that we shouldn't be doing this because I'm sure as fuck that sex complicates things. I wasn't lying about any of that. But we've crossed a line. A line I'm not sure I ever want to come back from.

16

AMBER

As I take the elevator up to Star's office, I hug myself, a smile playing on my lips thinking about last night.

I woke up to the agreeable scent of bacon wafting through the air, followed by the aroma of fresh coffee. Bronco had gotten up early to make me breakfast. I've never had anyone make me breakfast before. He also made poached eggs, buttering my toast like we're an old married couple.

I don't know how I feel about that, but I know that Bronco is one of a kind. I can't even put into words how attentive this man is without my eyes clouding over. Maybe this fucking your best friend thing could really work?

I poured my heart out last night. I was a mess. Yet, he comforted me in ways that I didn't think were possible. I know I've held back from him, and I don't expect him to understand, or forgive me, but it wasn't my intention to be secretive. In truth? I'm embarrassed about the tattoo. I hate it. Yet, I meant what I said; it *is* a reminder of how far I've come. Or at least that's what I used to think. Now I realize I've been living under a rock, and those old excuses I kid myself with no longer work. I've been carrying this around with me for so long, it's like the monkey on my back that I can't get rid of.

I bite my lip when I think about our conversation this morning...

"Mornin' sleepy head."

"Wow, you made me breakfast?" I yawn, sitting up propping myself against the pillows.

"Need to keep your energy up." He gives me a wink.

Here I was thinking this was going to be awkward.

"I think you used every last inch of my energy last night."

"I aim to please. How are you feeling?"

"Aside from my va-jay-jay feeling like it's been to pound town and back? I feel good. A little tired..."

He looks sheepish for a half a second, dipping his eyes to his feet in the most adorable way. "I didn't hurt you?"

I shake my head. "Hurt me? No, Bronc, you didn't. You were fantastic. I've just been out of action for a while."

"I've still got it then?" He places a hand over his heart.

I smirk. "You've still got it."

He sits on the edge of the bed. "And us? Are we cool?"

I pick up a piece of toast and bite into it, eager to tuck in, but not wanting to look like an oinker, either. "Of course, why wouldn't we be?"

"Well, that whole friends with benefits thing you keep goin' on about? This isn't that, by the way."

"It's not?" I tilt my head. "What is it then?"

"That implies that it's a casual thing."

"It is casual."

"Yeah, but you're not plannin' on seein' anyone else, right?" He palms the back of his neck.

"Wait, are you putting some alpha claim over me now we've slept together?" I can't help but laugh.

"Not sayin' you're my ol' lady, but we've got a good thing goin' on, can't deny our chemistry."

Of course, he wants me to be exclusive without the attachment, and to be honest, that kinda suits me. I don't want to be tied down, but he told me he was sick of playing the field. So what happens if one of us catches feelings for real? I can't say I'm immune to my best friend and all his charms. He's amazing.

"We said it was one night," I remind him, my chest tightening.

He gives me a pointed look. "So, we're done?"

"Last night was amazing, but remember all that talk about being friends, and it making things weird?"

"Are things weird?"

"No, but this isn't a normal situation." *I wonder for a second if I'm trying to reason with him, or myself.*

"Define normal. I know how you feel about relationships, but are you sayin' we can't do any of that again, or you don't want to?"

Of course I want to. I want to scream his orgasms from the rooftops, but I'm not sure the neighbors will appreciate that. "I didn't say I didn't want to, but all that stuff about feelings—"

"We can feel and not get heavy, right?"

"So we'd be friends with benefits," I reiterate. "You can say it."

"It's not that."

"So what is it then? It isn't like we're dating, we skipped that part and jumped into bed."

"I can take you out on a date. After all, I am your fake boyfriend."

"Ha-ha. We crossed a line, and it was fantastic, but we need boundaries."

"Uh, oh this sounds scary."

"You mean to tell me you're not gonna play the field in the meantime?"

He frowns. "I haven't been playin' the field for a long time. So it would bother you if I did?"

"Well, you know I don't sleep around."

"But you're also not looking for anyone permanent in your life." It's not a question.

My mind begins to race and I answer it anyway. *"I guess not."*

He opens his mouth, then closes it again. I don't like how he's holding back, but I have no room to talk. I held back some pretty big revelations, and I'm not sure I'd be so accommodating if the roles were reversed. We tell each other everything, and now he thinks I held back information. I feel sick about it.

"I don't wanna overcomplicate things. But I also don't want another man in your bed. There, I said it."

I arch a brow. *"Well, I just told you I don't sleep around, and you know that's true."*

"Right, so we're a thing?"

"I don't know what we are."

Is it just me, or did his shoulders just sag a little? We agreed on one night of amazing sex, and now it's hard to walk away, for both of us. Maybe I'm overthinking the whole friends with benefits situation?

"Maybe I should be a little more blunt?" he says.

"Maybe you should."

"Well, this could really work. I don't wanna fuck anyone else, and all the guys you date are morons."

"Thanks for reminding me—"

"At the clubhouse, we can keep up our fake dating charade. It'll keep Cupcake off my back and those other assholes off yours."

The words sting, even though they shouldn't. I don't want it to be fake, but I'm the one who just said all that stuff about feelings. *"Let me get this straight for a second. Are you saying you're not done with me?"*

He smirks. *"Oh, Princess, I don't think I could ever be done with you."*

My eyes go slightly wide, so I do what I always do and make

a joke out of it. "*You say that now, but then again, you did see me eat my weight in junk food last night, and that didn't seem to turn you off.*"

He laughs as I stab into my egg with the side of my fork, spreading it across my toast as I avoid his gaze. "*I like that you have a big appetite. I don't know where you put it all, but no complaints here.*"

"*You know this is madness,*" *I tell him.* "*And it won't stop everyone speculating at the clubhouse and poking their noses in.*"

"*So date me.*"

"*Bronco, if we date then it means something more, and I'm not sure I can give you that.*"

"*Well, if my dick's inside you, that means somethin'.*" *He shrugs when I almost choke on my mouthful of food.*

"*Bronco!*"

"*I'm kiddin'... sorta. You're the one who said I was too sexy for words.*"

"*That's because we shouldn't be fucking each other's brains out.*"

"*Funny, I didn't see a rule book statin' anythin' like that. We're makin' our own rules,*" *he states calmly.* "*If that's what you want?*"

I swallow hard. What do I want? I feel as if I'm giving him mixed signals already. I want him, but I don't want him to be my boyfriend because I'm scared of being hurt again. "*It's hard to know what I want, but I know last night was amazing. Let's just not put any pressure on ourselves until we figure this out.*"

He nips my chin. "*Fine by me. Now, eat up. I gotta go into the shop early and open up, then collect Titan on the way. What time is your meeting with Star?*"

Bronco assured me that Titan was more than fine on his own for the night. He likes a little me-time.

I texted her as soon as it was reasonable on a Monday morning, she said she'd fit me in today with no problems.

"Ten o'clock."

"And you're sure you don't want me to come with you?"

"I'll be fine, honestly. I'll let you know what she says."

He nods. "As long as you're sure."

"I'm sure, don't worry about me."

He watches me eat for a moment, not saying a word. When I look up at him, he gives me a chin lift. "I'll always worry about you, and I still haven't forgiven you for not tellin' me about your ex and the cult, and that tattoo."

I swallow my food, feeling the heavy beat in my chest. "I know, and I'm sorry. I should have. I don't like keeping secrets from you, but I know firsthand how bad your temper is."

"Don't worry about my temper, Princess, no matter what happens, I've told you if you need to confide in me, you can, I promise I won't go postal."

I don't know if he really means the part about not going postal, but I still smile. "Now get that goofy look off your face, or everyone at Iron and Ink will know you got lucky last night."

He stands, heading toward the shower, looking at me over his shoulder. "If only they knew how lucky I am."

His words still tingle inside of me. Bronco makes me feel like a million dollars, and here I was thinking things would be awkward between us. We just picked up where we left off, and that was that. I've decided to go with the flow and enjoy myself, don't overthink anything.

When I arrive at the correct floor, I'm greeted by Star's assistant, Halo.

"Oh, hey!" I say, surprised to see her since she just had a baby only a few months ago. Star had twins a few months back, so that's twice the fun, but she's only taking on a few clients on selected days. "I wasn't expecting to see you here."

She smiles brightly. "Hey, Amber, so great to see you! Romeo is with his daddy for a few hours, so I came in to help Star get on top of things."

"That's so nice of you. How are things with the baby? That baby shower was so cute."

She welcomes me inside, which is typical Halo behavior because she goes out of her way to make other people feel comfortable.

"Oh, he's such a good baby! I tell Riot he gets that from me," she giggles.

"Oh, totally, I can see that. He's a handsome little devil. That teeny tiny outfit he had on was so adorable." He was dressed in a gorgeous sailor suit, including the little hat.

She laughs. "Riot wanted a mini motorcycle jacket, but we couldn't get one to fit."

I laugh, too. "Starting them young, huh?"

"Something like that." She asks me to take a seat while Star finishes up on the phone. "So, how are things with you?"

"Mainly good," I say, knowing that I'm going to have to fess up sooner rather than later. "I'm here because I need help locating my sister-in-law, Erica. She left her niece with me almost a month ago, and I haven't seen her since. I'm running out of options, other than calling the police."

Worry lines form on Halo's forehead. "I'm taking it that's not her usual behavior?"

I shake my head. "She'd never leave Olive unless she was in some really big trouble." I take a breath. "And I'm just hoping it isn't our past catching up with either of us."

Halo squeezes my arm gently. "Well, that's why we're here, and don't worry, everything you say in this office is strictly private and confidential."

"I appreciate that."

"Star won't be long, but I do have some paperwork if you'd like to fill it in." She hands me a clipboard, and I already feel nervous about this whole thing. But paperwork is unavoidable, so I take it and smile.

By the time I'm done filling it in, Star greets me and we head into her office.

"How are the twins?" I ask.

A smile curls across her lips. "They keep us both on our toes, but motherhood is amazing. It's not something that we really planned, but I love it."

"I'm so happy for you."

"Thank you." Star smiles warmly.

Halo joins us, taking notes as I fill them in on the whole story. When I'm done, they both stare at me with slightly different expressions. Halo looks sad; her eyes watery. Star, sympathetic with a soft smile. I have to stop a few times, dabbing my eyes with a tissue. I also gave Star the handwritten note Erica left me.

"I have nowhere else to go, other than the police, but I'll be honest, I'm scared. The police aren't always helpful, and I know Erica would be really mad at me, but what choice do I have?"

"If you think she's in grave danger, then I'm not opposed to that," Star says. "From what you've told me, it sounds like she's trying to deal with a problem herself. Is there any way you think the church is involved?"

"I don't see how," I say. "They would have no way of finding us. We both changed our names, moved states, heck, I moved a couple of times. I know Steven and Vince wouldn't leave Illinois for anything, so I find it hard to believe it's anything to do with them."

"But there's a child involved, essentially, Steven could have filed a missing children's report, which I'll be checking. If that's the case, it could explain why she's being so secretive, and also keeping her daughter safe," Star says.

"I still don't know if Steven would do that. He doesn't like drawing big attention to the church, or his own actions. It isn't how they operate. They work better behind closed doors," I say. "Where nobody can see what they're doing."

"I'm sorry," Star says. "For what you went through, that can't have been easy."

I nod slowly. "It was tough, but we always believed we would escape. It took teamwork and a whole lotta luck. Erica is like a sister to me — the sister I never had. This just isn't like her."

"And you don't know about any boyfriends, or anything different with her at work?"

"No," I say. "I've called her workplace and they said she'd put in a leave of absence but didn't know when she'd be back."

"Okay, well, I think I've got enough to go on. I'll need a recent picture of Erica, cell number, email address, and her date of birth, anything you think that would be helpful."

"Okay, thanks ladies. I really appreciate this."

Halo puts her pen down, walks over and folds me into her arms. "It was very brave telling your story," she says. "We'll do everything we can to find Erica. Star knows people in all kinds of places that can help, with your consent, of course."

My eyes meet Star's as she says, "Sometimes I ask Rock and Jett for help with security footage and hacking. Is that going to be an issue?"

I swallow hard. "Won't they be obliged to tell Cash?"

"If it's on club time, then yes, but they can be discreet as long as the club isn't implicated. At the moment, Erica is missing, but this isn't a club related issue."

"I should probably tell Cash myself." I look down at my hands. "I didn't want to involve the club because this isn't their problem to fix."

"You know you're considered club property now you're dating Bronco," Halo chuckles. "So he'll want to jump in and involve everyone."

"That's what I'm worried about," I admit. I don't tell

them about our secret pact. They don't need to know any of that.

"I can't say I didn't see it coming," Star says, surprising me. "I think it's pretty obvious he's nuts about you."

"Really?" I try not to sound too confused. Is it really obvious? Or is Bronco just really good at charming women? He admitted he was trying to ward off Cupcake.

Star and Halo both nod in agreement. "He's not been seen with any chicks for ages at the clubhouse," Halo goes on, clasping her hands together excitedly. "That's a dead giveaway. It's sweet, if you ask me. Bronco saving all his cookies for his best friend, who was right under his nose all along. Aww!"

"It's early days yet," I add quickly "We're just seeing where things go. Now that Olive is in my care with some degree of permanency, that changes things a little."

"Well, Bronco is very reliable," Star says, shuffling the papers on her desk. "I never thought I'd say this, but in the last six months or so, he's really stepped up. Not only at the club, but with his own business, taking charge of the shop and running it all smoothly. He's put a lot of work in."

Everyone knows how hard Bronco works, and a big part of that success is his ability to adapt and put his mind to anything. I'm proud of him. I don't like lying to my friends about our relationship, but this little white lie about us dating isn't going to hurt them, right?

"I think I'll have to get some more ink now that the baby's born," Halo agrees. "Some of his work is freaking amazing."

I think about the tattoo on my wrist; the same one I covered up with makeup and my cuff this morning. The same one that Bronco wants to cover up with a new tattoo. My heart bleeds and melts at the same time. He was so distressed when I'd confessed what it was. I'd never seen his face change with the different emotions before. Confusion. Horror. Disbelief. Then anger.

I swallow down the guilt that threatens to rise. "It is. He really is talented."

"So, I'll do some digging, and I'll let you know what I come up with." Star gives me a small smile. "Don't worry, I've been doing this a while, and I'm confident we can find something. I'll probably start with bank records, and a phone trace."

"But her phone isn't in service," I say. "I've tried calling multiple times."

"We can still get a trace with GPS tracking, even if the phone is switched off."

I don't ask if any of this is legal or not. Instead, I nod. "Thank you. I really appreciate it. I just hope she's not gotten too in over her head. I just wished she'd have told me."

Star nods, tucking her hair behind her ears. "I'll call as soon as I know anything. In the meantime, if you think of anything else, even if you believe it's not relevant, let me know. The smallest details can often help more than you think."

"Okay, I will." I hug them both, then head out.

My heart is heavy, the dread in the pit of my stomach threatens to take over. I know Erica. She wouldn't do something like this. Then I realize; yes, she would. If Olive were in danger, she'd do everything to protect her. It just hurts that she can't tell me who or why, or how I can help.

This isn't nearly the same thing, but I catch a glimpse at how Bronco felt when he found out my secrets. I don't know why I did that to him. I saw the hurt on his face, and it's killing me. I never want him to think I'm being sneaky or secretive, but that's exactly how it must have come across. I'll make it up to him, I'll try and be a better friend. Or a friend with many benefits. I think I like the sound of that better.

17

BRONCO

I FEEL LIKE I'M WALKING ON CLOUD NINE. I'VE BEEN on my own personal high all day.

I'm usually a happy-go-lucky kinda guy, taking everything in my stride, but today I feel as light as a feather. I know Amber has everything to do with that, and I'm not sorry about it.

Even though I showered this morning, I can still smell her on my skin. That might have something to do with the vanilla body wash I used this morning with a hint of honey and almond. Not my usual scent, but it casts my mind back to our hot night in Amber's bed. Man, she's something else. I never knew sex could be even more intense when you actually like the person. *Really* like them. Everything felt different, and even though we made a pact we wouldn't get emotionally involved, I know I'm lying to myself.

I get jealous when I think about her with another guy, or if a dude even dares to check her out; that never used to happen until recently. I was elated when fuckface Ben had to cancel, and I got to take his place, even though we've been to watch the Pelican's heaps of times. Something is happening to me.

Last night felt different; I've never been nervous before, but that's exactly how I felt. Like the first date jitters.

Fuck.

Maybe this situation can actually work? We're perfect for each other — even if Amber may not see it that way yet. *What am I even saying? Am I really falling in love with my best friend?*

I guess that's hard to know because I've never been in love before, and I was one of the idiots who would ridicule the guys at the clubhouse when they got snagged. I was renowned for declaring that I was single and wanted to mingle. I constantly ribbed my club brothers about their balls being in a sling, and now look at me. My how the mighty has fallen. It sneaks up on you, that's all I know.

When I check my phone on my break, there's a message from Crystal.

> **CRYSTAL**
>
> Saw you on the kiss-cam last night. Uh, WTF? Why didn't you tell me you finally grew some balls?

I smirk at the text. It was Crystal who encouraged me to go for it and stop being a pussy. Last night I was so caught up in all things Amber, I forgot that someone I know might be watching the game and see the kiss-cam.

> **ME**
>
> I thought I'd put it up on the big screen to show the entire nation instead

> **CRYSTAL**
>
> From where I was sitting, it looked like she was the one who kissed you

ME

Fine. I didn't want to make her uncomfortable, sue me. I went in for the best friend side cheek, and she turned the tables

CRYSTAL

And I remember you saying this wasn't a date

ME

It wasn't until the kiss-cam thing, then it kinda turned into something else

CRYSTAL

Did you two have sex?

ME

I'm not dignifying that with an answer

CRYSTAL

OMG you horndog, you did!

ME

Look, it just happened

CRYSTAL

That's what me and Ryder said, then I ended up pregnant with Ade

ME

I'm not telling you shit about what happened bc I know about that girls group chat

CRYSTAL

I know about the Grumpy boys chat, too

ME

It's the WTF chat, if you really must know

CRYSTAL

I'll bet all you talk about is exhaust pipes and who can belch the loudest

ME

Wouldn't you like to know?

CRYSTAL

I want dirt, give me it. I am your sounding board after all

ME

Don't go sayin' shit

CRYSTAL

Pinkie promise, my lips are sealed

ME

I mean it

CRYSTAL

I promise! Now spill, asshat!

ME

You're wrong btw - it's Amber who's afraid of commitment

CRYSTAL

So you show her all the ways you can be reliable, it's not that hard

ME

I'm tryin'

CRYSTAL

So you're dating?

ME

> Yeah, I mean, sorta...

I can't tell her the whole truth, because even to my ears it sounds pretty lame.

CRYSTAL

> What does that mean?

ME

> Like I said before – she doesn't want commitment, and I'm a jealous dick, so we're perfectly suited

CRYSTAL

> Jesus. You're taking Nevada's advice, aren't you? Fuck buddies won't work, mark my words, bud

ME

> It's not about the sex, she's fucking amazing, Crys, I can't even describe it

CRYSTAL

> Aww, Bronco's in lovvvvve

ME

> I'm not in love. I'm not even sure if I'm capable of love, but this is a different feeling

CRYSTAL

> Does your heart quicken whenever she walks into a room?

ME

> Yeah...

CRYSTAL

Do you think about her all day every day? And when you're away from her, you're counting down the minutes when you'll see her again?

ME

Maybe

CRYSTAL

When she's in your arms, you feel a contentment that you can't describe?

ME

Okay, fuck off now

CRYSTAL

LOL you're in love

ME

FFS, don't tell her that, she'll run a mile

CRYSTAL

I'm insulted. I pinkie promised, didn't I?

I run a hand through my hair, my heart thrumming in my chest at her suggestion. I've felt differently about Amber for a while now, if I'm being honest with myself. While a feral, possessive part of me wants to take her and make her mine, the best friend inside me is saying she's not ready for that.

ME

I don't know what it is, but let me figure it out without you interfering, got me?

CRYSTAL

Moi? Interfere? I'm insulted. I'm also happy to be your wingman anytime. Being married and all, I know how this relationship stuff works

ME

I don't need a wingman

CRYSTAL

But I've always wanted to say that, I think you need unbiased moral support. After all, if you listen to anything Nevada says, god only knows what'll happen

ME

He's changed his ways, so leopards can change their spots

CRYSTAL

That's true. It can be done when you meet the right one

ME

What if she doesn't feel the same way?

CRYSTAL

That's why you show her what kind of man you are

ME

Doesn't she already know that?

CRYSTAL

She knows you as a best friend, not a potential life partner or anything more

I scratch my chin. Maybe Crystal has a point. Amber has only known me as a best friend, and I like to think I've been a good one. But she doesn't know me as a boyfriend, or anything even close. Maybe I do have to step up to the plate and show her what I'm capable of.

Even if she thinks we are only friends who fuck.

Jesus, I'm turning into a sap already.

ME

> Your words of wisdom are once again scaring the fucking shit out of me

CRYSTAL

> Happy to help, gtg. Remember, girls like pretty things

ME

> What does that even mean?

But Crystal doesn't answer, and my next client is here.

All through the appointment, my mind wanders and I realize I don't know when I'm going to see Amber again. We didn't exactly make plans, and Olive is back from Harlem and Indigo's, so that'll probably mean I won't be having sex in Amber's bed again anytime soon.

Last night was fucking amazing. The best night of my life. I didn't expect it to be anything less, but her warmth... that's the thing I love the most. She's warm, cozy, a princess, *my princess.*

I also haven't heard from her since this morning, and nothing since her appointment with Star. I shoot her a quick text after my client is finished up, asking how things went. It's around school pick up, so I don't expect her to reply. About five minutes later, my phone beeps with a message.

> **AJ**
> Star seemed confident. I told her everything, and she said she'd be in touch soon. I can only wait it out and hope for the best

> **ME**
> That's great. The sooner we find Erica, the sooner we can get to the bottom of it

> **AJ**
> I'm scared, Bronc. This is so out of character for her. What if she's in some serious trouble, or worse?

> **ME**
> You can't think like that. Sit tight and once Star finds something, we can go from there

The gray bubble fades in and out, and I wait for her next message.

> **AJ**
> Olive and I are having pizza for dinner, would you like to join us?

My heart quickens at the idea of spending more time with her so soon.

> **ME**
> Sure, I'd like that

> **AJ**
> Come over around 6, it's a school night so Olive goes to bed at 8

> **ME**
> Okay, did you want me to pick up the pizzas on my way?

AJ

You don't have to do that

ME

I don't mind, just send me what you'd like

AJ

That's sweet of you

ME

Sweet's my middle name, Princess

AJ

Olive asked if you can bring Titan. I know he's not great with people he doesn't know, but he's good with kids. She'd love to meet him

ME

I can bring him, but she'll probably take one look at him and scream

AJ

He just looks scary, he's really not that bad once you get to know him, and I showed her a photo

ME

Did you just describe me?

AJ

Ha ha

ME

Wait, since when did you have photos of my dog?

> **AJ**
> I always take photos of your dog. I especially like the ones where he's lying on his back asleep with his paws dangling in the air

> **ME**
> So much for killer instinct, he's supposed to be a guard dog

> **AJ**
> Not in this lifetime

> **ME**
> Cleaning up, I'll CU tonight

> **AJ**
> Copy that

My pulse isn't just racing, it's beating to its own drum. I didn't expect that I'd be seeing her again so soon, or if she'd even want to after this morning's conversation. It may have ended on a positive note, but I know how she likes to overthink things.

Maybe sex doesn't complicate things at all. Maybe it just makes everything better.

I take a quick shower when I get home, despite dreading washing away Amber's scent from my body, then feed Titan, telling him he's got to be on his best behavior. He really is great with kids, and hopefully if Olive doesn't freak out, he won't get his feelings hurt. Kids often take one look at him and burst into tears. He wags his tail and tries to make friends, then lays down with his face on his giant paws. It's as if he's trying to figure out what he did wrong. It isn't his fault, and I've come to adore his grumpy face.

I wear my usual attire: jeans, henley, boots and my cut,

nothing fancy. By the time Titan and I are in my truck heading to the pizza place, I'm whistling a tune.

Glancing sideways, Titan's staring at me.

"What?"

He's sitting upright in the passenger seat, giving me a noticeable side-eye. He's so judgy.

"You like Amber," I tell him. "And I'm sure you'll dig Olive, she's not annoying like some kids can be. I'm sure she won't cry or hide behind her aunt."

He yawns loudly, then lays down, his head on his paws.

"Keepin' you up, big fella?"

He yawns again as if he really does understand what I'm saying.

"Maybe you should have a nap before we get there, might put you in a better mood."

I stop to grab the pizzas and a tub of ice cream from the parlor next door, telling Titan none of this is for him when I climb back in my truck. Of course, he thinks everything that smells good is for him.

Rolling up at Amber's place just after six, I put Titan on his leash and tell him again about being a good boy. "We wanna make a good impression, and you lickin' Olive to death won't be cool." He looks up at me and I pet him on the head. "Who's a good boy?"

He yawns again, but it sounds like a howl. He clearly had a hard day sleeping on his giant bean bag the last ten hours since I left for work this morning.

I ring the bell, waiting out front as I hear footsteps moving toward the door, then Amber appears. "Hey!"

"Hey."

Then she sees Titan and bends down to pet him. "Titan! Oh, you look so handsome! Yes you do, yes you do!"

Of course, my dog laps it up and I feel a little jealous she's not scruffing me under the chin and calling me handsome.

"How was your day?" I ask as she stands again, taking the pizza box and ice cream out of my hands.

"Good, I haven't heard from Star yet, but I spent the entire afternoon doing inventory for the clubhouse and the Whiskey Shack to take my mind off things."

I give her a sympathetic smile. "Try not to worry."

"I should also say something to Cash if Rock and Jett may be involved."

"That might be a good idea, just so he's aware. I can go with you if you like, best to be above board.

"Thanks, Bronc." She squeezes my forearm and I feel it all the way down to my toes. "I really thought you were gonna say you already told him."

I hold a hand over my heart. "Said I wouldn't, and it wasn't my call. Not club business in the sense we're involved or anyone's in danger, so it wasn't somethin' he needed to know, but things are usually best out in the open."

"I agree."

I glance over Amber's shoulder to find Olive looking over at us curiously. "Hey, Olive," I call out. "I brought my buddy here to meet you, he wanted to say hi."

Amber smiles as she moves aside to let us in. Holding Titan's leash, I walk towards her up the hall as her eyes dip to my dog. Her eyebrows shoot up a little, but then her smile spreads across her face.

"Hi, Bronco, is this Titan?"

"Yep, in all his glory."

Titan sniffs her feet, then I tell him to sit — which he does — and waits for my next command.

"He's really big."

"He is, but he's a big softie, too. He loves belly rubs, stealing food off my plate, and takin' up all the room on the couch."

She giggles again. "Can I pet him?"

"Of course."

She reaches toward him tentatively and Titan sniffs her hand.

"Good boy," I tell him.

He tilts his head, his tongue shooting out to lick her hand and she squeals. "He's really cool!"

"I think he likes you."

"Really?"

Just as I nod, Titan rubs his head against her hand, encouraging her for more pets. "I think you made a friend for life."

He laps it up like a big ol' golden retriever, wagging his tail with excitement. He's putty in her hands.

"Way to go, bud," Amber laughs. "He is just the sweetest."

I turn to look at her. "He's a fierce, combative guard dog with a nose for trouble like you wouldn't believe." Just as I say it, he flops over, landing on his side and then rolls onto his back, begging for tummy rubs.

I slap a hand over my forehead as Amber and Olive both laugh.

"You were saying?" Amber nudges me in the ribs.

"Okay, he didn't really get that whole combative thing, unless it's someone he really doesn't like," I argue.

They laugh again.

"Let's eat. Olive, would you like to get the plates out and set them on the table?"

I've literally never had pizza on a plate before, but if this is what they do at mealtimes, who am I to argue?

"Okay, Aunty Amber, can Titan come, too?"

"Of course he can, but no feeding him," Amber warns.

"Even if he gives you those cute, sad, puppy dog eyes," I join in.

"Okay, I won't," she promises, skipping off to do as she's told.

I glance at Amber. "How's she doin'?"

She shrugs. "She misses her mom. I don't know how long I can keep lying. I know it's to protect her, but she needs her mom." Tears start to well in her eyes. "She's asking questions, Bronc, and I don't know how to answer them."

I'm crossing the floor in a few paces. Folding her into my arms, I kiss the top of her head. "It's gonna be okay. From what you've told me, Erica is a smart woman. I know this is hard, but you gettin' worked up won't help nothin', it'll only make you sad and stressed. Gotta be strong for her."

"I'm trying," she whispers. I can hear the tears in her tone.

"I know you are, and keeping things as normal as possible for Olive is the right thing to do."

"I was hoping it would buy me some time."

"It will. It's best to shield her from the truth, she's just a kid."

She nods. "I know that, I just have this awful feeling in my bones."

I pull back and she looks up at me. "Like I said, try not to worry. I know that's easy to say, but whatever happens, we will find her."

I don't expect what happens next... Amber reaches up onto her tippy toes and kisses me. It's chaste, but full of that sweetness that I adore about her. "Thanks, Bronc. Your pep talks always perk me up."

I place my hands on her hips and rub my nose against hers. "Anytime, *bestie.*"

"I felt you today," she whispers.

My eyebrows raise. "Where?"

"You know where."

My sly smile slowly turns into a full-fledged grin. "See, you can take nine inches. I don't know what you were worried about."

Her eyes widen as Olive comes running back into the kitchen, my dog on her tail.

We spring apart and I turn to Olive. "I got a tub of double chocolate chip ice cream for dessert from this amazing place next to the pizza shop," I tell Olive. "You're gonna love it. That's if you like chocolate?"

She grins. "I love chocolate!"

"Great." I clap my hands together. "I don't know about you two, but I'm starving."

We spend the next hour at the table with Olive telling us about her day at school, and how much fun she had at the sleepover this weekend. I know how she feels; I had an amazing sleepover myself, but I can't exactly tell her that.

She mentions her mom a few times. Once when Amber serves the ice cream, and another when she asks if her mom would let her get a dog when she comes back. I can see the angst in Amber's eyes and it kills me. I want to take her in my arms and tell her that it's all gonna be okay, even when I really don't know if it is. I don't want to give her false hope, but I also need to do some investigating myself. When I leave here tonight, I'm going to stop by the clubhouse and see if Rock or Jett have anything. What would be helpful is the name of this cult, and the asshole that Amber fled from. At least I'll be able to see if he's still in Illinois, running his so-called church. I know nothing good can come of me poking my nose in, but I need to keep on top of things. That feeling that Amber had earlier, about things not being right? I hate to say it too, but I feel exactly the same way.

18

BRONCO

We watch a little TV until it's Olive's bedtime. She's been curled up on the end of the couch, Titan by her feet, sleeping soundly.

"He's really taken to her," Amber muses when she comes back from settling Olive into bed.

"He really has." I smile. Titan is nowhere to be seen. "Speaking of my dog, where is he?"

"He's lying in her doorway, in full protection mode."

I yawn. "Good boy."

"Sorry, am I keeping you up?" She smirks.

"Someone did in fact keep me awake last night doin' very bad things to me."

"That's funny, someone did the exact same thing to me."

"Huh, guess we both got lucky."

"I guess we did."

I move closer, keeping my hands to myself even though I'm dying to touch her. Our lips meet and a soft moan leaves her throat. "*Bronc...*" Our kiss is feather light.

Knowing I probably can't take this where I want to with

Olive in the house, I pull back, kissing her forehead. "Did someone miss me today?"

"I don't know what you've done to my best friend," she sighs. "But I've been having withdrawal symptoms all day."

I smirk. "Miss me bad, that's good news for me."

"But not good news for me. I was counting stock over and over because I kept daydreaming."

"Daydreaming about me?"

"Yes, and your cock."

I grin slyly. "Stop teasin'."

She glances down the hall. The bedrooms aren't together, so that's one plus, but I didn't come here tonight expecting sex. I just wanted to be here, with them.

"Now I've had it, you've got me wanting more."

It's like music to my ears. "Even after you said you couldn't walk."

"I didn't say I couldn't walk, *Cassanova*. I said I felt you."

I'm still grinning when I brush one hand over her face. "You did, and I can't help feeling a little smug about that."

"I hadn't had sex in a while."

"You sure it's that?"

"Okay, maybe that missile between your legs played a part."

"A pretty big part if I'm hearin' it correctly." I kiss her again, her lips part as our tongues lightly touch. Again, it isn't rushed or needy, it's a simple understanding that comes from knowing someone so well.

"Behave," she whispers.

As she climbs into my lap, I chuckle. "Me, behave? You're the one sittin' in my lap, rubbin' that pretty pussy against my *missile.*"

"That's because you smell fucking amazing." Her mouth is on my neck and my dick is straining between us.

"It's just soap. I smell better when I use your body wash."

BRONCO

"Thief."

Our kisses grow faster, heat rising in my body at a rapid pace. I want nothing more than to strip her out of her clothes, shove my jeans and boxers down, and have her ride me on this couch. But we can't.

"I need to get some of that so I can jerk off to you in my shower."

"Oh, God," she sighs, her hips moving back and forth over my cock. "I'm going to come just from this."

"Gotta be quiet, we both know how loud you get."

"Olive is a heavy sleeper."

That's like music to my ears. "So get those pretty tits out and let me suck them."

She rises farther, pulling her t-shirt up and her bra down. Her glorious tits pop out and I groan, palming them with my hands as I cup one breast and sink my mouth over one peak.

She gasps, gripping my shoulders. "So good," she whispers. "Get more of me in your mouth, that's it—"

"Fuckin' perfect." I lave her tip with my tongue, moving to the other side as my cock begs to be let out.

I suck her pretty titties, working my way between the two as she grinds down on me. Her gasps and moans may be quiet, but they lead a trail straight to my dick.

"Bedroom," she groans. "Bedroom, Bronc."

"Need to fuck you with my mouth, *Princess*. Been a whole day without you on my tongue."

She shivers, and I know she's almost there. I pull her off and she yelps when I haul her up, throwing her over my shoulder as she smacks my ass. Carrying her to her bedroom, she lands on the bed with a bounce as I put a finger up to my mouth. "Shhh, you'll wake Olive, and then I won't be able to taste your multiple orgasms."

"Multiples?" she wines.

I ignore her, dropping to my knees as I pull off her sweats and panties. "Spread your legs."

She does as I say, and my, my what a sight she is with her tits hanging out of her bra and her pussy on display. I slide my tongue through her wet folds and she shudders.

"Oh, my God."

I do it again, this time swirling my tongue over her clit. I love teasing her, it's my new favorite pastime. "Taste so sweet," I murmur. "All this honey, just for me."

Her hand grips into my hair. "Only you."

"Good girl." I spread her with one hand, my mouth closing down on her clit.

She makes a garbled sound and I suck harder, knowing she's right on the edge. This time, I let her orgasm. She grinds against my face, her panting uneven and raspy, but barely any sound comes out of her mouth. Her head drops back and I reach one hand up to pinch her nipple and a shudder ripples through her body.

But I'm not done. I want more. I throw both her legs over my shoulders, pulling her hips so she scoots forward and I really dig in deep. I eat her like a man possessed, fucking her hole with my tongue as she comes unglued. Her next orgasm is faster, her pants heavy, and my name a whisper on her lips.

"Dick," she whispers. "I need your dick, Bronc."

"You're sore," I remind her, my hand already at my buckle as I stand.

"Shut up and fuck me."

I grin, dropping my jeans and briefs to my ankles as I reach for her feet. I'm standing, flush up against her, pulling her legs in front of my chest at an angle. "So glad you're flexible." I hold my cock, teasing the tip over her clit as she grips the comforter with both hands.

"I guess all those yoga classes paid off."

I tease her until she's writhing against me, begging me in

short, sweet gasps and when I can't take it anymore, I slide all the way in to the hilt. "Gonna be fast." I pull out and slam back in. "Got me so fuckin' worked up with that smart mouth of yours."

She cups her tits and I stare at them while I plunge in and out of her. She grips me like a vice, my dick throbbing as I try to make it last a little longer. Amber's grip on the comforter tells me she's close, and I am, too.

"So good, you're so sexy."

Her words are my undoing, and I spurt with ferocity as I come undone, clenching my teeth as she falls, too. I reach down to my cock, pulling out slightly as I watch my cum shoot all over her pussy and lower abs. I like to make sure I'm everywhere.

"Jesus." I'm a sweaty fucking mess as I plunge in, making sure I coat myself in all our juices, and pull out again.

"I should clean you up," she pants.

Oh, fuck, what?

"You're gonna—"

She reaches between my legs as she sits up, scooting toward the end of the bed as her hot little tongue licks my tip, and down my length as she does exactly that.

"Gonna have me revved up again in no time," I pant, watching her work between my legs.

"I think I'm addicted to your dick."

"You know that's a package deal. You can't get one without the other."

She looks up at me, her tongue swirling over my head. "Don't get jealous. I'm addicted to you, too."

I grin, cupping one side of her face. "Your mouth is gettin' dirtier the more you hang out with me."

"You're a bad influence."

I yank her to her knees, bending down to kiss her. Tasting

myself and her on my tongue, I groan. "Love seein' my cum spillin' out of you."

"Yes, you do tend to make a mess."

I smack her bare ass cheek lightly as she yelps. "Can't help that you make me crazy."

"I wish you could stay over again."

"Me too, but I get why I can't. I think my dog's right at home here, though."

He hasn't even been in to check on us. Right on cue, he lets out a growl.

I quickly pull up my jeans and underwear, securing my belt as I move across the bedroom. It could just be Olive, but Titan wouldn't make a sound like that. It's a warning.

I see him down the hallway, his tail straight, his stance ready for battle as he stares at the back door. I head his way, touching his head as I pass him. "Good boy, Tite."

I don't carry a piece, but I do have a knife inside my cut, which I realize is back on the couch.

"Is everything okay?" Amber asks behind me.

I turn. "Stay here, just gonna check stuff out. He doesn't normally act like this unless somebody is there."

"Oh, shit."

"Don't worry, just stay here. Lock this behind me. Titan." He follows me and I unlatch the back door. As soon as the door is open, Titan leaps out and runs into the backyard. I follow behind, trying my best to keep up with him, but he's super fast. This isn't like him at all.

I should've brought my fuckin' knife. When I find him, he's pacing back and forth at the edge of the garden. I don't see anyone, or any movement, but my dog's telling me otherwise.

"What the fuck?" I whisper, looking all around the small space.

Titan growls, then barks, coming to stand by my side.

"Was someone here?" I ask him. He growls low. If there was, they're long gone now. I pet his head. "Good boy."

I continue to check the rest of the space, but being small it doesn't take that long. I come up blank, but I trust my dog. Walking full circle, I knock on the backdoor. "It's me," I call out.

Amber unlocks the door and pulls it aside. I step back in, Titan at my heels. "Didn't find anythin'," I tell her. "But Titan wasn't happy, best to check it out." I don't want Amber to feel unsafe, but now I need to check on her security or get some cameras installed. I know there's a street camera, but nothing outside except a sensor light.

"Do you think someone was here?"

"I don't know," I say honestly. "But the good news is there's nobody out there now. Sometimes he just gets spooked." She bites on her lower lip. "Just keep the doors locked at all times, double check before you go to bed."

"I always do."

"Good."

Titan lays down again, half-way inside Olive's bedroom, his head facing us. I know him. I know that he doesn't just bark at nothing. I don't like the idea of anyone being around here at nighttime, prowling around Amber's house.

"I think it's best if I stay here tonight," I say. "Just as a precaution."

"Okay." She doesn't sound certain.

I grip her shoulders. "It's fine, I promise. I'll be gone early before Olive wakes up."

She nods.

I was gonna go see the twins tonight, but that'll have to wait until the morning. I'd rather be here just in case that was someone casing the joint, and they don't come back. Or better yet, they'll be met with my 150 pound guard dog. When it comes to security, Titan kicks into defense mode, and I kinda love that about him.

"Look after the kid," I tell Titan. He rests his head down on his paws, but his eyes are still open.

I check the rest of the house, door and windows, but everything looks normal.

We head to Amber's bedroom as she changes into her pajamas, and I slide my jeans and t-shirt off. "Sure you're okay with me bein' here?"

"Yes, of course. There have been some burglaries in the area lately," she says. "So who knows, it could've been someone trying to break in."

"I think you need security cameras." I frown. "I'll talk to the boys tomorrow, if you're cool with that?

"Do you think that's necessary?" There's a worried tone to her voice.

I pull her into my shoulder as she wraps an arm over my chest. "Nothin' wrong with updatin' security, *Princess,* especially now you have Olive for a little while."

"I guess not."

I kiss the top of her head. "Try and get some sleep. Titan will wake us up if he hears anythin'."

"He's so protective."

"Told you, once he gets pets — especially from kids — he's putty. She's made a friend for life."

Amber yawns. "He's such a sweet looking menace."

I chuckle. "He sometimes remembers his job, even though he spends most of his day upside down, dreaming of pork tenderloin and unlimited belly rubs."

She kisses my chest, making a humming sound. "I feel safe with you."

That's music to my ears, and as I glance down, I see her eyes squeezed tightly shut. "I'll never let anything bad happen to you," I say. "Or Olive."

"Mmmhmm." She's falling asleep, and I take it as a compliment that she feels secure enough to do that when I'm around. That's my job, regardless of our *situationship*.

"Always," I whisper into the dark. "I'll protect you for the rest of my life."

"The Kingdom of Faith?" I balk. "What in the actual fuck?"

"Yeah, well don't go tellin' Star I told you," Rock says. "I'll be wearin' my balls for earrings."

"I won't. Just need to make sure Amber isn't in any danger."

"I get that. With her sister-in-law missin', it makes sense to check it out, but these fuckers have means and ways of staying hidden. Not like they're gonna have a website; I already checked."

Yeah, that will be an issue, but surely somehow I can find out more intel. "Fuck. So what do we know about this fuckin' Vince dickhead?"

"Well, from what Amber told Star, and the little I've found online, he started this church twenty-something years ago, and in the last decade — that's when Steven joined — they've added over a hundred new members."

"And it's still in Illinois?"

"Looks like they haven't spread their wings that far out of their own nest."

I run both hands through my hair. Amber will be here soon for work, and we'll be talking to Cash about what's going on, just so he's in the loop. "Probably content corruptin' the minds of the innocent people within their reach," I mutter. "I'd like for him to be within my reach."

Rock looks up from the screen. "Damn right. How do all of these cults mass manipulate that many people?"

"Amber was a kid when her brother joined, she didn't have a choice."

His face sobers. "That sucks."

At least I have a name now, and I can do my own investigating. I give him a chin lift. "Got anythin' else?"

"I'm just workin' on security cameras. Star is doin' all the heavy liftin'."

"Speakin' of which, we're gonna need to get cameras around Amber's house. Last night Titan was on edge, and I know someone was out there."

"Got it. Tag and Harlem can set it up with Jett this weekend."

"That'd be great, thanks."

"You think it's somethin' to do with this dude? Or Steven?"

"I don't know, my gut tells me they're not done, but I don't see them leavin' Illinois all this time later to chase their wives. It still doesn't explain Erica."

"That's a dead end right now," he says. "But like I say, Star is workin' on the case, she'll have more information than I do."

I figured as much, but Star is a professional, and as much as I'd love to go barging in there demanding to know what she's found out, she'll only tell me to get the hell out. "Got it."

That uneasy feeling washes over me. If Erica was snatched, or worse, I don't know how Amber will take that news.

I thumb over my shoulder. "Gotta talk to Cash."

"I'll let you know if anything newsworthy comes up," Rock says.

"Appreciate it, brother."

I head out, stopping by the kitchen to say hi to Manny.

He's been creating some new dishes, and the boys have only been too happy to be guinea pigs with anything he cooks.

"Somethin' smells good." I stick my head in the doorway.

Manny is kneading dough when he looks up from the bench and grins. "Chicken pot pie, apparently I've been overdoing the beef bourguignon."

"Garbage, don't listen to anyone who utters that shit outta their mouths."

"So, how are things with you and Amber? Talk about a dark horse."

"Good news travels fast."

"Uh, we had to see it on the kiss-cam on the TV." Manny rolls his eyes. "Kept that kinda on the quiet."

"Things didn't develop until that night." It isn't too far a stretch from the truth. "And we've been friends forever, so we didn't wanna rush things."

He gives me a narrowed side-eye. Manny is known for his almost psychic-like abilities. He's very in tune with bullshit radars, too.

"Uh, huh."

"You would know, you were friends with Lace and Bandit before you all got together."

"I wouldn't say I was *friends* with Bandit. In fact, we started off hating each other."

"But you knew, right?"

He puts the rolling pin down, then lays the pastry very carefully over the top of the huge casserole dish. "I fell before he did because he hadn't quite come out yet, but me and Lace were pretty instant the first time we kissed. I think you should be friends before getting into any kind of relationship. The sex and lust is fun, but it wears off. If you don't actually like the person without all that, it'll never work."

As usual, the man talks sense.

"Exactly. Amber's so smart, funny, sexy, and we have fun together, and I've got the Pelicans to thank for it."

"Another one bites the dust," he sighs.

"We're just takin' things slow." Also not a lie. "Not claimin' her or anythin'."

Manny can't resist his next jab. "Hmm, so technically if she's not claimed, she isn't your ol' lady."

"Amber and I have an understandin'," I say. "And she's not one to be tied down like that. Blame her ex, he was an asshole."

Manny puts the pie in the oven, then turns back to face me. "I'll repeat it in case you missed it." He cups his hands around his mouth. "If she's not claimed, she isn't your ol' lady."

"Yeah, I got that part."

"Which means some other bozo could come along and sweep her off her feet, and you can't do shit about it."

"She wouldn't do that."

"Right, you know what I've discovered over the time I've been in this MC?"

"God help us," I mutter under my breath.

"It's that no matter how tough, independent, or mouthy our women are, they all still need one thing."

I frown. "And what's that?"

"Stability. Be the one true thing she can lean on, especially in hard times. The solid structure in her life that never waivers, no matter how big or small the mountains are that will arise. Women need dependability, no matter what they say."

"I like to think I'm all of those things."

"Good, then pull your finger out of your ass and claim her."

I fold my arms over my chest. "Amber doesn't want to be claimed, not yet anyway. Like I said, we're takin' things slow."

His brow furrows like he doesn't understand. "In that case, you better be pullin' out all the stops to worship her, brother, because a woman like Amber doesn't come along twice in one lifetime."

He's right. I of all people know that. I just can't tell Manny, or anyone else, how I really feel because it'll get back to Amber, and then she'll run a mile. I want to live in my bubble a little longer.

"You got any pie to go?" I try to change the subject.

Manny scoffs. "If you're takin' some to your lady love, then yeah, I might be able to arrange that."

I grin. "Spoken like a man who knows how to please."

He wiggles his eyebrows. "You have no idea."

19

AMBER

The meeting with Cash went well, and he's fully supportive if I need the club's resources to help find Erica. It's a relief, because although I've known Cash for years, I never want to just assume anything. Knowing the twins are working on my case, probably during club hours, felt like the right thing to do.

Bronco, on the other hand, is like a cat on a hot tin roof as I make my way to the bar to begin setting up. "What's wrong?" I ask him.

"Nothin', just gotta get to the shop and do some shit."

I cock a brow. "What shit?"

"Paperwork mainly."

Somehow, I know that he's not telling the entire truth. He forgets how well I know him, but I don't want to pry. "Okay, I'll see you later on maybe."

He gives me a chin lift. "You heard anythin' from Star yet?"

I shake my head. "Nope. God, Bronc, this is tearing me apart every day that she's missing. I don't know how much more I can take, and Olive is starting to ask more and more when her mom's coming back."

He folds me into his arms. "I know it's hard, babe, but you gotta try and hold out a little longer. You've got the best people working on findin' her, gotta believe that."

I try not to let tears fall. I've been a strong person for a long time, but it's taken me eons to get here. Now I feel as if it's all falling apart. If anything's happened to Erica, I don't know what I'll do.

"I miss her."

"I know you do, and with all the love she has right here from her family, you know she's gotta come back. Like you said, she'd never leave Olive unless it was—"

"Life or death?" I finish when he pauses.

"I wasn't gonna say that."

I pull out of his embrace. "But you were thinking it, because that's the reality. It's something I need to get a grip on and try to face. If all of this turns to shit and Erica isn't coming back, then I have to be strong for Olive."

His face softens, his eyes the most incredible shade of honey today. I swear they change color like one of those mood rings. "Yes, but it's okay to ask for help, and it's more than okay to let people help you."

"I just didn't want to be a nuisance to the club."

He strokes a stray tear that rolls down my cheek traitorously. "You're never a nuisance, babe, so don't ever say it. We're a family here, you know that."

He's right. The one thing I do know about the NOLA Rebels MC is the brotherhood they have extends to everyone. They really are just one big family.

"I know, but I worry so much. This isn't like Erica, Bronc. I don't know what I'm gonna tell Olive if she's not coming hom—"

He puts a finger over my mouth. "She will be comin' home, gotta have faith."

My eyebrows raise. "I used to have faith." I let out a breath I didn't know I was holding. "For a long time, but I lost that somewhere along the line."

"I didn't mean religious faith," he corrects. "Just the belief that you'll see her again."

Him and his woo-woo. I plant a kiss on his cheek. "You really are a good man."

"I tell myself that all the time." He moves his head and his lips find mine. It's soft, slow, and barely there.

My heart rate kicks up several notches. Before I know it, I'm clutching onto his shirt, pulling myself closer. I need contact like I need air. I need *him* like I need air. "You know how to distract me." I'm practically panting when I pull back. "I'll give you that."

"Not bad for a fake boyfriend."

I don't know why, but hearing the fake part hits home. Do I really want him to fake all of this in public because I'm the one who's running away? I know deep down in my heart that fuck buddies won't work forever. What happens when someone comes along that turns his head, and then where will I end up when this is over?

Do you want more? I want to whisper it, and I'm so close, but I'm afraid of his answer. Afraid of what it means when we eventually have our first fight. I'm looking for excuses, and I hate myself for it. I hate that I'm wired this way.

"Best I've ever been with."

As if he can see the hopelessness I feel, he cups my face and brings his forehead to mine. "What's goin' on in that pretty head of yours?"

I blow out a breath. "So much, Bronc, but now isn't the time or place. We probably need to talk."

"Uh, oh, don't tell me you're sick of me already."

I manage a half-smile. "I could never be sick of you, but I think my expectations going into this may be different from yours."

He pulls back, his furrowed features meeting my gaze. "You lettin' me down gently, *Princess?*"

"No. I just don't want to get hurt."

"I would never hurt you." The words are out fast, and I know he means them with every fiber of my being. "You know that."

I'm being ridiculous. I want to tell him. I want to hold him close and tell him he's the man of my dreams and I'm falling for him, but the words won't come out. "Later," I whisper. "I've gotta get moving." Reluctantly pulling away, I step behind the bar, wiping my eyes with the back of my hands.

"Babe, I don't want to leave you like this."

"I'm fine, Bronc, just being silly."

He opens his mouth to speak, but then his phone dings. Sliding his cell out of his back pocket, he reads the text and frowns. "I gotta go. I'll call you later."

"Okay." I try to sound brighter. I've never been one to take pity on myself, and I don't want to start now. "Have a good day. I'll call you if I hear from Star."

He nods, giving me a small smile. "Later."

He takes off, and I press my hands against the bar, taking several deep breaths.

When did this happen?

When did I fall big time for my best friend?

Maybe it was that night he beat up those two assholes; I definitely looked at him in an entirely new light after that. Or the hundred times we've hung out and he's done something super sweet, or was just there, doing what Bronco does best. A large part of my belief is that I don't deserve him. That he's too good for me, and I know I have to overcome that, but I don't know how. This wasn't supposed to be complicated, but I think we just went way past that.

BRONCO

"Cut City Boys?" I mutter to myself as I dial Ryder back. He picks up on the first ring.

"Got my message."

"Wait, I'm pretty sure that gang was taken out after we raided that shit hole in the bayou." I remember it well, and so would Hustler since they nabbed Audrina.

"Well, clearly we didn't get one of the assholes."

"What you doin' with him?"

"He's at the warehouse."

I scratch my head. "What's this gotta do with—"

"Prospect's been makin' sure all the club's interests are protected, along with JJ, Bullet, Chains, Pipes and Bandit when they're not workin' elsewhere."

"Okay." I knew they did regular checkups, but I'm not prepared for what comes out of his mouth next.

"Pipes caught one of 'em sniffin' around Amber's place."

My heart sinks into my stomach. "What the fuck?"

"Yeah, piece of shit won't talk."

I snort. "Oh, he's gonna do some talkin'. I'll meet you there. I'll let Cash know I'm still at the clubhouse."

"He won't be far behind you."

"Got it."

I hop on my sled, fury running through my veins. So Titan was right. Some asshole was snooping around last night, and now they're back again during the day. I hope this piece of shit is ready to suffer, because the one thing I know how to do is get a man to talk.

"Not sure he's the best person to be doin' this," Harlem mutters when I break another bone in this asswipe's finger. So far, he's on his third.

The howl that leaves him is pathetic. I slap his face, ignoring Harlem. There's something about a slap, rather than a punch, that's humiliating. "I'm only gonna ask you one more time, fuckface, and then I'm gonna cut your dick off. What were you doin' at my woman's place?"

He's a mess; bloodied and beaten up. Before I arrived, Tag and Harlem fucked him up pretty bad, and I'll admit, he's taken quite the beating. "I can't—"

I sucker punch him in the guts. "Wrong answer."

I go for his buckle, not envying the idea of touching his dick, but a man's gotta do what a man's gotta do.

"Wait!" he cries. "I don't know who sent me, but before the raid, some asshole was snoopin' around, askin' about club girls at the NOLA Rebels MC."

My gaze shifts over to Cash without even moving my head. He's livid. If there's one thing he or anyone in this club can't stand, it's when assholes go for the women. You just don't do that shit. Women, kids and pets are off limits.

"Some asshole?" Harlem stands next to me, Tag by his side, as intimidating as fuck. I'm just glad they waited for me until the real torture began. "Which asshole?"

"I swear I don't know! I got out of that shithole the night you raided it, slipped away from the pigs, too. I've been layin' low downtown because now that The Boss is gone, the rest of us—"

"The rest of you?" Tag pokes a finger in his face. "There are more?"

"Y— yeah, a couple of us got out."

"Gonna need that address," Harlem barks. "Now!"

"I'm literally dead if I—"

I snap another finger and he wails. "Not lookin' good for you now, Oswald, better rethink your next answer if you ever wanna use those fingers again. Next I move to kneecaps."

"No!"

He reels off some shithole downtown, and Cash sends a crew to check it out as I continue to circle him. "Not hearin' anythin' new, Oswald."

"Mississippi," he sputters. "Disciples."

I frown. "Disciples? What is that, an MC?" I've never heard of them, but Bane, the MC Prez over there for the Ridgehaven Hellions MC, Mississippi, definitely will have.

"No— not an MC—"

"Mafia?" I slap him again. "Spit it out, we haven't got all day."

"They're wannabe gangsters, but not like the mafia."

"White trash," I hear Rock mutter from somewhere behind. "Too many trailer trash gangs all up the Mississippi border, stretchin' into Alabama, then there's the hoods."

"Not hoods," Oswald stammers. "Disciple Lords have been keepin' a low profile for a while now, and tryin' to move into Cut City territory, you just happened to get to us before they did."

Cash comes closer, clearly this is news to him. We've got connections everywhere, including our allies, the Irish mafia right here in New Orleans. Big Papa who runs the underworld and knows every drug lord in town, including the Mexican Cartel, who still owe us a favor. But none of us were expecting this.

If Bane knew they were a threat to the MC, he would've

been in contact. The Ridgehaven Hellions is located outside of Jackson, but the MC have a second clubhouse in a cigar shop they own called Cigar Haven so they keep on top of everything that's going on with their arch rivals; the Jackson Skeletons MC.

I'm up in his face. "Anythin' else you forgot to tell us?"

"No— I swear it."

"Could've just said that in the beginin'," I go on. "Would've saved a whole lotta angst, on your part."

"W— what are you gonna do? I told you what I know!"

"You don't expect us to just let you go?" Tag gruffs, arms folded over his chest. "Doesn't work like that, asshole."

"B— but—"

"What's all of this got to do with snoopin' around my ol' lady's house?" I don't miss the arch eyebrows in tandem from Tag and Harlem, but choose to ignore it.

Ryder comes to stand next to me, nothing like intimidation tactics to get this piece of shit flapping his gums. He presses his lips together. "Think we're gonna have to resort to more desperate measures."

"Think you're right," I agree.

"No... no, wait!" Oswald protests.

I rough him by the scruff of the neck. "Last chance!"

"She was a person of interest, as all of the women of the MC are, they're the weak point."

Hearing his words makes my skin crawl. "What the fuck?"

"Gotta understand, The Boss wanted it that way," Oswald goes on.

"But he's dead," Ryder says. "So who's in charge now?"

"Nobody official, but those that got away want revenge," he sputters.

"Includin' you?" Harlem piques an eyebrow.

"No, I'm just one of the guards, nobody important. They won't even miss me—"

"That's good then." I smirk. "Looks like you just dug your own grave."

"That's not what I meant! I was doin' what they told me to do. Watch the girl, track her movements."

"So she can get snatched?" Tag barks. "That's how you get your kicks? Stalkin' women and children to get back at us when they didn't even do shit?"

For all of Tag's grumpiness, he sure as shit has his priorities in order. We all know Oswald is a dead man, it's just a matter of how much we can squeeze out of him.

"Wasn't gonna touch her, or the kid!" he wails.

"The kid?" Ryder looks at me.

"Amber's niece," I tell him.

Ryder doesn't even flinch, striking Oswald in the throat with one punch. "Fucker."

Oswald chokes and gags, gasping for air. With his hands bound behind his back and his feet tied at the ankles, he's got nowhere to go.

Harlem shakes his head. "Too bad you can't learn your lessons in this life," he says. "Never go after women and children."

"End this now," Cash barks, coming back into the warehouse. "I've heard enough of this shit."

I step away for a second, moving toward Cash. "This makes no sense. Amber has nothin' to do with any of this."

"She's attached to you." Cash is seeing red, I can tell by the annoyed look on his face, and the way his head looks like it's gonna explode. "That's how."

I palm the back of my neck. I didn't exactly see it that way, but I just said out loud she was my ol' lady. "I get that, but this just feels off."

Cash grimaces. "Sent a crew to the location. If this asshole is tellin' the truth then that'll be that."

"Too bad for them."

"Damn straight." Cash eyes our captive over my shoulder. "Don't like this. Feels like we dropped the ball, but I'll call Bane, find out what he knows."

"They did a good job of keepin' a low profile."

I walk toward Oswald with Cash. "What do the Disciples have to do with any of this?" Cash demands.

"They're the reason we attacked when we did and kidnapped that chick." He's referring to Audrina. "They want our turf. Apparently they made a deal with an MC in Mississippi, and that's how they're gettin' so much traction so quickly, doin' all their dirty work."

"Bane's gonna be thrilled. Big Papa won't be happy about this either, or the Irish," Ryder mutters.

"Fuck," from Harlem.

"Can we cut him now?" Tag gripes. "I'm bored."

Cash ignores them all. "That still doesn't make sense why you and the other goons are stalkin' the women of the MC. Are you workin' both sides?"

Sheer terror crosses Oswald's face. "What? No!"

"So we're goin' to believe all you want is revenge? You already tried that tact when one of our women was kidnapped," Cash goes on. "So you thought you'd try again?"

"Desperate times call for desperate measures," Ryder murmurs. "Right, Oswald?"

"No... it's not like that. I don't know what the others had planned, but some of the guys who got away want revenge. They've been cooped up like caged animals for months—"

"So instead of tryin' to be a decent human bein', you thought you'd go back to old tricks?" I spit. "This time you just shoot to kill, right?"

"I don't know what they were plannin', I was just told to track movements. I don't know what the others were gonna do, but there was talk of joinin' ranks with the Disciples, and with that..."

"With that what?" I grip his shirt again.

"Comes a sacrifice."

My eyes widen. "A sacrifice?"

"To initiate into a gang sometimes requires a loyalty test," Harlem says. "Killin' someone important to your enemies is usually goal number one, and since we all know women and children are the biggest threat and weakness we have, that's who they target."

"Are you fuckin' kiddin' me?" Cash barks, pushing past the others. "You are fuckin' done, asshole!"

"Wait! I didn't say that's what was gonna happen," he garbles. "It's just what I heard because some of the guys don't know what the fuck to do now The Boss is dead. Disciples are hidin' out, I don't know where they're based in New Orleans. I didn't have shit to do with any of this. I was never gonna hurt her!"

Harlem and Tag hold Cash back. We're not quite done with Oswald yet, and since I've declared Amber my ol' lady to the boys, he's mine to finish. That's how shit around here works.

"You expect us to believe that?" I shake my head. "You were just stakin' out a woman's home with no intention to hurt her even though you just admitted some of the low life's you hang out with struck a deal with the Disciples?"

The color drains from his face. "I didn't—"

"Save it." Ryder turns to Cash. "He's no use to us now, right boss?"

"Got it in one." Cash smirks, his eyes shift to me. "Finish this."

"Wait!" Oswald cries, but it's too late for him.

I pull out my blade, gutting him like a fish as he squirms around. "Fuck you, and fuck anyone who comes near NOLA Rebels property."

He garbles, his head dipping forward as he bleeds out.

Well, he had to know he wasn't gonna live; the plastic sheet beneath his feet should've been a dead giveaway.

"Sent the Nomad brothers to check shit out at the location, along with Jett, Rock, Hawk, Priest and Nevada," Cash says. The Nomad brothers are Brew and Haze; members of the MC, but they also do their own thing from time to time. "If any of these shitheads are there, they'll be sufferin' a similar demise to Oswald here. In the meantime, let's clean up and I'll call Bane as soon as we get back to the clubhouse."

"This shit fuckin' stinks," Tag grumbles. "Thought all this takedown crap was done when we wiped out the Cut City Boys the first time."

"I guess we weren't thorough enough." Harlem palms the back of his neck. "That won't happen again."

I wipe my blade on Oswald's shirt. Goddamn piece of shit. My only regret here today is not drawing out his suffering longer. I could've, but the idea that the women and the kids are still being watched, had me acting fast so I could get back to Amber and check on Olive.

Cash may even call a lockdown depending on what happens with the raid at Oswald's pal's place. We still have to find the Disciples, but I'm sure it can't be that hard. Not if the Ridgehaven Hellions have anything to do with it.

20

AMBER

"She's in New Orleans?" I stammer. I knew calling Star on my break would be a bad idea, because I start to pace, my mind whirling. "So she never left?"

"The bank records are telling me she's still in Louisiana, but mainly Baton Rouge," Star continues. "Which is a good sign. If she's using her bank account, then she's alive. The question is, what is she doing?"

"How do we know it's her?" I feel a lump in my throat. "Someone could've taken her card and used it."

"I'm sending through a photo, it's a little blurry, but Rock picked it up from one of the ATMs downtown."

I place a hand on the bar, thankful nobody is here at this time of day. The message comes through and I stare at it. It's Erica. Relief floods through me as I stare at her picture. "It's her. When was this taken?"

"A few days ago," Star says. "There's more."

I squeeze my eyes shut, not understanding any of this or what the fuck is going on. "Okay."

"There was a large deposit into Erica's account almost a year ago. When Rock traced where the funds came from, it led back to an organization that looked like a loan shark or one of those shady lenders who offer you money when the bank won't." I brace myself for what she's about to say next. "Then Jett did a little more research and once he was able to sift through the layers of red tape, he uncovered the last name: Olgetti."

"What does that mean?"

"Well, ever since the Mancini mafia were taken out a little while back, the Bratva in Chicago took over operations, leaving relative peace for a short time because the Bratva had no rivals."

Riot, who used to be a sniper, took out Chicago's mafia leader, and went undetected for years until Mancini's associates started dropping like flies. I remember it because it made the news. It wasn't Riot who was taking revenge, but a rival sniper, and she was the devil in disguise.

"I've heard about it," I say, wondering where this is going. "It made the nightly news over a year ago."

"I've done a little research myself trying to figure this out, and I can only come back to organized crime. The Olgettis also have ties to the Mancini family, but it looks like they're not taking over anytime soon. Bratva rules Chicago now, but underworld crime is still at an all-time high."

"My sister is involved in organized crime?" I can't even get the words out without stammering.

"I'm sorry to say that it's looking likely. My guess is she borrowed money and she can't pay it back. That could definitely explain her absence, and why she's keeping her daughter safe and you out of the whole mess."

"How much money was it?"

"Fifty grand."

I swallow hard. That's a lot of money. "Okay, but can we find Erica?"

"I tracked her cell phone but I had no luck. She did use her card at a motel in Baton Rouge, and that's where I think she still is."

"If you can track her, won't these Olgetti people be able to, too?"

"It's unlikely they have the kind of resources I have, so I think we're safe to say she's on the run, and rather than putting you and Olive in danger, she's taking matters into her own hands."

I shake my head. "This is insane. I don't even know what she needed money for—"

"She owed a lot in back rent, and other bills that were paid shortly thereafter. The debt was piling up."

"She never said anything," my voice is barely a whisper. "She could've told me, I would've helped."

Fury races through me. This isn't what sisters do. We're supposed to help each other out, not borrow money from shady dealers who probably want to kill her.

"I know this must be a shock, but I'm guessing this is what we're dealing with."

"So where do we go from here?" My eyes are still closed, I've no idea where to turn. My trust and faith is all with her.

"We're still trying to find out more about the Olgettis. If we can settle that debt on Erica's behalf, then she'll be in the clear, with interest and whatever else she's agreed to, the sum could be a lot more."

I start to pace. "I don't have that much money," I tell her. "I could rustle up some funds, but not that much in a short space of time."

"We'll talk to Cash, maybe make a payment plan to the MC if he agrees to get her out of trouble. I can talk to Luna and Tag."

Luna and Tag? I know they live in a prestigious area of New Orleans, but I'm not asking them for money. Tag made eyebrows rise when he bought the house Luna was living in for $1.9 million dollars just to keep her safe. She thought her parents had bought it and was living there paying them rent. The rent money — which would never cover the repayments — was going to Tag.

I don't know what the likelihood is of them or Cash doing shit, but at the end of the day it's not the MC's issue that Erica got herself into this mess. "I doubt Cash will agree. Why would he? And I can't ask Luna or Tag for money. I can find another way."

"I know this is hard, Amber, but your sister-in-law is in trouble. Enough to dump her kid and take off," Star reminds me. "The MC is a family, and we don't abandon our families. If her mess puts you and Olive in danger, then it's an MC issue. It seems like a reasonable enough explanation to Cash, not that I'm sure he'll be thrilled about it, but it would get the Olgettis off Erica's back."

"I'll have to think about it. I need to talk to Bronco." I can feel the tears building up. This is all too much. I have no clue why Erica would ever keep something like this from me. It's completely out of character.

"I understand. I'll be back in touch when I find anything else. In the meantime, sit tight. Rock and Jett are digging up security footage of the hotel. When I called them this morning, she already checked out."

"So we should head to Baton Rouge?" I'm grappling for something. Baton Rouge is a big place, and it would be like finding a needle in a haystack, but somehow being closer to Erica makes me feel like finding her would be a real possibility.

"We can't right now."

"Why not?"

"Talk to Bronco. The club is about to go into lockdown."

"Lockdown over this?" Panic rises in my voice.

"Not over this, over something else. The details are sketchy. Cash has called a club meeting in the next hour."

"Holy shit."

"I'll call you later."

"Okay, thanks, Star."

We hang up and I take a few deep breaths. This is just too much information.

Erica is in trouble with a crime family. She's still in Louisiana. She's heavily in debt and being hunted. The club is going into lockdown over another matter... My head might just very well spin off.

I pull out my cell and call Bronco. He doesn't answer. I quickly type a text, knowing he's unlikely to listen to a voice message.

ME

Call me when you get this, it's urgent

A few moments later, Hustler and a very pregnant Audrina come in through the clubhouse doors. Hustler's brow is furrowed, his face full of worry as I make my way toward them from behind the bar. Little Tilbury, their tiny chihuahua, is on her leash at their heels.

"Hey, is everything okay?"

Audrina smiles tentatively as Hustler sits her down on one of the booth seats, then places Tilbury on her lap. "I'm fine. Kinda hoping this baby will show her face any day now, because I'm so over being pregnant."

"But you're so cute." I smile.

Hustler still hasn't said anything, but when his eyes meet mine, I see concern there. "Everyone is moving to the clubhouse temporarily," he says, all business.

"Star just said something's going on, but she didn't know what."

"All you need to know is that it's for everyone's protection. Safer here where we can all keep an eye on things."

"What things?" I press. "Does this have anything to do with Erica?"

He shakes his head. "Separate matter, but still a concern."

"Shit, I've gotta go pick up Olive at three—" I panic. If we're going into lockdown, I need to get Olive's things.

"No need, Bronco is on his way."

"Bronco?" I did list him as an emergency contact when I enrolled Olive, so collecting her shouldn't be an issue.

"Yeah." He turns to Audrina. "Gotta go make a few phone calls, but I'll be right here."

She shoos him away. "Go, I'm fine. Amber's here, and the other girls will be arriving soon."

He kisses her chastely, then takes off toward the front of the clubhouse doors.

I take a seat next to Audrina. "Okay, what the heck is happening?"

Knowing Audrina would've heard some of it from her ol' man, she doesn't hold back. "There was a threat against the club with a rival underworld gang from Mississippi trying to infiltrate the Cut City Boys, or those that are left after the shoot out, and apparently they've been watching the women of the MC again, trying to find a chink in the chain."

"What the fuck is wrong with these people?" I half expect Audrina to correct me on my cursing, but she doesn't. She's the most lady-like of the ol' ladies and I don't think I've ever heard a bad word come out of her mouth.

"I don't know, but Cash was going to call Bane, the Prez of the Ridgehaven Hellions over in Mississippi, because that's his territory, and I'm guessing Bane knew nothing about it because he and the club are tight."

"You got all of this from one car ride over here?" I smirk.

She smiles a little devilishly, stroking Tilbury's head. "I have my ways, and I think West forgets I have ears."

I sober quickly, remembering Erica's predicament. I fill

Audrina in briefly on what Star told me, and she looks just as shocked as I am. "She didn't say anything about the debt? Why would she not come to you?"

I shrug. "Embarrassment, I'd assume. She's never been one to get into debt, not like that. I guess in her mind she thinks she's doing the right thing keeping Olive safe, and me in the dark."

"A problem shared is a problem halved." Audrina places a hand on her large belly. "Or so they say."

"Can I get you anything?" I wince because she looks really uncomfortable.

"Unless you have a special remedy back there for getting babies out, then I'm good." She smiles again, stretching her back as I rack my brain for something I could do other than make her a cup of tea.

A few moments later, Manny comes through the doors, several shopping bags in his hands. "Hey, ladies. I heard the news," he says by way of greeting. "I rushed out to get more supplies. If we're stuck in here for a few days, we're gonna need a shit ton of food."

"Hey, Manny." I run a hand through my hair. "Trust you to cook up a storm in the middle of a crisis."

He presses a kiss to Audrina's cheek. "I had to make sure our favorite Mama here has everything she needs."

"Please tell me you didn't go to the grocery store just for me." She looks mortified at the prospect.

He waves a hand. "I was out anyway when West called, and it's my pleasure to help a girl out." He gives her a wink.

"I don't know why we couldn't stop off home to grab my things. At least we have the hospital bag in the car, that's something at least," she sighs.

"You know your old man, always bein' protective," Manny sing-songs. "Are you hungry?"

I shake my head. "I'm okay, thanks, Manny."

"I don't want to burden you," Audrina starts. "But we were at Muso's when Hustler rushed me out of there, and I didn't manage to grab any lunch."

Muso's is Hustler and the club's cafe in the French Quarter.

"It's no burden to cook for a sexy Mama." Manny waggles his eyebrows. "Any cravings?"

"One of your famous BLTs would go down a treat." Audrina's cheeks flush slightly. I know she hates asking for things, even when Manny is more than obliging.

"Comin' right up." He gives me a chin lift. "You sure you don't want one?"

"Maybe you twisted my arm," I say, knowing I'll only offend him if I keep turning him down.

"Atta girl." He takes off happily, whistling a tune.

"Nice to see some of us are handling lockdown with poise and grace," I mumble, watching him go. "You'd think he'd be the one freaking out."

Manny was shot protecting Lace. He's a hero in my book, but he never acts like he's too big for his boots. He'll always do what's right for this club, and the way he shows he cares is by feeding everyone.

"We've all been here before," Audrina sighs.

I lean over and squeeze her hand. "This can't be easy for you, after what happened."

"I can't say that I'm thrilled hearing those monsters who kidnapped me are still at large, but I have faith in the MC, and I also realize that the cops weren't exactly as vigilant as the MC were when they showed up to rescue me," she says. "But I know Cash and the boys will not make the same mistake twice."

"You really don't need this kind of stress with the baby being so close to the due date."

"Tell me about it. West is beside himself, but I've been

down this road before. Even if my first pregnancy was almost three decades ago, some things you just never forget."

"Is it very different this time around? I'll bet Nevada was the wild child even in your belly."

She laughs. "He was a lot more active, and my morning sickness was worse. Now I'm older, maybe my body has changed so much that it doesn't feel as difficult as the first time. With Asher I was only eighteen."

"That's so young," I say.

"We were still in high school when I got pregnant. It was a lot. It was the only reason John and I got married. He was from a religious family, and mine were no better. I can't say I haven't had a good life, but it wasn't all roses. Since meeting West, it has become spectacular. Clearly the universe had other plans for me, and I'm the happiest I've ever been."

"And Hustler," I muse. "He walks around like the cat who got the cream."

"He's been such a rock. I've never been an equal in a relationship until I met him. I think because we were also friends before we got together, it really helped our relationship blossom. We knew a lot about each other before things got serious," she laughs. "We enjoyed each other's company without any pressure. Of course, we all know how that turned out."

"He couldn't keep his hands off you."

She rubs her belly. "Clearly I was never infertile like I thought I was."

Unlike Audrina, I know for a fact I can't have kids. It's the reason I let Bronco not use a condom and I don't regret that. Feeling him that close to me was something I wanted. Heck, I craved it. "It was meant to be."

"It was."

I'm happy for her and West, they're the cutest couple, and I know they'll make amazing parents.

My phone vibrates and I see Bronco's name dancing across the screen. "I'm just gonna take this," I say.

"No problems."

"Bronco?"

"Hey, sorry I missed your call, I was... uh, busy. Callin' to say I'm enroute to collect Olive, Hustler said he'd fill you in on what's goin' down."

"He did, sort of," I say. "But Bronc, I got a call from Star."

"What did she say?"

I fill him in and he's quiet for a moment. "Fuck, we gotta find her."

"I know, I'm freaking out. I just got off the call then Audrina and Hustler arrived, so I haven't had a second to process any of it."

"I'll be there soon."

"Shit, Bronc, if Erica's somehow involved with organized crime, this could end really badly for her."

"Shit's comin' at us from both sides," he says, alarming me further. "Just stay at the clubhouse."

"Okay, Audrina said something about some of the Cut City Boys being at large and some other gang from Mississippi were trying to infiltrate."

"So much for club business," he mutters. "Just sit tight, can you do that for me?"

"So the club really is going into lockdown?"

"It's just a temporary precaution, after what happened to Audrina, Cash isn't takin' any chances, so on that front we're all unanimous."

"I'm scared, Bronc. I've got Olive to think about now."

"She's safe here, you know that."

"I need to find Erica." I wipe the tears away. I didn't want to cry down the phone; in fact, it's the last thing I wanted, but being strong is taking its toll.

"Star's already found out where she's been, it's just a matter of pinpointing where she is right now."

"I get that, but if she has this Olgetti crime family after her, she might not have the luxury of time."

As much as Bronco may want to tell me to stop being hysterical, he doesn't. He lets me rant when I need to, and always talks me off the ledge when I'm close to losing it.

"Keep yourself busy for the next half hour and stop thinkin' about all the things that could happen," he tells me. "It's gonna be okay. We know Erica is alive, we just have to find out exactly where she is. If I have to drive to Baton Rouge myself, I'll do it."

"You'd do that?"

He grunts. "Of course I would. Erica's important to you, and then there's Olive to think of."

"I can't believe she did this. We could've come up with a plan together." I can barely get the words out. I keep thinking how terrified Erica must be, and how desperate she was to do what she did. I know how that feels because I've lived it. We both have.

"No point dwellin' on that now. She did what she did, and when she's back safe and sound, you can have it out with her then."

"Hurry back, but don't hurry... I mean, don't put yourself in danger..."

"I've got Titan with me, we're all gonna be fine. I'll be there soon."

"I lov—" I stop. *What the heck?* The phone goes dead. He already hung up. I swallow hard, not even bothering to wipe the tears away. My words are whispered so softly, I'm not even sure if they drift off my tongue when I say out loud, "I love you, Bronco."

Maybe I've always known it, or maybe I'm just feeling

emotional because of everything that went down today, but I know one thing. I can't live without him. I just don't know how to tell him that the game has changed.

21

BRONCO

"Then what happened?" I ask Olive as we drive toward the clubhouse. She's explaining her day with intense detail, and though she's well and truly missing her mom, I can tell she's fitting in and making the best of it. She's a good kid, quick to learn, as well as polite.

"Our teacher, Ms. Phelps, was so embarrassed, but everyone knows that she and Mr. Edmonds have been dating for a while now. She said yes, and then we all clapped and cheered."

Coach Edmonds and Olive's teacher got engaged today in front of the school when he dropped down onto one knee and popped the question. The kids were all extremely excited, and Ms. Phelp's blush resembled a tomato, according to Olive.

"I'm glad she said yes," I laugh. "Or poor Coach Edmonds could've been in a bit of a pickle."

"He was smiling from ear to ear," she announces, giggling.

Titan pokes his head through the console of my truck, and Olive turns to pet his head.

"Even Titan wanted to hear the story." I grin.

"How come you're collecting me today, Bronco?"

"Your Aunt got stuck at work, and I was in the neighborhood."

"Huh."

"What else did you do in school?"

"We had arts and crafts, and some boys called me Olive pit."

"You know boys are dumb sometimes?"

She sighs. "Yeah, I know." Then, "Bronco? What's your real name?"

I give her a side-eye. "How do you know it's not Bronco?"

"Don't most of the other men in the motorcycle club have nicknames?"

Clearly, I'm outmatched. "Yep, they do. I know a biker called Dufus."

She giggles. "Really?"

"Nah, but I do know one called Hubcap."

"And I know one called Meatloaf."

"I thought he was a singer?"

She giggles again, clearly having no idea who I'm talking about.

"My real name is Torin," I tell her. "My brother is called Ansel. Our mom has weird taste in names, but it means chief or leader in Irish Gaelic. I know what your name means, aside from the obvious; olive tree."

She turns to me excitedly. "What does it mean?"

"Its Latin name symbolizes peace and friendship. Olive is named after the goddess Athena who used an olive tree to win against Poseidon," I say. "Champions used to wear olive wreaths, worn as a symbol of victory. Then biblically, the dove returned to Noah's ark carrying an olive branch in its beak. From then on, the olive branch was known as a symbol of peace. Ever heard of the expression to extend an olive branch?"

"Yes." She smiles with her eyes, absorbed in my story.

"That's where the expression came from."

"Wow, how do you know all that?"

"I like woo-woo stuff," I laugh. "That's what my mom calls it. She's into reading palms, medicinal herbs and crystals and stuff. Plus, I was looking up Amber's name one time, and thought I'd check yours out."

"What does Aunt Amber's name mean?"

"It's from an old Arabic name meaning Jewel."

"Jewel," she whispers. "That really suits Aunt Amber."

"It does. And get this, in the bible it means divine glory."

"You're really good at this. What about Titan?"

"It's Greek for great strength. Before that, he was named Diablo, which is Spanish for devil; he didn't like that much, so I renamed him."

"I really like Titan." Olive pets his head as he tries to get farther in the front on the console, but he stops his movements, realizing he's too big.

The dog in question then lolls his head to one side, knowing we're talking about him. He settles his head back down and closes his eyes, letting out a sigh like he's hard done by.

"I think he likes you, too."

By the time we get to the clubhouse, Olive has used my phone to google all the meanings and origins of her friends' names. I've gotta hand it to the kid, she's enthusiastic.

"I can't wait to tell Cami and Ella." She beams.

I don't have the heart to tell her they'll be here tonight, but not for the reasons she thinks. Still, as long as all the kids are safe, what does it matter? There's plenty of bedrooms upstairs in the clubhouse, and Cash and Deanna will open their home with its three extra bedrooms, for couples with little kids. Trouble is, everyone is getting pregnant around here, and Audrina is ready to drop any day now.

I pull up in the lot and we climb out, letting Titan out of

the back. He immediately runs toward the nearest tree and pees on it. Olive giggles.

I'm anxious to see Amber and calm her. She sounded worried on the phone. While I can't exactly tell her what I did to Oswald — who's now at the bottom of the bayou — it seems as if the hits are coming from all sides.

The fucking Cut City Boys are still at large, teaming up with the Disciples to try and infiltrate into New Orleans undetected. Clearly catching Oswald was a blessing in disguise. Erica is on the run from gangsters in Chicago, who likely want to get the money first, before killing her. What the fuck is next? Not wanting to jinx myself, I touch the black obsidian around my neck. It's always brought me protective energy and helps me tap into my inner strength. It hasn't let me down yet.

Glancing sideways, Olive slides her hand into mine. My throat thickens. She's a sweet child, but very much still a child. Trusting. Innocent. And she's under my protection along with Amber. It was always meant to happen this way.

"Am I allowed to call you Torin?" she asks as I sling her backpack over my shoulder.

"Not if you expect me to answer."

She giggles, letting go of my hand to run ahead, trying to catch up to Titan.

I can't stop thinking about Erica. She's in fucking Baton Rouge, and I need to go there. It's one thing staying here to protect the women, but how do I explain to Amber that Erica's life is in serious jeopardy if we don't act quickly? If we found her, then so will the gangsters looking for her. Sure, Rock and Jett haven't pinpointed her exact location yet, but they will.

I debate leaving the clubhouse. Amber and Olive will be safe here, and Cash won't let them go anywhere. The only trouble is, Amber will want to come, and I can't have that.

She'll get in the way, and if these assholes aren't already on Erica's tail, they soon will be.

When I reach the clubhouse doors, Olive and Titan are already inside, careening through the space as Olive calls out for Amber. By now, there's a ton of Harley's in the lot, trucks, and some of the ol' ladies' SUVs.

As soon as I spot Amber behind the bar, I don't even hesitate. Walking behind, I take her into my arms as Olive takes off to find her friends. Since Indigo is sitting right at the end of the bar, Cami won't be far away.

"How you doin'?" I press a kiss to her forehead. Any preconceived notions about faking our relationship seem to have gone right out the window.

"I've been better. Can we talk?"

"Of course, they can look after themselves for a while." I lead her out of the bar toward the back where the offices are.

Cami and Olive are already talking excitedly about the "sleepover" at the clubhouse as we pass by.

"I'll be just a minute, okay, Ollie?" Amber says.

She nods. "Okay, *Jewel*."

Amber looks up at me. "What's that all about?"

I gruff a laugh. "I was talkin' in the car about names and what they mean."

"You know what my name means?"

"Sure I do. It's also an organic gemstone, not a mineral like some people think. It's made from fossilized tree resin."

"You have to stop talking like that." She grins. "You're turning me on."

I grip her hand harder, checking to see if Jas's office is free as I glance around. When the coast is clear, I pull Amber inside and close the door.

"What happened today?" she asks.

"Like I said, lockdown is for everyone's safety and a temporary precaution."

She places her hands on her hips. "Don't spin me that bullshit, Bronc. I know you better than that."

I run a hand over my face. "Shit got real today, that's all you need to know."

"Real how?"

"Like I said, we're not takin' any chances."

"So that's it? We slept together a couple of times, and now I just get left in the dark?"

"That's not what this is. This is me keepin' you safe."

"What were the Cut City Boys going to do?"

"Amber."

"Tell me. Please, Bronco, you can't keep me in the dark. We've never played by those kinds of rules."

"Yeah? Well things are different now."

"Different?"

I stare at her. "If you even have to ask that, then that tells me everything."

"Are we having a fight?"

"No. But we're not on the same page with everything, clearly."

Her eyes study my face and her lips part. "Did we go way past complicated?"

My lips twitch. "You think?"

She moves closer, her hand reaches for me and presses over my heart. "I don't want you to think I'm just saying what I'm about to say because I want you to tell me what's really going on, but somewhere along the lines, everything has become blurry."

I don't move a muscle. The heat from her palm is steady against the material of my shirt.

"I think I always knew, deep down, but I pushed it away. I was so scared of being hurt again. Of giving myself over to someone, not really realizing that I've been holding back, and for a long time that worked. But that doesn't work anymore."

I can't help it. I cup her face with one hand, the soft swell of her cheek as warm as her palm. "I don't want you to hold back. Say what you need to say."

"But you don't want to hear about the way the room spins whenever you're in it. How I'm breathy and needy when I don't see you for a day, and I'm counting down the minutes when I'll see you again." She grips my cut, and I let her. I need to hear this. "You don't understand how it felt being in your arms, and you being inside me for the first time. How well we fit, how much I want you to stay every night, *all* the fucking nights, forever—"

"What are you sayin'?" My heart is racing in my chest so loudly, I swear she can hear it.

"I don't know how or when it happened, maybe it was the kiss-cam, or it could've been before, but I love you, Bronco. I've always loved you, and I don't want you to run away—"

I bend my head, closing the distance as our lips meet and we kiss with a newfound purpose. Hearing her say those words is like music to my ears. My heart feels like a bird that's just been set free from a cage, soaring high.

"I'd never run away, *Princess,*" I mutter in between kisses. "I love you, too. I've loved you for so fuckin' long that it feels like a lifetime."

She moans breathily when I cup her face, deepening the kiss as our tongues meet. She presses her body against mine, groaning when my dick pushes into her hip.

"I love what I do to you," she whispers.

"I love what you do to me, too. I'll never hurt you. And trust me, I understand all of those things, because I've known it for a while."

"You have?"

I press my forehead against hers. "Yep, not afraid to admit it. I guess we were right about one thing, though."

"What's that?" She smiles, pursing her lips.

"Fuck buddies just doesn't work."

She slaps me on the arm. "Friends with benefits, remember?"

"Same thing."

"Jesus, are we really going to do this thing?"

"You know you can't stay away from me."

"More like I don't want to." She kisses me again, her hands roaming my chest as I grow harder with every movement.

"Glad to hear it. You know if you keep touchin' me like that, we're gonna fuck on Jas's desk."

"I think fucking on Jas's desk is a rite of passage for most of the members," she laughs.

I snort a laugh, too. "Can be quick."

"Nope. You're getting out of telling me what really went on."

I sigh. I thought she'd lay off after our confessional, but I guess not. "There was a guy at the house last night, I'm sure it was when Titan barked and spooked him."

She bites her lip, her face startled. "Really?"

"Yes. And he was with Cut City Boys doin' their dirty work, followin' the ol' ladies just like that last time, tryin' to find a way to get back at us."

"Holy shit."

"So you see now why Cash did what he did?"

She nods, tears brewing in her eyes. "Why are they doing this?"

"Because some got away and slipped under the radar, then another gang from Mississippi saw an opening in the neighborhood and thought they'd step on in. They won't. Bane will see to it that they never cross state lines." I stroke my thumb over her cheekbone where a single tear falls. I bring my thumb to my mouth to taste the salty speck. "I can't have people hangin' around the house at night, or anytime. They've been watchin', and we can't take the chance after Audrina's ordeal."

"Oh, my God."

"So when I tell you that you need to let me handle the thing with Erica, you gotta trust me that you're safer here. I don't want you or Olive in harm's way. I know you want to help, but I don't want to be worryin' about you when I have to leave."

"You're going to go after her?"

"If Cash okays it, then yes."

Her lips part as she swallows hard. "I can't let you do that, no, it's dangerous. These Chicago gangsters—"

"Are just like the gangsters we deal with here. Need to find out more about this Olgetti family, but if they've got a large operation, Cash may just agree to pay them out rather than takin' matters into our own hands. It'll only bring more danger to the club."

"I hate this," her tone is barely audible as she buries her face into my chest. "I hate that I can't just talk to her, tell her to come back and we're here for her, no matter what."

"She wanted to settle her own mess, and she thought she was doin' the right thing. I can only imagine how scared she is right now, and I can't stop thinkin' about it. Olive needs to have her mom back."

"I agree with you, but this isn't your mess to fix. It's not the club's either."

"And it's yours?" I question. "You didn't play any part in this, babe, just remember that."

"But she's my family…"

"That doesn't mean any of this is your fault, okay? I can't believe you carry all this guilt and shit around with you. You gotta let me in if we're gonna make this work," I say. "You gotta give me all of you, not just the parts you think I want to see. I want all of it."

"You want more?"

"Oh, I want a lot more."

"I'm trying," she breathes. "But with you it's effortless. I fell under your spell when we kissed properly for the first time at the game, but I knew something was up when I was mad at Cupcake for flirting with you."

"I don't want her—"

She places a finger over my lips. "I know that, but I still wanted to scratch her eyes out."

"So you'll listen to me and stay here when I go find Erica?"

She draws a long intake of breath. "Is this the part where I go all ol' lady on your ass?"

I press a chaste kiss to her lips. "No, it's the part where I bend you over the desk."

"We can't, Bronc. Olive is just out there, and might I remind you we're in the middle of a crisis."

"I can work fast."

She shakes her head, but her hands move to my belt buckle. "If I protest about you going to Baton Rouge, will you listen to me?"

"Nope."

"Just like that?"

I smirk. "I won't be goin' alone, so stop worryin'."

"I'm afraid," she admits, unzipping me. "I just want her home."

"And she will be, but it's better for us to find her than the Olgettis."

"You do too much for me."

"I do it because I love you."

She grips my dick. "I'm doing this because I love you, too, not because you're doing dangerous shit for me."

I grin. "Who cares? It's worth it. Lock the door."

She bites down on her bottom lip, then crosses the room to do just that. "Jas is going to kill us."

"Jas won't know, we'll be fast."

"I need you, Bronco. I love it when you're inside me. You make all the bad stuff go away." She yanks down my jeans and I groan when she grips my dick.

I would love to push her down onto her knees, fuck that pretty mouth of hers in record time, but then she won't get off and we can't have that.

"Fuck, I love it when you tell me what you want."

"I want you. I want you so fucking much."

I walk her backwards until her back hits the door, pinning her against it. I undo her jeans, yanking them and her panties down to her knees. "Gonna be hard and fast."

"Get on with it then."

I grin, then spin her around as she yelps, placing her hands on the door. I pull up her t-shirt so it's rucked up, yanking her bra down as I palm her tits. "You want this big cock inside you, pretty girl?"

"Hurry, stop teasing." She sticks her ass out and I chuckle, stroking my thumbs over her erect nipples. I wish I had time to worship them all fucking night long.

"Such a badass." Without warning, I line up, sliding my cock inside her pussy to the hilt. I'm a bastard. She's not even lubed yet, but I'm thrilled when I feel how slick she is from our dirty talk.

She mumbles incoherently, begging me in raspy breaths for more. Harder. Faster. *Take me, Bronco.*

I do just that. Pounding into her wet heat with every ounce of my being. Feeling like I'm the richest man in the world because of her words. She fucking loves me, and I love her. Finally, we can be honest about how we feel and it's like a weight has been lifted. She's my dream woman. She's everything.

"I love you," I mutter into her hair. "You're so beautiful. This pussy belongs to me."

"Oh."

"You got me?"

"Yes," she whisper-cries. "Oh, Bronc, yes, baby. Right there..."

I place my hands on her hips, pounding like a fucking lovesick fool, my balls slapping her pussy with every thrust. Her ass pushes back against me and one day, one day I'd love to take that little peach, too.

This is feral. Needy. Both of us panting and cursing as I get my fill. Not that I could ever get my complete fill of her.

Nothing and nobody is ever going to get in the way of our happiness. With every single beat of my heart, I'll keep showing up for her, letting her know that she can depend on me no matter what.

After all, it's the least I can do after all that she's given me.

22

AMBER

"Yes!" I cry, knowing we should not be doing this with all the crazy shit that's going on around us, but I also know that if I don't have him inside me right this very minute, I don't want to live another day.

"Feel how tight you are, squeezin' my cock like a vice," Bronco's words are right at my ear, and I shudder. I'm right on the edge.

I hiss, my core aching to come, the buildup is more than I can handle. "That's because I love it." My breathing is coming in hard and fast. It's like we're both unable to control ourselves.

I feel him tug my hair into his fist, and it's so damn sexy. "You love what I do to you, don't you, *Princess?*"

"Harder," I moan.

He pistons his hips as he rams furiously in and out, and I cannot catch my breath. Hell, I don't ever want to catch my breath. I was a fool to think that we could ever be intimate and not have feelings. I was kidding myself. We both were.

The way he stretches me feels so good. I never knew sex could be like this, even when it's hard and fast. Of course,

Bronco knows how to be sweet, but I also like him when he loses control. I do that to him, and it makes my heart beat faster in a way it never has before. I know we have to be quick, but what I'd give for him to take his time. To caress my body with his mouth. After being in his bed, there is no way I could ever want anyone else. There is nobody like Bronco.

When he moves his hand between my legs, brushing against my clit, it's all the friction I need and I explode so hard, I see stars. He follows behind, cursing as I feel him pulsing inside me, emptying his load as he grunts my name into my neck. One hand cupping my breast, the other gripping my hip.

"Fuck, that was good," he manages between pants.

"No question that we're well and truly in the honeymoon phase."

He pulls out immediately, cupping his dick as he reaches to the desk for the tissues. He wipes his dick, then me, and tosses the tissues in the trash can nearby. I'm still plastered against the door when he's zipping himself back into his jeans.

"You good?" Is it just me, or does he sound smug?

"I am now." I managed to peel myself off the door, tucking my breasts back into my bra and pulling my jeans up. "You're a bad influence."

"Me?" He thumbs his chest. "Pretty sure you reached for my belt buckle before I had the chance to stop you."

"Like you were gonna protest."

"I'm not just a piece of meat." Even he can't keep the grin off his face.

"I think we both know that's not true."

He pulls me to him and I yelp in surprise. "Cheeky."

"We should get back. Olive could be looking for me."

"Just like you to seduce me in the middle of a crisis with that sinful body of yours," he mutters in my ear.

I press my lips together. "I could say the same about you."

"Least I got a parting gift. I'll be dreamin' about you every second I'm gone."

I turn, my face dropping. "When are you leaving?"

"Tomorrow. I'm no good sittin' here twiddlin' my thumbs when we could be out there findin' Erica."

"You don't have to—"

He puts a finger over my lips. "We already discussed this, AJ."

"If anything happened to you, I'd never forgive myself," I whisper.

"Nothin' is gonna happen, babe, but the longer Erica is out there by herself, the worse this is gonna get for her."

"I just wish she'd call me. She hasn't even checked up on Olive." I try not to let the tears return.

"Only because she knows Olive is in capable hands with an aunt who loves her."

"You're just trying to make me feel better."

He brushes the hair off my face, tucking a lock behind my ears. "Not ever gonna tell you what you wanna hear, but sometimes you're too hard on yourself."

"I've always been this way. I've always pushed myself."

"That's because you're a survivor. What you did all those years ago is fucking amazing. Without your strength and resilience, you wouldn't have made it out of there."

It's true, even though I don't want to admit it. I was the one who instigated the entire escape. Sometimes I don't know where the will came from, but there was always a belief that something more than that place existed. There was more out there for me.

I vowed then and there; I would never, ever go back. Nor would I do anything that wasn't with my entire heart and soul. Bronco isn't the only one who's all about the vibe.

"I guess I've never really looked at it like that. I've kinda avoided thinking about it too much over the years. The things that were done to me and what I lived through were sheer hell, but I put it all in a box, locked it away and threw away the key." I shake my head at the memories. "I just wanted to move on with my life, but maybe there are still things in the past that I need to put to rest. Nothing can hurt me now. What happened is in the past, and I can't change any of it."

"Trauma can last a lifetime," Bronco says. "But I'm here for you in any which way I can."

"I know that." I cup his face. "You're my rock." I press my lips against his.

"You wanna be my ol' lady?"

I quirk a brow. "Is that even a question?"

"That a yes?"

"I thought we were taking things slow?" I can't even hide the smile that's playing on my lips.

He snorts. "Slow? We just declared our love for one another, then I fucked you against a door while pullin' your hair. I think we went way past goin' slow, babe."

I giggle. "You're right. It's the kiss-cam that did it."

"You gonna take credit for that for the rest of your life?"

"Maybe."

He rubs his nose against mine. "Smart ass."

"We better go."

"Yeah, got shit to do tonight."

I bite my lip, knowing he's talking about Erica. My heart hurts that he's doing this, but I also know there's no stopping Bronco when it comes to doing what he says he's going to do. I never want him to think he has to do my family's dirty work, but knowing that he's going to find Erica also gives me hope. I have to stay strong for Olive. She's all I have left.

"I love you, don't ever forget that."

His hand is on the door as he kisses me chastely once more. "Not as much as I love you."

Bronco

What Amber doesn't know is I've been conducting my own investigation for the last couple of days. I know she's a strong woman, and I don't wanna hide shit from her, but telling her that this isn't Erica's first debt to gangsters would devastate her. Maybe Erica didn't mean to get involved from what Amber has told me over the years; she doesn't strike me as the type of woman who's a troublemaker. Nor does she seem to be a person who would get tied up with the underworld. But desperate times call for desperate measures. I know how it feels to hit rock bottom.

"Another debt?" I lift an eyebrow at Rock.

"You know Star's gonna kill me for sayin' shit."

I give him a pointed look. "I'm lookin' out for Amber. I need to know stuff, especially since Cash okayed me goin' to Baton Rouge." I'm a little surprised he agreed. He's not an asshole by any means, but the club going into lockdown until the MC is cleared is no laughing matter. Of course, he's also not going to let an innocent woman be gunned down over a debt, not when she's Amber's family.

"Shit's gettin' real. You need a hand?"

"You offerin'?"

"Yeah, gotta let my ol' lady know, but I'm good to go."

Rock's ol' lady, Aspyn, is quieter than some of the other women of the club, but she's always around helping out wherever she can. Aspyn does a lot for local charities in New Orleans, and while she may have grown up with a silver spoon in her mouth, she definitely doesn't act like it.

"Ryder's comin', and Pipes," I say.

"Jett would come too, but Summer is workin' night shift, so he's waitin' around the hospital until she finishes."

"Thinkin' four of us will be enough."

"Hey." We both turn to find Stella leaning against the doorway. "Heard you're getting out of here. Any chance I can come with you?"

Silence ensues for a few seconds before me and Rock both burst out laughing.

Stella immediately bristles. "What's so funny, asshats?"

"You think your old man is gonna let you outta here when we're on lockdown to go to Baton Rouge?" I balk.

"Wait, you're going to Baton Rouge? What for?"

Great, me and my big mouth.

"Nothin'," Rock says. "Mind your business."

She flips Rock the bird. "I meant to go get some clothes. Dad literally threw me and Kai in the car and I was barely able to get anything. It takes work to look like this."

"Don't need to look good for anyone around here," Rock mutters.

"Twenty goin' on forty-five," I agree.

"Why does everyone around here treat me like a little kid?" she whines. "I'm almost legal enough to be in a bar, and a grown adult."

I smirk. "Tell that to your pops. He's the one who'll hunt any one of us down if we let you come with us."

She ignores that completely. "So tell me about Baton Rouge. What's taking you all the way up there?"

Rock glances at me. "You started this, brother."

"Hey, I've got ears." Stella waves her hands. "Stop bein' asswipes and tell me, I'll find out anyway."

"Don't you have somethin' else to be doin'?" I thumb over my shoulder. "Pretty sure Manny's lookin' for someone to help dish up the grub."

She places her hands on her hips. "So right away you try to put my ass in the kitchen?"

"He's one of your best friends." I shrug. "Don't go gettin' all worked up over it."

"Can see where she gets her temper from." Rock smirks.

She shoots daggers his way. "Fine, don't go gettin' your panties in a knot when I tell you what Cale Callaghan told me." She turns to leave, clearly knowing she's got our attention.

Cale Callaghan is one of the detectives always breathing down our necks. The very second he can pin something on this MC, he's here like a dog with a bone.

I frown. "Since when have you been talkin' to Callaghan?"

She shrugs. "He comes by the bakery." I notice the little smile on her lips.

"He's bad news," Rock reminds her before I can. "Don't go tellin' him shit about nothin' to do with this club, Stell, you hear me?"

She sighs loudly. "As if I would. Not dumb, Rock. I know my place around here. At least Indigo treats me with respect, unlike all of you."

"Since when has anyone not treated you with respect?" I'm intrigued now.

"Tag's always telling me off when I try to help. Dad treats me like I'm a teenager with pigtails, and he's always getting Kai to spy on me, even though Kai is younger than me."

"Ever wondered if it's because your pops cares about you?" Rock suggests. "Some kids don't have a parent who gives a shit about what they're doin' or who they're with."

"Great, now you're trying to make me feel bad," she grumbles.

"Stop changin' the subject. Spill what you know." I point at her. "Keepin' shit from us won't sit well around the table."

"You wouldn't, Bronco." Her tone suggests that in fact,

maybe I would, but she isn't quite sure. "That's a bullshit move."

I don't give her an inch. She's Harlem's kid, and she's smart. If there's anyone in this clubhouse able to get information out of a cop, it's her. I also don't want to think about exactly how she got that information. That's Harlem's problem, not mine. "Spill."

"Fine. I saw him downtown and he was asking about the Cut City Boys."

I sit up a little straighter. Stella may not be around the meeting table, but she's got ears, and all the women talk amongst themselves. We're not stupid. "And? What did you tell him?"

"I didn't tell him shit, but he told me to watch my back and don't be going anywhere alone."

"That's awfully chivalrous of him, but that's not groundbreakin'. You got anythin' more, because me and Rock are aging over here and we got shit to do."

"He told me the Cut City Boys were funded by some external organization, or were going to be before the raid," she says.

We both stare at her. Why would Callaghan, a clear enemy of the MC, tell her that?

"What the fuck?" Rock barks. "When did he tell you this?"

"A few days ago."

I give her a chin lift. "Which organization?"

"He didn't say."

Rock glances at me. "Gotta be the Disciples. Bane will know if he hasn't already started diggin'."

"Who are the Disciples?" Stella comes a little closer. "So they're based in Mississippi? Is it a rival MC?"

I shoot Rock a look. Great. Now she's got club business

information ready to share with the rest of the women. "Forget you heard that," I say. "He say anythin' else?"

"Just to be careful. Now that Cut City Boy's reign of terror is over, there's always some new threat to the neighborhood," she goes on.

I fold my arms over my chest. "Why's he so fuckin' interested in tellin' you shit? You shouldn't be talkin' to him."

"You can't tell me who I can and can't talk to, I'm a grown ass adult. He's also a customer, and he was just being nice."

Rock and I both snort. "Right," Rock mumbles.

"Don't tell him shit, Stell, I mean it," I warn her. "He's lookin' for anythin' he can to pin shit on this club, and you know what that means for all of us."

She shoots me an evil glare. "There you go again, treating me like I'm a child. I told you I would never tell him anything, but you attract more bees with honey than you do with vinegar, Bronc."

"I hope you're not givin' him any honey," I throw back. "The guys a first class asswipe, and he's only butterin' you up to see what you know."

"It's lucky I'm good at playing dumb then, isn't it? I love this club, and as nice as Cale is to me, that doesn't mean I'd give him anything. I'm smarter than that. He was clearly letting me know about the organization so I'd tell you, and I'm trying to figure out why he'd do that."

Rock meets my gaze. "She has a point," Rock says. "Question is, why's he stirrin' shit and talkin' to Stella instead of bein' a real man and comin' to the club directly?"

"Because she's a chick and he wants her to do his dirty work, and she won't tell him to fuck off, will you, Stell?"

She pokes her tongue out at me. "I'm not doing dirty work. He seemed genuinely concerned."

"Well, this club is quite capable of lookin' after its

property," Rock mutters. "Would be good to knock that prick on his ass."

"Don't be so awful, he didn't mean any harm," Stella says. "And like I said, if you go around bein' assholes to him, of course he's gonna take issue with every one of us."

I look at her pointedly. "You tell your old man what he said?"

She opens her mouth then closes it again.

"That's what I thought." I smirk. "He'd be pissed, probably ban him from comin' in Sweet Treats."

"It's not my dad's shop, it's Indigo's. The club may have bought in, but she has the majority say, and Indigo doesn't have an issue. I bet I could find out a whole range of things if I really wanted to."

I sigh. "Stella, usin' your looks and your body to get intel isn't what the club wants you to do, so don't be usin' that to try and get prospectin'. It won't work."

Her cheeks flush. "I never said that's what I'm doing!"

I glance over her patent faux leather pants and crop top. "Right."

"Yeah, and I'm sure Callaghan doesn't mind havin' you fawnin' all over him. Probably why he flapped his gums," Rock muses.

"You two are just the worst. I don't even know why I bother telling either of you anything," she huffs. "I thought it would be useful."

"It is useful," I try to soften my tone. We all know Stella is overly sensitive sometimes, and has that fiery Creole heritage, just like her dad. "We just mean don't be lettin' Callaghan drool all over you, or let him sweeten you up for information. At the end of the day, he's a cop. A cop who hates this club with a passion."

She pokes me in the chest. "You know what? Maybe I don't mind him drooling all over me, but just remember one thing. I've got a brain in my head, and I'm not afraid to use it, or show off my body if that's what it takes to get what I need to in order to help protect this club."

"That ain't your job," I say. "While it's appreciated, you don't need to work that shift. You could be puttin' yourself in danger unnecessarily."

"Fuck you, Bronco." She storms off before I can say anything else.

"Fuck," I mutter. "What did I say? She's the one goin' on about fuckin' Callaghan. What's his game plan?"

"Plant the seed, knowing that Stella will come back and tell the club. I don't know what his endgame is, but there's a message in there somewhere," Rock says.

I palm the back of my head. I've got a lot to do tonight, including going to Amber's place to grab some of her and Olive's stuff. Until we have final confirmation that the last of the Cut City Boys are dead, and Bane has control over the Disciples, this will be their new home.

"Too fuckin' right. The man's a dog for tellin' Stella shit. Can't be a man and come and say it himself." I shake my head. We gotta keep an eye on Callaghan because I don't like the feeling I get in my gut. He hates us primarily because we beat him to every single raid. Even when the NOLA Police force got all the credit for getting rid of the mob in New Orleans when Bella's father and uncle were at the helm, when in fact it was the MC, we didn't do shit about it. We were happy to be out of the limelight, and the only reason none of us got arrested was because Callaghan and his cronies couldn't pin it on the club. We did all the dirty work for him, and he gets all the medals.

"Why would he, when he's got a pretty little thing wound around his little finger," Rock replies.

"Yeah, gotta do somethin' about that." I just don't know what yet because I've got bigger fish to fry.

Callaghan issues can wait. First, we gotta go find Erica.

23

BRONCO

I slid out of bed early, ready to get on the road. Amber and Olive were in the room next door, and I couldn't sleep a wink. Even with Titan keeping watch, I was twitchy. I wanted to be with her, hold her, tell her everything was gonna be okay, but I couldn't.

I dress, pull my cut on and my boots, and slip quietly out of the room giving Titan a pat on the head.

"Stay," I whisper. He lays down on his stomach, paws under his chin, his ears prick up as our eyes meet. "Good boy."

I don't even get a few steps down the stairs when I hear her door open. I glance up and our eyes meet.

"Are you going without saying goodbye?" She appears at the top of the stairs as I turn towards her.

"I didn't want to wake you."

She's already in my arms before I even know what's happening. "I hate this."

"It's alright, I promise. I've got some of the guys comin' with me. You've got nothin' to worry about. Titan is stayin' here with you, he'll protect you."

Last night, Cash called a meeting to discuss the game plan

for the lockdown. Since all the Cut City Boys were now dead, officially this time, and Bane called to tell Cash he was on the way to Jackson to find out what the fuck the Disciples were doing, things were looking up.

If Bane can put a lid on things, then there is no more threat to the club or its members, and everyone can go back to life as we know it. Cash was pissed that the cops didn't get all the Cut City Boys during the raid on their compound. Which is just another reason to reiterate why MC club justice works way better than the law. Nothing is long and drawn out — aside from torture when it's needed — and we get shit done without messy, expensive trials with fancy lawyers who just wanna get paid. Their moral compasses don't exactly line up with ours the majority of the time, which is why I think most of the lawyers in this city are scumbags.

"Please be careful," she whispers.

I place a kiss on the top of her head. "I will."

"You still don't have an exact location?"

"No, but all hands are on deck. Rock will be with us, and he can keep in contact with Jett and Star. I'm gonna bring her home, babe. Just look after Olive and I'll be back as quick as I can."

She stares up at me, worry etched in her face with blinking, red eyes and puffy cheeks. "I love you. I'm sorry I didn't say it sooner."

I brush a knuckle over her cheek. "We may not have said it, but we both felt it."

"Yes, we did. That's what matters."

I press my lips to hers. "I love you, too. When I get back, we're goin' on a real date."

She laughs softly against my lips. "Was the Pelican's game not a real date?"

"Nope. I was a stand-in for fuckin' Ben. Have you deleted him from that app?"

"He wasn't on an app. We were texting, and I've already let him know I've met someone."

"Good, now you can delete his number." I deepen the kiss. "You're mine."

"Yes."

"My ol' lady."

"Are you asking to claim me, or just doing it?" she asks.

"Just doin' it because that's how it is between us. We don't need to put on pretenses, *Princess*. We know what we have."

"You know you could be a poet."

I snort. "Behave yourself. I'll call you later."

"Okay."

"I love you," I say again.

"Right back at ya, Bronco."

I reluctantly let her go, going half-way down the stairs before I turn around. Amber is still standing there in her pajamas, looking down at me. I blow her a kiss. "Wait for me."

"Always." She blows a kiss back.

I leave without looking back. If I see her sad face one more time, I'll turn around and drag her to my room and then I won't be going anywhere. I can't get distracted because we have a woman to find before anything bad happens to her, and time is of the essence.

24 hours later

They say finding a missing person is like looking for a needle in a haystack, but those people don't have a PI who can get blood out of a stone, and two hackers who are the best in the business. Erica had been zigzagging, and then finally, Star got a hit on her cell phone. Since she only seems to turn it on when she needs it, getting any kind of trace from that has been impossible up until now.

We've been keeping a base at the Baton Rouge Holiday Inn, working between the locations bouncing off Erica's cell, and her bank records.

"You know desperate people do desperate things," Ryder says as we wait in the lot for Rock and Pipes to finish fueling up.

"Know it. Just fuckin' hope the Olgettis didn't get to her before we do. She's still on the move, so that's a good sign, but if she's running around all over the city, then she's scared out of her mind, and I would be too."

"How's Olive been takin' things?"

I shrug. "She's got questions that we can't answer, but she's doin' good in school and makin' friends. Amber can't run with the 'mom had to go away for work excuse' for much longer, and Olive isn't stupid. She knows something's up."

"Poor kid. Not easy on her, or on Amber."

"She's takin' it well, but if anythin' happens... Erica is like a sister to her, they're close. It'll devastate her if we don't get her back."

"We will," he promises. "We're close."

Cash agreed to settle the debt until Erica can pay the club back. It's only because of Amber. She's been an integral part of the MC with her loyalty and work ethic. It's a lot of money, but it's not worth losing a life over. The most important thing right now is getting Erica back and her being able to start over. I want that for her and Olive, and for Amber.

With the news that the flames have been put out in New Orleans where the Cut City Boys are concerned, and with the cops now involved in sniffing out the Disciples, they've scurried back to Mississippi where Bane will be waiting. Of course, it's a good enough excuse for Bane and the MC to start a new beef with the Skeletons for letting it get this far, but that's on them to figure out. As long as they stay out of NOLA then we don't have to intervene.

The fact that we came so close to another threat wreaking havoc, tells the entire club and our allies we need to tighten our belts. That fight is for another day.

I call Amber while I have a few moments before we head out.

"Bronco, are you okay?" are the first words out of her mouth.

"I'm fine, *Princess*. What about you? How's everything goin' there?"

"Everything's good," she says. "Just been keeping myself busy, waiting to hear from you."

"I know, babe, and we're close, I promise."

I hear the fear in her voice. "You've done so much for me and for Erica and Olive, heck, this entire club, and she has no idea you're coming for her."

"Don't get all choked up. You know I'll turn this sled around and come find you if you do."

"We can't have that."

"No, we can't. How's Olive?" Even though I only left Amber last night, I still want to know.

"She's fine. She was happy to have a day off school to play with her friends."

"That's one bonus about bein' stuck there, I guess."

"Titan has been following her around like a hawk," she says. "I think he's attached."

I smile, but sober quickly. "He's a good boy."

"Please be careful," she whispers.

"Always am." I hear the straight pipes fire up behind us as Rock and Pipes climb onto their sled's. "I gotta run."

"Be safe, I mean it."

"I love you, AJ."

"I love you, too."

We hang up and I smile at my phone.

"What in the fuck?" Ryder's gaping at me. "When did this happen?"

I shrug. "It happened."

"You claimin' her?"

"When I get back, yeah."

He smirks. "Does she know that?"

"Yep, and she wants it. Nothin' like seein' your ol' lady wearin' your club colors."

"Another one bites the dust," Ryder laughs.

"It'll be that much sweeter when I'm back in my ol' lady's arms."

"Won't be long now. Gonna check out that lead Jett texted over earlier, could be goin' home sooner than we think," he says.

"Fuckin' hope so."

"We good?" Rock sidles up next to us.

I nod. "Let's ride."

Another 24 hours pass before we get anywhere. It's late when Jett calls and tells us to check out a motel on the outskirts of the city. It might be our lucky break. The boys have all seen the most recent headshot of Erica, so they know what she looks like.

Ryder and I step into the small reception. It's a shit hole. The musty smell that greets us tells me this place is in dire need of a decent clean. The curtains are raggy and barely hanging on by a thread. It stinks like smoke, too, and the carpet has probably seen more traffic than Baton Rouge itself.

There's a tiny woman behind the desk who looks like

she's seen better days. She's missing a few teeth, has a cigarette tucked behind her ear, and still has her hair curlers in.

"Evenin'." I give her a curt nod.

"How can I help you boys?" Her southern twang, mixed with the hoarse smoker's cough that follows, rattles around the room.

"Here to find someone." I hold up a picture of Erica. "Name's Erica Maxwell, she checked in today."

The woman doesn't even glance at the photo. "You lookin' for a room?"

"Nope, just some answers," Ryder says.

She coughs a laugh. "Well, answers cost money. You ain't in Kansas anymore, boys."

I glance at Ryder as his eyebrows shoot up. "You done this before, sweetheart?"

She turns her smirk over to him. "Who's askin', pretty boy?"

I roll my lips, dying to laugh, but instead I slide a fifty over the counter. "We're askin'."

She glances at the patch on my cut. "New Orleans, huh? My third ex-husband lived there, ran a strip joint. Was a goddamn fuckin' snake pit. The asshole probably drank himself into an early grave, if the juice didn't get him first."

"She here?" I wave the photo again.

"Yeah, she's here."

Relief floods through me. "Which room?"

She glances down at the book in front of her. The motel doesn't even have a computer. It's like we've stepped back in time. "Well, that kind of information is gonna cost you pretty pair a little more. I got bills to pay, and Baton Rouge ain't cheap these days."

Ryder pinches the bridge of his nose. This old bird is fuckin' fearless, I'll give her that. She didn't even blink at our

MC cuts, or the fact she's about four-foot-nine and we tower over her.

I slide another fifty across, but this time keep my hand on it. "Room number, darlin'."

She smiles, showing a toothy grin that almost makes me shudder. "One twelve, honey."

I give her a pointed look. "Gonna need me a key."

She turns without hesitation, grabbing a spare off the hook. "Don't forget to lock up when you're done, and don't take anything big."

It occurs to me that she doesn't give a shit who we are, or what we're about to possibly do to this woman, and that makes me fuckin' mad.

Ryder taps me on the shoulder as he leaves. "Let's go."

"If she's not home, there's a diner next door, open until late," she adds.

I nod, unable to thank her because she's a fuckin' scumbag, and I follow Ryder out. Leaving Pipes with our rides, we make our way up a flight of stairs toward her room.

I don't even bother knocking; it's not like we're pretending to be room service, or housekeeping. Expecting a kerfuffle, I switch the lock with ease and push the door open. It's quiet inside. There's a bedside lamp on, only highlighting what must be the worst motel room I've ever seen. The carpet in here is worse than the one downstairs, and it has that same musty, damp smell that has gotta have mold hidden in the walls.

There's nobody in the room, but there's a large bag on the bed, and a couple of boxes on the floor.

I slide the bathroom door open with my foot, but there's nobody in there.

"Jesus," Ryder says behind me, pulling his bandana up over his mouth and nose.

"Gonna need disinfectin' when we get back to the Holiday

Inn." Those are not words I expected to ever come out of my mouth. "Gotta check the diner," I say, rifling through the contents of the bag. There's mainly women's clothing, a book, a notebook, and a smaller bag containing bathroom items.

Aside from that, the motel room isn't somewhere Erica is going to call home for very much longer.

We head out of the room, back down the stairs and make our way to the front of the building. It's late, and when we head toward the neon flashing sign, there's only a couple of cars in the lot out front. The diner, as expected, isn't doing a massive trade at this time of night. There's two people sitting at the counter, talking to the waitress, then a couple sitting at one of the booths. Two other tables are occupied.

"Well, hello there, gentleman," the waitress coos, leaving her conversation to look us up and down. "What can I get y'all?"

I give her my sweetest smile. "Just coffee, darlin'."

"Comin' right up."

I glance around, spotting a woman with blonde, shoulder length hair with her back to us in one of the booths. It's gotta be her. I signal to the others I'm going ahead, Ryder next to me. I walk towards her.

Before I even arrive at the table, she glances over her shoulder and our eyes meet.

Well I'll be damned.

Fucking Erica.

I'm next to her before she can even react, blocking her exit as Ryder slides into the seat opposite her. I follow suit as Rock stands a few feet away, and Pipes guards the door. If the waitress is suspicious of us accosting this woman, she doesn't do shit. I don't rate the sense of security around here, or how everyone just looks the other way.

"No," Erica whispers. "I have more time. *Please.* You said I had more time."

"Erica," I say. "This isn't what you thi—"

She tugs on the lapels of my cut. "I'm begging you. I'll get the money. I have a daughter, I have to get back to her." Tears are already streaming down her throat. "I had a life, a pretty good life..." She starts to sob and Ryder looks over my shoulder as the couple a few tables away glance over.

"We're not here to kill you," I say.

"No? Then why did they send four of you?"

"Who's they?"

"The men I owe money to."

"The Olgettis?"

She turns her gaze on me, her desperation turning to anger. "If you already know the answer, why are you even asking?"

"We know everything, Erica. Amber sent us."

Her mouth opens, then closes again. "Amber?"

I nod.

"They've got Amber, oh my God! What about Olive, you bastards!" Her hand comes up to slap me, and I stop it mid-air.

"Fuck," Ryder hisses.

"Calm down, woman!" I whisper-shout. "You wanna get us all arrested?"

"Everythin' okay here?" The waitress suddenly appears, eyeing us cautiously. Maybe I discredited her too soon. She's staring at Erica. "Do you know these men, honey?"

"I... my... yes, it's fine." She smiles weakly and I don't think the waitress believes us, but she places the coffees on the table.

I reach into my wallet, pull out fifty bucks and hand it to her. "For your trouble."

She doesn't hesitate, tucking it into her bra under her uniform. "Well, y'all enjoy your coffee, there's plenty more where that came from."

Ryder rolls his eyes as I turn back to Erica. "Not lyin', and she's about half a second away from callin' the cops." I pull my phone out and dial Amber. "Here."

I hand her the phone as she wipes her tears, pressing the phone to her ear. Then, "Amber?" Fresh tears lace her eyes as she listens down the phone. "Yes, it's me, I'm... I'm here with some bikers—"

"Bronco," I mouth, pointing to my name on my cut at the left breast pocket.

"He says his name is Bronco. No, I... Amber, I don't know where to start... I know that... I know, but you don't understand. These men are dangerous, they threatened to kill everyone I love... Please, I'll explain, I promise." She starts to cry again and shoves the phone back at me.

"Babe?" I glance at Ryder who hands Erica a bunch of napkins. She takes them gratefully, wiping her eyes and blowing her nose.

"I... oh my God, Bronc, you did it. You found her." I can barely understand her through the tears. "I can't believe it."

"Sit tight. We're gonna leave first thing in the morning. She can ride with me."

"How is she?"

I glance over Erica once more. "She's fine. Shaken up, but she's alright, *Princess*. Gonna bring her home." Psychologically, I'm not so sure, but she's here and she's alive, that's all that matters.

"I can't even explain in words how grateful I am," Amber starts. "Truly."

"You can show me when I get back," I quip. "Get some rest, I'll call you first thing."

"I love you. Ride safe."

"Love you, too. We'll be fine."

I hang up and Erica stares at me. "Do you love each other?"

I run a hand through my hair. "It's a long story. We gotta get outta here, not sure if you remember but you're being hunted."

"I know. They gave me till Sunday, but I didn't believe them."

I turn to face her. "Right now, you gotta trust me. We're gonna fix this, but I need you to not do anythin' stupid. The longer we sit here debatin', the more danger you're puttin' yourself in."

She shakes her head. "I won't fight. I promise I won't."

"Good, because I've had about as much of Baton Rouge as I can stand." I contemplate leaving tonight, but the brothers are tired. We've been out all day. I can get another room with twin beds, watch Erica, and be on the way to New Orleans in the morning.

Ryder stands, taking a swill of coffee. He winces and slides out from the booth. "Gonna ride with me," I tell Erica, holding onto her arm as she grabs her bag. "Can go grab your shit from the motel, but we ain't got much room."

"I just need my things," she says. "Where are we going?"

"To the Holiday Inn." I tip my head to the waitress as she finger waves. I think the fifty bucks did the trick because there aren't any cops in sight. "I'll take you to see Amber and Olive at first light."

Once we're outside she turns to me, then flings herself into my arms. "You're an angel, Bronco, all of you—"

I let her hug me, knowing this woman has been to Hell and back. "It's gonna be okay. Amber's been lookin' for you, and I gotta tell you, woman, you better have a damn good explanation for why you left without tellin' her shit. She's been worried sick."

"I panicked," she whispers, her voice ragged. She's a wreck. "I didn't want any harm to come to Amber and Olive. Amber has already done so much for me."

"She loves you, and you're her family, but if you pull a fuckin' stunt like that again and hurt her, you're gonna have worse problems to worry about than the Olgettis, you got me?"

She glances up, her mouth opening and closing. "I... I understand."

"Good. C'mon. Let's get you something decent to eat and pretend this conversation never happened."

I need to get back to my girl.

24

AMBER

I stare at the phone. It's almost 2 am and I'm still in a daze.

He found her. He really fucking found her.

Bronco sounded tired, but also relieved. To hear Erica's voice... it meant the world to me. Sure, I'm mad as fuck at her, but I also love her so much that I couldn't yell. Not yet, anyway. When she gets back, there will be plenty to say.

I brace myself to talk to Olive, ready to explain that her mom is coming back today, and that everything is going to be okay from here on in. Erica can start a new life here with Olive; it's what she wanted to do before all this mess took over our lives.

I sink back against the island, relief flooding through me. A few moments later, I feel a wet nose nudge my leg. Looking down, Titan's sweet face peers up at me. He looks as perplexed as a dog ever could, the concern I see in his big brown eyes is unnerving. "Good boy," I whisper. "Such a good boy."

He nuzzles his head into my hand as I scratch him behind the ears, easing his tension. He mewls in contentment, and it's as if he really does feel all the angst around him. After a few moments, he flops at my feet, yawning like he's done a good job.

I owe so much to Bronco and to the club, and I know I can never repay it, but I'll do everything in my power to make sure the money is not only paid back with interest, but that Erica stays on the straight and narrow from now on. No more loan sharks, and no more running away trying to fix a bad situation only to make it worse.

I wish I could talk to Abigail about this, but it's a lot for someone in the MC to deal with, and I don't want her involved. She obviously knows I work for the Rebels, and often teases me about the hot bikers. If only it were that simple.

My mind brings me back to the present moment; I shudder at the thought of what Erica has been through, but also what she's put me through worrying about her. I've shielded Olive for most of it, but she's becoming more curious with her questions, and the kid isn't dumb. I never wanted Olive to be burdened with the actual truth, and it's been searing a hole in my heart as big as Texas. We always said we would never have any lies between us, and Erica broke that. I know it'll take some time to forgive her, but I also understand running. We've done it before, and when you're scared, you do things without thinking. I just wish she'd have come to me. This whole mess could've been sorted out.

I sigh, knowing that I need to get some rest. Olive has to be up for school, and I'm even contemplating letting her stay back today depending on when Bronco sets off. Cash made it clear that although the coast is clear now with Cut City Boys, we have to stay put until he gives the go ahead to go home. I'm assuming that'll be when Bronco comes back. As the MC Prez, it's his job to make sure everyone is protected under his roof. I get that, and as much as I want to go home and sleep in my own bed, I'm not going to make a fuss. The club has already gone above and beyond for me in ways that I could never dream of. So staying here a little while longer isn't an issue. Now that we have Bronco and Erica returning, my heart could sing with joy.

I came down to the kitchen to get a glass of water after Bronco's call. My throat is dry and hoarse from the crying jag I had just earlier. I tiptoe back up the stairs to bed, with Titan on my heels, and sleep finds me swiftly. I just can't wait for the morning light so Olive can be reunited with her mom again. It's all I've wanted for these last few weeks, and I can't wait for her to be back where she belongs: with her family.

I end up taking Olive to school the next morning. Of course, Titan rides with us because there is no keeping him at the clubhouse. Since Bronco won't be back until lunchtime, I want to get my house in some sort of order ready for Erica's return. Cash insisted that one of the prospects go with me, but since they're off doing other errands, the only other brother available is one of the Nomad Brothers. Brew, to be precise.

He's the broodiest, quietest biker in the entire MC, and while I don't feel uncomfortable with him, it feels kinda awkward when he folds himself into my SUV, pushing the seat back because he's so huge, and taking up all of the room in the front seat.

Olive chats the entire way to school, patting Titan's head as she rambles, and occasionally Brew gives her one or two word replies if she asks him something. Clearly this man has never been around kids before, but at least he tries.

After giving Titan a pat, Olive skips off happily through the gates, meeting up with Cami as she waves goodbye.

I climb back in my vehicle, waiting for Brew because he

stepped out. I've gotta hand it to the guy, he takes the job seriously.

"Is everything okay?" I ask when he climbs back in.

"Drive."

Okaaay then.

I've been serving Brew drinks for years, and I've barely talked to the man. Well, he's not the most verbose dude on the planet, clearly, but he does have something about him that I can't explain. It's like you feel 100% safe in his vicinity, while not wanting to get on his bad side at the same time.

He's acting a little on edge, and I don't know if that's something to be concerned about. Then again, this is Brew we're talking about. He's always on edge.

"So, are you back in town for a little while?" I don't know why I feel the need to make small talk, but it just blurts out of my mouth. He and his brother are nicknamed the Nomad Brothers for a reason.

"Depends."

"On what?"

He stares out of the front window, his jaw tight. "Shit."

"That's descriptive."

"You ask a lot of questions, like your niece."

"Just making conversation," I sing. "I realize talking is optional, but silence is just weird."

"I find it therapeutic."

I roll my lips. So he'd prefer silence. Okey-dokey then.

I keep driving, my thoughts running haywire about Bronco and where he is. He texted me early this morning to say they were fueling up at around ten, and they would only be a couple of hours away. The guys had gone a few nights with lack of sleep, so he didn't want to wake them early. Erica had crashed hard, but now she's riding back with Bronco.

"Sorry about the babysitting job," I offer a few minutes later. The silence is deafening and just feels weird.

"It's my job. I do what Cash says."

"Still, I'm sure you have better things to do."

I see him tilt his head in my periphery but I keep my eyes on the road. "Protectin' club property is important."

Oh, I'm Broncos unofficial ol' lady now, so I guess everyone knows. I don't make an argument about people being property, I know that it's just their way of making sure everyone is protected. "From what, though? The threat is over, right? Aren't all the Cut City Boys all dealt with now? And those Disciple people?"

"You know a lot about shit you shouldn't."

"I have ears, Brew, and I'm not stupid."

He turns to look out the window once more, muttering, "I don't make the rules. I just follow what Prez says. Conversation over."

Glad we had this talk.

When I finally pull up into the driveway, I'm ready to clean my house and change the sheets. I also need to do some laundry since we've been holed up at the clubhouse for the last three days.

To my surprise, Brew helps me lug two bags of our stuff into the house. I didn't expect him to be chivalrous, but it was a nice surprise. Titan follows us dutifully.

"If you like, I can leave the game on from last night?" I suggest when we're inside.

He gives me a chin lift, looking around the small space. "Got any coffee?"

"Uh, sure."

He takes a seat on my couch and I switch the kettle on, heading to the laundry room to start the first load. Titan sniffs around before folding his body in the middle of the hallway between the living room and the laundry, sighing as if that trip to school wore him out.

My house isn't that bad, but I definitely want new sheets on the spare bed, and I need to go to the grocery store later.

I can hear Brew switching channels on the TV and roll my eyes. Of course he's been here five seconds and he's the king of the remote control. Typical.

I strip the spare bed where Olive has been sleeping, pile that up in the laundry and make the bed with fresh sheets. By the time that's done, I make Brew a coffee.

"Sugar and cream?"

"Yep."

"Both?"

"Uh, huh."

"A little sugar or a lot?"

"A lot."

A simple please wouldn't go astray.

I make it, and one for myself with less sweetener, and walk into the lounge. He's got the news on, something I never watch at home because it's way too depressing.

When I glance up at the screen, I almost drop his cup. Titan jumps up immediately, running toward me. His ears are forward, his tail straight and he lets out a questioning mewl.

"Reports say the church named The Kingdom of Faith was purchased back in 2010, set on one-hundred acres, and was fully self-sufficient, luring members to its sect with promises of peace and religious freedom within the walls of the church," the reporter on the screen says. "What we now know is this organization was a coverup for exploitation of women and minors, unlawful acts and deprivation of liberties. One of the cult leaders, Steven Gallows, is tonight in custody charged with several varying offences from kidnapping to child imprisonment. Vincent Mead is still at large—"

"Oh, my God." The cup wobbles and I barely keep hold of it before Brew is standing, taking the cup from my hands,

Titan by my side. I mindlessly touch the top of his head, letting him know I'm not in danger.

"What's wrong? You know that fucker?"

I stand, frozen, staring at the screen as the woman keeps talking. I can't even hear what she's saying, but the caption on the TV reads: Illinois Cult Leader Caught. Another Founder On The Run. Links to Human Trafficking.

My legs wobble and Brew is steering me back to the couch and telling me to breathe. Titan sticks by me like glue, nudging me on the shin with his nose. His concern is so endearing. He's so much like his daddy.

"Ex," I try and whisper, but I don't even know if any words come out. "He's my ex—"

"Just breathe." Brew's dialing somebody, barking something into the phone about turning the TV on and recalling The Kingdom of Faith to whoever he's shouting at. He hangs up, then turns to me. "You got a history with assholes?"

I nod.

"Did you escape this cult?"

I nod again.

"Does he know where you are?"

I shake my head.

Brew scratches his chin. "If he's into organized crime and traffickin', there's every chance that he may be more equipped with technology than you think."

"We never had computers."

"They just seized a whole roomful of devices." Brew's words shock me. We weren't allowed any technology or mobile phones. They were strictly forbidden.

"What? We never had anything like that..."

"Had a whole operation. Now that fucker, your ex, he's on the run, not like he's gonna get far."

My skin prickles. "How long has he been missing?"

"News said five days or so."

I feel uneasy. I know Vince has no idea where I am, but that doesn't make this any easier.

He's out there somewhere. It's typical that Vince would run like the coward he is. I hope he rots in fucking Hell.

"Holy shit."

"This got anythin' to do with your sister-in-law's disappearance?"

I shake my head. "No. Completely unrelated."

Brew looks unimpressed, and it's the first time I've noticed he's shoved off his cut and is wearing a holster. Two guns either side of his chest look about as menacing as him.

"Well, let's just hope he doesn't even think about stopping here anytime soon." His eyes meet mine. "I don't miss."

I'm still sitting, trying to get my head around all of this. Titan makes a noise and I kiss the top of his head. I want to call Bronco, but I know he'll be riding and he'll think something's wrong if he gets a missed call. I mean, something is wrong, but that's not the point.

"I believe you."

"Any chance at all you think he'd try and find you?"

"For revenge before he goes to jail?" I hug myself. "Absolutely."

"Fuck."

"Though, I don't know where he'd start looki—"

"They had an elaborate set up, you'd be surprised what these fuckers can find out with very little information."

"I'm not even on social media," I whisper. "There's no way."

"Still. This ain't good."

"Did you tell Cash?"

"Not yet. I told my brother, he's gonna tell him and then we're gonna find the fucker before the cops do."

I frown. "But you don't even know him."

He stares at me. "You saw what he did to those women and children. I'm guessin' he did that to you, too? Took you against your will?"

I can barely get any words out when I say, "Yes, I had no choice. I was a child. My brother was supposed to take care of me."

A few moments go by, and I see the concern in his eyes. Maybe a little for me, and all those people he doesn't even know. Then it clicks. Bronco told me something years ago about Brew. He had a woman, and he lost her. She died because she was trafficked. He was never able to find her.

"You're a good guy," I say, not exactly sure why I say it out loud.

He snorts. "Why'd you say that?"

"Because I know you are. I can sense it."

His nostrils flare. "I hope they all burn in Hell."

"They will." I squeeze his forearm. He looks down at my hand. It's like he's unable to fathom human touch or something. "Good will always trump evil, every single time."

"What about those that don't live to tell the tale? Where do they go?"

"I'm sorry," I breathe. "About your..." I can't even bring myself to say the words.

Brew is one of the toughest, meanest men I know, yet he's standing here in my tiny house, looking like he wants to take on the world. "It was a long time ago." He looks away for a long moment, then comes back to glare at me.

"You'll see her again."

"In Heaven?" He snorts. "You really think there's a happily ever after for people like me? Let me tell you, Amber, there isn't, and you know what else? I like killing. I actually fuckin' enjoy hurtin' people who hurt others."

His words should shock me, but they don't.

"Vigilante justice?"

He nods. "Somethin' like that."

"Is that why you're in and out of the MC?" Even Bronco hasn't told me the whole story, but I got the general gist of it.

"There's always work to be done somewhere." It's almost like he's pissed that he wasn't part of this take down. All the way over in Illinois with people he doesn't even know.

"I agree. Scum of the earth are everywhere."

His deep, green eyes look pained. So much so, I have to look away. This man is strangely soulful in ways I never expected. "You've no idea."

Titan sounds off a loud bark right before a commotion at the door. I jump, and in a split second, Brew pushes me back into the couch and has a gun raised, pointed in front of him with both hands. Titan runs toward the front door faster than I can blink. *Holy shit, that was fast.*

Brew walks slowly to the edge of the loungeroom, and I swear to fucking God he's about to shoot when we hear:

"Amber? It's me!" Bronco yells through the house. Titan's bark gets louder as I hear Bronco greet his dog. Then, probably seeing Brew's gun pointed at him, I hear, "Holy fuckin' shit, Brew!"

"Sorry man." Brew lowers his piece. "Shit's just gone down, had me on edge."

"What shit?" I hear his heavy boots on the wooden floors before I see him.

"With the cult," he says it like he already knew about them.

Then it clicks. Did Bronco have something to do with this? I know he was overly interested in the tattoo on my wrist and where it originated.

"What the fuck?" And then he appears. Pushing past Brew, he reaches for me and I dive into his arms.

"Oh, I missed you so much." I'm a babbling mess.

"Vincent escaped from the compound, the feds raided it, and... and they found stuff, and Steven is in jail."

"Slow down." He kisses me on the forehead. "We'll get to that in a second, okay?"

I look past him and my eyes brim with tears. Erica's standing there, Ryder behind her as her hands fly up to her face.

She's in my arms in two steps when I cross the floor to get to her. We embrace and the tears fall freely. "Don't you ever do that to me ever again," I scold.

"I'm sorry," she whimpers. "I was in a lot of trouble."

"I know, but that's no reason to go AWOL on us. You could've been killed, Erica. You didn't think. What about Olive? What if you'd been killed?"

"I'm sorry. I had to get out of town. When they tracked me in Louisiana, I had to lead them away from New Orleans. I didn't want any of them knowing about you, or about Olive. If there was any other way—"

"We'll talk about this later." I pull back, holding her at arm's length. "I'm so glad you're back. Why didn't you call from a payphone?"

"Trust me, I wanted to. I was scared, Amber. You don't know these people, what they're capable of." She glances up at Bronco. "Then my saviors rolled up into the diner, and I thought they were there to kill me."

"Lucky you got us and not the Olgettis," Ryder mumbles from behind.

Tears leak from Erica's eyes. "I'm so grateful, Amber, for everything. I promise I'll never do something like this again."

I nod. Unable to say any more because I'm still mad, but also relieved. Then I have to break the news about Vincent and Steven.

"So, I just saw the Kingdom of Faith have been raided," I whisper. "You'd better come and sit down for this."

We move over to the couch, the boys hovering between the open space of the lounge and the kitchen. Titan settling himself at Bronco's feet. I swear Brew is pissed he didn't get to shoot someone.

"What the heck? He escaped?" Erica gapes.

"He won't be comin' here," Bronco assures us. "For one, he's not that smart, and two, if he does know where you are, he'll have to get past me and the rest of the club before anythin' happens."

I turn to Bronco. "Did you have something to do with the raid?"

He stares back at me. "Club business, babe."

Translation: *Oh, we're gonna talk about this later. You bet your ass we are.*

My head spins. Underworld figures. Erica being chased. Cults. Exes who want revenge. My brother being arrested and charged with a string of offenses. Could anything else possibly happen?

Bronco sits next to me on the couch, his hand reaching for mine. Titan drops down on the floor beside us.

"Thank you," I say. "For finding her. To all of you."

"Wasn't that hard, but if she stayed in one place for longer, it would've been easier."

Erica's eyes cloud over when she says, "I learned how to run from the best."

I clutch her hand with my free one, smiling even though we're both crying. "Don't ever leave me again. Whatever happens, we're sisters. And yes, I'm still mad at you."

"I'll make it up to you," she whispers.

"You don't have to do that. You just have to be honest with me. Olive will be so excited, I didn't even say anything because I wanted it to be a surprise."

"Could I come with you? To the school pick up?"

I squeeze her hand. "She's your daughter, of course you can."

For the first time in a long time, my heart feels lighter. Even though the madness hasn't quite ended yet, I know that no matter what, we will always fight for what is right. I will never just sit down and take anything. I vowed that to myself when I fled that awful place. I can only hope the cops catch up with Vincent before the MC do. Judging by the look on Brew's still scowling face, I'm betting he hopes the MC definitely gets involved in capturing him.

"Welcome home," I whisper.

Erica smiles. "I'm glad to be home, finally."

25

BRONCO

The light that lit up in Amber's eyes when she saw us makes me never want to up and leave her again. It's a miracle we got to Erica when we did. I mean, how long was she planning on running for? The Olgettis may have given her an extension on paying back the money, but I don't believe it. When these lowlifes want something, they take it. They don't ask. They don't bargain. They sure as shit don't give you extra time.

Now that Vincent is on the run, it can't be long until the law catches up with him. Until that happens, Amber won't be let out of my sight. Yeah, it was me who tipped off the feds, but little did I know that they were already building a case. I didn't tell them shit about Amber, and if she wants to tell her story, or testify against her brother — and Vincent when he's caught — then that's up to her. But they had to be stopped.

Amber looked destroyed when she found out the depths of their network. She had no idea they were involved in any kind of trafficking, and then luring women into the sect to do with whatever they wanted. Well, they won't be doing that from a jail cell.

"Mom! Mom!" Olive calls when she sees her mother and Amber waiting at the gate.

Erica sweeps Olive up into her arms and pulls her close to her chest, kissing her as she cries into her hair. "I'm back, baby. I'm back for good."

"I missed you." Olive clutches her, unwilling to let go. "I'm so glad you're back, Mom."

I get a lump in my throat watching them. I'll never understand why the fuck she did what she did, but that's water under the bridge now.

Jett made the transfer to the Olgettis with interest, and Erica is now under the protection of the MC. As far as the Olgettis in Chicago know, she's indebted to us.

Crystal and Deanna said they'd help Erica with a job in New Orleans, and there are plenty of teacher's aide jobs in the city. Jasmyne said she could do with a new assistant if that didn't pan out because Luna's too busy now with juggling the books at Rock's and Hustler's. Either way, Erica has options.

Amber hugs Olive too, wiping her eyes as Olive talks excitedly about what they've been up to this past month. It's all taken its toll on Amber. I want to take her away for a weekend, get her away from all of this once Erica is settled in. We've also still got that tattoo to take care of.

I look down at Titan. He's begging to go greet Olive, and when she gets closer and sees him, she sprints our way. I let go of his leash and he runs to her, half-jumping and licking her excitedly. She giggles, petting his head like they haven't seen each other in eons, when it was only this morning. I left Titan at the clubhouse while I was away because he knows everyone there, and he didn't leave his spot outside on the landing, right near my room, the entire time. Okay, he did escort the girls to school, but at least he listened when I told him to protect them. He's a good dog. Tough on the outside, but soft in the middle.

Amber wraps her arms around my neck, breaking me out of my reverie. She kisses me chastely on the lips. "Hey daydreamer."

I smile. "Happy?"

"Extremely."

"Let's go home."

She looks up at me. "Hey, I was thinking."

"Uh, oh."

She tightens her hold around my neck. "Wise ass."

"Whenever you think, I gotta brace for impact."

"That's so mean!"

I grab her ass and squeeze it, and she yelps, looking around to see if anyone saw. They didn't, and Olive and her mom are too wrapped up in each other to care what we're doing. There's only Titan at my side, looking up at us like he just remembered he's my dog.

"Titan doesn't think so, do you, boy?"

He barks loudly in response and we laugh.

Amber reaches down to scratch his head. "I wondered if I might impose on you."

I waggle my eyebrows and lower my voice. "Does this involve you sittin' on my face?"

She scowls. "Stop it! Be serious!"

I bump her with my hips as she tries to keep up the pretense of being mad, but she eventually gives up and her fake frown relaxes. "Sorry, go on."

"Well, once Erica is settled in, I wondered if I could bunk with you some of the time, give her some space. My house is pretty small—"

"Why don't you just move in?"

She stares at me. "Permanently?"

"Yup. I'm up for it if you are, but fair warning, there's still only one bed."

"You're the worst fake boyfriend I've ever had."

My lips turn up. "Glad to hear it, because you won't be tryin' out anyone else."

"Getting all growly on me now?"

"When was I not?"

"Fair point." She smiles against my lips. "You're pretty hot when you're growly."

"Speakin' of growling men, saw Brew went alpha on your ass."

"Oh man, that dude is something else." I lower my voice. "You should have seen him when the subject of trafficking came up."

"Yeah, babe, it's a sore spot."

"I can see why."

I take a breath, the vision of losing Amber in any way rattles my bones. I can't relate to Brew because I'd lose my mind if anything ever happened to her. "He's never forgiven himself."

Her eyes soften. "It's just awful."

"Life is pretty awful to a lot of people, but we gotta keep movin' forward."

She snuggles into my chest. "I know, but for a little while, I'd like to just live in our little bubble."

"That can be arranged. So when are you gonna move in?"

"When Erica is settled and feels safe again."

I kiss her on top of her head. "Whatever you say, *Princess.*"

"Are you guys gonna make out all afternoon or are we gonna get goin'?" Pipes rolls his eyes. I forgot he'd followed us, just to be on the safe side until Vincent is behind bars. Ryder and Rock head back to the clubhouse to report back to Cash.

"You got somewhere to be?" I quiz, looking over Amber's shoulder.

"Need a shower. Been ridin' for three days," he replies, giving me an unimpressed frown.

"Quit whinin' like a little bitch." I flip him the bird for good measure.

"We should get moving," Amber sighs. "I still have to finish the housework."

Cash agreed we could leave the clubhouse, but only under my protection, and that includes Titan and a prospect keeping watch until Vincent is caught. Nobody is taking any chances.

"We'll go back to the clubhouse first, grab your stuff and head back there. It'll give Erica and Olive more time to catch up," I say.

"There you go, getting all logical on me." She rubs her nose with mine and I hear Pipes make a pretend choking noise.

I ignore him, kissing Amber again as I flip him the bird behind my back, just in case he missed it the first time.

"You fell in love with my brain first, and my sense of humor," I remind her.

"How do you know that?" She leans in close to my ear and whispers, "Maybe I just wanted your dick all along."

I growl. "You'll be gettin' plenty of that, babe. Glad you're well rested."

She walks backwards and I hate letting her go, but I gotta drive the girls back to the clubhouse.

Once they're all seated inside, including Titan, I give Pipes a chin lift as he smirks.

"Another one bites the dust."

I shake my head, shoving him in the shoulder. "Just you wait."

"Nope, not gettin' snagged."

"You say that now," I mock. "But you wait and see."

Pipes pretends to play the violin and I make my way back to the driver's side, tempted to punch him in the fucking nose if he keeps it up. Yeah, I guess I am a sap for my ol' lady, and if that makes me a statistic, I'm more than okay with that.

I turn my head. "We good?"

Amber rests her hand on mine as I get the thumbs up from the backseat. "Yep, we're good!" Olive sing-songs with Titan at her feet.

I look at Amber. "You?"

"I'm perfect, Bronco." *I love you,* she mouths.

I love you, too, I mouth back.

It's been a roller coaster, but life is pretty sweet. It'll be even sweeter if I can squeeze the life out of that prick Vincent, but I'm sure he's too busy running from the law to bother finding his ex-wife and seeking revenge. If he does, I'll be waiting for him.

"Fuck, baby." I slide in and out of my ol' lady's slick pussy and grip the pillows beside her head. I'm gonna combust, but that'll be embarrassingly fast. We gotta be quiet because of the visitors down the hall, but the way she's squeezing my ass, begging me for more is making drawing this out extremely difficult.

"So good," she whispers. "More, Bronco, don't hold back."

I'm ramming her as hard as I can into the mattress and she's begging me for more. *Goddamn.*

I circle my hips in the way she loves and she tightens her grip on my ass. "Not holdin' back, baby. You just love my cock way too much."

"Not denying it."

"So fuckin' tight."

"Mmm."

She arches her back and wraps her legs around my waist. I

lift her ass slightly, getting deeper as I clench my jaw. "You better come soon, *Princess*. Can't hold on."

"Oh? And here I was thinking you were gonna 'fuck me all night long'." She giggles.

I rock my hips into her and she groans. "Oh, I'm gonna fuck you all night long, babe, but haven't been inside you for three whole goddamn days. Second fuck I'll draw it out."

"Such a romantic," she sighs.

I pick up my pace, needing the release. "Fuck, yeah."

She gasps when I grind my pelvis, brushing her clit, and all of a sudden she's hissing and gripping the mattress, trying to be quiet while she falls apart. I follow behind, spurting my load like a man possessed.

I press my forehead to hers. "You know you're mine now." I've always been gentle with the 'ownership' part of claiming an ol' lady because of Amber's past. I never want her to think that we're misogynistic assholes. We just care about our women and have deep love and respect for them, no matter what. It isn't what people might think it is. The women in our club always have a choice.

"I like being yours."

"You do?"

"Yes." She brushes my damp hair from my forehead. "Bronco, I'm not gonna break just because I had a bad experience."

"It was worse than bad. It was a nightmare for you."

She glides her thumb pad over my cheekbone. "Yes, it was, but that's in the past now. They'll find Vincent, and they'll lock him up. And I've decided that I will testify, if it comes to that."

I pull my head back. "Babe, you don't have to do anythin'"

"I know that, but for years I've hidden away, afraid to say anything, afraid of being caught. Well, that ends now. I don't want to live in fear anymore, and the others in the cult deserve a chance at life on the outside. It isn't their fault, just as it wasn't mine."

"We have BADVA, they can help if that's what you need."

Bikers Against Domestic Violence Association. The club has been heavily involved in the program of protecting women and children in court cases in New Orleans when they go to and from court. It's something Cash and Jett started, and are passionate about.

"Thank you. I appreciate that."

"Just know you have my support, and everyone in the club. Whatever you need, you got it," I say.

"What did I do to deserve a man like you?" Her gaze tells me everything. Her eyes are filled with love, appreciation and a little lust.

"You didn't do nothin', it's me that was too blind to see the obvious for far too long."

"All that matters is we got here."

"And you're gonna move in with me when Erica is settled."

She smiles softly. "I'd love that. I've waited so long to be happy, I don't want to wait for anything anymore."

I bend to kiss her deeply. "I think Erica is gonna like it here."

"She hasn't stopped apologizing since she got here."

"Well, I know she must feel terrible about what she did," I say. "I know it can't be easy, but I get why she did what she did. Trying to protect the ones you love sometimes comes at a heavy price."

"Don't you ever run away from me." Amber grabs my ass and I give her a lopsided smile.

"Like I'd ever do that."

"I missed you."

"I missed you, too."

"We're lovesick fools now, you know that right?"

I grin. "Yep, and I don't give a shit."

"Tell me something I don't know."

I kiss her nose. "You're the most beautiful woman I've ever seen."

"Trust you to blow it out of the water."

"Well, you asked."

"Do you think things will settle down again in the club?" she asks.

"They always do."

"And Vince? He's still out there."

"We'll deal with it if he even dares to come to these neck of the woods," I tell her earnestly. "And it won't be pretty."

She stares at me. "You shed blood for me, didn't you?"

"Club business. Sometimes the scum has to be dealt with in an inhumane way. It's what they deserve."

"I agree with you. We've seen so much mayhem these last few years. After Audrina was kidnapped, things seemed to get better."

"Within an MC, there's always gonna be shit goin' down, it's the life we live," I say. "But the important part is we all stick together. We're a family, and no matter what, we're always gonna be."

"So no more fake boyfriends for me?"

"Nope, your real boyfriend would get jealous."

She smiles. "He would, and he's really, really scary."

I buck my hips, still inside her sweet pussy. "He's crazy about you."

"He can't keep his hands off me."

"That's true, but he also might need another minute."

She laughs again, walking her fingers up my chest. "Is someone a little tired?"

"Fuckin' you is a full-time job."

She slaps my ass. "Funny."

I kiss her forehead. "Just so we're clear, I'm yours, too."

"Didn't doubt it for a second."

"Good." I pull out, then roll onto my back, bringing her with me.

"Bronco?" she whispers after a few moments as we try to catch our breaths.

"Yeah, babe?"

"I want you to tattoo me."

I turn my head to look at her as she gazes up at me. "Okay."

"I need this thing gone. I'm ready."

I kiss the top of her head. "We can look at some designs. You have anything in mind?"

"Maybe a bird, or something to symbolize freedom."

"Whatever you want. I promise it'll look so fuckin' amazin' you won't even remember the old one."

"There's also something I've been meaning to ask you."

"Anything."

She tries to keep a straight face. "Did you really tattoo Nevada's dick?"

I burst out with laughter, then Amber presses a hand over my mouth. "Fuck, babe, do you really have to remind me of that while we're in bed."

"So it is true."

"Haven't you heard about client confidentiality?"

"Right, but this is Nevada. Please tell me he paid you."

"It felt weird takin' money after havin' to do... *that.*"

She giggles. "That would've hurt."

"My emotional scars are worse, trust me. But I owed him. He's fuckin' nuts, by the way. Who tattoos a constellation on their dick?"

She snuggles farther into the crook of my neck. "You're clearly very talented."

"I am, and I'm gonna fuck you on my inking table."

"Oh."

"Yeah, you'll be sayin' more than 'oh' when I'm done with you."

"I'm looking forward to it." She presses a hand to my heart. "It feels like we've turned a corner."

"It'll be better from now on, I promise. And maybe we can go on a proper date."

"We haven't done book club for a while."

I rise up from the pillows. "Speaking of cucumbers..."

She pushes me back down, throwing a leg over my body as she straddles me. "Oh, no you don't, mister. No cucumbers here. I like my dick alive and well, and definitely not green." She reaches between my legs, my dick at half-mast but he's perking up by the second.

"You drive a hard bargain." I reach toward her and we kiss. It's soft, slow and passionate. Just like everything Amber does. She's the most amazing, brave, beautiful woman I've ever known, and she was right under my nose this whole time.

I've never loved anyone like how I love her. My heart beats to a different tune whenever I think about her or hear her name. That's what gave it away when I first fell for her. I embraced my feelings, not something I'm terribly great at doing, but my mom's always saying that sometimes it's the little things that count the most.

And I'm going to show her for the rest of my life that I can be that guy. The one who is completely crazy about her. She deserves to get all the things in life that she wants, and as long as she wants me by her side, I'll be there.

"You're everything to me, Bronc. I love you so much."

I grip her ass, her breath hitching in her chest. "Sit on my dick and say that again."

She grips my now hard cock and, wasting no time, slides down on it. We both groan. "I love you."

"I love you more, *Princess*. Gonna show you exactly what you mean to me every single day. I'll never stop showin' you."

"You already do."

And I fall, yet again, more in love with my best friend as every second passes. Her warmth. Her glow. Everything about her I want to love and protect.

My Princess.

Forever.

EPILOGUE

Amber
One week later

Bronco lays the stencil on my skin, over the tattoo on my wrist that I've despised for so long.

"Kind of poetic, isn't it?" I muse.

Bronco looks up. "What is?"

"The day I get this covered up is the same day Vince gets arrested."

Bronco's nostrils flair. "Trust me, I had the boys lookin' for him, but he's fuckin' slippery."

"Bronc, you've done enough for me and my family."

We don't talk about what we know: Vince had a van with rope, tape, a taser and other "kidnapping" equipment including guns and knives. I'm convinced he was coming after me, especially after I told my entire story to the cops and they'd shared that Vince had a search history with my name all over it. He was looking for me. That bastard was going to go on one more hurrah before he ended up dead himself, or captured by the police. He'd been looking for me for a long time.

"He should do himself a favor and end it in prison," Bronco mutters. "Just wish I'd gotten to him first."

"You've done plenty, and I love you for it."

He pecks me on the lips. "Lie back, relax, and let me know if you need me to stop at any time, okay?"

I nod. "Okay."

I'm just glad this day has come. I'm thankful that Bronco is the one to do it. I wanted it to be him.

Bronco leans over and kisses me upside down. Fucking hot. "Then when I'm done, I'm strippin' those little cock teasin' shorts off you, pullin' those panties aside, and sinkin' my dick into that sweet pussy."

His words. I make suggestive noises and he presses another kiss to my skin, my forehead this time. "Let's see if you last that long," I tease.

"You distract me and I'll just draw out your next orgasm."

"You're mean." I poke my tongue at him and he chuckles.

Then — and fuck me if I don't die a little inside — he puts a pair of glasses on.

"What the heck?"

He focuses his gaze on me. "What?"

"You wear glasses?"

"Only to ink in."

"Since when?"

"Since... I don't know, forever."

"But you don't need them for reading?"

"I can wear them more often if you're gonna get all hot and bothered over it." He wiggles his eyebrows suggestively.

Holy mother of God. I have a vision of him naked, fucking me from behind in this very room, wearing just those dorky glasses. *Give it to me now.*

"I think that could definitely be my new favorite thing, aside from your dick."

"You gonna let me start, or are we not even gonna get past first base?" he demands.

I roll my lips. "Are you this rude to all of your customers?"

"Only the ones who give me lip when I'm tryin' to concentrate."

"Fine. I'll behave."

"Any final words to your coverup?"

"Yes." I place a hand over my heart. "Fuck you."

Bronco laughs, turns on the machine and I close my eyes. While this is a poignant day, I just want to enjoy what it also means.

No more running, looking over my shoulder, or worrying about Erica and Olive.

I get to be a normal person with my boyfriend, a man I can't stop kissing.

And I wouldn't want it any other way.

"You really like it?"

Tears well in my eyes. The three doves are amazing. They symbolize myself, Erica and Olive. Each bird is flying under the other in different directions, but also together. Because of the dark tattoo that was underneath, Bronco had to create a darkened skyline. It's so beautiful, I can't hold back the floodgates.

"Bronco, it's fucking amazing!" I dive into his arms, pressing kisses all over his face.

"Shit, I thought I'd fucked up for a second." He pushes my hair behind my ears. "I'm glad you like it."

"Like it? I love it. It's perfect, just like you."

He smiles as I continue to admire myself. "Proud of you."

"Because I sat still?"

He presses a kiss to my lips. "No, because you're brave, and I dig that about you."

"You're the sweetest man." My heart rate accelerates tenfold. "I want you, Bronc. I want you right now."

"Glasses on or off?" he teases.

I kiss him this time, deepening it when I part my lips and my tongue seeks his. "On," I pant. "I want you, hurry."

We're all hands as he rips his t-shirt off at the same time I lose my tank and my bra. He doesn't even get his jeans down all the way when he's pulling my back to his front, gripping my ass. "I told you what I'd do to you when this was over."

"So do it." With my feet on the floor, I bend over the chair and stick my ass out.

He comes up behind me, yanks my shorts down, and my panties. I wiggle my butt and he groans. I turn back and his eyes meet mine. Fuck, those glasses...

"I request you wear those all the time when you're fucking me," I declare.

He smiles, then parts my legs with his knee, grabs his shaft and rubs it through my folds as I hiss. "So wet already," he groans.

"That's because I've been so turned on with you inking me."

He circles my clit with his head, then he's at my entrance, trying to push in. I stick my ass out farther, begging him with my needy pants. With one thrust, he's deep inside me and I jolt at the movement. "So fuckin' perfect," he murmurs. "Wearin' my ink, talkin' like that." He slides out, then rams back in.

"I love wearin' your ink."

"You want more of it?"

"Yes."

He starts to move his hips and I groan, my body on fire just for him, just like it always is. We've been through some ups and downs, but nothing could prepare me for the love that was waiting for me all along with my best friend. He was right there for so long, I was just too blind to see. As long as I live, I'll never stop loving him.

He helped bring me to the place that I am today, encouraging me and being an amazing friend the second I got to New Orleans. I'm more confident with him by my side, and I'm loved in his arms.

We were meant to be together, and I'll never stop thanking my lucky stars.

Bronco

I ram in and out of my woman. She's so damn fine. Wearing my ink and talking like that, I'm gonna come fast. "Gonna be fast, babe," I groan. "Feels too good."

"I can ride it and go slower, make it last."

I spank her ass cheek and she yelps. "You callin' the shots now?"

"You love it when I call the shots."

I watch my cock disappearing in and out of her, and I try to hold on, but it's too much. We fucked this morning, too, but I'll never get enough of my girl. I ram in harder, hitting it so damn deep and she grinds back against me. "Yes, right there."

She's close, and when her back arches, I ride it home as she grips the seat until her knuckles turn white, moaning on a ragged breath. I follow behind, hot spurts of cum filling her as I grip her hips and hang on for dear life.

"Fuck, that was hot."

"You railed me," she pants.

I snicker, pulling out as I feel between her legs. "You're gonna walk around like that for the rest of today."

"Can I at least get a tissue?"

"No. Gotta protect your ink before you leave, and give you the proper care instructions."

"So professional."

I spank her ass and she yelps as I bring my fingers to her mouth and tell her to suck.

She groans and I close my eyes, breathing in the scent of her hair as I inhale. "You're so fuckin' perfect."

"I love the ink," she whispers when I pull my fingers from her mouth. She turns in my arms. "I love I have a piece of you now."

"You'll always have a piece of me, sugar."

There's no other place I want to be, aside from in her arms.

Three months later...

"Torin, pass the mash potatoes, sweetie," my mom says as we sit around the table in my apartment. I do as she says, glancing sideways at Amber as she smiles at me.

My mom loves Amber. In fact, in the three days she's already been here, the two have been inseparable. I know Amber misses her mom who she lost at an early age, so when Mom asked her if she'd like to have a girls' day out of shopping and lunch, I've never seen her so excited. Even if my mom does tell embarrassing stories about me, I don't care if it's my girl's smile I get to see at the end of it.

Amber moved in a month ago, and we've been redecorating and making it a little less 'bachelor pad' and more 'happy couple.' New furniture was high on the agenda, including a bed, couch and turning one of the spare bedrooms into a mini library, just like the one Amber had at her house. I know how much it meant to her, so I got the Ikea bookshelves she loves so much, and put them together one day while she was at work. Fuck me if that shit is a bitch to figure out. Reading is something Amber enjoys, and while we still have our monthly book club, I really just read the books so I can hear her talk about what she liked and didn't like. Granted, I don't always read the books, or I skip to the smutty parts, but Amber still won't let me near her with a cucumber.

"This is delicious, sweetie," Mom says, tucking into the roast chicken we prepared. Mom is traditional on Sundays, and what Mama says goes.

"It's so good," Olive agrees, stabbing a carrot like butter wouldn't melt in her mouth. I know she's giving Titan food under the table, and he'd do just about anything for chicken.

Erica smiles across at her daughter. "We're lucky to have such amazing people in our lives."

My mom smiles in return, patting Erica on the hand.

Well, things certainly turned around for the better. Erica got a job pretty quickly as a teacher's aide, and she wants to finish her qualifications and teach kindergarten. It may be a while before the club gets their money back, but Erica has started a payment plan, and took on some night shifts at the Whiskey Shack Grill for some extra money. We love having Olive whenever we can. Since Erica was happy to take over the lease on Amber's place, everything has worked out for the best. And I have my girl in my arms every single night.

Vincent is in jail, and will be for a very long time, along

with Steven and several other men from the cult. They'll get what they fucking deserve one way or the other, and frankly, I don't have any sympathy. The sad fact is, not all of the women were like Amber and Erica and wanted to leave. They're so brainwashed that they'll likely stay where they are and try to rebuild their lives, or move on to another cult, probably with similar values to the one they were in because they don't know any better. My blood boils when I think about Amber's forced marriage and how young she was. The fucker is lucky he got caught by the cops, because what I did to that fuck face Oswald would be nothing compared to the hours I'd make Vincent suffer. Jail is too good for a sack of shit like him.

"You'll all have to come out to my home sometime," Mom says. "Get all that city grit out of your hair. It'll be fun."

Mom's in her element, of course, because she knows Amber is the real deal. Not only have I never brought a woman home to meet my mom before, but she's heard all about Amber for years when we were best friends.

The conversation we had when we were alone went something like this...

"I told you to follow your heart a long time ago," she tells me, slapping me upside the head.

"Ow Mom, what was that for?"

"She could've been snapped up by any eligible bachelor in all this time. You have to pay better attention to your intuition. Maybe you need to unblock those chakras?"

I roll my eyes. "Ma, my chakras are fine. We found each other, didn't we?"

Her face softens "I suppose that's true, but I brought a rose quartz bracelet for Amber to wear, it'll help keep your love strong and grounded. Unconditional love will open up those chakras in no time at all."

Mom doesn't worry if Amber may not want to wear gaudy, chunky jewelry; the thought wouldn't cross her mind. "They're *open, Mom, trust me. We've already declared our feelings for one another."*

She stops what she's doing, her eyes brimming with tears. "You've said 'I love you'?"

I take a breath. I'm not usually one to confess my feelings, especially to my mom, but I thought it might keep her off my back. "I've always loved her," I say simply. "It's just expanded now, that's all."

She envelopes me in a big hug that I didn't see coming, and I squeeze her back. "I'm so happy."

"I'm very happy, too," I confess. "Like you once told me: good things come to those who wait."

She pulls back, wiping her tears. "Right, but don't be so slow next time. You want to keep that girl, Torin, you've got to dig deep and give her all you've got. Promise me."

I smile down at the tiny woman who could kill a man at ten paces. "I promise. Now pull yourself together. Amber will be here soon and she can't wait to meet you..."

I smile, thinking about how my life has changed so much in the last three months. Things have only gotten stronger with the two of us, and even though I've always known Amber is a strong woman, she's proved it more to herself than anyone else during this whole ordeal. I'm so proud of her. Overcoming trauma like that isn't easy, and I take my hat off to her every day for putting one foot in front of the other.

I'm always gonna be an overprotective asshole, but that's just my nature.

As Titan comes toward me, nudging me with his head, I lean to pet him behind the ears. "Good boy," I tell him as Amber's hand joins the other side as she chats away across the table.

A few moments later, she must feel my gaze because she turns to look at me and my lips curl up.

I love you, I mouth.

Her soft smile turns into a grin as her cheeks flush. The idea that I can still make her blush sends heat to my dick.

I love you, too, she mouths back. *Always.*

We're just one big, happy family. And that's all I've ever really wanted, along with the love of a good woman.

Nothing can ever compare to that.

ACKNOWLEDGMENTS

Thank you for reading Bronco & Amber

I hope you enjoyed their story!

If Bronco is your first read from me, thank you so much! If you're already a reader and are following along with the series, I hope you enjoyed book 12 of the series.

I appreciate all of the love you all show me and my biker boys.

For those of you that may be new to my books, NOLA Rebels is a spin-off from my best selling series Bracken Ridge Rebels MC set in Arizona. That series is complete with 12 books 😊

Appreciation to my ARC team! And to all of those who may have signed up with Author Agency or Literally Yours, I appreciate the chance you've taken on my books!

Special thanks:

Hugs to my twin sister Dakotah Fox for, once again, being the shoulder to lean on (and cry on!) for being my sounding board, proof reader, and everything in between

The Outgoing Bookworm – Michelle – for being my alpha reader and making sure those pesky time lines and ages of the characters are spot on

My Beta team: Kylie, Tara, Anshul – thanks again for making me laugh with your comments, and for all the helpful suggestions as well as repeating myself five thousand times! Appreciate all your help

To my PA and friend Angelica for working tirelessly in the background and supporting me and Dakotah with our Street Team. I look forward to working with you extensively this year, best of luck keeping us organized LOL You're the best!

If you can spare the time to leave a review on GR and/or Amazon and BookBub if you loved Manny or any of my books that would be greatly appreciated and it helps me so much as an little indie author. Links are on the following pages.

The next book in the series will be Ryder and Crystal, releasing 30th May 2025.

See full trope list and a sneak preview and pre-order link below.

Be sure to check out my private Facebook group (links to follow) as I update this page regularly before anything gets released on other social media channels. I will also be sharing special snippets and scenes for Ryder's book there.

Love from Australia, MF xx

WANT MORE?

RYDER: NOLA REBELS MC Book 13. PRE-ORDER here: https://books2read.com/NOLARyder

Tropes
Childhood friends to lovers
Married couple
Protector
Rival families who disown them
It's always been her
Sexy dares

Marriage in trouble
Easy going MMC - until you cross him
She was a spoiled princess
He rescues her

... keep reading for a sneaky excerpt
(Please note this sneak peek is subject to change before editing)

PART I
THE PAST
RYDER

PROLOGUE
RYDER

Age Eighteen

I'VE GROWN UP WITH CRYSTAL CARTWRIGHT MY entire life. She's two years younger than me, but she's always been in the thick of it with us boys. If it wasn't her attempting to be part of our gang when we played cops and robbers, or trying to keep up on her bicycle when we took to the muddy hills of the mountains just for fun, she was bossing us around like she was in charge. And it used to be annoying, heck, it still is, but she also got cute overnight and the boys in our neighborhood are starting to notice.

I'm best friends with her brother, Luca, and my neighbor Torin. Luca and Crystal also have a little sister, Casey, who is the exact opposite of her sister and has no interest in hanging out with us. Luca was pretty mean to Crystal growing up, never wanting her around because she whined all the time, and got on all of our nerves, but I also felt sorry for her. She's her parents' little princess and they smother her in bubble wrap.

Now that she's, she's calmed down a lot, and no longer wants to be part of our secrets, or hang out with us. Crystal is one of the most popular girls in school, cheerleader extraordinaire, she's smart as well as cute and can cut you with words when she really gets mad.

If only our families got along, it would've been a match-made in heaven since I practically live at Lucas's place. He moved out into the pool house, so I don't have to run into his parents.

Oh, both of our parents hate one another. I'm from the wrong side of the tracks. Luca and his sisters come from a privileged upbringing on the other side of town.

They have a big home. Shiny new cars. Threads that cost a bomb, and all the electronics you can imagine. They holiday every year in Florida, or Mexico, or somewhere far away from here. I've always liked Louisiana, but coming from a small town where there are distinct differences between the rich and the poor, makes me want to leave this shithole behind and never come back.

Unlike me, they have loving parents, but they're also strict. They've never really approved of my friendship with Luca, but they tolerate me because I try not to get into trouble. And then there's Crystal. *The princess*. She gets everything she wants because she's their miracle baby when they thought they couldn't have more. Then they had Casey, so I don't know how that shit works. I'd go as far as to say Crystal's spoiled, but she'd strongly disagree which is funny, she wouldn't know any different. Still, it never stopped her hanging out on my side of town, in fact, it's like her and Luca wanted to get away from their perfect little life some of the time. Slum it with the poor kids. At least Torin can relate.

My step-dad, Wayne, is a drunk, and I have a mom who would rather stay out late with her buddies than worry about being a parent. Nobody cares where I am or what I'm doing. My dad walked out on us leaving mom with all the bills. Soon, we were packing up and moving when the bank foreclosed. I never saw my real dad again. I'll never forgive him for what he did, or what he put my mom through. Then again, she was never really invested in being a mom, but that doesn't make it alright. Then there's my step-brother Stu, but he's not even worth talking about. He hates me, and he blames me for anything and everything, especially his dad's drinking problems which started long before he met my mom.

It didn't help that growing up I had a stutter, and every now and again I still lose my words. Of course, Wayne, and asshole Stu ,used to think it was hilarious to mimic me as a child, they don't do that much anymore, but the sting still hurts when I think about how horrible they were. Worse than any kid in the playground, and always when my mom wasn't around.

Now I'm 18, I'm on my own and I prefer it that way, but I've been looking after myself before I was even in double digits. It's nothing new. I'm moving to New Orleans, and needless to say I won't be going to college. We don't have the money, and even if we did, I don't have what it takes to stick out more years of my life in school. I'll get an apprenticeship, or a job, or both. Anything to get out of Greenlark.

Neither Luca or Crystal care that me and Torin are both from the other side of town. They don't act like little rich kids, even when Crystal is having one of her tantrums, she's never unkind for the sake of it or looks down on others. Maybe that's why I've always liked her. She's kind. Thoughtful. Sweet.

I've always known Crystal had a schoolgirl crush on me, but I thought she'd grow out of it over time. I'm not gonna make it with my best friend's sister, but in the blink of an eye, something changed.

I sit back on the couch, recalling what happened a few nights ago...

I wake with a start, feeling someone slide under the duvet next to me. A few seconds later, my eyes spring open and I sit up ready to fight. Fighting is something I'm used to when my stepdad likes to throw punches. Hence, Luca let me sleep on the couch since their parents are away for the night. "What the fu—"

"It's me, Ryder," *Crystal whispers.*

I stare at her, my heart beating wildly because I forgot where I was. "What's going on"

She's wearing tiny sleep shorts and a tank that barely contains her rack; something I shouldn't be noticing even in my sleep deprived haze. My eyes snake down her body, and even in this dull light, I can see the rise and fall of her chest as she stares at me.

"I think you know." *She slides her palms up my chest and I recoil back.* "We've been getting close lately—"

"Crystal, stop it. What are you doing?"

She doesn't listen, snuggling her nose along my jaw. "Ryder, I've noticed how you've been looking at me, and I wanted to give you something before you leave town. I've thought about it a lot."

I don't want to ask, but the words still leave my mouth; "Give me w...what?" *Oh, no. I can't find my fucking words.*

"Me." *She cups my dick and I shoot up off the couch. She rolls back, her eyes wide with confusion. Okay, maybe we flirted a few times, but nothing ever happened and nothing is ever gonna happen with Luca's little sister.*

"You don't want me?" *Her eyes look glassy, even in this light. Such a soft, shade of blue they don't even look real.*

Oh, and I didn't say that. Crystal is beautiful, she always has been. A perfect face. Blonde hair that resembles corn silk. Athletic build with long legs. But that's just the thing. She's a kid. Even at 16, she has no clue what she wants. As appealing as having her for the very first time might be, I have to call her bluff. Her first time can't be with someone like me. It should be special.

"N...not like this. This is wrong. You're Luca's sis...sister."

She places her hand on my arm, just like she used to do when we were younger. When kids made fun and she was the only one who didn't laugh at me. "It's not wrong if we both want it, come on Ryder, don't be a pill. It's my virginity, not a marriage proposal. You've had sex plenty of times."

I stare at her like she's grown another head. Then her eyes dip and she giggles. Okay, my dick responded to her closeness, but that's not the point. I cover myself up with the duvet, fearing it's way too late to hide it.

"You don't want to lose your virginity to m...m...me." *Why the hell is my voice so thick? Why the fuck can't I speak? I feel like I swallowed a bag of marbles.* "You need to go before Luca finds us."

"He's in the pool room, he'll never know."

"No, Crystal."

"What if I don't want to go?"

"Don't be a brat," *I growl.* "I k...know you're used to getting what you want."

"That's not all true, I'm not getting what I want now."

"Spoken like a true brat."

She narrows her eyes. I can't deny it. I've been with a ton of girls, but they weren't my best friend's little sister. Me and Torin, hang out at the mall, or at parties. It isn't like I'm forcing chicks to get with me. Apparently I have a baby face, and they like my dick. I'm blessed, but this blessing is staying right in my pants where she's concerned.

"You could say it with a little more conviction," *she snaps.*

I take a breath. I know I can control my stutter if I just fucking breath... "Crystal. You're a great girl, you know I like you, but as a friend. You and me just aren't gonna happen, Sugar." *I have to let her down gently, hoping she'll go away. The temptation of her splayed out like that before me, all breathy and needy makes my dick throb. Focus!*

Crystal isn't used to being denied. Her nostrils flair at my rejection. Christ, I'm doing this for her own good! Can't she see that?

"So what if I'm Luca's little sister? I'm a woman now—"

"Not legally."

She folds her arms over her chest. "You don't want me." *I can see the tears in her eyes and it kills me. It fucking kills me.*

I grip her chin. "Crys. You're gorgeous, and any guy would be happy to have you in his bed, but you're too young. You're only sixteen. You don't wanna do anything stupid you might regret."

"So now I'm stupid?" *She recoils, trying to get away from me.*

"I didn't say that."

"I can't believe this!"

"It's not because I don't want to," *I blurt, only making it worse.* "I mean, you're really pretty, but we can't. It's wrong, you're like a sister to me. I could never forgive myself."

"You're really pathetic, you know that, Ryder?"

"Don't be mad at me." *I try to catch her arm before she stomps off, but I'm too slow.* "One day you'll see that this was the right thing to do. We can't lie to Luca." *And you're only 16. I don't do underage chicks...*

"One day you'll realize what you threw away." *Her eyes are filled with tears, her cheeks pink with humiliation.* "And you'll be sorry."

"Crystal, don't leave like this." *But it's too late, she's running away, taking the stairs two at a time to get back to her room.*

I punch the pillow. Fuck.

She can say what she wants, but this was the right thing. How could I ever look Luca in the eye again after defiling his little sister? I couldn't. That's the short answer. I care about her too much. In fact, until this moment maybe I didn't quite realize exactly how much I care.

I don't miss the middle finger she gives me as she stomps up the stairs.

She might hate me now, but she'll realize when she gets older that I don't want it to be the asshole that took her virginity, and couldn't offer her anything more. Because despite what she says, they always want more. Since I'm leaving town, how would that even be fair to her? She's still a kid in my eyes. She doesn't know what she wants, and me railing her will only complicate things. Even if she is right about one thing, I have been looking at her differently lately, but that's on me. I would never act on it. Hell, I'll beat anyone if they even touch her. We both know it, but it's not because I want her for myself, it's because I've known her since she was little. That's what you do around here, no matter what side of the tracks you come from. You protect the ones closest to you. You protect them at all costs. I won't be the monster she needs to be protected from. No matter what.

I cover my face with my hands, knowing that she'll hate me forever.

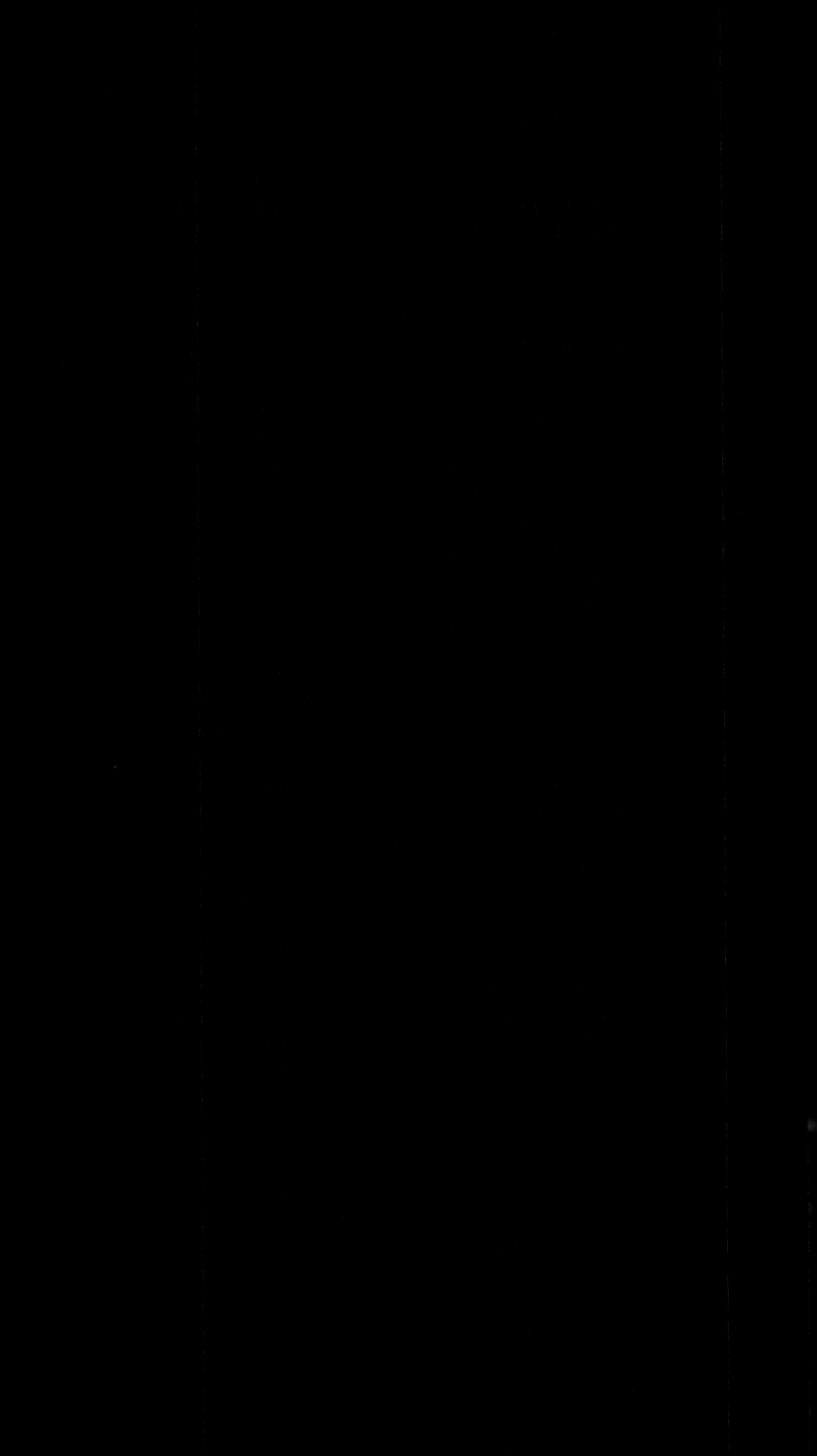

1
CRYSTAL

Age Sixteen

I WAKE UP, EXPECTING THE HUMILIATION TO BE gone, but it's not. It's worse than ever.

How am I ever going to face Ryder again? More to the point, I've ruined everything between us.

He can say what he likes, but he did flirt with me, on more than one occasion.

He's always been sweet, more so as we got older and not only that, Ryder turned from a boy to a man almost overnight. His muscular body, his bright green eyes — too pretty for a boy, as well as those long lashes I'd die for — then there's his laugh. His smile. The way he looks out for me, for all of us. Somehow, for years on end, Ryder took on the role of protector, and I can't say that I mind it.

This however? This is humiliation at its finest.

Rejection.

His words stung, especially the ones about me being a brat. I never asked to have parents with money. I don't think I act like I'm spoiled, but I guess he must really think that. And that does nothing for my temper. Mom says it's my Irish blood that gets me fired up, and she might be right, but whatever happens now, I can never face Ryder again.

"Hey."

I sit up with a start, my heart pounding as I hear Ryder's voice from the doorway.

He came to me?

I clear my throat. "What do you want?"

"I wanted to say I'm sorry, Crys. You know I didn't mean to push you away."

Oh, no. He's only going to make it worse, and now I'm going to cry in front of him.

"Go away."

"Not until you say we're cool."

"Why does it matter?" My anger is masking my humiliation, but I plow on. "It isn't like you care."

"Can I come in?"

"No."

He ignores me, coming into my room and now I'll have the memory of him like this. Shirtless, in his boxer shorts, a contrite look on his face.

"I never meant to hurt you. You're mad now, but in a few year's time, you'll see that I'm not all that bad."

"I never said you were bad."

He drops his head, then sits on the end of my bed. I always imagined him in my room, but never like this. In my fantasies, he was doing a whole lot more than sitting.

"But I am bad, Crys. And I'm not just sayin' this to get you to feel sorry for me, but we're different you and I. I'm a loser who'll probably amount to nothin', you have the whole world at your feet and every opportunity in the world."

I sit up, my brow furrows in confusion. "So do you."

He shakes his head. "I'm not going to college, Sugar."

"But you said—"

"I know what I said, but kids like me don't get to do that when you don't have money."

"But there are other options, community college, night classes—" I panic at the idea that he'll be leaving, even though I know it's inevitable college or not.

"You had to have known that." His eyes are so pretty in the morning light. They sparkle like pretty diamonds, but they also look sad.

"I... I honestly didn't think about it."

"I'm gonna go get a job, an apprenticeship probably. I don't know yet, but I do know that I've nothing left in Greenlark."

"Well, that's great you have plans." I beam. "I mean, you've always loved fixing things, and there's nothing wrong with not going to college." Of course, I've had it beaten into me that college is the only way. My parents wouldn't just disown me if I decided not to go, they'd probably cut me off, too.

He swipes a hand through his hair. "Yeah." Somehow his answer isn't quite what I expected. He seems... sad about it. His shoulders sag, his whole demeanor is off, and my gut wrenches.

"Ryder?"

He looks up.

"What do you want?"

"I don't know what I want."

"No, that isn't true, in all the time I've known you, you've always been sure of everything."

"Maybe I'm not sure about this," he says. "Maybe I really don't know where the road is gonna take me."

"I don't want you to leave."

His lips curl up. "Everything changes, Sugar, otherwise we'd never learn anything or go anywhere."

"You have opportunities too." I feel I need to reiterate

that. Just because he's poor doesn't mean that he can't have a good education, right? "I mean, scholarships—"

"Wayne broke my pitching arm and ruined any chances I had of baseball as a career." He looks away, and I could cry. I could really cry my eyes out. I forgot all about that. Ryder was the star pitcher, and everyone knew he was destined for great things. Nobody knew what really happened, but I knew. I always knew when he'd been hurt. He'd be real quiet. Shy away from talking, and even ignore me. And I'd see the bruises.

"Jesus, I'm sorry, Ryd." I move to my knees, leaning over to squeeze his hand. "I didn't mean to bring that up."

He shakes his head, bringing his eyes back to mine. "You don't have to feel sorry for me. It wasn't meant to be. I wasn't destined for an easy life. I've come to terms with it."

A tear leaks from my eye and he reaches toward my cheek, catching it on his thumb. I want to tell him that I love everything about him. That he's beyond perfect and he won't have to worry. He's got a good head on his shoulders, despite his horrible parents.

"I want to make it better," I whisper.

"That ain't your job." He brings the pad of his thumb to lips, and licks the moisture from the tip. "Your job is to make something of yourself. Be a good girl. Stay in school, but do one thing for me?"

I'd die for him, if that's what it took. "Anything."

He nips my chin. "Don't go throwing your virginity at just anyone, you got me? Don't let a precious gift go to the wrong guy, because guys are gonna try, Sugar, and they won't care once it's gone, they'll move on to the next available girl."

Oh, God. I want it to be him. I want it to be him so much.

"But I want you."

He shakes his head. "You're not destined for a small town life. It won't be enough for you."

"Then I won't stay."

"Of course you won't, but with me, that's all you'll have."

"No."

He goes to stand.

"Please don't go," I whisper, clinging to him.

He bends, and I almost think he's going to kiss me. His head dips, and then he plants his lips on my forehead. "Take care of yourself."

"No! Please Ryder, don't go!"

"What the hell is going on here?" My dad's voice booms from the door.

I look over and my eyes go wide. "Dad?"...............

**Pre-order here:
<u>https://books2read.com/NOLARyder</u>**

ABOUT THE AUTHOR

Mackenzy Fox is an author of contemporary, enemies to lovers, motorcycle and dark themed romance novels. When she's not writing she loves vegan cooking, walking her beloved pooches, reading books and is an expert on online shopping.

She's slightly obsessed with drinking tea, testing bubbly Moscato, watching home decorating shows and has a black belt in origami. She strives to live a quiet and introverted life in Western Australia's South-West with her hubby, twin sister and her dogs.

FIND ME HERE

My books are all available on my website:
https://mackenzyfox.com ⬇️

My reading order is located on my website under Book Directory 🤍

Tiktok: https://www.tiktok.com/@mackenzyfoxauthor
Tiktok backup account: https://www.tiktok.com/@mackenzyfoxbooks
Tiktok Fox sisters: https://www.tiktok.com/@thefoxsisterswrite
Face book: https://www.facebook.com/mackenzy.foxauthor.5
Instagram: https://www.instagram.com/mackenzyfoxbooks/
Goodreads: https://www.goodreads.com/author/show/20852435.Mackenzy_Fox

Don't forget to join mine and Dakotah's private Facebook Group: The Den – A Mackenzy & Dakotah Fox Readers Group here: https://bit.ly/3dgQfKk

Sign up for my newsletter:
https://landing.mailerlite.com/webforms/landing/g2l8y8

You can also find all my books, ARC sign ups, book links and giveaways here in one easy spot: https://linktr.ee/mackenzyfox

ALSO BY MACKENZY FOX

<u>Bracken Ridge Rebels MC:</u>
Steel
Gunner
Brock
Colt
Rubble
Bones
Axton
Nitro
Gears
Knox
Hutch
A Bracken Ridge Christmas - extended epilogues

<u>NOLA Rebels MC:</u>
Cash
Jett
Hawk
Harlem
Tag

Also by Mackenzy Fox

Rock
Priest
Nevada
Riot
Manny
Hustler
Bronco
Ryder
Pipes
Stella

Bad Boys of New York:
Jaxon

Mr. Series Taboo Collection:
Mr. Bentley
Mr. Petrov
Mr. Devereaux

ALSO BY MACKENZY FOX & DAKOTAH FOX

Medici Mafia Fortress Series:
Fortress of the King
Fortress of the Queen
Fortress of the Heart
Fortress of the Soul
Fortress of the Damned
Fortress of the Brave
Fortress of the Cursed

Bassett Brothers Bourbon - Stoney Creek Series: (small town)
Celeste & Callan - Prequel Novella
Grayson & Hartley - Book 1
Gabriel & Skye - Book 2
Brooklyn & Eden - Book 3
Beau & Autumn - Book 4
Georgia-Blue & Hudson - Book 5

Quick Burn Series:
Ruler Breaker Romance - Sports;

Also by Mackenzy Fox & Dakotah Fox

Huxley
Nash
Wolf
Shepherd

<u>Silver Pines Series:</u>
<u>Small Town Christmas Little Holiday Novels</u>;
Snowed In
Snowed Out
Snowed Under

<u>Standalone:</u>
Broken Wings (contemporary romance)

Made in United States
Orlando, FL
27 May 2025